# The Milk of Human Kindness:
## Lesbian Authors Write about Mothers and Daughters

Edited by Lori L. Lake

Regal Crest Enterprises, LLC

Nederland, Texas

ISBN 1-932300-28-7


First Printing 2004

9 8 7 6 5 4 3 2 1


Cover design by Donna Pawlowski


Published by:

Regal Crest Enterprises, LLC
PMB 210, 8691 9th Avenue
Port Arthur, Texas 77642-8025


Find us on the World Wide Web at
http://www.regalcrest.biz


Printed in the United States of America

# CONTENTS

# INTRODUCTION

The conception of this anthology took place in the dark, late at night, in a dream. I awakened at two o'clock in the morning with a directive ringing in my ears: "Put out a call for submissions for stories about mothers, and you will name the book *The Milk of Human Kindness*." The voice sounded male. Insistent. And very bossy. I rolled over and fell back to sleep.

Somewhere around four a.m. the voice awakened me once more, but this time, I was feeling groggy and rather cranky, and I didn't want to listen to this shrill crank who was interrupting my slumber. My partner woke up and asked me to please stop thrashing around. I tried to, but every time I slipped off to sleep, I heard the voice: Milk. Milk. Human kindness... Call for submissions...

At five a.m. when Diane rose to get ready for work, I said, "I've had some really odd dreams. You're not going to believe this, but I think I'm going to put together an anthology and call it *The Milk of Human Kindness*. I've been dreaming about it all night." Diane's response was to roll her eyes and say, "That's all you need — another project. But if it means you'll sleep better, by all means do it. I would certainly like to get a good night's sleep for once."

I didn't act right away on this message from beyond and continued to have the same dream, so finally I got out my Shakespeare plays and hunted through *MacBeth* for the phrase, "the milk of human kindness." The heartless Lady MacBeth, who easily out-evils many male villains, worries that her husband is "too full o' the milk of human kindness/To catch the nearest way." In other words, she's not sure MacBeth has the guts to go for the glory. She intimates that she can make any sacrifice and that she will work to move her husband forward under any circumstances. It's such a reversal of all that we so often expect from a woman, a mother, a wife. A mother is supposed to be unselfish, caring and nurturing, full to the brim with love and kindness. What better typifies that than a woman giving her milk to an infant in a literal sharing of body and self?

On one end of the motherhood spectrum there are the Lady MacBeths and on the other end are their opposites: women who give their all and would die before any harm came to their families. Don't most mothers fall somewhere in the middle, though? I came to the conclusion that not every woman is full of the milk of human kindness; and yet, few are as diabolical as Lady MacBeth. What did other writers think? What were their experiences and perceptions? I put out a call and asked for stories, essays, and memoirs about relationships between mothers and daughters.

What I received surprised me. Most authors came at the topic from the point of view of the daughter, but a few told their stories from the mother's perspective. In every story, there was a straining for understanding, for knowledge and growth, even if the characters in the story or the "I" of the piece paid a high price for it. The contributions to this collection affected me deeply. Some caused me to think about them for days. Others made me chuckle with familiarity. Three, in particular, brought me to tears. I felt in awe of the power of these women's narrative voices, of what they survived, of what they envision, and of how they can write with such clarity and passion.

We have in this collection twenty-three stories of love and loss, happiness and heartbreak. They're written by women in their 20s all the way up into their mid-70s; some write full-time as a career while others write when they can; all have published at least one book featuring strong female characters and feminist themes. They hail from all over the United States and from Canada, Britain, New Zealand, and Australia and represent 25 different presses. Some of them are mothers, godmothers, surrogate mothers—and all of them have graciously shared at least one aspect of their ideas, beliefs, and thoughts about mothers and daughters.

Each author's contribution is prefaced by information about her and her work. Some of the authors represented here in this collection have written a dozen or more books; some are newer writers still breaking into the field. For the most part, details of book titles and publisher information have been omitted from the prefaces. To see a list of works for each author and contact information as well, please turn to the bibliography at the back of the book.

If you are touched by any or all of these stories, please feel free to contact the authors. As I have worked on the stories with all of these talented women, I have learned that each is blessed with more than a little milk of human kindness. And besides, through their efforts, this book has been birthed into being, and I am no longer merely dreaming of its reality—it's here!

Lori L. Lake
Twin Cities, Minnesota
August, 2004

Once upon a time, in very recent history, there were no books celebrating lesbians. We dedicate this collection to all the women who never had lesbian stories to read, and we hope girls and women never again lack for stories that reflect their lives and times.

"No song or poem will bear my mother's name. Yet so many of the stories that I write, that we all write, are my mother's stories."

~Alice Walker, *"In Search of Our Mothers' Gardens"*

## Cameron Abbott

Cameron Abbott lives in New York City with Michele, her lover of 19 years.  In the Seventies, she attended a talk by Rita Mae Brown at Cazenovia, and she says, "Apart from developing a huge crush on her, I found her words inspirational.  It only took me another 20 years to get off my butt and write a novel myself."

Cameron is a successful lawyer, law professor, and arbitrator who has MA, PhD, and JD degrees. She has capitalized on that knowledge in her writing, and both of her suspenseful romance novels are set in the professional and legal world. A voracious reader of lesbian novels, she turned her hand to fiction in 2001, and the result was *To the Edge*, which quickly became an international bestseller.  Her second novel, *An Inexpressible State of Grace*, was released in January 2004, and has been chosen as an Insightout book club selection.

# Train Tracks

## Fiction by Cameron Abbott

THE TRAIN AMBLED south through the lush countryside, charting a course roughly parallel to the New Jersey Turnpike. Well, it was actually much more than an amble—this was the high-speed Acela, after all—but compared to the air shuttle she could have taken, the train was practically crawling. And that's just the way Kate wanted it.

"I don't want to hassle with airport security," she'd told Ellen while cramming underwear into her overnight bag. She picked up her keys and jiggled them for effect before dropping them into the side pocket. The key-ring had a small Swiss army knife attached too securely for easy removal, and she always feared that some alert security guard would stop her if it showed up on the x-ray scanner. Of course, she could just check the bag containing her keys, but she hadn't bothered to mention that to Ellen.

"Anyway, after you deal with airport traffic into La Guardia and out of BWI, plus the long drive into Baltimore, it ends up taking about the same time. And I can spread out on the train. It's more comfortable for getting work done."

She was rambling, she knew it, and Ellen knew it, too. Anything to avoid thinking about what lay ahead.

"Kate, it's okay, I was just curious." Ellen put her hand on her lover's arm—gently, tentatively—and quietly searched her face. Kate knew that look: wondering what she was feeling, ready to shoulder any burden Kate asked of her, hoping she would use these last few minutes to talk about it. Letting Kate know that she was there for her, as she had been for the last ten years.

But Ellen wouldn't ask, wouldn't pry—she knew Kate wouldn't talk about it in any meaningful way until she was ready, and that might not be until she called later that night. Or the next day. It might not be until Kate returned from Baltimore.

Over the years, Ellen had become very adept at reading the lexi-con of Kate. And vice versa.

Kate zipped the bag, turned, and kissed her. "I'll call you from the hospital," she whispered.

IT WASN'T UNTIL the train was half an hour south of the Newark stop that Kate pulled out the tray seat in front of her to set up her laptop. She fired it up, accessed the summary judg-ment brief she'd been drafting, and stared at the screen, trying to get her head back into the argument.

"Plaintiff's construction of this terminology strains the bounds of credulity, because..." That's where she'd left off. She'd been searching for the perfect phrase to capture the outra-geousness of her adversary's position when her secretary had buzzed her that her sister Janice was on the line. Her flurry of emotions had been swift: first annoyance at the interruption, then surprise that her sister even knew her office number, and finally dread. Whatever it was, she was certain she didn't want to hear it.

"Mom's in the hospital. It doesn't look good."

Her heart skipped into overdrive, but she took a deep breath and forced her voice to remain calm.

"What happened?"

"She fell. It looks like a broken hip. But there may be some brain damage, too. She isn't making any sense."

*Does she ever?* Kate bit off the remark before voicing it, oddly aware of some tiny sliver of family allegiance—or maybe just human empathy—making itself known after all this time. She glared back at the screen in front of her. "Well, what do the doc-tors say?" *Let's get the facts before charging off on a wild stam-pede to Baltimore.*

"That you should get down here. Now."

She waited a few beats, debating whether to ask one last question, the one she hated herself for even considering. But eventually she did, just barely, in a half-whisper she regretted immediately.

"Has she asked for me?"

Janice gave her usual sigh—the audible, disgusted one that came out as something between a yawn and a moan. "Just get down here."

THE SCREEN CONTINUED to stare at Kate, patiently await-ing the bolt of inspiration from her that would finish the sen-tence. And she continued to stare right back at it. She usually had no problem working on the train. People tended to keep their voices low, and the gentle rhythm of the tracks usually lulled her into a peaceful state of utter concentration. But not today.

She lifted her eyes from the accusatory blinking cursor and stared outside at the trees and embankments whipping past at a dizzying speed. The objects in the distance were discernable; they didn't appear to move as quickly, and her eyes could therefore focus on them for a few seconds. But the landscape closer to the train tracks appeared and was gone in a fraction of a second, things buzzing by so swiftly that her brain barely had time to register they were there at all, much less identify them. The trees and telephone poles in the middle distance were the most fascinating. If she tried to take in the scene as a whole, everything whizzed past in a kaleidoscope of blurred images; but if she focused on a single object, she could just barely make it out before it disappeared. By sheer force of will, her gaze on that telephone pole, or that shrub, seemed to suspend them for a moment, making them stand out in a field of whorling, blinding motion.

Although she knew the trees weren't moving—she was the one traveling 100 miles per hour—it didn't appear that way from the comfort of her seat. No wonder the Renaissance thinkers had such a hard time with the notion of a sun-centered solar system. From a stationary point, it really did appear that you were standing still and the rest of the universe was moving past you. It's all a matter of perspective, and although Copernicus and Galileo had it right, old beliefs die hard. It would take another few centuries for technology to catch up and prove what they had intuited by simply opening their minds.

While her eyes played their focus game, her mind soon drifted into a game of its own, reviewing a myriad of flashcard images zipping through her consciousness before they could quite register.

A smack across the face, hard enough to leave her cheek stinging for long moments afterward as she sat blinking, uncomprehending, at her mother's clenched jaw and cold glare. She was five years old, and they were living in the three room rental on Trinity Street, in the heart of Baltimore's Little Italy. She hadn't meant to knock over her glass of milk; she was just reaching for a piece of Sara Lee crumb cake, and her elbow hit the glass before she realized it.

An invitation for the familiar litany that punctuated so many of her childhood days: "All right, clumsy, you just get a towel and wipe that up! You think we can afford to throw good milk on the floor? You think you father's out there working every day so you can throw his good money down the drain? And no crumb cake for you. Not until you learn some respect!"

It was fear, of course. She'd figured that out long ago – her mother's constant fear that the money wouldn't stretch far enough, they wouldn't make the rent that month, they'd be out on the street and humiliated in front of the whole neighborhood. As poor as they were, her mother had been even poorer as a child. Kate never had to eat ketchup sandwiches for dinner, as her mother had (or so she claimed). Even though, from time to time, her father gambled on the ponies riding at Pimlico and joked about the day when his ship would come in, there was always food in the refrigerator and electricity turning on the lights. Still, her mother lived in unremitting dread that it would all be taken away. And she did her best to teach that fear to her daughters every day of their lives.

Kate hadn't known her mother's mother. She knew only that her grandmother, with the heavenly name of Celestina Bertucci, had raised her children alone and had died when Kate's mother was only fourteen. Kate's uncle Dominick had taken over and supported himself and his sister Maria until Maria's marriage two years later to Jamey Howard, the quiet hardworking Irishman who became Kate's father.

If her mother were anyone else, Kate might have felt some compassion for her. Functionally illiterate, having dropped out of school at fourteen; always an outsider in their small Italian neighborhood, having been raised a Protestant and worse, marrying Irish. "Shanty Irish," her mother would hurl at her father during their weekly knock-down, all-out arguments. But he'd just smile at her, the curl of his lip saying what he dare not: that she was no better, a dirt poor WOP, and probably a bastard to boot. Still, for all their fighting, they were a united front when it came to Kate and Janice. When Maria Bertucci married red-headed Jamey, she took control of his life, just as she would take control of her daughters' lives when they came along a few years later. It always seemed to Kate that he'd handed over the reins with too little resistance. Then again, Maria Bertucci Howard was a force not easily resisted.

"Get your head out of that book and find something to do," her mother railed at her one day when she was in the fourth grade. She *had* something to do, of course. She was reading *Little Women*, and her teacher had even commended her when she'd selected the book during Library period that day. But her mother wouldn't care about that. "You know they're calling you a book-worm and a smarty pants, don't you?" she said with an all-knowing wag of her head.

"They" could only refer to the women in the neighborhood who swapped gossip every day at the pork store on the corner or in the evenings when they all sat guard on the sidewalks in front of their respective houses, perched on lawn chairs beside the white marble stoops of which they were all so proud. Forever trying to fit in with the gaggle of big-haired madonnas, her similarly-coiffed mother would chime in on a discussion about tomato sauce (which everyone called "gravy"), or the quality of the prosciutto this week, but her comments often went ignored. After all, the hallmark of a good cook is in the enthusiasm of the eater, and with an Irish husband, she was seen to be cooking for a dull and uneducated palate.

"Why don't you go show your new bike to Frankie Perillo?" her mother continued. "He got a new bike for his birthday last week. You could ride around together."

The last thing Kate wanted to do was ride around the neighborhood with that moron. Francesco Perillo thought he was God's gift to creation, just like his father and everyone else in that family. They lived in the gaudiest house on the block, and owned the whole thing, from the ugly mermaid fountain taking up the entire patch of front lawn, down to the Baroque portico festooned with hundreds of curlicues and angels. You'd think his father was the Pope instead of the owner of a hardware store five blocks over. Still, they were the richest family around, and the prospect of getting invited to one of the Perillos' backyard barbeques or wedding showers (with so many cousins, there were always a lot of showers for *something* in that house) was an incessant theme in Kate's home.

"I don't wanna play with Frankie Perillo. He's stupid and a bully," Kate said.

"You watch your mouth," her mother hissed, glancing quickly at the open front window to make sure no one was within earshot.

"I'm supposed to read this for school." That was technically a lie. But since she wasn't Catholic, she didn't worry about having to confess it later.

"Keep it up, girl," her mother sneered. "See where it gets you. No one wants to marry a smarty-pants. It's no good for a girl to be too smart."

*Yeah, look where all your brains landed you,* Kate wanted to say. But by the ripe old age of ten, she had already learned where the line was and knew better than to cross it.

"You could do a lot worse than Frankie Perillo."

Kate rolled her eyes and groaned. "Ma! Please!"

"What'd I say?"

The thing was, Kate didn't really care if her brains were a turn-off to boys. All of her girlfriends giggled about how cute Johnny Nunzio looked in his altar boy get-up, but she was much more interested in how sweet Angie Balducci's voice sounded when she sang "You're a Grand Ol' Flag" after the Pledge of Allegiance every morning. They'd sat together ever since first grade because their names were so close alphabetically, and they'd become best friends. But Angie lived too far away to visit after school—on the whole other side of Italy, a good 20 blocks away—so her friendship with Angie was basically useless to her mother.

And Angie liked her brains. She always asked Kate her opinion about everything, and when she'd say Kate was the smartest person she knew, Kate struggled to hide the smile she felt ready to beam across her face.

They used to talk on the phone every night. "It's about homework," Kate would say in answer to her mother's scornful look. But Kate's mother had put an end to the nightly phone calls last month. The phone company changed the billing plan, and now they had to pay for every call, so Kate's mother had laid down the law: no phone calls except in an absolute emergency (and probably not even then). Kate actually got hold of the notice from the phone company and, after reading it carefully, tried to explain to her mother that incoming calls were free, so if Angie called Kate, it would be Angie's phone number that would get charged. But her mother, who could barely read herself, suspected Kate was trying to pull a fast one and stuck to her initial edict. The distinctions between incoming versus outgoing calls were clearly too subtle for Maria Howard, who knew only that her husband had announced they'd be charged for "every call." Kate suspected that pressing the point would simply earn her another smack—not for being fresh, but for implicitly using her intelligence and education to show up her mother.

THE TRAIN PULLING into Wilmington roused her from her reverie. She knew from long experience that it was another forty-five minutes to Baltimore. Since there was no car rental outlet at the train station, she figured she'd grab a cab to the hospital and deal with renting a car later. She'd definitely need a car, if for no other reason than her certainty that, at some point, she'd have to make a quick getaway, and she refused to be dependent on someone else to drive her.

It had always been that way in the Howard home. Explosions erupted out of nowhere, like summer heat-lightning materializing on an otherwise humid but benignly cloudless day, and while her father usually retreated into a can of Natty Boh or Carling Black Label, her sister and mother would end up raising the roof with escalating insults that eventually were glossed over but would never be forgotten. Kate had no reason to think that anything had changed in the three years since she'd last been there. If anything, everyone in her family appeared to get worse with age, their subtle personality quirks blossoming into more neuroses with each passing year. Her father's love of a good brew, her mother's hair-trigger hysteria over anything outside her control or understanding, Janice's growing resemblance to their mother. And Kate's aloofness from them all.

"The Shadow" her father had started calling her when she was about fifteen. She'd float in and out of the house without a sound, every nerve in her body poised for the assault, silently praying for them to not notice her. It never really worked. Her mother was an omnipresent force, a multi-faceted spyglass peering into every corner of their lives. Nothing was too small to escape her notice (and therefore her criticism), and a cigarette ash on Kate's white sweater was cause for just as great a tirade as cutting school to go to the movies. No matter how silently she crept down the hall in the middle of the night, as soon as she reached the kitchen to sneak that piece of cake, her mother's inner motion-sensor was triggered, and her sharp voice would cut through the dark quiet: "That's right, keep stuffing your face. You're gonna be as big as Aunt Concetta."

Ironically, for all her mother's harping at "Kate-the-child" to stop spending so much time indoors, she was no happier when "Kate-the-teenager" granted her wish by spending every possible minute outside the house. No, she knew Kate was smoking pot and popping pills— although she never actually saw it, Kate was extremely careful about that—so that by her teens, the chant of Kate's early childhood was played in reverse: "Why can't you stay inside for once?" her mother would call out to her as she slipped through the front door. "Where are you going?"

"Out," Kate would call back. She still couldn't bring herself to ignore that voice altogether.

"When will you be back?"

"Later."

Kate avoided her house for a lot of reasons. She didn't want her mother to see her when she was high—which was practically all the time—and she didn't want to answer a lot of questions about where she'd been and who she'd been with. The drugs were the least of it. Although her father sometimes roused himself to accuse her of meeting up with a boyfriend down by the playground, the truth was far worse: she had a girlfriend.

It had started at a slumber party two years earlier. Kate, then thirteen, was invited to a birthday sleepover at Gina Martino's house. Since the Martinos were a family deeply embedded in the community — they owned the pork store and had cousins on nearly every block — Kate's mother was more than happy to give her permission. "You just make sure you thank the Martinos real polite, and don't eat like a *gavonne*. Be friendly to Gina's brother, too. You never know."

"Ma!"

"I'm just saying."

Gina had invited Luisa Andolino, a new girl in the neighborhood who had just started school with them. "They just came over," Gina explained, meaning that they had just arrived from Italy (the real one). "They're my mother's cousins." Thus the Martino clan grew, but since everyone liked the Martinos, they all accepted the Andolinos right away. Especially Luisa.

It didn't hurt that Luisa was devastatingly beautiful — or so she seemed to Kate. Long dark hair streaming down her back, with a flowery old-fashioned hairband keeping it all out of her face and showing off her intense blue-black eyes, which were framed by dark, perfectly shaped brows. Her nose was just right — not too long, but not an inconsequential little pug like the one Kate had inherited from her father. To Kate, Luisa Andolino was simply a perfect Madonna out of the Italian Renaissance. *Belissima*.

Kate hadn't gotten a chance to be nice to Freddie Martino that night. She hadn't seen him, which was just as well because he certainly would have spread it all over school if he'd witnessed the girls' kissing game. Luisa had been the one to come up with the idea, suggesting that they "practice" on each other and insisting that all the girls "over there" (in her little town just outside Naples) routinely played this game in order to ready themselves for the day when they'd be kissing a boy. "Is no big deal, *si?*" she'd said with a shy smile.

For the rest of her life, Kate knew, she just *knew*, that nothing would ever come close to the heavenly softness of Luisa's lips, the musky, earthy smell of her face, the heart-stopping moment when Luisa turned to her and pressed her mouth against Kate's. The girls' game that night went on for only an hour or so, but Kate and Luisa continued their game privately for another four years — until Kate's mother found the love notes Luisa had written.

The memory of that nightmarish afternoon never failed to slam into Kate's chest with the force of a tidal wave, as if she were seventeen all over again. Luisa had telephoned her at the

Five 'n' Dime, where Kate had an after-school job at the checkout counter. Kate could barely make out what Luisa was trying to say, with all that crying interspersed with Italian, which always seemed to come out more when Luisa was upset. But understanding finally began to dawn on her — and with it, abject fear.

"They *know! Capisce?! Sua madre! Le lettere di amore!*"

"My mother?! Oh God..."

"*Si, si!*"

Kate made some lame excuse at work and dashed home, but she knew the situation was unsalvageable the minute she stormed through the front door. Luisa's mother was seated on the sofa and gave Kate a hateful stare before pointedly turning to face the other side of the room. Kate turned to her mother and barely registered the venomous glare on her face before launching into her self-righteous defense.

"How *dare* you go through my stuff! Those letters are *private!*"

"You shut your filthy mouth!" her mother hissed.

It was over, really, before it ever began. It was over, she later realized, before she'd even walked through that front door. Their mothers had put their heads together (no mean feat, considering how high the hair was piled up), and had decided on the only possible course of action. Luisa was sent back to Naples to live with cousins. And Kate was grounded, basically for life. Their fathers had not been consulted, of course. "For your sake," her mother had ominously intoned. "You know what Andolino would do to her if he knew?" Kate's father was a different story. She knew he'd laugh it off (which he eventually did — there was no such thing as a real secret in the Howard home), but he was also powerless to countermand an order by her mother.

To Kate, the strangest thing about the whole episode was how her parents and the Andolinos had remained friends. Although Luisa never returned to Baltimore, her parents kept the neighborhood apprised of her doings: her graduation, her eventual marriage (a development about which Maria Howard took great pains to inform Kate several years later, with a little sniff of satisfaction), and the birth of her first child seven months after that (the timing of which Kate took pains to point out to her mother, and thank goodness she was, by then, too old to slap). Her parents' ongoing cordiality with the Andolinos shouldn't have come as a surprise — although Mrs. Andolino had often voiced her conviction that it was Kate who had led Luisa into "that sin." No, the fact that Kate's mother prized her standing in the neighborhood over everything else, including loyalty to her daughter, was one of the sad truths of Kate's childhood, and it was unrealistic to expect anything different.

THE CLATTERING OF the train over the bridge of the wide Susequehanna River reminded her that Baltimore was now only about half an hour away. Baltimore, where her mother lay helpless in a hospital bed. She couldn't quite picture it. This giant, this tower of unspeakable will and fury, who was everywhere, at all times, monitoring and commenting on the slightest movements of every creature within her sphere—with scorn, derision, fear. It just wasn't possible. She tried to visualize the scene, the quiet form in a hospital bed, but she couldn't quite do it. Instead, another series of images crowded up against the picture she was trying to conjure. Images that had been lurking just under the surface of her consciousness, fleeting and disparate, from here and there over the years. Too numerous to singly identify, each too inconsequential to have been memorable, but all now tumbling feverishly through her too-weary mind, as if to spin a web that was as yet unrecognizable.

Her mother in the midst of a frenzy during Kate's trip to Baltimore during the third year of law school. The firestorm could have been about anything—how "uppity" Kate was becoming now that she'd put herself through school and was almost a lawyer, perhaps—but the fight was not the focus of her attention right now. Instead, the image that flitted through Kate's mind was the moment when, in the middle of ranting, her mother had opened the refrigerator and put a bottle of Clorox on the top shelf.

Fast-forward to the next freeze-frame: a few years later, several months after she and Ellen had moved in together, when they'd visited the old Baltimore neighborhood because Kate had a hankering for steamed crabs. Kate's mother, like any Baltimore native, had been cracking crabs since the cradle, and yet at one point during the backyard feast, she'd picked up a spice-covered claw and quietly asked no one in particular, "Now what do I do with this?" The assembled neighbors and family members had joked that Maria had had too much to drink.

Next frame: in a visit a year or so later, her mother complimenting her on a necklace she was wearing, and laughing with a little bit of embarrassment when Kate pointed out that she'd given the necklace to Kate the previous Christmas. And the stoney look of confusion when, the very next morning, her mother had again complimented her on the necklace and asked where she'd gotten it.

There had been no defining blow-up, no single tantrum that

marked Kate's formal estrangement from her family. She'd just sort of drifted off. She kept in touch to varying degrees over the years — occasional emails with Janice, calls to her parents' home every few weeks. But she hadn't found the time to visit for three years now, and her invitations urging her parents to visit New York were concededly half-hearted. *They're busy being grandparents to Janice's brood*, she told herself. A trip to New York is too expensive, too much trouble for them. But the truth was that she had an ordered life — a good job where she was respected and well liked, a beautiful lover who was as devoted to her as her family was not — and the disruption that her family's presence would entail just wasn't worth it.

Even their telephonic connection had waned recently, she realized. When she called her parents these days, it was her father who almost always answered the phone. Retired now, he was no doubt sitting around the house watching soap operas and getting a head start on his Natty Bohs. But there was that one time she'd called a few months ago, when her mother had answered the phone. She'd picked it up on the fifth ring and yelled "Who is it?" as if holding the receiver far from her mouth. Kate had laughed and said, "Ma, it's me, Kate."

"Kate?"

"Kate. In New York. What are you doing?"

"New York?"

"Let me take it, Mare," she heard her father say in the background. "Kate?"

"Dad? What's up with Mama?"

"Oh, nothing. She just gets confused, you know."

Kate had let it drop. If he didn't think it worth going into, neither did she. But looking back on it now, she realized that bizarre exchange had been the last time she'd actually spoken to her mother.

And then there was the comment by Janice in one of their rare phone calls last month. She'd mentioned she wasn't going to drop the kids off at their grandparents' house until Dad got home from the Orioles game. "Oh, it's too much for Mama to handle them alone," she'd said. Kate hadn't thought anything of it. Three kids were very likely too much for any one adult to handle alone. Then again, maybe it was something more.

AS SHE WATCHED the conductor walk through the car, it occurred to Kate that they must be very near Baltimore, and she was suddenly seized in a vise-grip of undefined panic. Forcing herself to remain calm, she brought all of her highly-paid problem-solving skills to bear and ran through the likely culprits.

Her mother might be dying—no, as much as that was certainly a possibility, it wasn't the immediate cause of the suffocating dread that swept her. The fact that their peculiar phone call a few months back might be their last conversation, that was closer to the mark, but still not quite there. And then it hit her, a swelling realization that engulfed her in a black pit of desperate, aching motherlessness: her mother might not really *be* her mother anymore. She might live on—if one thing was certain, Maria Bertucci could never be felled by a simple broken hip—but she might, for all intents and purposes, be irretrievably lost. And with her, all of the chances that Kate had thoughtlessly squandered over the years, opportunities to have a conversation without fighting, to resolve any of their innumerable differences. To find acceptance.

It was absurd, truly ridiculous, to imagine any real connection with the woman who, for Kate's entire life, had been a relentless grinding force hell-bent on molding her into a shape that simply would not fit. But as the thoughts and feelings continued their free-fall through the dark, a glimmer of something new found its way through the despair. A fleeting glimpse, really, no more than gossamer that melted as soon as she touched it, but which left something real in its wake. Not a thought so much as a sensation: elusive, undefined, but something to dwell on later. She couldn't quite capture it, it was gone before she could even really see it, but it left her with the mystifying notion that maybe, just maybe, in the twisted world of all that was her mother, that relentless grinding had been a sort of gift. As if her mother had been the grain of sand that formed a pearl.

"Baltimore! Next stop, Baltimore Maryland."

"ELLEN?"

"Honey? How is she?"

Kate tried to shield her tear-streaked face from the people passing through the hospital corridor.

"I don't know. They say it's too soon to tell."

"Well what is she like? Is she conscious?"

"Yeah, she's sitting up. She held my hand and kept kissing it and telling me I was beautiful."

"You're kidding."

"But then she asked me who I was."

## Georgia Beers

Born in 1968 in Rochester, New York, Georgia Beers continues to live there with her partner of ten-plus years and their two dogs. She works in the field of advertising specialty and print sales, but with a degree in Mass Communications (emphasis on broadcasting, minor in theater), she is the first to say, "I am a salesperson who *so* does not belong in the sales field."

When asked where she gets her ideas, she says, "I find influence and inspiration everywhere. Truthfully, for lesbian fiction, any beautiful woman I see could potentially end up a character in one of my stories. Current events get me thinking. I also read a ton of fiction — lesbian and hetero — and I always find influences there. TV shows, movies, my friends. There isn't a lot that *doesn't* influence my writing in one way or another." Georgia is currently at work on her third novel.

# The Tuesday Before Thanksgiving

## Fiction by Georgia Beers

I LOOK IN the mirror. Again. That's got to be the fifth time in the last fifteen minutes. My hair is still neat, albeit much grayer than I'd prefer. It's cut a little shorter than usual, but I've found it's much easier to deal with this way. I fluff it with my fingers and wonder what Devon will think of it. I push it behind my ears, fiddle with my necklace. Then I roll my eyes at myself, heading for the living room to check the pillows on the couch and straighten the stack of coasters on the coffee table for the third time.

I'm nervous. And I hate that I'm nervous. I shouldn't be nervous; there's no reason. This is *my* house. She's *my* daughter. *I'm* not the one who has to be impressive. I have all the power here. Don't I?

*My daughter is a lesbian.*

God, I hate that sentence. It shows up, unannounced and unwelcome in my head every so often, tearing my attention away from whatever I'm doing at the time, taunting me. It's been appearing for almost five years now, and I'm only just beginning to realize it isn't a lie and it's not going away.

*My daughter is a lesbian.*

I return to the mirror, finger-comb my hair once more, and think back to the telephone conversation with my daughter the previous week.

*"We'll get there some time on Tuesday. We'd like to be able to spend some time with Aunt Ce, too. Then we can help you Wednesday night with the turkey and stuff so there won't be so much to do on Thursday."*

*"We?"*

*An uneasy silence. Then, "Yeah. I'm bringing Holly with me. I'd really like you to meet her. That's okay, right?"*

Of course it's okay, *my head screams at me.* Tell her of course it's okay, that her friends are always welcome here. *But this*

*Holly...she isn't just a 'friend.' That fact makes the words stick in my throat longer than they should.*

"Mom?" *Devon's voice is worried, unsure.*

"Of course it's okay," *I manage to grind out.*

"Great." *She sighs with relief as she says it. It occurs to me that part of her must have been worried I'd actually say no. The realization shames me.* "Give a call if you need us to bring anything or pick anything up along the way, okay?"

"Okay. Drive safely. Don't speed."

"I'll be careful. I love you, Mom. And thanks."

"I love you, too, Devon."

I suddenly wonder if it's because she's got a boy's name. Is that the first mistake I made? Starting her off confused, right from the beginning? My fault, not hers.

I sigh, peering out the window and letting my thoughts drift to my expectations of this Holly. Definitely not a boy's name. At least *her* mother doesn't worry about that. I conjure up a picture of what I'm anticipating, and cringe as my brain tosses me an image of a large, manly woman with many piercings and tattoos. The crew cut, black motorcycle boots, and pack of cigarettes rolled into the sleeve of her t-shirt round out the entire portrait and I shudder involuntarily.

I remember back to when Devon first told me. She was just about to leave for college. My sister Celia says I shouldn't have been surprised, that all the signs were there during Devon's childhood. She hated wearing dresses, she loved to play in the dirt with trucks, and she wouldn't touch any of the dolls I kept buying for her. In school, she excelled in sports, playing softball, basketball, and volleyball and was voted to All State in all three. She did date a nice young boy named Chad for a short time. They went to the prom together. I thought he was very sweet, but he stopped coming around one day, and Devon never really went into detail. She'd get mad when I'd pry, so after a while, I stopped asking questions. She seemed so angry so often, and I tried not to make it worse.

"I'm a lesbian, Mom." One day, she blurted it out. Just like that. "I'm a lesbian, Mom." And then she went to meet up with her friends. The little brat dropped a bomb on me and ran off. Then she avoided me like the plague as best she could. I knew we should talk about it, but I honestly was in such a state of shock that I had no idea what to say. I dropped her off at her dorm, gave her a hug, and told her to call if she needed anything. Each of us cleanly avoided the subject all together. Then I cried the entire ride home.

Each time she came home for a holiday or a long weekend,

there was something new about her. First, there was the hair dye. She bleached a blonde streak into her beautiful dark hair right in the front. I could have killed her. She resembled a skunk. A month later, she came home with a hoop in her eyebrow and a nose ring. I tried hard to keep my comments to a minimum, but I made it clear I didn't approve of the look. She thought I was constantly on her back, but she had no idea how much I was keeping inside. I'm surprised my head didn't explode. She glared at me for the entire weekend and I glared back.

Then the biggest blow came, right after graduation. She was offered a job in Chicago and she took it. My heart broke. Yes, she could have gone much further away from our little hometown in Upstate New York, but it's still far. About ten hours by car or a couple by plane, and I'm not a big fan of flying. Or driving. Needless to say, I've often wondered if she took the job to get away from me. I think all mothers wonder that at one time or another. I was devastated for weeks after she left, and I still get melancholy when I remember that time in my life. Her father left us when she was a toddler, so it had always been just me and Devon, just the two of us. The idea of her leaving me alone nearly destroyed me. I'm still not sure how I managed to survive without her here.

I'm suddenly snapped out of my reverie by the ringing of my phone. "Hello?"

"Hey." It's my sister, Celia. We talk on the phone at least half a dozen times a day; it's ridiculous. It's also a huge comfort. Celia's support is a big part of the reason I was able to keep my sanity after Devon left for Chicago. "What time are the girls arriving?"

The girls? She obviously knows Devon is bringing that Holly with her. Devon keeps in better touch with her aunt than with me, and I often find that it gets under my skin. "They should be here any time," I say evenly.

"Are you nervous?"

"Nervous?" I fiddle with the fringe on a toss pillow. "About what? Why should I be nervous? What's there to be nervous about?"

I can almost hear Cece roll her eyes. My big sister always could see right through me. I hate that. "About meeting her."

"Why should *I* be nervous? *She's* the one who should be nervous." I wonder if my sister is buying any of this false bravado of mine. I'm sure she's not.

"She sounds like a nice girl."

"You've talked to her?"

"A couple times when I've called Devon. She seems very bright."

I try to ignore the jealousy that wells up. How come I've never spoken with this Holly? Is it because I tend to call my daughter at work? "That's nice."

"Oh, come on, Marti. Lighten up. This is important to Devon. She really wants you to like Holly."

I grind my teeth against the fact that Celia knows so much more than I do about my own daughter. "Mm." It's all I can manage to say.

"Marti." Celia's voice becomes firm, what I call her Big Sister Voice. "This trip is extremely important, do you understand that? Stop being so old-fashioned. Your daughter being gay isn't that big a deal, you know." I can hear the sudden smile in her voice. "It's actually kind of hip. You should watch *Will & Grace* once in a while."

*I do watch Will & Grace,* I think, pouting.

"Holly could be The One." She says it quickly, almost as if she wants to get it out before she changes her mind. I can somehow feel the capital letters.

"What?"

"All I'm saying is, Devon really loves this girl. She might be it. Give her a chance."

There's a knock at the door and commotion in the foyer, and I have no time to absorb the little tidbit of information my sister's just plopped into my lap. "Damn it, Celia," I hiss into the phone. "Why don't you just wait until the very last minute to tell me something like that?" I hang up on her laughter and go to greet my child, whom I haven't seen since last Christmas.

I'M SHOCKED WHEN I turn the corner and see her. We stand and stare at one another, and my daughter grins knowingly the entire time. Gone is the blonde streak and her rich, cocoa brown hair is past her shoulders and all one color again. The eyebrow piercing is gone as well, though I do detect a small diamond stud still glittering in her nostril. She's dressed neatly and casually in a pair of faded jeans and a black, v-neck sweater, and she looks incredible. The smile on her face and the gleam in her dark eyes are like icing on the cake. She looks happier than I can ever remember.

"Hi, Mom." She holds out her arms to me and we hug tightly.

"It's so good to see you, honey," I say softly, and I mean it.

"You look terrific. I love the new hair cut."

My hands go to my hair self-consciously. "Thanks. *You* look terrific."

She blushes and steps aside, and for the first time, I take a good look at the woman with her, the woman I'm intending to hate. Well, intensely dislike anyway. She's not at all what I'm expecting. She's a tall, stunning blonde, and she's smiling politely in my direction. Her khaki pants and navy twin set are simple, but tasteful. Her blonde curls cascade to her shoulders in controlled waves. There is a friendly sparkle in her blue eyes.

Devon's voice softens as she makes the introductions. "Mom, this is Holly Carter. My girlfriend."

Holly holds out a hand to me and I take it, trying not to stare at the woman, not to grip her hand too tightly, as a father might do to a boy courting his daughter. Her handshake is firm, confident, but not overpowering. "It's nice to meet you, Mrs. Scott."

"Please," I say. "Marti. Mrs. Scott makes me sound old."

Holly nods, still smiling. "It's nice to meet you, Marti."

"Same here." I didn't expect her to be so pleasant. So pretty. So polite. I'm still shaking her hand. I realize with surprise that my daughter has brought home the All-American Girl.

"So," Devon says, obviously trying to keep us from falling into an uncomfortable silence. "Let's get our bags upstairs, and then we can visit."

I finally let go of Holly and the two girls head up to Devon's bedroom. For a split second, I hope Devon will lead her friend to the spare room, but even I know I'm being ridiculous. Of course, they'll stay in the same room. Of course, they'll sleep in the same bed. Of course. I sigh and saunter into the kitchen.

TWENTY MINUTES LATER, both girls join me in the kitchen as I'm preparing dinner. They've changed into fresh, unwrinkled clothes and look relieved to be out of the car.

"Damn, that's a long drive," Devon says, pulling out a chair and plopping down at the table with a sigh.

"All you have to do is move closer," I respond automatically as I unwrap the chicken. My answer is practically the same every time, and Devon usually gets annoyed with me. This time is different.

"Maybe one of these days I will."

I don't turn around to face her, but I can feel my own shock plain on my face. I never knew that the idea of moving closer to home even crossed my daughter's mind. I struggle hard to keep myself from jumping on her response.

"What are we having?" she asks, pulling the subject out from under me.

"Chicken cutlets."

She cheers from her seat, and I smile. Every mother knows her child's favorite dish and I'm no different.

"Can I help?" This comes from Holly, and I turn to meet her gaze. She gives me a sideways grin that's quite charming, and I try hard to resist it. "Or at least watch? I know how much Devon likes your chicken cutlets. I hear about it all the time. I'd like to learn how to make them for her."

"So you do the cooking?" I ask.

"I try to keep Devon out of the kitchen. It's for our own safety." We both chuckle.

"Hello? Sitting right here." My daughter's protest is feeble and she knows it. She hates to cook. She always has.

"Well, come on over here," I say, trying to keep any reluctance out of my voice. After all, *I* want to make Devon's favorite meal, and I'm not really thrilled to have this Holly stealing my thunder. Part of me, though, is flattered, and I move over a bit to make room for her at the counter. When she stands next to me, her statuesque figure is even more prominent. She's at least three inches taller than I am, and her perfume is a subtle, musky scent I like immediately. I hand her the meat tenderizer, which looks like a hammer with teeth. Then I gesture at the boneless chicken breasts on the counter. "Beat the hell out of these. Do you have a boss or somebody who's gotten on your nerves lately? That helps. Get them good and flat."

Holly smiles wickedly and goes to town.

I mix up the seasonings and breadcrumbs in one dish and the eggs in another. Then I get out my electric frying pan. The thing is ancient, but it works, and chicken cutlets are just not the same done in a skillet on the stove. I pour in the oil.

"No fat in that," Devon comments, raising her voice over Holly's pounding.

"I've made them the same way your entire life, Ms. Health Nut. You never complained before."

"I know. Hey, Mom, do you have anything to drink? Wine, maybe?"

I realize what a great idea it is. A glass of wine would be wonderful at this moment, especially for me, as I share cooking duties with my lesbian daughter's lover. "I bought a couple bottles of your cheap junk. They're in the fridge. If you could open a bottle of the Merlot on the rack, you can pour your mother a glass of that."

"Hol?" she asks.

Holly stops her pounding to answer. "A glass of Merlot would be great. Thanks." She gestures to her project. "How's this?"

"Good," I say.

"That was fun. You're right; smashing heads makes it even more entertaining."

I nod and take her through the next step, checking to see if the oil's hot enough. Then we dip each breast into the egg, then the seasoning, and finally place them into the pan.

"What's in the seasoning?" she asks as Devon hands us each a wineglass.

I hesitate for a second, wondering if I can play the 'it's a family secret, I can't tell you' card and get away with it. I know Devon will pounce all over that, so I go for honesty instead. "A little bit of everything. Bread crumbs, basil, oregano, parsley, salt, pepper, parmesan. It depends on your mood and what you have in the house."

Holly nods with understanding, then sips her wine. "Oh, this is nice."

I glance victoriously at my daughter, who playfully sticks her tongue out at me before drinking her White Zinfandel.

"So, Mrs. Scott," Holly begins, then corrects herself. "Sorry. Marti. Devon tells me you work in the office at the elementary school."

"That's right." I nod, pleasantly surprised once again that my daughter talks about me in any way, shape or form. "I've been there for..." I do a quick calculation and my eyes widen at the total. "...twenty one years now. Good Lord."

"I remember Mrs. Pritchard in our office. She was the nicest lady. When you're seven years old, it really helps to have a familiar, friendly face you can turn to for help." She grimaces sheepishly. "Our school was huge. I got lost constantly."

Devon chuckles from her seat. "She's still lost constantly. She has no sense of direction whatsoever."

"I do, too!"

"Sweetie, you don't, and you know it."

Holly sighs in defeat.

"I don't either," I whisper to her, surprised by my sudden desire to be conspiratorial with her. "Devon's father always made fun of me; I'd get confused and turned around so easily. He, on the other hand, could find his way home from the center of the earth."

"Well, I think your daughter inherited that."

"I think so, too. Lucky for us, huh?" I sip my wine, trying to ignore Devon's grin.

THE GIRLS DON'T let me move after dinner. They clean up around me and start a pot of coffee brewing, and I'm a bit embarrassed by how good it feels to be pampered. I tell Devon I made a coffeecake and to bring it out. As Holly is wiping down the table, Devon calls to her. "Honey, you'd better give your mother a buzz and let her know you made it here in one piece."

Holly looks up at me. "May I use your phone?"

"Of course. It's right in the hallway."

She excuses herself politely as Devon brings me a steaming mug. "This is the first Thanksgiving she's spent away from her mom in twenty-eight years," she says quietly.

I'm both surprised and impressed, but Devon returns to the kitchen to finish the dishes before I can respond. I suddenly realize how much it says about my daughter that Holly is willing to give up Thanksgiving with her family to be here. I'm also sad for Holly's mother. It's not easy to feel the stinging absence of your child during the holidays. I know this from experience. I stir sugar into my coffee, lost in the reminiscence of time gone by.

Both girls return to the table a few minutes later with their own mugs, the coffeecake, and plates and forks.

"Everything okay at home?" I ask Holly, much to my own surprise.

"Yeah." She seems a little melancholy and I find myself longing for the smile I was beginning to associate with her presence.

I feel my Mother Sense kick in, and I can tell something is bothering her. A mother knows these things and has no choice but to explore. "You're sure?"

Holly sits and meets my eyes. "I'm sure. Thank you. It's just a little weird being away from my mom this time of the year. I think she's having a hard time of it, even though she doesn't want me to know and doesn't think I can tell."

I smile at her ability to read her mother and I figure Devon can probably read me just as accurately, though I'd be hard pressed to admit it. "Where does your family live?" I feel Devon's eyes on me, and I suspect she's surprised, but I ignore her.

"Cleveland."

"Are there a lot of you?"

"I have two younger brothers. One is in college and one still lives at home."

"And are they home now?"

"Yes."

"Then your mom isn't missing *all* her kids. That makes it a little better for her."

Holly nods and sips her coffee, absorbing my words. "I suppose."

"You and your mother must be close, what with you being the only girl."

"We are. Very."

"And your dad? Is he still around?" Even after all the years, I still feel badly that Devon's father isn't.

Holly smiles. "My parents have been married for thirty years. They're wonderful together."

For some reason, I find myself surprised that Holly comes from what seems to be a perfectly normal household. "Have they met you?" I turn to ask my daughter, honestly wondering.

She nods enthusiastically. "They're really great."

Holly chuckles. "I tease my parents about the fact that they love her more than me. When my dad calls and Devon answers the phone, he'll talk to her for twenty minutes. I get five and he's done with me."

"Hey, I can't help it if he's dazzled by my charm." Devon's smile is wide and I know instantly that she has a soft spot for Holly's dad. Part of me is relieved she finally has somebody in that role. The other part is a little jealous, hurt that I was never able to fill the whole void for her.

"Charm has nothing to do with it," Holly chuckles. "He just thinks you're cute."

"I *am* cute."

"And humble, too."

Their easy banter brings an involuntary smile to my face, which catches me off guard. I can't remember the last time I saw my daughter so relaxed and playful. I'm unprepared for the way it warms my heart. Deep down, I know Holly is at least partly responsible. I'm not sure how to deal with that.

*My daughter is a lesbian.*

Funny how that phrase pops up at the most inopportune times.

The phone rings and Devon jumps up before I can move a muscle. I smile as I have a quick flash of her as a ten-year-old who loved to answer the phone. Holly and I sit in silence listening to Devon talk. After a short time the identity of the caller becomes clear.

"Aunt Ce," we say simultaneously, then laugh.

Our chuckles die down and we sit quietly, sipping our coffee and picking at the remainder of the coffeecake. Internally, I'm having a battle with myself. I want to break the silence. I want to make this Holly more comfortable. At the same time, I don't want her to think she's won me over so easily. I hold tightly to my stoicism.

Suddenly, her eyes light up as she looks over my shoulder

into the living room. "You're reading Mary Higgins Clark."

I nod, following her gaze to my book lying open, pages down on an end table.

"Have you read them all?"

I nod again. "I have all the hard covers."

"Me, too," she says enthusiastically. "I have them all out on a shelf at home. Do you have a favorite?"

I'm suspicious about her; is she intentionally trying to find common ground with me? I want to let her know that I'm on to her, but the question about the books intrigues me. I never really thought about it before, and I tap my finger against my lips as I ponder. "It's been so long since I've read some of them, I can't remember them all. I really liked the one about the doctors...it was one of the early ones...which one was it?" I wrack my brain for the title.

"*The Cradle Will Fall*," she says, grinning widely.

"That's the one."

"Definitely my favorite, too."

*Isn't that convenient?* I think, narrowing my eyes as she continues with her praise for my favorite title. *Devon must have given her this information.*

"It's so well constructed," she continues. "I'm always amazed by the fact that she's still going strong after all these years."

"I just saw an interview with her on one of the morning shows recently."

"I think I saw that, too. On the *Today* show?"

"She was pushing that book." I point to the one I am currently reading. "She's very charming."

"And classy," Holly adds. "She's a very classy lady."

Before I realize what's happening, I find myself sucked deeply into conversation with her about our favorite authors; many are the same. Tami Hoag, Sue Grafton, Steve Martini, Lisa Gardner. I realize that my daughter couldn't have possibly given her girlfriend a list of *all* my favorite authors, that we really *must* have the same taste in literature. Slowly—and totally against my will—I'm discovering Holly to be intelligent and witty and fun to talk to. Devon returns, and we're so deep in conversation that we don't notice for several minutes. She lingers in the doorway, and when I finally look up, she grins my way. I resist the urge to childishly stick my tongue out at her.

"Aunt Ce says hi." She looks at Holly. "We're going to meet her for breakfast in the morning, okay?"

"Sounds great." Holly turns her blue eyes my way. "Will you join us?"

I'm extremely flattered that she even asked, and I pretend I don't see the quick flash of panic that shoots across Devon's face. I somehow even manage not to let it offend me. I'm well aware of how close my daughter and my sister are and, despite my occasional jealousy, I don't want to infringe upon that—even though I often wonder what they talk about. "Thank you, but no. You two go and have a good time. I'll see Celia on Thursday."

Devon tries—unsuccessfully—to mask her relief, and I mentally shake my head and roll my eyes. "Mom, you've got a Blockbuster card, right? Should we get a movie?"

I'm happy they've decided to stay in for the night, tired from the drive. I expected them to run out and meet up with Devon's school friends. I begin to wonder if she might actually be content here with me. The thought warms my insides a bit. I hand over my Blockbuster card and try to give her a ten-dollar bill.

"Ma, please. It's okay. I've got money."

"Sorry. Old habits." I chuckle to cover my slight embarrassment as I return my money to my wallet. Does a mother ever stop wanting to take care of her child? I don't think so.

I'M UNPREPARED FOR how quiet the house suddenly seems once the girls leave to rent a movie. They've only been here for a few hours, but already I miss the company. I take my coffee cup into the kitchen and rinse it out. As I turn, I notice the evening paper on the counter. The headline seems distortedly large to me.

*Bush Says No to Gay Unions.*

I pick the paper up curiously and read the article. It's not a pleasant one. Many in the government want to specify that marriage can only occur between a man and a woman. A gay man interviewed says he's fine with that, as long as there is an alternative for gays—a union of some sort.

*"I've been with my partner for seventeen years, but when he dies, I won't receive his Social Security benefits, nor would he get mine."* He goes on with a list I was never aware of. *"If he's in the ICU at the hospital, the doctors can legally deny me entrance to see him. We had to go to a lawyer and have specific paperwork drawn up so that I can make his medical decisions, should something incapacitate him. If President Bush wants to make marriage a religious thing between a man and a woman, fine, but he needs to take all the civil, non-religious benefits that go with it off the table. That's where the problem lies. Separation of Church and State."*

I'm not at all politically savvy. I hate politics; I always have. I think there is way too much lying and twisting of the truth to do anybody any good, and I try not to dwell on that fact. I usually avoid reading articles or watching any news reports about the President or the government because I get too disgusted by all the double-talk. I know that's not a very responsible attitude for an American, but I can't seem to help it. This article, however, has captured me, and as I read on, it occurs to me just how many members of the government and the religious sects are against equal rights for gays and lesbians. I can feel the hatred and intolerance of some of them as it almost drips off the paper. I half-expect it to burn my hands. Honestly, it's a little frightening. Continuing with the article, it doesn't seem to me that the gays and lesbians are asking for special treatment, as many accuse them of doing. It appears to me that they're just asking for equal treatment. I could be wrong, but the whole argument seems quite simple to me.

*My daughter is a lesbian.*

It hits me like a ton of bricks and suddenly, I'm plugging Devon's name into every "gay" or "lesbian" or "homosexual" in the article. My stomach churns.

I never wanted my kid to be gay. What parent does? I've had a difficult time dealing with it—and that's probably the understatement of the year. If I'm going to be honest, though, it's mostly because of me...because of *my* life and *my* image and *my* reputation and *my* desire for her to have the traditional wedding and *my* expectations of having a son-in-law and two-point-five grandkids. I realize, for the very first time in the seven years since I've known about my daughter's sexuality, exactly what she's up against in the world. I can feel my heart cracking in my chest for her. My eyes well, and I don't wipe the tears as they course down my cheeks. I don't want this adversity for my child. I don't want people calling her a sinner or a pervert or a lesser American.

"She's a good girl," I whisper into the silent kitchen.

I take the paper to the recycling bin and bury it beneath a bunch of empty cans and bottles. I don't want to see it again. I don't want to touch it or read about it or even think about it. I want it to go away.

*My daughter is a lesbian.*

And right then, at that very moment, I understand that it will *never* go away.

AS I LIE in bed that night, my mind is swirling with a million different thoughts. I could have stayed up longer with the girls—Lord knows my brain isn't ready to settle down for the night—but I wanted to give them a little space. We watched *Miss*

*Congeniality*. Both Devon and Holly seemed rather smitten with Sandra Bullock while I was busy drooling over that handsome young man who used to be on *Law & Order*. Despite my occasional distraction by thoughts of the newspaper article, it was a pleasant evening, though it became a bit obvious to me that the girls were overly conscious of their proximity to one another. I think they were nervous about making me uncomfortable. I appreciated that—I probably *would* have been uncomfortable—and that's the reason I pretended to be tired and turned in. I stretched and yawned and put on a good show. Still being on Chicago time, Devon said they were going to stay up and channel surf for a while. So now I lay here, sleep so far away I don't expect to see it at all tonight. It's a curse of middle age, or so I'm told.

I'm thirsty and I'm bored. I sigh and blink at the ceiling. My book is down in the living room, which doesn't help me at all. Also, I know there are six fresh bottles of Poland Spring water in the refrigerator, and the more I think about them, the thirstier I feel. I finally get up, annoyed with myself, and open my bedroom door, which is right at the top of the stairs. I strain my ears, but hear nothing except the television. The lights are off, too, from what I can tell. All I see is the eerie blueness cast by the screen, though I can't actually see into the living room from up here. The last thing I want to do is walk in on something that will be seared painfully into my brain forever. I debate for several minutes, but after still hearing nothing but the television, I make my move.

I tiptoe down the stairs, thankful that I know where each and every squeak resides. As I reach the bottom, I can see the couch as it faces the TV. I stop, shadowed by the darkness, and am inexplicably touched by the sight.

Both the girls are on the couch. Devon is leaning with her back against the arm and her feet stretched out. Holly is sitting in front of Devon, tucked snugly between my daughter's knees and leaning back against her chest; they're almost spooning. Devon is still awake, her eyes on the TV, but Holly is sleeping soundly.

I can't seem to move. I just stand there watching them, feeling simultaneously like a voyeur and a guardian.

Devon tightens her arms around Holly as Holly shifts a little in her sleep, burrowing more deeply into Devon's body. Devon smoothes a few stray, blonde locks of hair off of Holly's forehead and places a soft kiss there, and I'm shocked by the fact that it brings tears to my eyes. Even in nothing but the weird, ethereal light of the television, I can see the love and devotion on my daughter's face; it's as clear as if I was standing over the two of them, only inches away. Today seems to be a day of realizations and firsts for me as once again, I'm struck by something I never before understood. It hits me like a truck: my daughter is completely and utterly in love with this woman. And as I watch, she rubs her cheek against the top of Holly's head and smiles a gentle, easy smile of contentment.

*My daughter is happy.*

I wipe at tears that unexpectedly roll down my cheeks, take a deep, satisfied breath, and make my way silently back up to my bedroom. All of a sudden, I'm very tired, anxious to get some much-needed sleep so I can be up early and spend as much time as possible with the girls while their visit lasts. I smile. Then maybe we can discuss the arrangements for Christmas.

*My daughter is happy.*

## Meghan Brunner

Meghan Brunner has lived in Minnesota all her life and is blessed with the love and support of blood family, her partner of four years, and an extended circle of heart-kin. Though she is the youngest author collected here and is, as she puts it, "riding the tails of the Gen-Xers," she's already written two complete novels, the first of which, *From The Ashes*, was a 2003 Gaylactic Spectrum nominee.

Meghan has an undergraduate degree from the University of Minnesota. Her focus in her writing, thus far, has been upon lesbian dramas of urban fantasy and magical realism. When asked what has influenced her writing most, she says, "The voices in my head have been giving me stories for years. I'm afraid that if I don't write them down, they'll hunt me down and tie me to a chair until I do."

# A Mother Just Knows

## Fiction by Meghan Brunner

THEY SAY THERE are some things a mother just knows.

With her copper-red hair and olive-green eyes, no one would mistake Ryna for a child of my blood. Aside from our common slightness of build and lack of height, there is little resemblance between us. Even so, Ryna was and will always be the daughter of my heart... and after six years of trying with her father, I had begun to realize she was the only child I would ever have.

At only ten years her senior, I usually felt more like a big sister or an older friend than a mom. I had missed her first words, her first steps, her first laugh, her first tooth...but I had been there for those first squeaking notes on her fiddle, and I watched helplessly as her first romance — with a fellow named Josh — dashed her young heart and hopeful fantasies. And I cried for weeks after she went to live with Angela, her biological mom, so she could attend high school for three years.

I like to think that love makes a mother. I'd told myself that for years. But during that sweltering August not long after she'd turned sixteen, for the first time, I *felt* like a mother.

I watched her with Niki, and I just *knew*.

I'd never thought of Ryna as lesbian, or bi-, or anything, really. Not even straight. She was just herself — proud, defiant, and passionate. When she brought Niki and Tanek to our camp at Pendragon Renaissance Faire decked out like Gypsies and introduced them to the family, we all knew they belonged. She had already adopted them as we soon would. She loved Tanek as the brother she'd never had — but her love for Niki transcended family ties.

She had been infatuated with Josh. But with Niki... I think that was the first time she was really, really in love.

And it was the first time I was really, really in hate. I had been furious with Josh for breaking my Ryna's heart, but the scars he left caused her former gusto to turn to shy wistfulness. And that I could never forgive.

And, as a mother, it was something I could not ignore.

RYNA WATCHED WITH a faint smile as her step-mom, Kaya, retrieved a last scarf from the dirt-browned plywood of Caravan Stage's floor. The cobalt-and-gold fabric matched Kaya's outfit; she draped it artfully over one shoulder as she sauntered toward Hollow Hill and the enticing, spiced smells of curried chicken and tabouli. *And a kiss from my father*, the fiddler thought with a knowing grin.

Early evening had come to Pendragon—thank several gods—though Ryna wished it had brought some relief from the day's muggy, suffocating heat. It was Labor Day—the third day in a row that Pendragon's cast had spent trying to look chipper for the patrons while sweating their collective skins off in layers upon layers of garb...and Ryna had loved every blessed, familiar second of it.

She plopped down beside the luxuriously furnished, open-faced Gypsy wagon nestled behind Hollow Hill's grassy mound. The variety show that had just ended had been Niki's first time belly dancing on stage, with only a few spotty lessons from Kaya as preparation. Niki still glowed with triumph, and rightfully so—hell, one dance and already she had a fan club. The slanting, orange light outlined her like some mystical being, standing among the cheap wooden benches, absently clinking her bangle bracelets as she chatted with her admirers. Even after three days of ninety-billion-degree heat and crappy shower facilities, she looked beautiful and poised. One of the Fae, surely... no one with Niki's feline grace could be mortal. Someone to protect, to cherish, to love. A woman worth dying for.

A touch of breeze toyed with Niki's wavy, caramel-brown hair, and Ryna let herself imagine her hands running through the silken strands, braiding them as she had that first time in the school cafeteria. Maybe Niki would agree to come on the road after they graduated, travel from faire to faire with the other Gypsies? Ryna had been saving up to build a Gypsy-esque trailer of her own, but to design it for the two of them to live in together... to be able to show her friend the world of Magick and wonder that awaited outside their drab small-town high school with its narrow-minded locals...

Lost in daydreams, Ryna almost didn't notice as Kaya folded easily to the ground beside her, battered leather mug in hand, and shook hair the same shade as Niki's from her eyes.

"You love her, don't you," Kaya said quietly, more statement than question.

Ryna glanced at her stepmother, then quickly away, sure she matched Niki's burgundy garb. "How'd you guess?"

"You nearly fell into Robyn Hood's pond because you were too busy watching Niki to pay attention to where you were walking," Kaya teased.

Ryna put her head in her hands briefly. "Gods. That obvious?" She barely stopped herself from asking who else knew.

Kaya laughed, a sound like faeries dancing. "Princess, there's nothing wrong with it. Love is beautiful."

"I know," she said with a sigh. "Even if Angela doesn't."

She could feel the wave-fierce rush of protectiveness ripple through Kaya, though her voice remained deceptively calm. "Your mother's been giving you a hard time?"

"You are my mother, Kaya. And nothing I can't handle. She's convinced I'm hot for Tanek because *she* thinks he's cute. She'd put me in psychotherapy if she knew the truth."

"Are you sure? She worked here too, even though it was a long time ago."

"I'm sure. She lives for beige power suits and expensive manicures at the spa. Ramen makes her gag. She's not our people, Kaya. She just played at belonging until she could score a man with big bucks."

A small smile quirked Kaya's lips at that. Ryna wondered suddenly if her stepmother had feared Angela would usurp her position—and snorted. *Not bloody likely.*

"Niki's quite the catch," Kaya pointed out, deftly returning to her original topic. "Smart, funny, caring, beautiful—a lot like a certain redhead I could name."

"She thinks of me as a sister." Tears caught in Ryna's throat just at the thought, which was ludicrous. It wasn't as if Niki had ever given her firm hope, after all.

"Do you know that for certain?"

"I did an asking spell a few months ago. Just to see if there was—you know—hope."

"And?"

Ryna shrugged, turning careful attention to plucking the blades of grass near her moccasined feet. "She falls a little in love with everyone, Kaya."

"So she's a little in love with you."

Ryna fell quiet for a moment, watching her love, trying to banish the claws that squeezed her heart, trying not to let the pain show in her voice. "I can't live with a little, Kaya. I can't. I don't know how. I love people with everything I have—or not at all. And...and if she—"

"I know, princess." Kaya reached up, gently brushing tendrils of sweat-dark hair from Ryna's face. "And sometimes you have to accept that love is beautiful however it comes and be grateful for what you have. But sometimes...sometimes little things can sneak up on you."

Ryna tried for a flippant smile, tried to not make it all matter so much, tried not to think how at the end of the day she'd have to leave this incredible woman and go back to the shrew who had birthed her. "So you think it's okay if I sneak up on her?"

"I think that never knowing what might've been is the worst way to live a life. The rest is up to you." She kissed the crown of Ryna's head as she stood with the light grace of a pixie. "And I think that, should you wish to plot an ambush..." Kaya gave her an impish smile and a wink.

Ryna grinned. *Only two more years, and I can come home forever.* "Thanks Kaya."

The smile that touched Kaya's eyes carried a lifetime of tenderness. "Any time, princess. Any time."

I HAVE NO idea what thoughts raced through my heartchild's mind as I left Ryna there, watching the woman who'd won her love but not claimed it. I would like to think my words granted some courage, unraveled a bit of the uncertainty Josh had planted in her soul. Even all these years later I can't think of him without that fierce undercurrent of anger. But even though Angela took her from me for three years, Ryna returned with hugs and gratitude. It makes me think that I am, maybe a little, the mother I aspire to be.

What I aspire to be...what every mother aspires to be. To foresee every disaster, to prevent everything we predict. But what woman, what mother, can do that? Children are ours to hold, but their lives are their own. We may need to stand by, unable to shield them from the world's hurts, but we are never truly as helpless as we believe. Our hands may be bound, but our arms can always be open.

And sometimes, no matter how old they or we get, a mother's kiss can still heal her daughter's wounds.

## Carrie Carr

Carrie Carr likes to call herself a "true Texan." She was born in the Lone Star State in 1963 and has never lived outside of it. Currently a resident of the Dallas-Fort Worth Metroplex, she lives with her partner of 5+ years whom she legally married in Toronto in September 2003.

As a technical school graduate and a quiet introvert, publishing her fiction — particularly lesbian-based books — was something she never expected. She says, "Living on a farm probably influenced me the most because I had to use my imagination for recreation. I made up stories for myself, and my only regret is that I didn't save the ones I had written down and hidden away when I was growing up."

She has recently completed the sixth installment of the Lex/ Amanda series and is at work on two stand-alone romances.

# Hiding in Plain Sight

## Memoir by Carrie Carr

MY SHAKY HAND stretched upward, found and gripped a cold, metal object, and pulled it from the high shelf. Then, through bloodshot eyes, I took a long moment to check over the small-caliber revolver. Everything appeared to be in order, so I trekked back through my family's quiet house. On my way to the back door, I dropped a sealed envelope on the kitchen table, then gathered up the cordless phone and the fifth of Captain Morgan's Spiced Rum.

The immaculately kept yard held no interest for me this day, as I slipped the gun into the waistband of my jeans and tucked the phone under one arm. Moments later, I was at the far end of the yard. I struggled with the heavy back gate, finally able to pull it open far enough to slip through. The back alley was vacant at this time of the day, for which I was thankful. I didn't want or need an audience.

Once through the gate, I sat down against the fence, leaned back, and closed my eyes. A wave of despair washed over me, and tears leaked out .The pain of hiding who I was to everyone I loved was wearing on me, and I could think of no other way to get through the agony that was my life. I pulled the gun from my jeans and looked at it carefully. The snub-nosed thirty-eight belonged to my mother, although she had never actually used it. It had been a gift from my father on their last wedding anniversary, and he kept it cleaned and loaded for her.

After an entire life of denying who and what I am, I had finally come to the sad realization that I was the one thing my father and brother had railed against for as long as I could remember—I was gay. Almost thirty years old, and I knew I should have gotten a clue years ago. Some of the people I worked with had been trying to get me to "come out" for the past couple of years, but I vehemently denied their good-intentioned pestering. Five years prior, I'd had a brief relationship with another woman, but in my denial, I chalked it up to loneliness and experimentation.

Placing the gun in my lap, I picked up the cordless phone and prepared to dial nine-one-one, to let them know where to find me so my family could be spared that awful detail.

I GUESS I should start at the beginning. I grew up in the heart of the Bible belt, in a small town in the western part of Texas. Non-descript houses with more dirt than grass in their yards were the norm, and my family moved around often from one to the next. Though my immediate family was close, I often spent Sundays with my grandparents, much to my own chagrin. My grandmother was a devout Baptist, and my grandfather was a drunk — mainly, I think, to counteract my grandmother. Looking back, I can't really blame him much. Hell, both their kids ended up as drunks, too. Probably for many of the same reasons. They say the apple never falls far from the tree, and I'm a living example of that. Like my father, and his father before him, I ended up an alcoholic, too.

Throughout my early life, I never felt like I fit in. Whenever I made new friends in the neighborhood, it seemed my father would find "a better house" and have us move. I finally gave up trying, and my mother soon became the best friend I ever had. She was the one person I never wanted to disappoint, and she always seemed proud of my few achievements. I lived for the smile on her face, and in some instances, I still do.

Small towns have even smaller minds, and ours was no exception. Women were expected to marry, have children, and take care of the house. Most did just that. My mother wasn't any different, despite working at various part-time jobs while my brother and I were growing up, although she did her "job" with as much love and humor as she could. When she married my father, his mother didn't think mom was good enough for her son, and therefore, she didn't speak to her for the first several years of my parents' marriage. When mom finally delivered the first grandchild, me, they grudgingly accepted my mother into the family. My Dad's sister was basically the same way until I was grown, and to this day, she still looks down her nose at my mother.

I looked up to my parents, as most children do. Although my father was rarely home, I placed him upon a high pedestal, and I would do anything to gain his approval. But he was also a product of the small West Texas town, and his bigotry and small-minded opinions came back to haunt me years later.

I remember back to one Saturday afternoon, when I was

twelve, Dad took me to a café for lunch. We had spent the morning building fences together, and he decided we deserved a break. He seemed proud of me. I was strong, bright, and was one of the best helpers he had around the family farm. Since my younger brother was always sickly and frail, I was raised as the son my dad never had. For the longest time, I thought this was why I grew up the way I did, not being interested in boys. But I know now that's not the case.

We had just sat down at a table when our server stopped to see what we wanted to drink. He was soft-spoken and his mannerisms were almost dainty, but he was polite and professional. After he left, Dad bent his wrist at a funny angle and lisped, "I'll be back in a moment with your drinks." He shook his head in disgust. "Damned queers."

At the time, I didn't understand why Dad was so upset, but his tone upset me, too. As time went on, I started to feel uncomfortable every time he acted that way, but I wasn't sure why. In order to look good to him, I nodded my head and laughed. "Yeah," I agreed, putting on a face of false bravado that I didn't feel. I was terrified what would happen if he knew the truth about me.

As I grew up, I understood my father's cruel words and even uttered them myself at one time or another. I hid my confusion over my sexuality under a harsh exterior, knowing that if I took it out and studied it, I wouldn't like what I found. My high school years were spent with acquaintances more than friends, people who I could go out with to the movies, but not close enough to share my private thoughts with. Like girls my age, I developed crushes, but mine were always on other girls, and my shame and fear of reprisal kept me quiet. Instead of posters of young hunks on my walls, I put up pictures of men I admired, which kept me out of trouble. I suppose that's why Clint Eastwood adorned a spot over my bed, instead of the Farrah Fawcett poster I secretly coveted. Burt Reynolds and John Wayne were also prominent figures in my room instead of the "boy of the week" adorning the covers of the teen magazines. Not even I could go that far to hide an image of the "normal" teenage girl I wasn't sure was there. It was hard enough having to listen to the childish titterings of my friends when a boy would walk by, when I didn't feel anything at all.

When I was barely twenty, my father was fired from his executive position at a local company. The whisperings around town were that he had some shady dealings, but nothing was ever proven. The facts didn't matter to me. All I knew was that my upper middle class life was turned upside down. I was working at a restaurant as an assistant manager, and when my father decided to pack up the entire family and move hundreds of miles away, I balked. It wasn't me who lost her job—why should I leave my work and my friends just because my father ruined his career? So, the rest of my family moved away, while I stayed behind. This was another decision I ended up regretting.

Throughout that time, I talked to my mother on the phone almost nightly. She was still the best friend I had, and the longer they were gone, the angrier I became. In my eyes, my father ruined all our lives by moving them so far away. I hated the fact that I was alone and had no immediate prospects of changing that. So, in order to wash away the pain, I drank. It was a running joke where I worked that I'd come in every morning hung over—but it didn't stop me from going home in the evenings and drinking myself into a stupor.

I think the separation was even worse for my mother—at least according to what my younger brother told me. My father met up with a man who ran a janitorial company. In his wisdom, Dad invested my parents' entire savings in this company, and both of them worked there. The hard and stressful work nearly killed my mother. I don't think I've ever forgiven him for that. The man he partnered up with took the money, shut down the company, and left town. So, once again, my father and mother had to start over.

Hundreds of miles away, I continued trying to drown the pain and shame of my father's firing. At the restaurant, I became friends with another woman who was two years younger than me. Her family treated her badly, and so, being the gullible fool I was at the time, I allowed her to stay at my small apartment. She slept on my couch, and during the weeks that followed, we became even closer friends. Sandy would hug me, and I gladly accepted the contact, since my family was so far away, and I missed them so much.

One cold night, Sandy slipped into my bed and snuggled up behind me. Half asleep, I asked, "What are you doing?"

"It's cold out there. Please, can I sleep in here with you?"

I hated to be mean to someone who was so nice to me. "Sure."

After that, she slept in my bed with me every night, and it wasn't a big deal—at least it wasn't until the night she started kissing my neck. Before I could say anything, she rolled over on top of me, and her mouth covered mine.

That was a surprising night for me. Sandy was very demanding in bed, and she ended up being even more demanding at work. Although I was the assistant manager and she was just an employee, her constant looking over my shoulder and snide comments were making me a nervous wreck. She wanted to work the same hours as I, and if she wasn't scheduled, she'd make excuses and stay around, anyway. Any time I spoke to another woman, whether it be an employee or a customer, suddenly it was "flirting", and I closed myself off just to keep the peace. Around that time, my drinking got heavier. Without me realizing it, we became "a couple." She was trying to get into the Army, so she told me we had to keep our relationship a secret, which was okay by me. Considering how my father acted throughout my life, I was terrified of my family ever finding out.

After a year of being told what to do, when to do it, and not being allowed out of the apartment for anything, I knew I had to find a way to break off the relationship with Sandy. Any time I brought it up, she would cry and then threaten to kill herself. I'll admit I was weak, and so I stayed. Finally, a phone call from my brother did what nothing else could. He told me my mother was sick, and he was worried about her. That was all I needed to hear. I made the decision to move away to be with my family, no matter what Sandy said.

Once I returned to my parents' home, Sandy wouldn't leave me alone. We were hundreds of miles apart, but she still wanted a relationship with me. Again, my nerves became frayed by her demands and phone calls. She threatened to "out" me to my parents, and then to kill herself. One night, in a drunken stupor, I finally told her to go ahead.

She must have gotten the point. There were no more phone calls or letters from her. The last I heard, she worked for a discount store selling fake jewelry.

Living with my parents once more took a bit of adjustment. I had lived by myself long enough to know I enjoyed it, but I realized my family needed me at home. With my father's work future uncertain, I had to help pay the bills, which I didn't mind at all.

For years then, I worked and ignored the way I felt. My mother's health improved, and we often went shopping or to the movies, and she was the best friend I had. Although she had never said anything derogatory about homosexuality, I had no idea how she felt, and I feared losing her if I ever owned up to who I really was.

My friends at work continued to tease and harass me, some of them telling me I needed to step out of the closet I was hiding in. I ignored their taunts, all the while aching inside to be who I wanted to be. I had even started exploring Internet resources — of course using an assumed name — learning about what it was like to be a lesbian. I made friends online who didn't care what my sexual preference was, and that was the only time I was truly happy. But the freedom I'd found on the computer was no substitute for the real thing, only making the pain worse. The longer I surfed online, the more I wanted to be free of my inhibitions. I spent sleepless nights, drinking and crying, afraid of losing my family, yet all the time feeling I was losing my mind.

THAT BRINGS ME back to the alley. All is quiet, since everyone is at work. I look at the gun in my lap, and then, to gather my courage, take the bottle and tip it up to my lips. The alcohol burns my throat, but the tears in my eyes are from a deeper pain. I'd rather die than see the looks on my parent's faces when they find out I'm gay. Even though I'm not in a relationship right now, I would have liked to find someone — but that search would have been difficult to make in secrecy.

Tired of hurting, I set the bottle down beside me and pick up the gun. I stick the barrel of the revolver into my mouth and close my eyes, saying a silent apology to the people I love. Before I can pull the trigger, I feel like someone is watching, almost begging me not to end my life. My hands shaking, I remove the gun and open my eyes, but there's no one around. The feeling is still with me. I know that I'm alone in the alley, but it's as if someone has asked me to stop.

Shaken and still clutching the weapon, I gather up the phone and the bottle of rum and retrace my steps back into the house. I put my mother's revolver away, making certain to wipe my fingerprints and tears from its surface. Now that I've decided not to kill myself today, I go back into the kitchen and pick up the envelope I left on the table. It takes me only a moment to tear up the letter, but I feel a bit better for doing it. I can always write another one later.

THAT NIGHT, I slept fitfully. Unusual dreams invaded my slumber, and whenever I awakened and then fell back to sleep, I'd pick up right where I left off. This continued for several nights until I thought I'd lose my mind. In an attempt to exorcise the visions that whirled through my brain the moment my head hit the pillow, I started to write them down. It didn't take long before I had a story started, so I did what any closeted lesbian can do — I posted the story to an Internet site. Before long, people were reading the story that started out in my dreams. One woman, in particular, seemed very interested. And not just in the story.

We started out as friends, this woman and me. She told me

how the story called to her and how she identified so closely with one of the characters in it. Over time, our friendship blossomed, and we realized how much we had in common, and how much we had grown to care for each other. For the first time in my life, I fell in love. She was thousands of miles away and had complications of her own, but we swore someday to be together, no matter what.

I continued to write my narrative, which by then had turned into a novel, and when it was finished, a publisher approached me. I was so excited! Me, a published writer. My elation turned to fear when I realized I could no longer keep my secret life a secret, not any more. My family would have to be told, since my novel was a lesbian love story. The one thing I had feared for a long time would finally happen. I'd have to "come out" to my family: to my redneck father and brother and to my mother — the one person who I never wanted to lose.

As I kept my long-distance relationship going, I searched for a way to talk to my family. I decided to tell my mom and not even worry about my dad or brother. Suddenly, it was like the opportunity to be alone with her slipped from my grasp time and time again. There was always someone else around, and something else going on. For weeks, whenever I'd work up the nerve to talk to her, something would happen, and my chance would be lost.

Meanwhile, I finally had a chance to bring the woman I loved to Texas for a visit. We were to travel to California together, and, first, her plane stopped off in my town. She'd have a layover of several hours, so we could spend time together before traveling on.

My fear and my happiness continued to wage war against each other. I met my love at the airport, showering her with flowers. We went back to the house I shared with my family and spent a wonderful afternoon together. I gave her a ring, she accepted it, and I knew she was the person I would spend the rest of my life with. I wanted my family to know about her, about us, but we would leave before they got home from work.

We've never been the most touchy-feely family, nor do we spend a lot of time talking out our feelings. Even though I've always felt loved by my parents, I could probably count on one hand the number of times I've actually been told "I love you" by one of them. So, in true family form, I wrote them a long letter, explaining who I am, and who I love. Being the coward I am, I left it on the kitchen table, in the same spot where months earlier my suicide note had lain. I figured that when we came back from California, if they hated me, I'd at least have my love to help me.

California was a wonderful trip and over much too soon. We rode back to my family's house in the back of a limousine I had rented for the occasion. Terrified at the reception we'd get, I led my lover into the house. My mother was there, all smiles. She hugged me, and at that moment, I wanted to cry. Mom was warm and welcoming. Was it possible that she hadn't read the letter? Did she not know about my secret? Later, the three of us sat in the living room talking about the trip. My mom gave us each a bottle of water, then sat to listen to our tales. I was hungry and offered to run up to the nearest fast food place and pick up lunch for us all. As I stood, I looked down at two bottles of water: my lover's and mine. "I can't remember which one is mine."

"I don't think it really matters, does it?" my mother retorted, a sneaky smile on her face.

She was right, of course. Considering our long weekend, I doubt if drinking out of each other's water bottle would bring harm to either of us. Seeing the smile my mother wore, I knew not only that would everything be okay, but for the first time in my life, so would I.

FIVE YEARS LATER, I'm living a life I could only dream about before. I no longer drink, and I'm feeling pretty good about myself.

My lover and I have a beautiful house, her teenage daughter and I get along beautifully, and I stay home to write full-time. My family is probably the biggest surprise, though. My mother, who was always my best friend in the world, is still a huge part of my life. We live less than a mile away from my folks, and we see them several times a week. They often come over to spend part of the weekend with us. We actually talk a lot, now, about all sorts of thing— things I would have never thought possible. All those years, it turns out, my mother had a pretty good idea about me. I think she kept it to herself, in hopes that I'd work though things on my own. I know that having a lesbian for a daughter isn't something she aspired to, but she's come to terms with who I am, and I think she's proud of me. She only wants me to be happy, and even she knows that being gay isn't the easiest thing in the world. Yet, she's always there for me.

Mother is still one of my biggest supporters. She gives my partner flowers for Mother's Day, and the two of them have developed a great relationship. We all enjoy each other's company, and seeing the two of them together, laughing, brings joy to my heart that I never thought I'd know.

I think back to that day in the alley and realize that I almost lost all of this, before I could find it. That's something that scares me a lot. I'd like to think that Mom was there, somehow, instead of at work. Maybe deep down inside, I knew what my death would do to her, and to the rest of my family. I'd have never met the woman I'm planning on spending the rest of my life with, and I would have lost out on a lot of close friendships that I've developed these past few years.

I thought that coming out would ruin my life as it was, and I was right. In my old life, I was a drunken, angry, closeted woman who hated herself, and her life. Because of the love and support of my family and my partner, I'm now a sober, happy, *out* woman who feels like she's the luckiest person in the world.

Sometimes, the only person you are hiding from is yourself.

### Caro Clarke

Born in Ontario, Canada, Caro spent her childhood in various oil towns from Alaska to Newfoundland until her family finally settled in Calgary, Alberta. She studied medieval history at various universities, ending up at Somerville College, Oxford University, where she graduated in the mid-Eighties with a D. Phil. She taught for a while but soon found she had no patience for academia and moved to London to work for various small publishers and in a gay and lesbian bookshop. In between times, she has been a carpenter, a minder (bodyguard), a freelance editor, and now works as Webmaster and freelance web consultant.

Always, writing has been central in her life. She has written one critically acclaimed novel, *The Wolf Ticket*, many short stories, and writes poetry as J. P. Hollerith. Caro has also written articles for NovelAdvice.com, an online magazine for writers.

Currently Caro lives with her lifetime companion Fiona in a flat in Little Venice, in west London, England where she is at work on her next writing project.

# Winterreise

## Fiction by Caro Clarke

MAGGIE WAS ABOUT to sit at her favourite table when she heard sobs. She looked around the coffee shop to see if anyone else was rising. How strange—they all seemed absorbed by the Schubert on the loudspeakers. She took her coffee and went to the back.

"I couldn't help noticing..."

The young woman raised her head from a wad of coffee-shop napkins. Her eyes were swollen, her face blotched, her mouth a tight hook.

"Oh, my dear," said Maggie. "What's the matter?"

The young woman put the back of her hand against her cheeks. "It's nothing—it's—" an effort at a smile crumbled. "Oh, you know— Sometimes—y-you just want your mom."

Maggie settled in the chair opposite, favouring her bad knee. "From your accent, I think that your mother isn't to hand."

"Chicago."

"That's a shame. Why not talk to *me* about it, whatever it is?"

"I couldn't, I—"

"I'm a good mother-substitute," said Maggie. "I've got two girls of my own."

"I really...can't." The young woman's face betrayed her; Maggie dared to pat the hand holding the napkins, saying, "Give it a try. I've probably dealt with more than you can imagine."

The young woman's uncertain glance paused at Maggie's silver hair, at the soft skin of her neck, at the lines around her eyes. She hesitated, then said, "It's my—my—" a breath, "girl-friend."

"Hmm," said Maggie encouragingly.

"She wants to split up."

"Hmm?"

"We've split up." The young woman's eyes flooded and she disappeared behind her napkins. "She's left me."

"Why?" asked Maggie.

"I d-don't know!"

Maggie offered the packet of tissues she carried for such situations. "Someone else?"

A violent shake of the head faltered, stopped. "She didn't say she'd— yes. She has."

"How long since she left?"

"A week. It's only really hit me now—that, you know, it's true."

"You used to come here?" asked Maggie. "With her?"

"All the time! I didn't—I never meant to be here today, but we always come on Saturday mornings and I was on auto-pilot and then I sat down and she wasn't here—and—and it was *real*."

As the young woman wept, Maggie surreptitiously read the tear-blistered notepad aslant on the table. *Dear Sophie*, it said, then *my darling Sophie, I can't*, something washed out, then *anything you want*, ending with *always be you*, a shaky signature *Jess* and a *P.S.* left unfinished. Strange these days to see someone writing a real letter, Maggie thought. So much more satisfying than sending an email and, thank goodness, more easily not sent.

Time to distract. She asked, "How long were you together?"

"Nine m-months. Almost ten. I thought—I should have known, I just—I mean, when she moved in with me, she didn't bring all her stuff. She only needed a backpack and a c-couple of boxes to move out. She never even *planned* to stay."

Maggie thought the darling Sophie had probably spent her final week spiriting away her belongings. She asked, "Are you stranded?"

"What—for money? No, it's my apartment. I covered the rent anyway." Jess's mouth twisted as she controlled herself. "I guess that's lucky for me. I thought this was—that she was—"

"Forever?"

Jess nodded.

"You met at college? Your last year?"

"How did you know?"

Maggie nodded at the scarf slung over the third chair. "College colours. But I think you're not a student now."

"No, I'm working. We met in the spring, just before exams. She's still there. A grad student. She moved in as soon as I got an apartment. I was so happy—" Jess's face crumpled. "I love her, I'll always love her."

"I doubt it," said Maggie.

"What?" Jess looked up from her tissues.

"I'd be surprised," Maggie clarified. "It rarely happens with a first love."

"Uh..." Jess looked as if she had been hit with cold water.

"When you're young, it seems as if summer will last forever. Then winter slaps you in the face. I remember when my eldest girl came face to face with her first winter. It was heartbreaking."

"Lots of people fall in love and stay there."

"Lucky them, relocating to the tropics," said Maggie. "Most of us don't. We get gloves and woolly hats."

"I can tell when winter's coming: it's fall and the leaves turn colour. But I didn't know Sophie was going to walk out on me. I mean, we'd just finished painting the apartment—"

"Painting can cover up more than blank walls."

"I *like* making a home," said Jess. "I *like* cooking breakfast and being, you know, a couple."

"But she found out she didn't?"

Jess's head jerked in pain.

"Maybe nest-building was all you had to offer—"

"Oh, *thanks*."

"—or maybe it was all you had to offer each other. I know couples who've turned serial DIYers to hide that fact." Maggie took a sip of latte. "How was the sex?"

Jess choked. "My mom would *never* ask me that!"

"It's the heart of things, isn't it?"

"We—" Jess flushed. "It was great at first. But since the new term—she started saying we were too middle-aged. Too suburban. She had—this idea of herself," said Jess tentatively. "You know, a free spirit."

"She reminds me of my eldest," said Maggie, nodding. "Passy doesn't like being held down. She insists on her independence. Heaven forbid she should be stopped from going wherever she wants to! But when something happens, she races home to all those dull domestic comforts. The difference is that your ex"—she saw Jess flinch at the word— "has run from one nest to another. Passy's never played fast and loose—at least not that I know of, though she teases my neighbour's boy, which isn't right, because he's on a short leash."

"Sophie was never cruel. That's why I'm so—so *shocked*."

"She's still a student. It's a child's life. You've left that behind." Maggie looked at her. "Maybe too quickly. At your age, you should still be exploring the world, establishing your territory, enjoying yourself. What is it that you do?"

"My job? I work at a picture library. We supply photos to newspapers and magazines."

"Do you like it?"

"Sophie said it was boring. It isn't, you know. We sell work by all the great photographers. I studied one of them at college. I do some art myself—digital stuff. Nothing serious."

"Why not?"

"I'm not that good."

"You think so, or you know so?"

"*Now* you sound like my mom. It doesn't pay anything."

"But if you love it?" asked Maggie. "The stillness and focusing on things? My Sarah's like that. She can stare at something for hours. She notices every single detail. Passy teases her when she's absorbed, but I know she's seeing things, or seeing *into* things, in a way that's beyond me."

"Is she an artist?"

"In her own style." Maggie smiled. "I really don't know what she's doing half the time, but I trust her instincts, even though I sometimes lie awake at night until I hear her door swing shut. She has this curiosity, this need to watch the world."

"I'm an observer, too. It was Sophie who made things happen. Her friends were always over at our—my—place."

"She supplied the social life?"

"She was *fun*." Jess wept again, but Maggie noticed that the tears stopped sooner. "I never learned to make friends—I come from a big family—I always had my sisters—"

"Sisters are the best friends you can have," said Maggie. "I see that every day at home. My two are very close. Even when they squabble, next minute I'll find them in the kitchen sharing a treat."

"My sisters and I were like that. We sort of brought each other up." Jess gulped. "We always got on. I miss them. I was going to move back home after I graduated, but Mom said to stay where I was myself and happy, even though she doesn't really like me being, you know, a lesbian. So I stayed here for Sophie. I'm such an idiot!"

"Your mother sensed what you needed."

"I don't know. We don't talk much about feelings. She says you have to learn life by yourself—but I don't want to learn *this*!"

Maggie handed her fresh tissues and waited until she mopped up. "Winters don't last forever. Spring always comes."

"When? When for me?"

Maggie considered her. "About six months, maybe eight."

"Oh, *God*."

"And after at least one lover."

"One—? No way! That's horrible."

"Rebounds happen," said Maggie. "People can't live in perpetual winter."

"So they, what? Take a spring break?"

"Exactly. It's the sign that your spirit isn't broken, that you're getting ready to leave the cold behind."

"I can't live that long feeling like this—I want it to *stop*."

"I don't think so," said Maggie. "If it stops, it means you've stopped loving Sophie. And you don't want that, not yet."

Jess hid her head behind drooping hands. "I can't."

"Sophie took the easy way," said Maggie meditatively. "It's all *why suffer when you don't have to?* But everything needs its season." She cocked her head to Schubert's melody still falling like snowflakes from the loudspeakers. "If you face your *Winterreise*—your winter journey— you'll learn that you can survive this, and worse than this."

"Is that what you say to *your* kids?"

"When they get into their own kind of trouble, yes, I try to tell them how long it will take to mend. They don't understand, of course—but then, they see time differently. To me, six months is nothing."

"Is that all life is? Learning to deal with pain?"

"Didn't I mention spring?" asked Maggie. "I promise it's there. For instance, my Sarah and I weren't always close. Then she had a car accident and I had to take care of her for quite a while. We both learned about each other. Before, I'd tried to make her do what I said. Now, I just want her to be herself. Before, she used to be out that door no matter what, but now we can spend all day together, simply enjoying each other's company."

"I remember having pneumonia," said Jess slowly. "My mom had to take time off work. She was burned about it."

"Not about that. What we mums get angry about is having to make hard choices. She wasn't mad at *you*."

"It seemed like it," said Jess.

"It seems to *me* that your mother made a hard choice between having time with you or supporting you."

"She didn't choose: she had to. My dad left."

"It's always a choice," said Maggie. "Don't take hers for granted."

Jess began to speak, then stopped. "That's something I never thought of."

"Would I be right if I said that she was always there when it was important?"

"I *wish*—well, she couldn't be. She missed my high school graduation because of renovations and when Holly had her first concert—"

"The *really* important things."

"Like us being sick? Yes, for that. And she sure dropped everything when Amber got arrested for drunk driving."

"My two are on my mind every single minute of the day," said Maggie. "Even when I'm not with them. Especially when I'm not with them. It's no different between you and your mum."

Jess's mouth trembled. "She—I guess so. If she was here now, I guess she'd be telling me the same things you are—okay, not everything, not about sex on the rebound—"

"She'd be thinking it," said Maggie. "And I think she'd have something to say about your flat, too."

"Don't tell me I've got to move!"

"You need to reclaim it. Buy it new curtains. Re-arrange the furniture. Paint every single wall again."

"I can't paint Sophie out!"

"You can," said Maggie. "Not today, probably not even this month. But it's too easy to make a shrine out of loss. I know. I had a third girl, my youngest. She died."

"Oh, I'm so sorry!"

"It was years ago," said Maggie. "The other two didn't really know what had happened, only that Steffie was gone and they were sad. I admit I made an altar of Steffie's things: her toys, her blanket. I'd find one of her hairs and couldn't throw it out."

Jess gave a breath of inarticulate sympathy.

"At the beginning, you can't help it," said Maggie. "That's how grief is. But eventually you put it away. I've learned that the sooner you can start, the sooner it helps." She pushed away her coffee mug and leaned forward. "Now, what about Christmas?"

"Christmas?"

"It's not far away, is it? You were going to spend it with Sophie?"

"Yes, I'd planned a traditional—and—and Sophie was going to make—"

"Can you afford to go away?"

Jess nodded, blinking hard to stop tears.

"Why don't you go home?" asked Maggie. "You could use some *real* mum-time."

"Are your kids spending it with you?"

Maggie laughed. "They always do. I buy the biggest turkey I can find and every year they eat so much that they fall asleep on the sofa just as I'm settling down to watch the Queen. Strangely, when I sneak into the kitchen for a midnight feast, there they are with room for more!"

"You all sound really close," said Jess mistily.

"Christmas is for family," said Maggie. "Any kind of family. Go to your mother this year. You need her. Maybe next year you'll be spending it with your true love."

"I thought I'd found her," Jess said stonily. "She doesn't exist."

"I've noticed that people who've been raised with love tend to find it waiting for them when they grow up."

"How will I know when I have—when I really have?"

"Because that's when summer never ends." Maggie sat back. "First things first. You have to walk through this winter. Your sisters are only emails away—have you been in touch with them yet? No? Have you phoned your mother?"

"She's so busy with the new store—"

"She'll make time," said Maggie.

"You—yes. I should call them. Her."

Maggie looked at the clock. "I'm afraid I have to go now, but it's time I did, isn't it? You're probably talked out. Will you be all right?"

"I think so." said Jess. "I'll remember—to wrap up warm."

"Good girl." Maggie eased to her feet, patted Jess's shoulder, and left the shop.

All the way home, she replayed what she had said. There were so many kinds of mothers in the world: the ones who loved like wool and the ones who loved like linen, the ones who stood over you like roofs and the ones who stood beneath you like bridges. It was hard enough to know which one to be when the daughters were your own. She hoped that Jess would be brave. She hoped she had helped.

"I think I did a good job," she said to herself as she unlocked her front door. "I hope so." Dropping her library books onto the hall table, she called, "Patience! Sarah! Mummy's home!"

And her two Siamese cats bounded down the stairs to greet her.

## Katherine V. Forrest

With the publication of *Curious Wine* in 1983 and subsequent books in the next several years, Katherine V. Forrest became a major figure in then-nascent lesbian literary tradition. Her highly accessible novels contained positive portrayals of lesbians struggling mightily with self-identity in a society that neither understood nor accepted them. She helped to revolutionize the publication and availability of novels reflecting lesbian lives.

Born in Windsor, Ontario, Canada, Katherine now lives in San Francisco with her partner Jo and their beloved cat. She teaches classes and seminars on the craft of writing and is known for her advocacy and encouragement of other lesbian writers.

Twice winner of the Lambda Literary Award for Best Lesbian Mystery, Katherine has also been honored with the prestigious Pioneer Award from the Lambda Literary Foundation. She has been profiled in virtually every major lesbian and gay publication in America, as well as in numerous magazines and newspapers abroad. Katherine says, "I stand on the brave shoulders of every lesbian writer coming before me." Hundreds of lesbian writers in this new millennium stand on Katherine's shoulders.

# Jeanie

## Memoir by Katherine V. Forrest

WHEN I WAS fourteen, my adoptive mother was taken from me by a cancer which had begun five years earlier in her left breast and spread to her spinal cord. She was forty-two. Eighteen months later, my father, age forty-four, died of a heart attack. Having been surrendered to these parents for adoption when I was an infant, I had in effect lost two sets of parents by age sixteen which, as someone has mordantly pointed out, makes me very careless indeed.

Two years later, at age eighteen, I left my dark world of grief in Canada for a fresh beginning in the United States. Adding to a devastating loss beyond all my imagining was a new distress—the suspicion that I was not like other young women my age, and in the most abhorrent possible way: I was attracted to my own gender.

I would shed my skin and start all over again, I vowed, and this rebirth would not include falling in love with one's own gender. That person was anathema to me, just as she was to the world I knew.

Crossing a border did not, of course, transform the fundamental me. I tried my damnedest to be heterosexual, but the homosexual world, whose existence I discovered in the pulp novels of Ann Bannon and Paula Christian, drew me irresistibly. In the seedy gay bars of Detroit I gained sanctuary of sorts; but there was limited comfort in a sixties' lesbian society whose rigid rules of behavior required declaring oneself as either butch or femme. Since I seemed to possess (or lack) aspects of both sexual types, I was a misfit even among my own kind, in what I knew to be my natural milieu.

Out of the ink-black clouds that seemed permanently fixed over my life, lightning struck once more. A cousin, out "slumming" in Detroit's tawdry downtown bars, spotted me and sounded the alarm to my Catholic relatives. Called on the carpet, I was instructed by a white-lipped aunt that my presence in such loathsome places was beyond the pale and would turn me into a deviate and an outcast from all decent society.

Again I fled, to another new beginning — this time in California. It was 1961. I was twenty-two. I was completely on my own. I hated myself.

Within a few months I met a woman and established my first long term relationship. We hid, performing all the usual subterfuges and pretenses of the day, including paying for an apartment with an extra bedroom. We lived in isolation, revealing ourselves to no one, including my partner's family, retreating from any gay people who happened to pick us up on their gaydar. As our time together wended its way toward five years, my partner found more and more need to "relax" with her vodka gimlets. And I became ill, seriously, for a time.

With my self-esteem free falling toward zero, I turned twenty-seven. I passed my days being inconspicuous, in full protective mode inside a fortress. No way lightning would ever strike me again — I had shut down my life to prevent it.

Onto this arid landscape, like a mirage, Jeanie appeared.

IT WAS 1966. I was working at Technicolor Corporation in Hollywood. Years earlier, up until the post-war era of World War Two, Jeanie had worked there as a switchboard operator-receptionist; she had left to raise her son. When Danny turned seventeen, Jeanie shed her marriage and returned to her old job, where she found me.

Twenty years older than I, reveling in her newfound independence, Jeanie was confident and at ease with being a sexual woman in all the ways that I wasn't. She had found herself a male friend, Vern, who shared her fun-loving, adventuresome ways, and she was exuberantly exploring her expanded horizons. "What in the world are you doing here?" she challenged me. "How come you're not out there doing something with your brains? How come you're not having *fun*?"

In those days there was no way could I tell her I was a lesbian, but I did relate my tales of tragedy and tribulation which she listened to with the profound empathy of a mother. "Kathy, life is a schoolroom," she told me. "*Everything* changes, nothing stays the same." I shrugged at these platitudes. But over the next few years the reality of those words would sink into my marrow and alter my entire perspective so that the words would become a mantra.

Jeanie did not judge her son's choices in life; her measurement of him was his own sense of personal well-being. She lavished on Danny her complete acceptance, belief, and pride. I was gratified to discover that I had somehow become another, very lucky beneficiary of the same maternal warmth and generosity of spirit. Daily she bathed my self-esteem in affirmation and praise and approval. My entire being seemed to respond — to strengthen. A new horizon became nebulously visible, one that seemed possible for me to reach.

She became, unknown to herself, my teacher, my surrogate mother. The touchstone to my womanhood, my principal role model in a way that connected powerfully with my identity. Trusting her, and with no sense of pressure or coercion, I began a surreptitious checklist of my own femininity, embarking on an ever-so-cautious quest to lay claim to my individuality, not as a lesbian, but much more basically: as a female. In the mirror held up by this heterosexual woman, I began, for the first time in my life, to learn how to be comfortable in my own lesbian skin.

Did I come out to her? For a long time I did not and could not. Being around her was like having my soul warmed over a fire. Even as I gained confidence and consolidated my gains, I couldn't risk losing the approval and acceptance that were the healing force in my life. Did she guess? With Jeanie's concept of life as a schoolroom, to her I was simply a slow learner. One day my embryonic sexuality would blossom and I would pair up with someone like her fun-loving Vern and emerge into the fullness of my life.

It would be seventeen years before I was far enough along on the continuum of my coming out process to reveal all my secrets to Jeanie. The publication of my first novel, *Curious Wine*, was a final step, a graduation ceremony, a formal coming out into a lesbian life I now lived openly, into a community I called my own and to which I had dedicated my professional life.

If she ever wondered over the course I had set for myself, with characteristic consistency she did not worry over it. My path might not be anything she could imagine choosing for herself, but if it was right for me, then my happy and healthy life was all that mattered. She read each of my books as I wrote them, to discern my world and my life in it — expanding her politics as she expanded her understanding of my part in the battle for gay rights.

THOUGH THESE ARE the historical facts of my relationship with Jeanie, to this day she still defies full definition. She was more than a sister, more than a friend. More than a mother in the non-judgmental way that she opened me to the entire interpretation of myself. When I met the woman with whom I would spend the next twenty years of my life, I would not have had the courage to reach out for that love had Jeanie not come into my life to begin the restoration of my self-esteem and to send me on my journey toward self-acceptance.

Much of what is beautiful in my life today is composed of what the women in my life have given to me. Like Jeanie, I too have played the "nurturing mother" role in my personal life, I have helped in the healing of other women. I ask myself, was I simply lucky to have had Jeanie happen to me? Or do we motherless women look for mothers when we most need to find them? And does the need for a mother ever leave?

What about that willingness of so many of us to bestow that gift of mothering within ourselves onto others? Do some of us bear within us a mothering template so that a hurting child of any age can be taken into us?

Among women, our deeper friendships contain, along with love and warmth, elements of nurturing, protectiveness, guiding, mentorship, and wound-binding.

As do our lesbian love relationships... Along with how much mothering? Sometimes, among the negatives involved with the necessity for stretching our wings, we move on from those who have loved and tended us well; yet it is a distinguishing characteristic of our lesbian relationships that more often than not we retain close ties with our former lovers. Perhaps it can only be safely said that somewhere amid our complex relationships, the definition of "motherhood" is satisfied in all but the biological sense.

At every stage of our being, life is, as Jeanie says, a schoolroom. But it is other women who teach us to search for what we need, teach us to open ourselves to the healing they offer. Those of us who retreat behind fortresses of our own design are on a track toward self-obliteration. The irony of our often difficult lesbian lives is that in loving our own gender, women remain an everlasting strength and beauty in our lives, nurturing and healing and loving us.

To this day I have never been able to adequately explain to Jeanie how essential she was to my survival and healing all those many years ago. I'm not sure that I have explained it even now. But perhaps when she reads this she will at long last understand something of what she did for me and why she means so very much to me today.

## Jennifer Fulton (Rose Beecham)

Born and raised in New Zealand, Jennifer Fulton brings a unique worldview to her writing. She says, "Everything is material. The unspoiled world in which I grew up will always influence my writing. So, too, will my travels. In writing my lesbian novels, I owe a debt to the work of Djuna Barnes, Katherine V. Forrest, Claire Morgan (Patricia Highsmith) and those doyennes of pulp fiction, Ann Bannon and Valerie Taylor, just to name a few. " She parlayed that material and those influences into a number of lesbian novels including a mystery trilogy written under the pen name Rose Beecham.

Formal education in Library Studies and English Literature prepared Jennifer for the 'real job' her parents thought she should have, and she spent many years in the rat race as a communications consultant in the public and private sector. She has since segued into full-time writing and is at work on both lesbian-themed novels and historical mainstream novels. Jennifer now lives in the U.S. with her partner and teenage daughter and is at work on multiple projects including the reissuance of and addition to her Moon Island series.

# Color Blind

## Fiction by Jennifer Fulton

IT'S IMPORTANT TO repaint rooms. You never know when décor could matter. Joan Turner thought visitors should enter her home and be struck immediately by the color scheme and those special touches that stamp a room with the owner's personality—her genuine black forest cuckoo clock, the porcelain slave-girl head with the turban and earrings, once her mother's. And her alligator jaw collection, compellingly displayed along mantel and walls, the jagged yellow teeth a reminder that evil lurks in the shallows.

Joan thought this was a lesson youngsters should learn early. She had made it her business to show her three children the swamp where her Daddy had trapped Solomon, the 'gator that hung over the fire when she was little. Locals gave him that name because he was smart. You never saw him until it was too late. No one knew how many children he'd eaten for breakfast, God have mercy on them. To illustrate her point she had plunged a long stick into the murky water and watched her children leap back as a thrashing tail responded.

Even after his head was mounted on cherry wood, Solomon's all-seeing eyes were unsettling. Joan could understand why Danny, her husband, had rigged up a pair of sunglasses over them. Nowadays Solomon hung in the living room she'd just finished painting. Walls that had been Orange Grove were now Navajo Sky, a turquoise color like that necklace Danny had brought back with him from a car dealers' convention in Albuquerque a few years ago.

There was still a quart of that orange paint sitting in the garage. Maybe she would use it to brighten up the hallway. Only a slob needed neutral tones to make their entryway look clean. There was nothing wrong with Joan Turner's housekeeping. You could eat off her floors.

The cuckoo chimed four o'clock just as Joan stepped back to inspect the walls for uneven patches. There was nothing worse than show-through when the paint dries. The kids would be home from school soon. She could imagine their startled faces. It must be like magic, she thought, to leave the house in the morning and come back in the afternoon to find it transformed. To maximize the impact, she cleared away the dropcloths and newspaper and straightened up the room.

As always, the children tried to feign nonchalance.

"It's blue," Danny, Jr. remarked.

"Be careful. It's still wet," Joan said.

"It's better than the orange," Frank commented.

Paulette, her youngest, studied the room with sullen disinterest.

"Well?" Joan demanded. She was not going to allow a twelve year old to spoil the moment.

Paulette did not even look at her. "I'm going to Linda's."

"Oh, no, you're not."

"But Mrs. O'Hara says I can. Linda asked her."

"Well your father says you can't," Joan said. "Tonight you're staying home for a change."

For a moment Joan had the ridiculous idea that her daughter was going to punch her. She took an automatic step back and caught her heel on the hearth rug. Next thing she knew, her hand was wet with paint, and her perfect wall was ruined.

"Now look what you did!" she yelled.

Paulette was already halfway up the stairs. Her retreating feet paused, and she hung over the banister, hollering, "How come you never paint the sewing room?"

Joan marched to the bottom of the staircase. "Don't you get fresh with me. You can stay in your room 'til you're ready to say sorry."

"Me apologize to you! That's a joke, right?"

"Don't make me tell your father," Joan warned.

This was met with a brazen peal of laughter. "What's he gonna do, Mom? Wanna tell me? Come on — the sewing machine isn't that noisy!"

It was always the sewing machine with that girl. Was it Joan's fault they couldn't afford store bought clothes for all their children? It was easier to make for a girl than for boys. Paulette always had nice new dresses. Joan would probably make another one tonight. Her daughter was better dressed than she was.

"When's Dad coming home?" Danny, Jr. asked.

"Do I look like a psychic?" Joan snapped. "He's at the club."

A groan. "He said I could use the car."

Joan shrugged. It was not her problem, not when there was a palm print that wanted painting over. "If you're in that big of a hurry, why don't you go find him?"

Without another word about the new décor, Danny, Jr. stalked off.

"I can fix the wall, Mom," Frank offered, the paint roller in his hand.

"You're a good boy," Joan said. At least one of her brood appreciated her. She could only imagine what their home might look like if she let things slide.

IN HER ROOM, Paulette sat on the bed. Her walls were onto their twelfth color in four years. Barely had the paint dried over one when her mom would be painting the next—Paulette had no choice what color. Her mom said that way it would be a surprise. As if new paint could ever be a surprise in the shifting canvas of their house.

Only the sewing room was spared. Fancy new colors were for others to enjoy. Her mom laid it on about making do with faded peach.

Paulette wished she could stand in there just for a moment and be transported back in time to the drab comfort of the house they'd moved into when she was eight. But the room was always locked except for the evenings when her mom shut herself in there, radio blaring hit songs from the seventies over the mechanical whir of the sewing machine.

Danny, Jr. said you could murder someone and she wouldn't hear a thing.

DANNY TURNER, SR. liked his steak rare and his women hot. That's what he told friends who came over. Joan always giggled when he said it. When a man tells a joke, his wife should laugh. That was a valuable lesson her Momma had passed on. Joan told Paulette the same thing over and over, but she was one of those girls who asked for trouble instead of avoiding it.

Tonight, in front of Uncle Wolf—not a blood relation but an old family friend—Paulette waited 'til everyone had finished laughing, then said, "Oh, I get it. He likes women. Yeah. That is funny," and laughed like a hyena, all by herself.

"Eat your dinner," Joan said. It was just like Paulette to embarrass her in front of company.

"I'm all done." She picked up her plate. "Can I go to Linda's now? Please. We're doing a homework project together."

"We've got company," Joan protested.

"She can go." Danny, Sr. spoke with his mouth full. "Be back by nine. I want those golf clubs cleaned before you go to bed."

Looking to cash in on this rare benevolence, Danny, Jr. piped up. "Can I use the car, Dad?"

Danny reached in his pocket and tossed the keys over. "You're not insured. Remember that, son."

"Yes. Thank you, sir." Danny crammed the rest of his meal down his throat and excused himself, leaving his dirty dishes on the table.

Joan had given up trying to teach her oldest to clean up after himself. He had his father's genes. She and Frank cleared up after dinner and washed the dishes. Danny and Uncle Wolf relocated to the den, where they would play cards, drink beer and watch cable for the rest of the evening.

"I've got sewing to do," she told Frank once all the wet dishes were stacked.

"Okay, Mom. I'll finish up here if you want."

Joan kissed him on the top of his head. Frank was small for thirteen, much smaller than his sister. Paulette took after Danny's side, big boned and big mouthed.

"You're a good boy," she said.

Frank picked up the dish towel. "'Night, Mom."

IN THE DARK, Paulette listened for the sound of Uncle Wolf's car changing gears at the stop sign half a block away, then got out of bed. She stuffed two pillows under the bedclothes and piled her quilt high over the lump they created. Then she stood behind her door.

Along the hallway, a toilet flushed and in the sewing room her mother turned up the radio. Paulette's palms slithered around the cold steel shaft of a Callaway 7 iron. One at a time she wiped her hands on her pajamas. The door swung open and her father shoved one foot behind him to close it. Stepping out of his shoes and pants, he shuffled over to the bed.

As usual he stood there for a moment in his shorts, waiting for her to lift her head. In the dim glow of her Cinderella nightlight, he bent over the lump. "Wakey, wakey."

Confident her range was about right, Paulette said loudly, "Hey Dad!"

As he glanced over his shoulder, she brought the club down hard, landing a chopping blow to his temple. He did not fall as she had expected, but staggered toward her. This time she swung in a wide arc, smashing him across the face. It made a dull, wet crunching sound, like biting down on a mouthful of freshly shelled peas.

He landed hard on his knees, groaning, clutching his head.

"No. Stop. Please," he begged, sniveling and trying to crawl to the door.

It was funny, Paulette thought, that's exactly what she used to say. She answered, just as he had, "Shut up," and struck him again.

Danny Turner sagged to the floor, his arms flopped out on either side. He still seemed to be talking. It came out like a baby's gurgle. She walloped him around the head a few more times, until he was completely silent. Light suddenly drenched the room. Squinting, Paulette thought it must be the light of our Lord Jesus or an angel come to take her father up to heaven. But that seemed an unlikely destination, so it came as no surprise to see her mother in the doorway, holding a newly finished yellow dress.

Joan said nothing at first. Her eyes widened and she made a strange little sound like a hiccup. Then with her foot, she gave the inert body a prod. "Go downstairs and get a couple of those big trash bags," she instructed. "Don't wake your brother."

When Paulette returned, the yellow dress was wrapped around her father's head like something an Arab might wear. Her mother pulled one of the trash bags down over this and said, "I'm calling your aunt."

Aunt Julie had moved north to live closer to them after she divorced her no good husband a year ago. When she arrived, ten minutes later, and saw Danny's bare legs sticking out from under the plastic, Aunt Julie declared, "About time!" She took one of her heart pills, then said, "I think we better get his pants back on him, the filthy pig."

The two women dressed his bottom half and put on his shoes. Paulette's mom lay the golf club on top of him.

"Take a leg each, you two," Aunt Julie said, flicking off the bedroom light and lifting him under the armpits.

As noiselessly as possible, they carried the body down the stairs and out the back door into the garage where Aunt Julie's pickup was parked. They loaded the body on board, then Paulette's mom went into the house for his golf clubs. She shoved the bloody 7 iron in with the set and tossed them onto the pickup.

"Go back upstairs and wait in the sewing room, dear." She handed Paulette a key. "Keep the lights on, and sit at the machine. There's some yellow fabric left over from your new dress. Just keep sewing over it 'til I get home. That way no one will know I've gone out."

THE NEXT MORNING, in the middle of breakfast, the police came. Joan showed them into the living room. They took off their hats and asked her to sit down.

"That some 'gator," the younger of the two officers observed, gazing up at Solomon.

Joan had set him back in his usual place that morning, and she'd removed the sunglasses. He looked more dignified without them.

"New paint?" the older officer said.

"Mom did it yesterday." Frank sidled around the door. "So we'd get a surprise when we came home from school." Ogling their uniforms, he continued, "Wow, are you real cops?"

"Frank. Hush," Joan said, then explained to the two officers, "He wants to be a police officer one day. It's his dream."

"Well, son, maybe when we're done talking with your mom, you can come out and take a look at our patrol car."

Frank went brick red with excitement. "Yes, please, sir."

"Run along now." Joan closed the door and turned to the officers, gratified her redecoration had made a favorable impression. "Is it my husband? Is he in trouble again?"

The older of the two cleared his throat. "Ma'am, when did you last see your husband?"

"At dinner time last night. He had a friend over to play cards. Then later on he went out."

"Any idea where he was going?"

Joan shrugged. "I gave up asking ten years ago. What's this about? If I need to bail him out again—"

"Ma'am. I'm sorry to have to tell you this but your husband was found dead on Emerald Vale golf course this morning."

"What? I don't understand—"

"It appears he was murdered with one of his own golf clubs."

"Murdered?" Joan raised a shaky hand to her face.

"I'm afraid we need you to come downtown with us to identify the body."

Numbly Joan stood. The younger officer placed a gentle hand against her back and opened the door for her. Joan liked that. It was a long time since anyone had treated her like a lady.

"I'll get my coat," she said. "If you don't mind waiting."

PAULETTE WAS SITTING on her bed when her mom came into the room.

"I have to go down to the Police Station," she said, closing the door behind her. "Your father was found dead at Emerald Vale this morning, and I need to identify the body."

"What's going to happen?" Paulette whispered.

"You're going to stay home from school today because I just told you the terrible news. Then we'll bury your father."

"And that's it?"

Her mom looked around room. They had cleaned the walls after she got back the night before, and the rug Danny Turner had bled on was now in the basement, waiting for the next garbage collection.

"I'm thinking I'll paint this tomorrow," she told Paulette. "While I'm at the morgue, you can decide what color you'd like."

### Gabrielle Goldsby

Around the age of nine, Gabrielle was very ill for a month. Every few days, her mother walked from her job in downtown Oakland, California to a used bookstore to buy copies of every Nancy Drew she could get her hands on. Gabrielle read the first 25 mysteries in a two week period, and she credits her independent, single mother with inspiring her love of reading and therefore her writing.

Gabrielle was born on a military base in Colorado in the early Seventies. She now lives in Portland, Oregon with Melissa, her partner of six years. With a Bachelor of Science in Criminal Justice Administration and a Minor in Ethnic Studies she seems well-suited to write lesbian crime fiction such as *Wall of Silence*. But Gabrielle is interested in trying her hand at many genres including historical fiction, and *The Caretaker's Daughter* is the result. While working as an Administrative Assistant for a finance company, she is currently working on her third novel.

# Long Way Home

## Fiction by Gabrielle Goldsby

"IT LOOKS MORE raggedy than I remember," I said gruffly. What I was thinking was how much I missed its raggedness. I had probably passed these houses thousands of times in my life: first peddling a pink Husky, then a mustard orange three-speed, and finally, driving a multicolored 1973 Chevy Vega. I hadn't paid much attention to them then, but seeing them again brought to mind something else from the past: an old nightgown. It had been washed and dried so often you could almost see through the material. I have yet to feel cotton softer against my skin. The feeling of comfort that nightgown gave me was worth the teasing I suffered at the hands of my partner, Dee. I could remember feeling a sense of loss every time I slipped it, old, dingy and threadbare, over my head. One day I would no longer be able to argue against throwing it away. Oakland felt like that: old, raggedy, and threadbare. But also familiar, comforting, warm, and mine.

"Remember that old nightgown I used to love?" I asked Dee.

"Yeah, I used scraps from it in that quilt I made for you."

"I miss that nightgown."

Dee nodded and looked out the window. "Five years is a long time to be away from home, Genean." She covered my hand with hers and I smiled though I didn't look at her. She always saw too much in my eyes. She knew what I meant, even when I didn't say it. It's one of the reasons I love her, one of the reasons I want to spend the rest of my life with her.

"This is my mother's home, and where I grew up. *My* home is with you." I didn't have to look to know she was wearing that crooked little smile of hers. I could feel it in the squeeze to my hand.

"I know, sweetie, but your home is also where your mother is." I shrugged and Dee let the subject drop. "For some reason I thought your mom lived closer to the airport."

I bit the inside of my lip to distract myself from the nausea that passed over me in that instant. I'd told Dee the bumpy take-off had caused the nausea, but in truth, it had started the moment we left our home in San Diego.

"We could've taken the freeway but..." I struggled to find an acceptable explanation. "I wanted to see..." Dee gave my hand another squeeze and I stopped trying to explain what she already knew. I had deliberately taken the long way because I was nervous. Sometimes I wish she didn't understand me so well. I grimaced and tried to ease the button of my jeans away from my navel.

"Your stomach still bothering you?"

"No," I lied. "I just I haven't seen my mother in a while, and she doesn't know...."

"She doesn't know about me."

"I was going to say she doesn't know about *us*, Dee."

She was quiet for a moment. "What do you think she'll say?"

I shrugged and glanced over at her. Her expressive blue eyes were hidden behind the lenses of her sunglasses. "I don't know."

"You can't even guess?" Dee chuckled, the nervousness in her voice mirroring what I was feeling.

"I know it's hard for you to believe, growing up in a family like yours, but we just never talked about gays or lesbians at all."

"What do you mean *a family like mine?*" The nervousness seemed forgotten for a moment and indignation crept in.

I laughed. "Look, I'm not cracking on your family. But I bet your mother made your breakfast and your school lunch in the morning, and was there waiting for you when you came home from school."

"Yeah. So what? A lot of people's mothers did that."

"None of my friend's mothers did, sweetheart. They didn't have time. Most of them were going it alone like my mom. I made my own school lunch while she was getting ready for work."

I drummed my fingers on the steering wheel and idly watched a woman, no older than my 26 years, drag three dirty-looking kids across the street. The youngest of the three was leashed and had a hood over his head in the over 70-degree weather. He grinned and pointed at our rented SUV as he said something I couldn't hear. His mother yanked his leash, and he obediently stepped up on the curb. The light changed, and I gave the car some gas.

"Hey, is that Skyline?" Dee pointed to a monstrous building

squatting behind several tall gates. I glanced at the building and back to the road, my mouth twisting lightly with distaste. This is one area that hadn't changed. The gates appeared as impenetrable as they had when I was a kid. I slowed to a near crawl as we bumped over four speed bumps obviously placed there to keep people from speeding in front of the school. A bright yellow sign blared, "SPEED LIMIT 15 MPH" as if the kids at Bishop O'Connell deserved better than the 25 miles an hour that the rest of America's children warranted.

"No sweetie, that's Bishop O'Connell." I was sure I said it lightly or at least I thought I did. Ahead, the light turned red, and I stopped the car at the intersection.

I could hear the question in Dee's voice as she repeated the name. "Bishop O'Connell," she said as if tasting it.

"Skyline is about 5 miles that way." I pointed with my chin, unwilling to release her hand.

"Was this school expensive?"

"Mmm hmm, very. It's one of the best schools in the Bay Area, though, so I guess it's worth it."

"Did you want to go here?"

I shrugged. "I wanted to go to school with my friends. None of them could afford to go there. Neither could I, come to think of it." I babbled on to keep myself from thinking too much. "When they first put up that gate it pissed a lot of people off. They couldn't stop the neighborhood kids from playing basketball on their court, so they put up these fences. People around here took it as an insult."

I sunk down low in my seat and peered at the pristine white basketball nets hanging from the hoops. "I guess they were right. Look at that, bet it's the only school in Oakland that still has basketball nets." The light turned green, and I could feel myself growing more and more tense as we drove down Truman Street toward my mother's home.

"I hate this," I blurted out.

"No, you don't. "

"Yeah, I do. I hate the way this is making me feel. Why do I need to do this? If you were a man—"

"If I were a man you would have dumped my ass four years ago. If I were a man I wouldn't be about to meet your entire family. If I were a man I wouldn't get to sit and hold your hand while your legs are up in those damn stirrups so that some doctor can stick a—"

"Okay, okay." I chuckled. "I get your point. I'm just saying I hate the fact that I feel so scared."

"Everyone is scared when they come out to their family. I

thought I was going to throw up when I first told mine."

"That was different. You were 16 years old. I'm 26. I shouldn't feel so... well shit, I shouldn't feel like this."

"Sweetie, I think it's natural to feel scared."

I continued speaking as if I hadn't heard her, determined to keep the silence and the fear from creeping in. "Besides, I'm not so much worried about my family. I mean if they don't accept us, then they can kiss my ass."

"You're more worried about your mother."

"Yeah, I have no idea how she'll feel. I mean she just doesn't... we never talked about these kinds of things."

"I still can't believe that."

"No, I mean she had friends who were gay. They were mostly men, but other than that, I don't know that it ever came up. Don't get me wrong. I always knew that there were people in this world that had same sex relationships. But it was always twice removed, if that makes sense."

Dee nodded, and I made the final right turn onto my mother's street. "That's where Cindy and Brin used to live." I pointed at the once immaculate house. It was hard to believe that the brown, nondescript house had once been the best looking one on the block. Now it seemed to slump down in back of its two small squares of wizened grass as if to hide. "See that lattice right there?" I pointed with my pinky, but didn't remove my hand from the steering wheel. "For some reason the previous owners decided to plant grapes that crawled up that lattice. All the neighborhood kids would try to eat them, which would result in a grape fight because they were the nastiest grapes ever. I think they were wine grapes." I prattled on. Shriveled vines still clung to the lattice, but there was no sign of the once leafy grape vines. The thought that the kids who lived here now had one less benefit than I did made me sad.

Two houses past the old Williams house, I grinned. Now this house looked exactly like I remembered it. "Mrs. Heartwater's," I said.

"Where?" Dee craned her head as if to get a glimpse of the old woman who I'm sure would be in her early 80s if she were still alive. Mrs. Heartwater's favorite pastime was to lean out of her window and flip off all of us kids with gusto.

I eased the rental up to the curb in front of my mother's house. The lawn was a lot greener than I remembered it, and the big, green bushes skirting the porch had been professionally pruned. She had also obviously painted the porch. "The house didn't look like this when I lived in it," I said, dimly aware that I was annoyed because the house had not fallen into disrepair in my absence.

"This is it then?" Dee asked softly.

I nodded. "This is it."

I was just about to suggest we leave to go have some coffee before actually ringing my mother's doorbell when the black iron gate that had protected our front door from who-knew-what swung open. A short, brown-skinned woman stepped out onto the porch, a huge smile enveloping her face. Before I even realized it, I had opened the car door and was jogging down the driveway to envelope her in my arms. I tried to join her on the small front porch but realized that I would tower over her making our tight hug nearly impossible to maintain.

"Oh, my God. You're so short," I said through a sob. Had it really only been five years? The brown hair that had been down past her shoulders was now cut stylishly short and was almost completely silver gray. The braces she'd gotten while I was in college were now gone, and the teeth gleaming back at me were perfectly straight and white.

"I missed you, baby girl," she gushed into my ear as we held on tight. I didn't need to turn around to know that Dee, who had made a far more graceful descent down the driveway, was now standing shyly behind me. I could almost hear pieces shifting into place. My life was finally whole.

"Hey, Momma. It's been too long," I said in a voice thick with tears. It *had* been too long; I knew that and so did she. The only problem was how to tell her why.

"Hey, Ann. She's here," a voice hollered. I cringed as my cousin Nora pushed through the iron gate and onto the porch. She grabbed me around the waist, wrenching me from my mother's arms, and smothered me with two overflowing double D's. "Ann," Nora shouted, "get out here."

"Umpf. Ann is here, too?" I asked just as Ann burst onto the porch and began jubilantly pounding on my back. Ann was married with three kids, and still managed to be more butch than either Dee or myself could ever be. Hell, she even co-captained a women's softball team.

After detaching my face from one cousin's breast, I hugged the other and began to introduce my lover of four years to my family. I felt a sudden surge of awkwardness. *Do I introduce her as my roommate? My friend? My best friend? My lover?* Certainly she was all those things and to just say one seemed, well, a betrayal. My mother stepped forward then and took the issue out of my hands.

"You must be Dee. I've talked to you so many times on the phone I feel like I already know you. Come on in here, you two.

We were just about to sit down for brunch." I watched as my mother pulled Dee into the house, my cousins following close behind.

As they disappeared from my view, I heard Nora explain to Dee, "My momma and Genean's grandmamier were sisters..." I remained outside staring out at our rental car, trying to figure out why being home felt so alien. Everything was unbearably familiar, yet so foreign. The air was still, as if the entire neighborhood was waiting for me to tell my secret. Or waiting for me to go inside so they could steal my shit. With that thought in mind, I hurried down the steps to retrieve our luggage.

After lining the luggage up on the sidewalk, I picked lint off the driver's seat, cleaned the rearview mirror with a tissue, folded the car rental agreement neatly and placed it in the glove compartment, fully aware that I was avoiding something. Hell, I was avoiding everything. But it was unfair of me to leave Dee in the house with a bunch of people she didn't know. I picked up both bags and started down the driveway. A tall young man in pressed, baggy jeans and neatly clipped hair stepped out onto the porch with a huge grin on his face.

Gone was the acne-plagued skin of years before. The body that had always been thin, but out of shape, now looked tight and strong. He, unlike my mother, seemed to have grown two feet taller in my absence.

"Hey bro, when did you get in?" I called out, feeling light-hearted for the first time since starting this trip.

"Last night. Look at you, girl." He made a big pretense of looking me up and down as he sauntered down the drive to meet me. "Where'd you pick up them hips?"

"That's from good eatin'."

"Uh huh. I wonder about what you been eatin' out there in Southern California." I hit him in the chest and blushed furiously. I had always had the impression that Terrell suspected I was gay. Even if he did, I didn't think he would tell my mother. The same way I didn't tell her when I caught him in bed with some neighborhood girl when he was 16. He was my little brother and when you have a mom who worked and went to school at the same time, you learned to take care of each other.

I grinned up at him as warmth and familiarity stole over my body. "So you're getting married, huh?"

"Yeah, she can't wait to meet you, but she's sort of shy. You know, afraid you all won't like her."

"So you have Momma invite Nora and Ann over?" I popped him on the arm. "You so smart."

He laughed and shrugged. "She'll have to meet them at

some point. We're a package deal." The humor in his eyes changed to affection as he looked down at me. "So, what about you? When are you going to start thinking about settling down?"

I smiled and felt my ears heat up. This was my brother, and here I felt like I was talking to a stranger. "Let's get you nice and tied up first, then we can worry about me."

He lifted our bags as if they were two sack lunches. "Come on, girl, let's get inside before they eat up all the food and Dee and Erica along with it."

I nodded and slowly followed Terrell into the house. He left the bags by the dining room doorway and hurried to his seat. Dee was already seated at the table, looking glassy-eyed at the food. Two cakes graced the table in front of her, leaving barely enough room for her large white plate. One was a two-layer chocolate, and I imagined I could smell its tart chocolaty frosting from my place at the front door. A large ham and a chicken sat to her left near another plate, presumably mine. Potato salad, candied yams, string beans, mashed potatoes, homemade macaroni and cheese, stuffing, the golden brown tops of dinner rolls, and a humongous gravy boat filled the rest of the table. My mother sat at the head of the table with Ann and Dee to the right of her and Nora, Terrell and the person I assumed to be my brother's fiancé to the left. The expectant look on their faces made me nervous until I realized that they were simply waiting for me to sit down.

"Y'all go on and eat," I said to no one in particular, "I'm just going to drop these in the bedroom." Without much more than a glance back, I struggled momentarily with the bags before heading toward the bedroom that had been mine for so many years. Gone was the waterbed of my teen years. Gone were all the Nancy Drew books that had lined the bookshelves I had made myself. And gone was the old sewing machine I'd used as a desk to do homework on. I dropped the bags and sank down to the edge of the bed. Apparently my mother had gotten herself a new bed because the one that I was sitting on now had been in her room for years. I grimaced at the floral design and the teal green walls. The carpets looked freshly cleaned, and there were no pictures on the wall. This was a guest room now.

The sounds of plates clacking and people talking brought me out of my reverie. I felt horrible that I had left Dee out there by herself, but it was all I could do not to run from this place that held so many of my childhood dreams.

I rose and reluctantly returned to the dining room just as Nora, around a mouthful of something, proudly told Dee, "Too bad you don't get to meet my brother, John. He has a lot of white friends."

"Oh really? Where is he today?" Dee asked as if Nora had just said John was a Capricorn.

"He works a lot. He'll be at the wedding though." Nora waved her hand in the air dismissively as if John's working too much was something she didn't understand but tolerated. She turned to her sister. "Ann, where's Calvin's black self?"

I winced. I love my cousin Nora dearly, but I had forgotten about her propensity for using the darkness of Calvin's skin as an insult.

"Calvin is my other brother," Nora explained, and I was shocked at the slight note of pride in her voice. "You need to meet him, too. I bet you've never seen anyone as black as him."

"Actually," Dee said, "I believe Genean showed me pictures of him. I thought he was quite handsome." Nora and Ann looked at Dee as if waiting for the punch line.

Ann finally said, "Are you sure you're talking about my brother, Calvin? Real tall, dark, pink lips, nappy hair?"

"Yeah, I'm pretty sure she said it was her cousin Calvin."

Nora laughed. "Girl, how long you staying for? We might have to hook y'all up."

I took that as my cue to step into the fray. "So where is my plate?" I said aloud, even though I knew where my plate was and that it would already have food on it.

"Right here next to Momma," Terrell said, pointing with his fork. Everyone in my family talked with their mouth full. It was the only way we could have conversations around the dinner table, especially if my mother or aunt were cooking. You couldn't help but shove food in, so it was either talk with food in your mouth or don't talk at all.

For the first time, since I had sat down at the table, I noticed the fine-boned, light-skinned girl sitting to my brother's left. She was shyly picking at the food on her plate and cutting her corn-bread with her fork. I looked over at Dee. Her fair complexion and blue eyes made her stand out as she picked up a turkey leg and bit into it with her eyes closed.

"Can you pass me the gravy, please?" Dee said to my brother, mouth completely full, eyes focused on her plate. I couldn't have felt more proud if she had simply reached over everyone's plate and grabbed that gravy boat herself.

Cousin Ann stabbed in Erica's general direction with her knife. "Girl, I thought Terrell said your family was from the south. Don't you know how to eat cornbread?" Erica laughed nervously and looked to my brother for help.

"Ann, leave her be," my mother said sternly, fork halfway to her mouth. "She can eat how she wants."

"Yes'm," Ann said and concentrated on eating her own food.

I looked around the table. A lull in the conversation allowed my mind to wander to the woman who was not sitting at the table with us. My Great Aunt Joan, Ann and Nora's mother, had fought cancer for years before it finally took her life. It dawned on me then; with my grandmamier living in Georgia and Aunt Joan gone my mother had become the matriarch of our family. I looked at the meticulously coiffed silvery hair and did some quick math in my head. Fifty-six years old now. She seemed too young for such a role.

"How old are you, Ann?" I asked.

"Thirty-two," Ann said around her food. "Why?"

"Just thinking about Aunt Joan is all. Trying to remember how old she would be."

"Momma would be about sixty-six, wouldn't she, Nora?"

"Yeah, sixty-six or sixty-seven."

I nodded. My mom was the same age as my aunt had been when she died. What if something had happened to her before I had a chance to talk to her? What if she never knew why I avoided coming home? I looked on as she used her knife to slip butter into the middle of a piece of cornbread before crumbling it and mixing it into her collard greens. How thin and small her hands looked. I blinked back tears just as she looked up.

"What's wrong, G?" she asked. I cursed the emotional tears that, over the last few weeks, crept over me like a ghost. I focused on the warmth of Dee's hand on my leg as she expertly continued to eat while trying to comfort me under the table. Dee had a long history of groping her girlfriends under the table. The thought choked a watery giggle from my throat.

"I'm just glad to be here, Momma."

Loudly, Nora said, "We're glad you're here too, girl," and any annoyance I had felt with her vanished under the love I saw in her face. It made me feel...well, horrible. Dinner forks clanked and conversation resumed. I could hear Dee's voice every so often, but I was too lost in my own thoughts to discern what was being said. Nausea swept over me as I pushed food around on my plate in the hopes that no one would notice that I wasn't eating.

A small push to my thigh made me pay attention to the last part of what my mother was saying. "Since your grandmamier's plane lands about an hour before I have to meet with the caterer, would you and Dee mind picking her up tomorrow?"

"Of course not, Momma." My mother stared at me for a moment, and I busied myself buttering a roll I knew I would not eat. My stomach still churned slowly over the miniscule food that I forced myself to eat on the plane. The rest of the meal passed, though I barely have any memory of it, other than accepting cream and sugar when coffee was served to me, and laughing when the musical tones of Dee's amusement penetrated the fog of anxiety that had enshrouded me.

Just before 10:00, I walked my brother, Erica, Ann, and Nora to the door along with my mother and stood outside to wave goodbye to them with promises of catching up the following day. I stood on my mother's porch and felt like a traitor. This had been my home once. Now I felt like a guest who had over-stayed her welcome.

My mother looked at me quizzically. "You want to go out back and sit a bit before we turn in?"

I nodded and followed her back through the living room with its new furniture and nearly white carpet. We found Dee in the kitchen washing dishes much to my mother's chagrin.

"Oh, no, Dee, don't you worry about that. Why don't you come out back with us? I'll load the dishwasher up before I go to bed, and Mrs. Nelson will unload it in the morning."

"Who's Mrs. Nelson?" I asked, my curiosity momentarily quelling my fear.

"She's the lady who comes in every other day to tidy up."

"You have a ...wait a minute. Since when could we afford a housekeeper? When Terrell and I were here you made us..." I could feel my eyes grow wide..."Oh, I see how you are. Using child labor and stuff. What kind of mess is that?"

Dee laughed. "My mother got someone to help her after all of us kids moved away too. You two go on out back. I enjoy washing dishes. It helps me to unwind."

"I'm the same way," my mother said as she patted Dee on the back.

"You're the same way?" I feigned anger. "What do you know about washing dishes? 'Cause near as I can figure, you haven't washed dishes since 1981."

"Girl, come on here." My mother laughed, put a mug of hot coffee in my hands, and pushed me toward the double doors that we had utilized to go out into the backyard for all of my child-hood. Gone were the rustic stairs I had tumbled down and up so many times that I still carried some of the scars. A deck the size of the bedroom I had occupied now dwarfed the backyard. My mother sat on a rocking swing and patted the space next to her.

It was cold out and shockingly quiet. I could hear water run-ning and the jangle of silverware as it was dropped into a drainer. "It's really quiet tonight."

"More quiet than San Diego?"

"Yeah, we live downtown.

"Really? Near Horton Plaza?"

I smiled as I remembered how thrilled my mother was with Horton Plaza when she came to visit. "Yeah, sorta."

"Well, that's good."

"Mom..." I said softly. "Momma, I need to tell you something."

"I figured as much."

"I...it's about Dee and..." I paused struggling to remember why it was necessary for me to have this conversation, at this very moment.

"What about Dee? Is she alright?"

"Yeah. Yes, she's fine. She just...well we've been trying to um... She wants to have a child. And no, before you ask, there is no man in her life."

"Really? Well, I can't say as I would willingly become a single parent but...I am really glad things worked out that way." My mother chuckled.

This was harder than I'd imagined. I took her hands in mine. "She won't be a single parent, Momma," I said, and then rushed to continue. "We've been together for nearly four years. She's my lover. We decided we would have a ceremony next month in Hawaii, and I was hoping you would come.... if you want to. And it isn't just her who wanted a baby—it's me, too." I had to turn away to catch my breath. Oakland once again seemed to wait in silence. I heard her inhale before she snatched her hands from my grasp. The swing jerked as she stood and, with her back to me, stared off the deck in the direction of the orange trees I had gleefully raided as a child.

"I'm still the same person you..."

"Don't you tell me who you are. I *know* who you are."

I drew in a breath. It had been a long time since I'd heard my mother so angry. Certainly not since I had become an adult.

"Is that what this is about? What it's been about all this time?" Her voice seemed hurt, bewildered.

"What ..."

"You haven't been home in five years, Genean. Five years. At first I thought you didn't want to come here...that you were ashamed of where you were from."

"Ashamed? Ashamed?" Tears of frustration and anger prickled at the back of my eyes. "I was never ashamed. Oakland made me who I am."

She turned to me then, her eyes flashing. "You stopped coming home because you're gay?"

"Yes. No. I never intended on not telling you but...there

never seemed to be the right time."

"Why didn't you tell me when I came down for your graduation? Why not then? You obviously were together then. Telling me I could have your bed and you would sleep with Dee! Do you know how guilty I felt about that?"

"Momma, please. Listen to me."

"No, you listen to me! When did I ever give you the impression I would love you any less because of who you sleep with?"

I held up my hands in placation and spoke softly. "That's just it, Momma. I don't just sleep with her. I wake with her. I eat with her. I want to start a family with her. I love her with everything I am."

My mother was silent for a moment. "I didn't mean to suggest—"

"I know, but it's really important to me that I get this right. I'm sorry I waited so long to tell you, but part of the reason was because I was afraid you would think... well you always seemed to think that my relationships weren't...real. You know, introducing them as my little friend. Momma, Dee is so much more than that. She's my wife."

I let the silence that followed last as long as she needed it to. "Was I wrong?" The humor in her voice was shocking after the solemnity of the last few moments.

"About what?"

"About your little male friends. You were never serious about any of them. They were never around for longer than six months."

"No I suppose you weren't, but...Dee is different, Momma. We have a commitment. That's why we want to have a ceremony."

"Does your brother know?"

"No, and I'm not going to tell him until after he comes back from his honeymoon. This is *his* time. I don't want to steal his thunder."

"Well, I think he suspects. He's made comments about you and Dee for a few years now."

"You're kidding? Come to think of it, he said something outside when we came in. I thought he was just being his normal crude self. And you still never suspected?"

"To be honest, no. Because I thought if there was something important to you, you would always tell me. I thought you knew you could always tell me anything."

I stood up and touched her hand. She was a bit too thin now. When had that happened? When had her hair become nearly as silver as my grandmamier's? I remembered wide hips and immaculately groomed nails, mocha-colored skin that always glowed, and that nice wonderful smile that wasn't diminished for one moment by the braces she got.

"I'm moving back to Atlanta in May," she said.

I sucked in a breath. "What? Why? You said you would never go back!"

"I know, but your grandmamier is getting older and I'm worried they're not taking as good a care of her as they should."

"But what about your job?"

"I've been there 34 years, Genean. I'll be eligible for my full retirement benefits next year. In Atlanta, I could afford to fix up your grandmamier's house, put a ramp in for her, all sorts of things. Besides, with you and Terrell gone, there isn't much left for me here."

My heart fluttered against my ribcage. She was leaving...in less than a year. I had been a two-hour flight away from her and now, now it felt like she would be halfway around the world.

"You don't want to just move Grandmamier here?"

"No, she would be more comfortable in her own home, and besides, Atlanta has changed a lot since I lived there as a kid."

The distant city lights made the tops of the orange trees glow, as if their leaves were dipped in silver. "Atlanta is a long ways away," I said, not looking away from the trees.

"Next door can be a long ways away if you don't try to stop in for a visit every now and then."

I placed my hands on her thin shoulders feeling tall, awkward and undeserving. "I'm so sorry." I folded her into my arms, feeling about as low as I did when I cut a hole in her hardwood floor to store my buried treasures. "You're disappointed that I didn't tell you sooner, aren't you?"

"If—when—you become a mother, you'll learn that your kids can hurt you like no one on this earth can. But they'll give you more joy, too. It'll make it all worthwhile."

"I really am sorry, Momma."

"Me, too," she said, and it made me feel worse because she really seemed sorry, only I was pretty sure she didn't mean it the way I did. In those few words, she had told me in a way only a mother could that I had messed up. I had wasted years by avoiding the possibility of my mother not loving me because I was afraid. Regardless of where she moved, I resolved to make sure we saw each other every few months. I closed my eyes tight and made her a silent promise.

"When will you know?" she mumbled against my shoulder.

"When will I know what?"

"About the baby."

I sucked in a breath and chuckled. "Oh, I don't know," I said, my stomach churning again. I had one nerve-racking situation down, and now I had to deal with another. "We decided to wait to do a pregnancy test until we got back. But um, maybe I can run down to the store and pick one up later."

"Why wait until later?"

"You mean do one now?"

"Yeah, I mean you should go buy one of those tests down at the grocery store *right now*. Ms. Dee and me need to have a long talk. I had no idea I would have two new family members to celebrate." The smile in her voice told me Dee was in for a long grilling, but I had nothing to worry about.

"Don't be too hard on her, Momma. She wanted to tell you three months after we met. I was just... I don't know, scared."

She nodded. "I won't lie to you and tell you that I understand fully. I mean, being a lesbian is...well, just not something I've ever even thought about. But why you felt so strongly that you would rather stay away than tell me...I don't think I'll ever get that."

"I know," I said sadly. "I'm so sorry."

"You don't have to keep saying that. Now go to the store."

"Yes, ma'am," I said and watched her head back into the house.

I could hear her say something to Dee; there was a moment of silence, and then Dee's voice clearly said, "She finally told you."

The shadows of my mother and Dee merged briefly then separated. I heard them both laugh and a soft drone as one of them, I think it was Dee, began to talk. I leaned back against the railing and looked up at the stars. The deck was new, but the view wasn't. I hoped like hell our child took after Dee and not me. I had caused damage to my relationship with my mother and, no matter how much she loved me, no matter how accepting of our relationship she was, I knew it would take a long time, a lot of love and a lot of honesty to get our closeness back.

The hurtful part was that even though I'd feared her reaction, I had always known she would still love me. I never truly doubted it. I had let fear keep me from telling her. I had wasted so much time. My eyes were watery long before I realized how lucky I was that I had a mother who loved me and partner who I was not only in love with, but who was also my best friend.

A plane hummed overhead, interrupting my thoughts. I watched its glinting burgundy light descend toward Oakland airport. People coming, people going, lives changing and evolving, just like mine. I turned toward the house but stopped short of opening the door. Reluctant to interrupt my mother's and Dee's conversation, I changed course and went through the back gate.

As I climbed into the driver's seat of the rental car, it dawned on me that one day—one day soon perhaps—I would be a mother, too. I imagined I could smell traces of Dee's perfume mingling with my own anxiety, and then a vision of my partner calmly explaining to my mother that it would be me carrying our child brought a smile to my face. I started the car and pulled away from the curb, already plotting the shortcut that would bring me back home quickest.

## Ellen Hart

After spending twelve years as a kitchen manager/chef at a large sorority at the University of Minnesota, Ellen Hart always likes to say it was either the real thing, or commit murder on paper. Hence, she became a mystery writer. Ellen's first novel was published in 1989, and since then, this prolific writer has penned nineteen more mysteries in two different series. The Jane Lawless series was the first with a lesbian protagonist ever to go from a small press to a mainstream New York publisher. The Sophie Greenway culinary mystery series has been called "Nick and Nora for the new millennium!"

Ellen is a five-time winner of the Lambda Literary Award for Best Lesbian Mystery, as well as a two-time winner of the Minnesota Book Award for Best Crime & Detective Fiction. *Entertainment Weekly* recently named her one of the "101 movers and shakers in the gay entertainment industry."

Ellen teaches mystery writing through the University of Minnesota's Compleat Scholar program and at The Loft, the largest independent writing community in the nation. Now that their daughters have grown up and started families of their own, she lives in Minneapolis with Kathy, her partner of 27 years, and their two darling dogs, Busby and Newton.

# Mother Memoir: A Coming Out Story

## Memoir by Ellen Hart

ALL MY LIFE I've been drawn to mystery in one form or another. My mother, and my relationship with her, will always remain the most profound mystery of my life.

When I was in my twenties, all I could see were the difference between my mother and me. To be sure, we *are* very different people. But in my forties, I started to notice similarities. Now in my mid fifties, I've begun to examine both the negative baggage my mother passed on, as well as the gifts. Life is a mixed bag, as we all know. We certainly don't get to choose our parents, but neither do our parents get to choose us. The lesson there, at least in my case, has to do with love and frustration, admiration and anger, and, ultimately, understanding and acceptance. No mother-daughter relationship is simple, but when you throw sexual identity into the soup, it can be explosive.

I want to tell you my coming out story. Along the way, I think you'll get a sense of some of the conflicts—but also the love—that defined my relationship with my mother.

In the fall of 1992, my third novel, *Stage Fright*, had just been published. I was still working full time as a chef/kitchen manager at the Delta Gamma sorority at the University of Minnesota. On weekends and evenings, I did promotional events—bookstore signings, radio interviews, library talks, whatever came up. At the time, I was not only in the closet with my mother about my relationship with my partner, Kathy, but I was also in the closet about my writing. Not only would my mom have objected to the lesbian main character in the books, but being a fundamentalist Christian to the right of Jerry Falwell, she thought mystery novels were satanic. I still remember the day I took her grocery shopping—when I was writing my first book—and she did a good ten minutes on how terrible "those sorts" of books were.

For ten years, my mother and I had been part of a fundamentalist Christian group called The Worldwide Church of God. I'd attended Ambassador University, the church's college in Pasadena, California, and graduated in 1971 with a degree in Theology. I left the church soon thereafter. The reason I left had a great deal to do with the sexual and moral corruption in the ministry, especially the head ministers, but also had perhaps even more to do with my growing feminism. My mother eventually left the church as well — not because of the corruption so much as because she felt she'd found too much doctrinal error. In her own studies, she'd discovered the truth, and the Worldwide Church of God no longer represented that truth.

My mother had always been the poster child for the iconoclastic spirit. My partner, Kathy, thinks it's because she was a full-blooded Norwegian. She was just too damn stubborn ever to be wrong. Although she proclaimed loudly and often that she'd made many mistakes in her life, nothing she was ever involved in at the moment was a mistake. She believed what she believed with total fervency. And what she believed was not only right, it was *righteous.*

My mom was an only child. She grew up in Hettinger, North Dakota, a town her family had helped found. Her father was a banker, mother a typical housewife. Marjory Rowena Anderson was a strikingly beautiful young woman who loved to date, wear beautiful clothes, and generally have a good time. She looked a lot like the movie actress Paulette Goddard. She met my father in the late thirties, when the clouds of war were lowering over Europe, and married him in 1939.

She often told the story of how they first met. It was a blind date, and she wasn't terribly impressed. When my dad asked her out again, she said no thanks. My mother laughed when she recalled the look on my father's face. He was dumbfounded. Herm Boehnhardt was a big man on campus: cool car, great clothes, handsome, financially clever, with a job on the sports desk at the *Minneapolis Morning Tribune.* Nobody had ever turned him down before. When she finally did agree to see him again, he took her home to meet his mother. My father's mother later told him, "She's the one. Don't let her get away." By that point, my father agreed.

I'm not sure where my mother's confidence came from, but she had a view of life that told her what *she* thought about the world — or an idea, a person — was more important than what the world thought of *her.* She passed that on to me. Frankly, that particular life lesson was one she might have liked to rescind. As much as she wanted me to be happy, she also wanted me to make the same choices she had. I think many mothers want that from their daughters, and mine was no exception. In a way, if we get married, have children, share the same religious and political opinions, it validates their choices and their lives. The fact that what I believed was more important to me than what *she* believed always galled her. She spent a great part of her latter years trying to convince me of her points of view. Only problem was, the beliefs she held changed so often that it was hard to keep up. But that never seemed to bother my mother. Or, more accurately, she never even noticed.

My mother believed that public education was a waste of money. Public education also passed on a lot of Godless liberalism and should be done away with for that reason alone. All women should home-school their children. She thought Democrats were lying cheats, out to ruin the country financially and morally. She believed in the International Jewish Conspiracy — the Bilderburers ran the world. All political figures were puppets. She saw no reason for welfare — anyone could get a job in this country and support themselves just fine. If they didn't, it was because they were lazy. All minorities were lazy. The Pope was the Antichrist. Sometimes the Jews were God's chosen people, sometimes they were behind all the evil in the world. Women should stay home and not work. The business world was for men. Men were smarter than women. The soul passed into the child's body through the father. Women were catty and small-minded. (Except for her.) She decried all the violence on TV, but loved James Bond movies. When we went out, she couldn't imagine why there were so many cars on the road. People should stay home. City water was polluted. All food was polluted. Doctors didn't know anything. You should drink vinegar every day. You should also drink hydrogen peroxide — it was good for you. Wheat grass was good for you. Sugar kills more people than anything else. It should be banned. Coffee was a drug, just like cocaine. Nobody should drink it. Potatoes were part of the nightshade family — they could kill you. So could tomatoes. Corn was for pigs. Humans shouldn't eat it. Right was good and left was bad. In her sixties, heaven and hell didn't exist. It was a Catholic doctrine that wasn't in the Bible. By her eighties, heaven did exist, and she was going there after she died. Income tax was illegal. Homosexuality was a sin punishable by eternal death. I think intellectuals were in the same category, but it's hard to remember now. She didn't leave me a handbook — just lots of tapes that run in my head.

I've often written about my mother in my books. Any author who tells you their writing isn't a form of therapy is lying. In my most recent mystery, *Death on a Silver Platter*, I describe a woman very much like my mother:

"Simply put, Millie Veelund was a bigot. She preceded most of her pronouncements with 'I'm not prejudiced, but—' The spirit of Joe McCarthy was alive and well and living in Minnesota. Margaret Thatcher was her political hero, as was Ronald Reagan, except that he was involved far too much with those Jews over there in the Middle East. Then again, he'd taken on the labor unions and won. He had a good heart. Millie Veelund was Archie Bunker without the twinkle. She used religion and politics like a flame-thrower. She was human Agent Orange. Danny hated her. And he loved her. And that was the problem."

You get the picture. Not only was my mother a cantankerous, self-righteous, know-it-all, but she revered ideas—believed they ruled the world. She passed that knowledge on to me. In fact, ideas do rule the world, and those you come to accept and call your own profoundly affect who you become.

Perhaps you can see why the thought of coming out to my mother was a scary one. I was of two minds about it. I thought she might never want to see or speak to me again. If that happened, I didn't know what would happen to her. By that time in her life—her late seventies—I was her primary caregiver. She was able to stay in her house largely due to the help Kathy and I gave to her. If we became estranged, I feared for her future. But I wondered if her natural iconoclasm might kick in and she might be okay with the fact that I was a lesbian—not condone it, of course, but she'd be willing to live with it. The bottom line was, would her love for me—which I never doubted—be greater than her need to condemn.

Back to the coming out story. The winter that *Stage Fright* was published, I had been asked to do a noon radio program at a U of M station. My mother didn't get out much, and since I wrote under the name Ellen Hart (Ellen is my middle name, Hart is the last part of my very unpronounceable last name), she wouldn't have put the two together if she'd seen something in the newspaper. But...she did listen to the radio. The show I was asked to be on wasn't terribly popular. Actually, I figured that only people surfing the dial—or a few shut-ins—would be listening.

After the show was over and I'd returned home, I got a call from my mother. Her first words were a question. "Do you know who Ellen Hart is?"

I panicked. I saw my entire life pass before my eyes. "Who?"

"Ellen Hart. I just heard her on the radio and she had a

laugh just like yours. You two could be sisters."

"Really?"

"She writes mysteries."

"Oh?" I tried to sound normal.

"It was amazing. I guess we all have doubles out there some-where."

We moved on to another subject, but that was the turning point for me. I knew I had to tell her the truth. Not only did I need to come out of the closet about my sexuality, I had to come out of the mystery closet as well.

The week after I was almost busted was a busy one. I had book signings every night until Friday. On Friday night, Kathy and I, armed with three of my books, drove over to my mother's house. I remember thinking: this is it. This may be the last time I ever walk into this house, the last time I talk to her face to face. And yet, part of me couldn't believe she'd toss me out on my ear.

We walked into the kitchen. My mother smiled at us, invited us in, asked if she could make us some tea. (Tea was okay at that point. Later, it got put on the list of items that could kill—espe-cially herbal teas.) She was always happy to see us, and always very gracious. (Unless she was in the middle of a tirade.) In fact, my mother was an incredibly kind and generous person to those she loved. As I pointed out before, humans are an almost insane mixture of qualities.

Before I even took off my coat I said: "You wanted to know who Ellen Hart is."

"Yes," she said, moving over to the stove. "I did."

"I'm Ellen Hart."

She looked over at me. "Well...I thought so!"

I handed her the books.

"Let me get my glasses," she said, limping out into the din-ing room.

I looked at Kathy. She looked at me.

"Sit down in the living room and I'll join you in a second."

Kathy and I continued to shoot each other meaningful glances as we took up positions on either side of the picture win-dow. This wasn't what either of us had expected.

Finally, my mother sat down in her chair and turned on the light. She opened one of the books and started to look through it. "I knew that was your laugh on the radio the other day. See, I wasn't wrong."

"The main character in the book is gay."

"Oh?" She kept paging through *Vital Lies*. The irony of the title wasn't lost on me.

"And there's something else you need to know about me,

Mom. Something I haven't told you before."

"Yes?" she said, glancing at the back of the book.

"Kathy and I are partners. We've been together for sixteen years."

That stopped her. She looked up, her eyes moving back and forth between us. I couldn't read the expression on her face.

She studied us a moment more, then returned her attention to the book. "Oh, I know that," she said, almost matter-of-factly.

I nearly fell out of my chair.

"How did you get this published?" she asked.

"It's a *mystery* novel, Mom."

"Yes, I see that."

And we were off and running. She had so many questions. Did I have an agent? How did I know I could write a book? Where were the books sold? Just in Minneapolis? All over the world! She was fascinated.

We talked for about an hour. When Kathy and I left, we were in a daze. We went to a restaurant, ordered some food and a couple of beers, and just sort of fell apart. Neither one of us knew what her response would be, but although it hadn't been, "Well isn't that wonderful. You're lesbians!!" it also wasn't the end of the world. She hugged us both before we left the kitchen. Kathy and I had both been under so much tension. And now it was over.

The next day my mother called me. She still had lots of questions—not about the lesbian thing, but about the published writer thing. She actually sounded proud of me. During the conversation, we did a little walk down memory lane. She discussed all the guys who'd proposed to me over the years. "I could never see you with that one, but Greg, now he was the one for you."

When I pointed out that Greg was also gay, she stumbled a little. This was a different world than the one she'd grown up in. And she wanted me to know something—to make her position clear: She didn't approve of my "lifestyle." She never would. She thought it was wrong and felt that one day, I'd understand that too.

I listened to her, let her talk as long as she needed. She deserved an opportunity to express her feelings. But when she was done, I said, "I didn't tell you what I told you last night to seek your approval, Mom. I just needed you to know. And one day, I hope you'll see that my choice was a good one—the right one for me."

And that was it. We never really talked about it again.

In the coming years, as I continued to write, my mother grew ever more proud of my accomplishments as a writer and a writing teacher. When my tenth book was published, she sat next to me at the publication party as I signed books. She attended other publication events, too, always sitting right next to me at the table. I look upon those moments now as golden.

My mother died in March of 2000. The months before her death were hard ones for her. She was as frail and thin as a sparrow. When I came to visit, to bring food to prepare for her, to strip and put clean sheets on her bed, or to look through a photograph album as we sat together on the couch, I always had the sense that she was looking at me hard — trying to memorize me. Though we agreed on very little, we did agree on one thing. We loved each other. I understand now that that love was the bridge over which we met and talked, and finally, where we healed the wounds of our differences.

## Lois Cloarec Hart

Born in 1956 in British Columbia, Canada, Lois Cloarec Hart grew up as an avid reader, but didn't begin writing novels until later in life. Several years after joining the Canadian Armed Forces, she received a degree in Honours History from Royal Military College, and on graduation switched occupations from air traffic control to military intelligence. Having married a CAF fighter pilot while in college, she went on to spend five years as an Intelligence Officer before leaving the military to care for her husband, who was ill with chronic-progressive Multiple Sclerosis.

Lois's first book, *Coming Home,* was a fictionalized version of her life with her late husband. Initially her writing was therapeutic exercise to deal with the difficulties of caring for a quadriplegic, bedridden loved one. She wrote by his bedside, whether he was in the hospital or at home and says, "The story was never intended for anyone's view except my writing mentor, who had encouraged me to begin in the first place. After a year's work on it, however, I decided to risk putting it out there for others to read. It came as something of a delightful surprise when readers related so strongly and positively to my first story, and that feedback encouraged me to continue writing. My husband lived long enough to see the book come out with his picture on the cover, but passed away before the second book was published."

Since the death of her husband, Lois and her partner of three years have commuted between Calgary, Alberta, and Atlanta, Georgia.

# Grandmother's Cup

## Fiction by Lois Cloarec Hart

IT WAS HER great-grandmother's cup, now the last surviving dish of a set that had been carefully packed a century before for a journey from the Old World to the New. The porcelain was wafer-thin and chipped, and the hand painted English roses had long ago lost their luster, but Meredith cherished it. She had hoped to pass it along to her only daughter, and then, God willing, to see it in the hands of a granddaughter some day.

Now, as they had done so often in the past, she cradled the teacup with hands that had surrendered the smooth suppleness of youth. Fragrant steam curling up from the old cup whispered around Meredith's face as she bowed her head, stubbornly fighting the tears that had threatened to overwhelm her time and again on this terrible morning.

The dreams she had nourished since her daughter Danielle's birth thirty-six years before had just been shattered in one bitter confrontation. What was it called? Oh yes, 'coming out.' It was such an innocuous phrase for the words that had left her heartsick, and as bereft as if her youngest child had just died.

After presenting her husband with three sons, Meredith had been delighted when their fourth and final child was a girl. She'd had no illusions about her own place in the universe. She would not change the world. Her name would not outlive her. She would leave no legacy but her children and their children. And that was fine with her.

She knew that inevitably her boys would forget the old tales she had told them as youngsters, but she had faith her daughter would carry her mother's stories on to the next generation. That had always been the only immortality of the women in her family.

Meredith was satisfied to be what she was: a devoted, God-fearing wife and mother, living a quiet, unspectacular life in the suburbs. She loved her stolid husband and boisterous sons, but though she strove to be an even-handed parent, she had always reserved a special love for her youngest child.

She wondered now if God was punishing her for that—for loving her daughter more profoundly and powerfully than she loved her Heavenly Father.

"Please...don't take her away from me."

It was a prayer...it was a plea...it was her heart speaking directly to the God she had worshipped devoutly all her life, but the only sound in the kitchen was the steady ticking of the old clock over the sink. No sense of peace filled her. No sudden insight illuminated her thoughts. Time did not roll back, and the sound of her daughter slamming out of the kitchen vowing not to set foot in her mother's house again until hell froze over still echoed in her ears.

A tiny, bitter smile, no more than a barely distinguishable quirk of her lips, broke the frozen plane of Meredith's face. Dani had always been volatile, so unlike her staid parents. All of her children had inherited a mercurial temperament, though God only knew from whom. It had been a source of both frustration and intrigue to the older woman, as she watched her exuberant brood grow and thrive.

How she, the epitome of peaceful domesticity, had borne and raised such a pack of extroverts was beyond her, but she was proud of every one of them, especially the daughter who over-achieved her way into an early high school graduation and a plethora of scholarships to the colleges of her choice.

In the years that followed, while her brothers embarked on more traditional paths of careers and marriages, Dani traversed the globe, acquiring degrees and taking up new professions as easily as most people took up golf. She had a restless energy never satisfied by conventional measures of success, and no six-figure income, impressive title, or corner office ever appeared to sate her inner drive.

Dani's return to her hometown the previous year had shocked Meredith. Convinced that it would only be a matter of time before her vagabond daughter moved on again, she resolved to simply enjoy the younger woman's presence for as long as she was in the area. Much to her surprise, Dani had apparently settled quite contentedly into a job advocating for literacy and educational opportunities for underprivileged youth.

Her daughter quickly reintegrated with a circle of old friends and her brothers' families, and appeared to genuinely enjoy the abundance of nieces and nephews that inundated every family gathering. It gave Meredith hope that perhaps her daughter was finally ready to settle down and raise her own family.

She tentatively suggested a few nice, church-going men as potential dates, but Dani gently stonewalled her, good-naturedly informing her mother that she was perfectly capable of conducting her own social life.

Unwilling to push, Meredith backed off, and resorted to listening carefully at family functions to glean bits of information. It wasn't that her daughter was particularly reticent, but eavesdropping generally produced a fuller picture than Dani's edited version of her daily life. As the fly on the wall, she learned about the joys and frustrations of her daughter's work. She became well informed on the abysmal record of her daughter's softball team, and she now knew in intimate detail about her daughter's Doberman's abscess, but there was nary a word about any gentlemen callers.

If Dani talked about anyone, it was her best friend, Adrienne. They had picked up their childhood friendship again with an ease at which Meredith marveled, given the 19-year lapse in their relationship.

Rising from the table, Meredith carried the teacup to the sink and watched the amber stream swirl down the drain, her mind finally contemplating the realities she had nervously ignored for so long.

Adrienne was the only child of her best friend, Iris, who lived right next door. As young wives, Meredith and Iris had both moved into a brand new subdivision forty years earlier, and through the years they forged an iron-clad friendship. Both would drop everything to help in emergencies, and they had each honoured the other in naming their daughters.

Meredith had been there for Iris through the sorrow of two miscarriages before her friend was finally able to have Adrienne. And it was Iris who had called the ambulance and stayed right with Meredith the day her husband, Gary, collapsed in the backyard with a non-lethal heart attack. Meredith had been prepared to provide moral support for her best friend when Adrienne confessed her orientation to her mother the day after high school graduation, but Iris hadn't needed the traditional consolation of chocolate-iced brownies and a friendly shoulder to cry on. She cheerfully accepted her daughter's pronouncement, and through the years had even occasionally fixed up her mortified child with eligible young women, though to Meredith's knowledge, Adrienne had remained resolutely unattached.

Iris had confided that she had been sure that Adrienne was gay pretty much from the moment she was sent home from school for beating up a bully who preyed on the other girls for their lunch money. Privately, Meredith had shaken her head, as she had done many times watching her best friend's liberal, laid back, free thinking, child raising practices. She would never have criticized Iris openly, but, though she suppressed it firmly, she couldn't help feeling the slightest tinge of moral superiority when comparing her more conventional children to Adrienne.

Iris's daughter had been the neighborhood tomboy and had endlessly instigated adventures through the fields and play-grounds of their children's youth. Despite the age difference, Meredith's three sons, Brad, Bill, and Brian, had followed Adri-enne's lead as eagerly as Dani.

Dani.

Staring out the window at the neatly cut lawn and the hedge separating  Iris's back yard from her own, Meredith grimly forced herself to reevaluate Dani's childhood. There had been piano lessons, and dancing recitals, and pretty, frilly dresses to wear to birthday parties and church, but for all the trappings of femininity, Dani had been as much of a tomboy as her best friend, Adrienne.

She was more likely to be found playing road hockey with her brothers than amusing herself with the profusion of dolls that generally ended up discarded under her bed. The selection of make-up that her mother bought her for her sixteenth birth-day went untouched, discovered by Meredith years later at the back of her daughter's sock drawer. Dani had been furious when her brothers had all gotten BB guns one Christmas, and she had not. Against her mother's orders, she had cajoled her middle brother, Billy, into teaching her how to shoot out in the woods behind the subdivision. In her last year at home, she showed up after school one day on an old motorbike she had used all her hard-earned savings to buy. When her parents demanded that she get rid of it, she fought them tooth and nail. She lost, but cir-cumvented their orders by keeping the bike inside an abandoned barn several miles away. She rode it surreptitiously until the day she left home for college, when she'd sold it to Billy for a hun-dred and fifty dollars.

Meredith shook her head ruefully. The first thing Dani had done on settling back into her hometown was to conscript Adri-enne into chauffeuring her to all the local motorcycle dealer-ships, until she found a huge black and silver bike that she handled with ease, but which scared her mother half to death. And as always, as she had been all throughout their childhood, Adrienne was Dani's staunch ally, cagey confidante, and gleeful co-conspirator.

The two friends were as inseparable now as they had been as children. You just couldn't keep those two apart. Meredith's memory turned to the countless times the best friends had begged their mothers to have sleepovers. Had they... No, she didn't want to know.

Seizing a dishrag, she dampened it and briskly scrubbed at the already pristine counters. She really didn't want to know about it at all, but Dani made that impossible today by forcing her to confront the truth she would never have accepted on her own.

Painfully, her mind resurrected every detail of this morning's conversation...

THE OLD SCREEN door screeched, and Meredith paused in finishing up the breakfast dishes to see her daughter burst through the door. Amused as always by Dani's inability to enter a room quietly, she smiled at the younger woman.

"Good morning, sweetie. You just missed your father. He's gone over to help Brad and the boys work on the new deck. I know it's not the best way to spend a Saturday, but I thought for sure you'd be joining them. Heaven only knows you're handier with a hammer than Brian and Bill."

Her youngest shook her head. "Maybe later, Mom." Pulling out a chair, she dropped into it, and Meredith winced at the sound of the wood creaking as Dani leaned back on two legs.

"Oh honey, please don't do that. One of these days it's going to break and you'll end up breaking something, too."

Obediently Dani rocked forward and planted her elbows on the table, folding her hands under her chin as she eyed her mother's preparations for tea. Meredith chatted amiably as she turned on the kettle and, as always when it was just the two of them, pulled out the last two cups of great-grandmother Abigail's set. It was only as she poured the water over the bags that she realized her daughter had been uncharacteristically quiet, letting her mother carry the bulk of the conversation.

Curious now, she set a cup in front of Dani and pushed the box of sugar cubes toward her. Settling into a chair across from her daughter, she sipped her tea and waited. She was surprised when the younger woman merely toyed with her tea and didn't say anything. Typically, within moments of sitting down at her mother's table, Dani would've blurted out whatever was on her mind. As she watched her daughter suck in a deep breath, Meredith became concerned.

"Honey? Is something wrong?"

A slow smile played across Dani's face. "No, actually something is very, very right, and it's time to tell you about it."

Meredith was startled by the gentle glow in her daughter's

eyes and the radiant smile on her lips. She had never seen Dani
so suffused with happiness. Suddenly, she bolted upright in her
chair.

"Oh, my heavens! Danielle Iris, you've found someone!"
Leaning forward, she covered her daughter's hand with her own.
"Oh honey, that's wonderful! Now tell me all about him. Who is
he? Where did you meet him? Is he a local boy? Do I know
him?"

Dani laid one hand over her mother's and squeezed gently.
"I have found someone, Mom. Someone I love like I've never
loved anyone else in my life. Someone I want to spend the rest of
my life with, and..." she met Meredith's gaze directly, "...some-
one who feels the same way about me."

"Sweetheart, that's just wonderful! Tell me all about him. I
want to know everything!"

Shifting uneasily, Dani's gaze swept the kitchen, and
Meredith was puzzled by the younger woman's underlying nervousness. Patiently she waited, determined to accept her daughter's choice even as she prayed that he wasn't a married man or
someone equally unsuitable.

When Dani remained silent, she probed gently. "Honey?
Talk to me."

Abruptly, Dani stood and circled the kitchen until she came
to rest with her back against the fridge. Crossing her arms and
bracing her legs, she stared at her mother. Despite the unmistak-
able defiance in her eyes, Dani's voice was low. "Mom, I'm going
to tell you everything, but you have to promise to hear me out,
okay? No flying off the handle halfway through. Promise?"

Somewhat insulted, since she did not consider herself an
irrational or unreasonable woman, Meredith nodded her head.
She was becoming increasingly concerned at the way her daughter was treating what she had assumed would be a joyful
announcement.

When Dani began to worry at her thumbnail, Meredith knew
something wasn't right, but she stilled her instinct to cross the
room and wrap her daughter in a reassuring hug. Whatever it
was, they would work it out together. There was no problem her
daughter could bring to her that they couldn't resolve somehow.

"Mom..." Dani stopped, then tried again. "Mom, there's
something I've been keeping from you for a long time. I didn't
really think there was any need to tell you because there were
always thousands of miles between home and wherever I was at
the moment. And I probably took the path of least resistance. As
Billy would say, I was being a goddamned, lily-livered, yellow
bellied poltroon."

Meredith couldn't help a smile. She couldn't begin to count the number of times she had chastised her middle son for his unusual and colourful language as a boy. He delighted in finding insults that his buddies wouldn't understand, and frequently practiced them on his siblings, at least out of his mother's earshot.

Dani grinned too, and seemed to draw strength from the shared family memory. "Anyway, as I said, it didn't matter...until I moved back here. Mom, at some level you've probably known this for a long time, but I need to make it official, so to speak. I need to be honest with you because I have to be honest with her."

Confused, Meredith shook her head. "Her? Who's her, honey? What are you talking about? I thought you said you'd met the man you wanted to..."

Then the pieces of the puzzle slid tidily into place, and Meredith sucked in an anguished breath, staring at her daughter as dread settled in her stomach.

"It's Adrienne, Mom. We're in love, and we're planning to spend the rest of our lives together. She's the one I've been looking for all these years." Softly, as if amused at the irony, Dani added, "And she was waiting for me right here in my own backyard. Talk about clueless!"

Meredith choked out, "But you're not like...her! You're not—"

"Yeah, Mom, I am. I always have been; I just never told you."

Dani's voice was unyielding, but Meredith felt like she desperately needed to reason with her daughter, to reach her logically and rationally, and all would be right again. Buying time as she mustered an offence, she blurted out, "Why?"

Sighing, Dani pushed herself away from the fridge and returned to her seat at the table. "Why what, Mom? Why am I a lesbian? Why didn't I tell you as soon as I figured it out for myself? Why Adrienne? Why now?"

Disturbed by the shrillness of her own voice but unable to modulate it, Meredith cried out, "All of those! Why, Dani, why?"

The younger woman shook her head wearily. "Some things just don't have answers, Mom. It took me a long time to come to grips with it myself, and then it just felt too private to share. As for Adrienne, I think we both knew there was a pretty powerful chemistry between us, but as long as I was only breezing through for visits, we never did anything about it. Once I moved back here, it was like we picked up where we'd left off. We became best of friends again, and then we became more. Now we're talking about buying a house and moving in together, so it's time to tell our families."

Meredith stood so abruptly that her chair toppled over. The words that streamed out of her mouth shocked her, but she was helpless to stop them.

"No! I won't have it! You're not like Adrienne! She's...she's...seduced you! You always followed her around like a puppy dog, and now she's using that to fool you into thinking you're something you're not. You have to get away from her influence, Danielle! You have to pull yourself out of her circle. She's bewitched you, honey! Don't let her do this to you! She's depraved! You're so much better..."

Dani stared at her mother, open-mouthed, face blank with shock at the attack on her lover. Then galvanized, she jumped to her feet, kicking her chair back as she planted her hands on the table. Eyes blazing, she roared at her mother, "Don't you dare talk about her that way! Depraved! You've known her all her life. How can you say that? She's the kindest, most loving woman I've ever known, and I thank God every day that she waited for me to come to my senses!"

"God! Don't you dare invoke His name to dignify this perversion of all that's right and good and normal!"

The two women screamed the searing words across the table, both furiously refusing to back down, and both knowing intimately how to wound the other.

"Who are you to define normal! You've never even left this podunk place to see there's a whole world out there beyond your narrow vision! There are millions of people like Adrienne and me, and all the bigots and all the invocations in the world aren't going to make us disappear! I don't give a flying fuck if you approve of us or not! I'm not going to live my life in some rigid little box defined by a book of fairy stories written by a bunch of ancient misogynists!"

"Don't you use that kind of language to me, young lady! This is still my home, and I will not have God's word blasphemed by someone who has clearly lost her way! If you're so blessed proud of who you are, then why have you run and hidden yourself for all these years? I think you're ashamed! Ashamed and well aware that what you're doing is wrong! Well, you're right—it is wrong. And I don't care who she is, no girlfriend of yours is ever going to be welcome under this roof!"

A small voice within struggled to be heard, warning Meredith she was going too far—saying things that would be difficult if not impossible to take back, but she didn't care. A profound sense of betrayal drove her tongue, and it was only when Dani swept her cup off the table in one furious motion, sending it shattering across the floor, that shock aborted her rage and her fury began to ebb. But before she could utter any conciliatory words, her daughter spun away and strode to the back door. With icy precision, she threw one last gibe over her shoulder.

"If my lover is not welcome here, then it'll be a cold day in hell before I ever set foot in this house again!"

With that Dani stormed out, slamming the screen door with such force that Meredith momentarily thought it would come off its hinges.

Lover.

Her daughter had called another woman her lover. Numbly, Meredith listened to the roar of Dani's bike racing down the alley, then she righted her chair and sank into it.

Lover.

The little mop-haired girl from next door who had bounded into her kitchen countless times looking for her best friend and Meredith's homemade cookies was now her daughter's lover.

Her mind simply couldn't wrap itself around that knowledge, so she forced herself to say it.

"Dani is...Dani is a lesbian. Dani and Adrienne are lovers. They are in love...with each other."

Saying it out loud didn't make it any easier to believe or accept, so she tried it several more times.

The words hung in the air, like balloons that had lost most of their helium, and still her heart refused to allow the truth in.

She had no idea how long she sat there, numb and exhausted by the emotional confrontation, but eventually her gaze drifted to the shards of porcelain littering the kitchen floor. She forced herself to rise and tear off paper towels to mop up the spilled tea. As she pulled the broom and dust pan out of the closet, her mind turned to the time her sons had broken six of the cups at once when an errant football smashed into her china cabinet.

Meredith had been furious at the boys for shattering the irreplaceable antiques, and had grounded the lot of them for two weeks. She grieved the losses and carefully stowed the last two cups on the uppermost shelf of her kitchen cabinets. The cups were only brought out to share tea with Iris, and later, when she was grown, with Dani.

Now, as she delicately picked up the bigger fragments, and swept the tiny slivers into the pan, she felt a far greater loss, even as she righteously struggled to cling to the remnants of her wrath. Finally abandoning the dustpan, she dropped the broom and remaining crouched, wrapped her arms around her knees as she rocked back and forth, fighting for control of her careening emotions and determined not to break down.

MEREDITH WONDERED IF she would ever feel normal again as she mechanically wrung out the dishrag and draped it over the edge of the sink. She was glad Gary and the boys were occupied all day building Brad's deck because it was taking everything she had to hold herself together, and she couldn't face the inevitable questions once her husband saw how distraught she was.

Lost in her depression, Meredith barely noticed the light tapping on the screen door, but groaned inwardly when the door creaked open.

Without turning around, she said, "I don't know why you even bother to knock, Iris."

A familiar voice sounded softly behind her. "I wasn't going to take the chance you'd tell me to keep out."

"You know?"

"Mmm hmm. Addy called me a few minutes ago. Dani's over at her place crying her eyes out, so I figured you wouldn't be in much better shape."  A chair scraped, and Meredith heard her old friend sit down at the table. "Got any of that tea left?"

Automatically putting the still warm kettle on to boil again, Meredith refused to turn around, only asking bitterly, "Did you know?"

Iris sighed deeply. "I knew."

That stung. "How long?"

Her best friend couldn't help a rueful laugh. "Oh Merry, I've seen the way Addy looks at Dani since they were kids. I expect I've known longer than they have. However, if you mean how long have I known they're a couple, then I guess it's been about four months."

Meredith flinched. A couple. Was that really how her best friend saw their daughters?  Well, it was easier for Iris. She'd had years to adjust to the idea of her daughter as a...

Grimacing, Meredith pulled a couple of mugs out of the cupboard and wordlessly set them on the table. Iris raised one eyebrow at the unusual selection, then her eyes fell on the dustpan, which still sat abandoned on the floor.

"Aw, shit, Mer. I'm sorry. One of your grandmother's cups, eh?  How'd it happen?"

The warmth in her friend's voice—the sympathy Meredith had relied on for more years than she could remember, was almost more than she could bear, and she stood rigidly, hands wrapped tightly around the top rung of a chair.

"Dani. She broke it."

Wisely, Iris did not rise to offer one of her usual hugs. Meredith felt so brittle she was sure if her friend touched her, she would shatter just like the cup.

"She must have been really upset. She knows what those cups mean to you."

Stiffly, Meredith pulled out the chair and sat down. Fixing Iris with a gaze that was both angry and accusatory, she snapped, "You have a gift for understating the obvious."

Her friend didn't even flinch. "Merry, we have to talk about this. I know you're in shock. I know you're hurting and confused."

"How could you possibly know those things? You were the one who was ready to throw your daughter a party when she announced she was gay! How could you possibly relate to how I feel? Did you feel like you'd been kicked in the stomach by a Clydesdale? Did you see all your dreams go up in smoke in one instant?"

Iris sighed, but didn't back off. "No mother wants to see her child have to endure being different in a world that persecutes those who are different. I knew Addy was going to have a hard go of it, and my heart ached for her on that account. There's no way I was going to make her life any tougher by not being as supportive as I could, but don't you think there have been times when I've thought how much easier it would've been if she'd fallen for Brad or Bill? Of course I have! But she didn't have a choice, Merry, and neither does Dani. We do. We have the choice of accepting our children as they are, or turning away, hurting them and ourselves. Don't turn away, hon. I know how much you love your kids. Don't think you can cut one of them off without feeling like you're cutting your own heart out."

Meredith felt the pain overwhelm her again, and she struggled to suppress the tears, furious at how out of control she felt. She was undone when Iris reached in her pocket and pulled out a tissue, pushing it across the table with an affectionate smile.

"'S okay. Go ahead and let it out. I can guarantee you it won't be the last time our kids make us cry."

The sight of those loving eyes regarding her with endless patience and understanding finally loosened the rigid check she had been maintaining on her emotions. She had no idea how long she cried, but was aware that at some point Iris snagged a box of tissues and handed them to her one by one. When the torrent finally eased, she couldn't help a watery smile at the mound of spent tissues piled in front of her.

"Yeah, yeah, we'll put our egg money in Kleenex next

month," Iris teased lightly, her eyes watching Meredith closely. "Feeling a bit better?"

Meredith sighed deeply. She couldn't deny that while the bout of tears had left her drained, she no longer felt as brittle. An exhausted peace had settled over her.

Several more tissues mopped up the remains of the crying jag, while Iris poured them both some strong tea.

Raising their mugs, they tapped them together in a deep, unspoken understanding. Over the years they had met in one kitchen or the other to deal with the endless quandaries their children presented them. They had negotiated the mazes of childhood and youth together, stronger for their differences, but united when it came to loving their children and wanting the best for them.

After several long, bracing swallows, Meredith opened her heart to her best friend. "You know I love Adrienne like one of my own, don't you, Iris?"

Her friend smiled and nodded. "You might as well have. Dunno how you could tell her from the rest of your brood half the time anyway."

Meredith laughed at that. It was true. Adrienne had merged seamlessly with her children, and there was always room for one more whether they were heading for the lake, barbequing in the backyard, or making pull taffy on a wintry Saturday afternoon.

"She and Billy were usually the messiest two," Meredith said in fond remembrance. Then recalling herself to the topic, she went on, "So you know it's not that I'm objecting to Adrienne herself, right?"

"Uh huh. You'd have flown off the wall at any woman Dani fell in love with."

Iris' words were delivered wryly, but with a bracing undercurrent of honesty, and Meredith flushed with shame. She had behaved so badly, and even if Dani were eventually able to forgive her, she didn't know if she'd ever forgive herself. She wondered how much Adrienne told her mother about what had happened that morning.

Embarrassed now, she couldn't meet her friend's eyes, until a sugar cube bounced off her shoulder. Startled, she looked up to see Iris grinning at her.

"I've known you, what, forty years?"

"Forty-one and a half," Meredith mumbled.

"And in all that time, this is probably the first time you've gone whacko. Hell, you even sailed through 'the pause' without missing a step. I think you were way overdue for a psychotic episode, so don't be so hard on yourself."

Meredith couldn't help a rueful snort. Psychotic episode? She guessed she deserved that.

"The point is, Mer, that this hit you out of the blue, and you reacted on instinct. I know you just want what's best for Dani, and she knows that, too."

"Does she? My God, after what I said to her. Oh, and I was so terrible about Adrienne, too. Dani will never forgive me for what I said about her—"

"Partner," Iris filled in helpfully. "You're gonna have to bone up on the lingo, old friend. Dani and Addy are partners, and from what I've seen, they're in it for life, so you might as well get used to it."

"Partners." Meredith tried the word on thoughtfully. Then looking at Iris with troubled eyes she asked, "Doesn't it ever bother you that you won't have any grandchildren?"

"Who says I won't?" Iris challenged with a grin. "Now that the girls are together, they might just decide to have kids, too."

"Kids? But how on earth..."

Iris uttered a mock groan. "That does it. I'm taking you to the next meeting of PFLAG."

"Your Wednesday night group?"

"Yeah, PFLAG. You'll meet people who have been in your shoes and know all that you're feeling right now. They're good people to talk to, and they'll help you understand that your child's horizon is only different, not limited."

Chiding herself for not having paid closer attention over the years when Iris had lauded her group, and unwilling to examine the reasons that she hadn't, Meredith returned to what was uppermost on her mind. "What if Dani won't ever speak to me again, Iris? What if I can't mend our relationship after the terrible things I said?"

Her eyes filled again at the thought that she might have driven her daughter away for good, but Iris took her hand firmly and gave it a good shake.

"Now don't you even be thinking that way, Merry. You and Dani have always been as close as Addy and me, and a fight, even a knock down, drag out, lung-screeching battle, isn't going to change that. Good Lord, if Will and I broke up every time we had a brouhaha, we'd never have made it to our 35th anniversary!"

Meredith couldn't help smiling at the mention of her friend's late husband. They had had a passionate, but oft times volatile relationship, and she had hosted both of them in her guest room on occasions when they were too furious with each other to spend the night in the same house.

Iris looked at her speculatively, then walked to the sink, returning with the last antique teacup, which had been drying on the rack. Setting it carefully between them, she sat down again.

"Look at it like this, Mer. As fragile as this cup is, it had to travel thousands of miles and survive untold trials before ending up on your table here, a century or so later. It's beautiful, it's vulnerable, but as delicate as it is, it's been a survivor. It's also irreplaceable, so you gotta cherish it—take care of it. I don't doubt that Dani's hurting right now. Hell, from what Addy told me, Dani's as big a mess as you at the moment. But your relationship isn't going to crumble. You're gonna have to do some work, but you two will tough it through, because to do anything else is unthinkable."

Meredith considered her friend's reassuring words, then sadly pointed at the pieces of the other cup still lying in the dustpan. Softly she said, "Sometimes you break things beyond repair, Iris."

Heaving a deep sigh, Iris rolled her eyes. "Okay, screw the metaphor. All I'm saying is that you love Dani, and she loves you. Her love for Addy isn't going to change that one bit, so as soon as you can, you reach out for her and you hold her as tight as all get out, and you tell her that no matter what, you'll always be her mother and you'll always love her."

Stunned by the heartfelt passion in her friend's voice, Meredith could only nod. She prayed she'd be given the chance to make things right.

Her words lighter now, Iris teased, "Hey, you know you should be delighted that Dani fell for the girl next door, and not some woman half a continent away. Now you can count on keeping her at home from now on."

With a small grin, Meredith retorted, "Unless Dani convinces Adrienne to travel the world with her." She broke out laughing at how her best friend's face instantly fell. "I'm just pulling your leg, Iris. Dani seems very content to have settled back home again. I'm sure our girls will live here happily every after."

And as she said that, Meredith realized she was starting to believe it. She had a long way to go before she looked at Dani and Addy as matter-of-factly as she regarded her sons and their wives, but she thought now that she would eventually get to that place...if she could secure her daughter's forgiveness.

Iris reached out and swatted her arm. "Don't scare me like that, woman! I'd lose my best flea marketing partner if that daughter of mine ever moved away." Then, glancing at her watch, she said, "Oops, I gotta go." Standing, she eyed Meredith seriously. "Are you gonna be all right?"

Meredith considered the question, then slowly nodded. "I think so. I have some pretty big fences to mend with Dani, however I do think we can eventually get past this morning. I'm going to give her some time to cool off before I call her though."

"Good," Iris said with satisfaction. Then winking, she added, "I'm guessing you'll see Dani sooner than you expect."

Meredith stood and rounded the table. "Oh, what—you're a soothsayer now?"

"No, let's just say I read the tea leaves." Iris grinned and opened her arms to her friend. Meredith gratefully took the comfort her friend offered and squeezed the other woman tightly.

Arm in arm, they walked to the back door. As they parted, Iris took Meredith's hands and held her gaze for a long moment. "Just remember, Merry, this is a beginning, not an ending. Addy and Dani have been friends for almost as long as you and I have, and if we've done anything for them, we've shown them how important friendship is. I think that bodes very well for the strength of their union."

Meredith nodded, silently grateful for the steadfastness of the woman she had called her best friend all these years. She held the screen door open as she watched Iris walk along the path towards her house. Then, startled, she saw Dani come around the corner of the hedge, and she wondered if her daughter had been waiting at Iris' house while the two older women talked.

Dani and Iris stopped to exchange hugs as they passed, and Meredith heard Iris' words clearly.

"You're perfect for each other, sweetie. I always knew it, and I'm so glad you do now, too. You've always been like a second daughter to me, and I'm thrilled to see our families united."

Meredith saw Dani glance uneasily at her at those words, but Iris just shook her head. "Don't you worry, Dani-girl. You just go on and talk to your mother. Everything's going to be all right."

After another hug, Iris went the last few steps into her house, leaving Dani walking slowly towards the screen door where Meredith stood watching her.

She stopped a few feet away and said sheepishly, "I heard Satan is issuing ice skates to the denizens of hell."

For all the tea in China, Meredith couldn't have stopped the smile that crossed her face, nor did she want to. She simply stood aside and held the door open for her daughter to enter. Her words were soft as Dani brushed by her. "I wasn't sure you'd come back—certainly not so soon."

"Addy made me," Dani admitted as she stood awkwardly just inside the door. Her eyes fell on the dustpan, still sitting in the middle of the floor. Spinning around to face Meredith, worried eyes searched her mother's face. Without preliminaries, she blurted, "I'm sorry for the things I said, and I'm so sorry that I broke grandmother's cup."

"I'm sorry, too," Meredith said, "but none of our words are etched in stone, and there's still one cup left to pass on to you."

Dani choked, and her eyes glistened. "You still want me to have the cup?"

Her own eyes suspiciously damp, Meredith nodded. "Of course. Who else should it go to? Besides, who knows? You and Adrienne may have a little girl to pass it on to one day."

And as she held her sobbing daughter tightly, Meredith decided it really was that simple. Her daughter had chosen a mate, and whether it was the one she'd have chosen for her was irrelevant. It was never her choice to make, and that was fine. It was her choice to support her daughter, and that was right. Iris was correct. She could no more have cut Dani out of her life than she could've cut her own heart out.

And that was love.

## Karin Kallmaker

Californian Karin Kallmaker is a person with real staying power. When she met her current partner, Maria, at the ripe old age of seventeen, she knew they were a forever thing. Twenty-seven years later, they're still together and are raising two children, Kelson and Eleanor. She's also had staying power in the literary world. Since the mid-Eighties, when she first began exploring the writing realm, she has published twenty-three works of lesbian fiction with many more planned.

In college, Karin took all the English and Humanities courses she could while still earning a practical business degree. Then for many years she was an accountant in the non-profit sector. She was finally able to quit full-time employment to become a part-time writer and full-time mom.

Karin and her alter ego, Laura Adams, have thrice been nominated for Lambda Literary Awards in Romance and Science-Fiction/Fantasy. Her novel *Maybe Next Time* won the Lammy for Best Romace in 2004, and she was just recently selected for an Alice B. Reader's Appreciation Award. She says, "I was deeply influenced by Katherine Forrest's *Curious Wine*. It set for me the standard of what I hoped to write. Someday, I might write something that fine." Readers around the world seem to think she has met that standard. Some consider her the most widely read lesbian author writing today, and at the rate she is going, she may well end up being the most prolific. She does, indeed, seem to have the staying power.

# Dangling Earrings

## Memoir by Karin Kallmaker

MY MOTHER WOULDN'T let me pierce my ears until I was sixteen. She wore clip earrings, very nice ones. They were gold, mostly, and might have a faux stone of some sort, and they always looked elegant. They were the earrings of a suburban married woman.

For many years I was, by all outward appearances, a suburban married woman. Funny, huh?

I think she was hoping I'd chicken out when she insisted the piercing be done by the family doctor – not at one of those places with a piercing gun. She made it sound like my lifetime health was at stake. At the time I thought she wanted to brand me tragically uncool forever. But I accepted the terms as not piercing my ears was simply not an option.

All the other girls had pierced ears. They wore pearl or gold studs, very sophisticated. Some of them even wore hoops. And we had all heard the story of the girl who wore hoops, and while she was playing basketball someone's finger got caught in one and tore her entire ear off. So a girl who wore hoops was flirting with disfiguration, really walking on the wild side.

When the doctor pierced my ears, I nearly fainted at the sight of my own blood. That might be why the left is slightly lower than the right. My mother was very concerned about infection. My best friend of course knew of a girl whose piercing had become so infected that her entire ear had fallen off. For a long time my mother had me wear gold posts to ensure everything was okay.

After about six months of gold posts, I found out my mother's unspoken motivations in regards to pierced earrings. Clip-on earrings were dainty, small, discreet. Anything heavy would have to clasp the ear too tightly for comfort.

Not so with pierced earrings! Pierced earrings could *dangle*.

They came in all colors of the rainbow. They included stones and feathers and figures in miniature. Beads, wire, hoops — there was no limit to self-expression with pierced earrings.

Nice girls, my mother told me after I asked about using my allowance to buy really big silver hoops (they were so cool, nearly touched my shoulders!), didn't wear jewelry like that. It wasn't a safety issue. It was a matter of good judgment. There was no telling, you see, what anyone would think of me if I wore "flashy" jewelry.

And so I learned how important what other people thought was, and how highly influenced other people could be by something as simple as earrings.

MY RELATIONSHIP WITH my mother is not one where I can ask if she was afraid even then that other people would know I wasn't ... normal. Did she fear that if I wore those big silver hoops, or dangling feathers, other people would cluck their tongues and whisper, "baby dyke in the making" to each other? It's probably more likely that she feared they would whisper "tramp" or "trash." Or, even worse, "hippie."

The following year I fell in love with my best friend. She didn't have pierced ears, and not only that, she didn't want them. She was a non-conformist, something my parents didn't realize until it was far too late. It took me several years to talk her into getting them pierced. We went to a place with a gun. She wore gold studs for a really long time because I was very concerned about infection. I loved her and didn't want her entire ear to fall off.

EVEN AFTER FALLING in love (and having lesbian sex) my earrings were still small, still discreet. The price of gold was off the scale, so I couldn't indulge that much. I got pearl studs on my eighteenth birthday, which I still have. The earrings never were a good predictor of who I really was, though. And if I had the kind of relationship with my mother where we talked about such things, I'd tell her that.

TODAY, MY JEWELRY box has many drawers. I like to buy earrings when I travel so I don't just pick out a fashion statement but a memory or association as well. Today I needed something green — ah, the New Zealand greenstone was perfect for mood and fashion. The dangling, unfurling carved koru frond stands for growth and new life. It doesn't really matter if nobody knows that but me.

My partner (the same girl I fell in love on the edge of 17)

gives me at least one pair of earrings a year. Many of them dangle. Recently, a friend gave me a pair of dangling purple books, exactly the sort of thing a nice girl in the 1970s didn't wear. Exactly the sort of thing a 40+ femme lesbian author would, especially if they matched her shoes.

Now I sport an extra hole in my left ear. I didn't go to a doctor's office. This time it was a tattoo and piercing parlor. I did not faint, but then there was no blood that I saw. So in my left ear there is a permanent gold hoop. It doesn't dangle much, and it is discreet in its own way. Elegant, even.

But it's not the earring of a suburban married woman. However, much of me resembles a suburban married woman, and because fashion and times have changed, that small discreet hoop I hope tells others, even friends and family, that I am not quite what they think I am. Look closer, and I'll surprise you.

I do know that my mother did not plan on being the mother of a prominent lesbian romance writer. She has had to come out to her friends about it. If I had the kind of relationship with my mother where we discussed such things, I'd suggest a piercing so she, too, can announce "not quite normal and danged proud of it" status to the world.

But we don't discuss such things. Sometimes I wonder, having never come to a meeting of the minds about the importance of earrings, if we lost the ability to really converse about more important things. I mean, if you can't discuss the politics of earrings, how do you discuss the politics of being a dyke?

MY MOTHER'S EARLY lessons in the importance of worrying about what others think have stood me in good stead. Without them, I doubt I would have gotten that extra earring. Had I not known to what degree others view and judge me from appearance only, I wouldn't have decided I needed to control the message as carefully as I had.

Think of the relief of the grocer, the cleric, the hair dresser. I did something that affirmed to myself who I am, and, if my mother's theory is correct that total strangers are obsessed with judging by appearances, then I have done a public service for thousands of people I will never meet.

All things considered, that's a lot of mileage for a gold hoop that dangles a bit. Even if, just before a haircut, it can hardly be seen. But I know it's there. And I hope to have the kind of relationship with my children that will let me tell them that how they feel about themselves, on the inside, is more important than the opinions of strangers.

However, because one of the vexing experiences of being a

parent is learning that your mother was right about some things, I will also impress upon them, as my mother did me, that *my* opinion of them is the most important thing of all. With luck, that will last until they are sixteen. I'd settle for fifteen, and it might really work as my kids have two moms, and they both tell them the same thing.

I KNOW MY mother spotted the new earring the first moment she saw me after I'd had it done. She didn't bring it up though. I wonder sometimes if she thinks that it's a shame we don't have the kind of relationship where she could say, "What did you do to your ear?" I know that I think it's a shame, sometimes. But she still wears the same kind of clip-on earrings, and I still hanker for earrings that dangle. We are who we are, and I don't think that will change.

I suppose some people would think that was sad, but as a parent myself, I have to admire my mother's consistency. That same consistency of outlook about what dangling earrings might convey to other people is the same consistency that has provided unwavering, albeit undemonstrative, support of my relationship for these many long years. It is the same consistency of character that provides tasty treats for grandchildren, always, and thoughtful evaluation of coloring projects.

It is, after all, the same thoughtful evaluation of my writing projects that I brought home from an early age. We don't talk about my writing in terms of anything but what I do for a living, but that fault is largely mine. I sometimes write about sex, and I'm pretty sure she knows that. It's just too intimate. I don't want to explain about, well, anything to do with sex. She didn't explain much to me, and I'm returning the favor. So, like dangly earrings, we avoid the topic and preserve harmony.

There's a lot to be said for harmony. We preserve it by not discussing touchy topics. We can talk about gay rights—my mother believes my partner and I ought to be able to marry. Voucher programs for public schools is safe. Certainly the pros and cons of presidential candidates can be aired.

But we don't talk about earrings, and it's better that way. We are who we are, and that's not going to change.

I don't think I'll tell her about the tattoo.

## Marcia Tyson Kolb

A freelance writer, fiber artist, and ardent gardener, transplanted North Carolinian Marcia Tyson Kolb raises heirloom roses for both business and pleasure. She lives and works in a cottage surrounded by gardens and birds where she is raising exotic finches in the company of her four parrots and one dog. The birth of her first grandchild has added a new element of richness to the tapestry of her life.

For the last half-decade, Marcia has been the impetus behind Dragonfly Cottage, an Online Community For Lesbians, where she is better known as Erzulie Dragonfly. She has been teaching "Wabi-Sabi Writing" classes for over 20 years and now teaches the course online. In the latest of her 30 years of freelance credits, the preface to her book *Living Wabi-Sabi: An Imperfect Perfect Life* was profiled in the October 2001 *Utne Reader. Girlfriends* magazine named her "Girlfriend Of The Month" in January 2002, calling her "Wabi-Sabi Woman." Her article, "A Normal Lesbian Life," appeared in *Curve* magazine in May 2002.

# The Evolution of Motherhood

## Memoir/Essay by Marcia Tyson Kolb

I ONCE WROTE a book called *VOYAGE OF THE STRANGER: The Peregrinations Of An Adopted Child.* In the book I explored the phenomena of the adopted child as never quite fitting in as seamlessly as biological children. Many of us, when we talk amongst ourselves, carry that same image of the little child with her nose pressed to the glass, on the outside looking in. It is an apt description of the lesbian woman in society today. Sometimes accepted, sometimes not, but always feeling a little outside of the circle, not the accepted and desired "norm" in this culture.

To that end, our relationships with our own mothers are tantamount, I believe, to how we will perceive our relationships with the other women in our lives, and relate to and with them, for better or for worse.

In addition to having been adopted, I searched for, and found, my biological mother when I was 26 years old and the mother of two small daughters myself. It was disastrous. She tried to sue me for harassment and invasion of privacy—even though I had approached her very cautiously and privately with assurances that I was not looking for a mother, nor did I want anything *from* her, but information that could affect the welfare of my own children. My relationship with my adoptive mother was irrevocably damaged due to the fact that she was often drunk, neglectful, and emotionally abusive, and I had been sexually abused from age 6 to 18 by my father and by another man who worked at our house. She did not protect me, and I was once again cast adrift on a lonely sea.

I bring in here the question of nature vs. nurture in two perhaps interesting ways, the juxtaposition of which have made for a difficult if not near impossible road for me to travel in my own life.

In the book I mentioned at the beginning, *Voyage Of The Stranger* (which never sold, as some books are not meant to, but a couple of times came close to selling, no, this book was a step-ping stone along the way to my own path of self discovery and coming out, which I would not realize for years after writing the book), I examined the place in my life that "The Original Seed Carrier," as I called her, The Birth Mother, had, as opposed to the Adoptive Mother, the one who would take over the care, the nurturing, the maintenance, and the upbringing of the child. If these relationships equal a lost land + abandonment again by the adoptive mother in physical, or psychological terms, what you are going to end up with is a child cast adrift on a lonely sea looking ever and always, for "The Mother."

The second question in the "Nature vs. Nuture" conundrum is that question we all get asked, especially if we were sexually abused: "Were you born a lesbian, or did you become one because of the abuse?" My question is perhaps unanswerable as certainly my abuse at the hands of not just one, but two men, for so many years, would have made many, if not most women, afraid of sexual contact with a man, but there were early intima-tions and proof of my lesbianism all throughout my life, from grade school, through high school and college, to young adult-hood when I was a married mother of three. It was not acted upon, but it was an unquenchable fire, a deep longing, that, like the soulful, vibrant sounds of a cello, resonated through my body, echoing through my heart, all four chambers calling out for a woman.

In November of 1998 I met the woman who would rock my world and catapult me out of the 25 year marriage I was in to a gentle and kind man, to that place I had longed for, but nothing, no thing, prepared me for the reality of this world. I was 44 years old. I had left my parent's home for my husband's home at 20, within 2 years had our first child, and by the time I was 29 had three children.

On the cusp of my first pregnancy, just weeks prior to find-ing out I was pregnant, I went in to the hospital with my first nervous breakdown, unable to handle having sex with a man, even a dear and gentle one. I remained in the hospital for a month undergoing physchotherapy, hypnosis, and daily visits with a psychiatrist, and a lifetime of memories, visions and nightmares of the abuse came pouring out. I left the hospital on anti-depressants, tranquilizers, and sleeping pills, and found out, three weeks later, that I was pregnant, making it necessary to go off of all the medication cold turkey.

The intervening years were spent in and out of therapy, with doctors afraid to delve too deeply because I was barely staying afloat emotionally to raise my three beloved children, they who came as angels to tether me to the earth. Supported by a kind and generous and loving man, a wonderful father to our children, we became parents, not partners, the sexual side of our marriage melting away into nothingness, and my longing for a woman grew alongside my growing children.

Throughout those years, most of this was unconscious, and I exhibited many of the symptoms that today have been named by the wonderful lesbian psychiatrist I have seen for nearly 5 years. My diagnoses are: PTSD2 (Post Traumatic Stress Disorder, Type 2, the kind considered treatable, not curable); BDP (Borderline Personality Disorder); and I have been diagnosed as a "Highly Sensitive Person" with a severe anxiety disorder. (You can read Dr. Elain Aron's book on the HSP to understand more about this, but it does not mean "sensitive" in the artistic sense of the word. For me, a trip out into the world is like being in a place where the loud speakers are on full blast all around me all the time. The reverberations of the world and even the most mundane activities shake me to my core, so that my world, at times, is a living nightmare and my only solace, retreat.)

The longing for the mother never dies. I remember my mentor and Muse and at the very end of her life, my friend, May Sarton, writing of becoming an orphan after her mother died when May was not a child but a woman. That state of orphanhood is felt no matter how old we are when we lose our mother. When we lose not one but two mothers, if not physically, but emotionally, and are battered or abused or neglected by the mother in whose care and keeping we have been left, we long to run to a woman who will soothe our spirit, run her fingers through our ruffled hair, make sense of the world, bandage our wounded knee, tell us everything is alright. And if we are lesbian in our soul, the flight to a woman will be a complex one fraught with difficulties. We long for the mother; we love the woman; the woman hates us for not fulfilling the needs of a mother she might also have, or the reverse, and we go tumbling down some hell-hole into heartache and abandonment over and over again.

I do not, nor can I, nor would I presume to try to speak for all lesbian women, but I have had the distinct experience for nearly five years of running a website for lesbians around the world, and I have heard similar stories so many times, they become leitmotifs running throughout my own life story. A woman with "mother issues" connecting in a relationship with another woman with "mother issues" of her own is a ticking time bomb.

Is it insurmountable? No, of course not. Nothing is impossible in my book. But I carry a lot of other baggage, too, of abuse of other kinds, and after leaving my marriage, finally, at 45, for a woman who almost immediately left me as soon as I'd left everything to be with her, and 2 years later, getting rid of everything I owned to go cross-country to be with a woman who didn't want to be in a relationship as soon as I got there, my abandonment flags fly at half-mast around my heart all the time now. The doors to my heart finally slammed firmly shut, and, after yet another nervous breakdown, I turned toward a new reality that looked very much like one that would be lived out alone, with my birds (a great many), my dog, my books, my weaving and fiber art, my children, and a small world I had created of my own making, in addition to the thousands of women I meet, counsel, and teach online through *Dragonfly Cottage Community For Lesbians* and through my *Wabi-Sabi Writing* classes. It's a journey to the soul through the written word, a way to find compassion for self and others through writing. Even my classes are no longer taught in person but sent out online from my seclusion, where I answer hundreds of e-mails each week, write, and tend this unusual world of my own making.

Finally, without a mother there is a void in a woman's life that is like a gaping hole the size of the Grand Canyon. With no other choice, no mother, no woman beside me, I turned to the deepest mother I could understand, Mother Earth, and I began to garden, and I gardened with a vengeance.

The first garden I created, in the years prior to leaving our marriage, was a very large garden in the shape of the body of a woman. I didn't even know what I was doing. I was trying desperately to reconnect with the Earth and all her motherly qualities, and every fiber of my being was crying out for the arms of another woman. One day in she walked, and I was gone.

Today, too, I garden with a vengeance, and my connection to my garden and my animals are my deepest connection to a spiritual source I have ever known or imagined. I finally found the Mother I looked for. She was the Earth beneath my feet. And as I walk amongst my plants, my black dog at my side, the wild birds at numerous feeders outside, the insects, the wildlings, and the countless birds I live with inside, I am beginning to settle more deeply, and the gaping wound that was the Mother-hole is beginning to close.

One might think that could be, if not the end of the story, the beginning of the end, but that is not how life works. It is inevitable that the door to our hearts will begin to crack open, and we will peek out. The longing for a woman still lives. And very recently I found out that my middle child, precious daughter, is pregnant with her first child, due almost exactly on my fiftieth birthday. As I enter Cronehood myself, I become a Grandmother, and my daughter has her own child. She will carry inside of her the mother issues I have created for her. This is the Wheel of Life and its continual, unending turning. 'Round and 'round and 'round she goes, and where she stops, nobody knows.

## Lori L. Lake

Lori L. Lake was born in Portland, Oregon and moved to Minnesota in 1983 with her partner Diane after graduating from Lewis & Clark College. She worked as a supervisor in a government office for almost two decades, but resigned at the end of 2002 so she could devote full-time attention to writing, teaching, and reviewing.

Lori has been most influenced over the years by many teachers, professors, and writers. In general, she has been inspired by Anne Tyler and Ray Bradbury, and in particular by Dorothy Allison, Katherine V. Forrest, Ellen Hart, and Jenifer Levin.

Lori loves to read. She facilitates a mystery reader's group at Amazon Feminist Bookstore in Minneapolis, and she writes book reviews for Midwest Book Review and various GLBT online writing sites. She is the editor of "The Crown," which is the newsletter for the Golden Crown Literary Society, and she serves as associate editor at Just About Write. She is now working on a mystery and the fourth book in the "Gun" series.

# The Bright Side

## Fiction by Lori L. Lake

IN THE DAZZLING light pouring from the noon time sun, the front of Mel's parents' gray two-story house looked shabby and washed out. The cedar shake siding showed cracks, and as she drew closer to the cement stairs, Mel noticed the trim also needed scraping and painting. She shifted her mini-daypack to her left hand and opened the screen door. After a quick tap with the rusting knocker, she turned the doorknob, stepped into the cool front room, and shut the door behind her.

From down the hall she heard the TV. "Mom?" she called out. "Dad?" She glanced around the house, wondering where her parents' scruffy little poodle was.

She set her bag on the rocking chair near the window and stood marveling at how a visit home was like stepping into the past, into a museum of family antiquities and new acquisitions. The living room was an odd mix of new and old. Long gone was the old couch, kept for over fifteen years, that Mel, her twin sister Izzy, and their older brother Nate had bounced on, entertained friends from, and laid all over when they were sick. Ten years ago, the same month Mel and Izzy turned 20, her parents bought something new. Overstuffed, pale rose in color, and covered in a satiny material, it sat, resplendent, and entirely unused. When it was first delivered, Mel sat on it and found it comfortable, but she'd never touched it again.

The new sofa was quite the contrast to the old shag carpet, meticulously kept up, but ugly cocoa brown just the same. Mel's eyes scanned the room. The same circa 1950 knockoff Goya paintings. The same wingback chairs on either side of a never-used fireplace containing two well-dusted ornamental logs and a clear glass pitcher of fake pink flowers. The ancient German beer steins on the mantel. A lighted corner cabinet contained her mother's collection of Birds of Prey. Eagles, falcons, owls, kestrels—Mel wasn't even sure what all the various figurines were, though her mother, who was a member of various associations like the Raptor Research Foundation and The Peregrine Fund, could name each of them and discuss their habitat, prey, and mating rituals. Mel had always thought her mother should have worked at a zoo.

Following the distant, tinny sound of a laugh track, she moved through the living room, down a narrow hallway, and to the doorway of her parent's bedroom.

"Dad?"

The double bed was made, and a white-haired man lay on top of the bedspread reclining against a stack of pillows, his head tilted slightly to the side. He opened his eyes. "Ahhh..." A sharp cough cleared his throat, and he said. "Hi, honey. Come on in. I was just watching a little TV." He scooted up, wiped at his mouth with his pale fingertips, and waved toward a white wicker chair on the opposite side of the bed. "Where's your mother?"

"I don't know." Mel shrugged, then sat. "She didn't answer when I came in."

He picked up the remote from on top of the flowered spread and hit the mute. From her seat, Mel saw a TV game show was playing, but she wasn't sure which one it was. Somebody had apparently won a new refrigerator, and the woman was jumping up and down with her over-large bosom coming close to hitting her voluminous chin.

Her father wore olive green khakis, a white button up shirt, and a black sweater. Mel squinted and saw a splotch of something yellow on the chest of the shirt, but before she could ask about it, he said, "So what are you up to today? Off work?"

"No, it's my lunch hour, Dad. You called and asked that I stop by?"

"What?" He frowned. "I asked —" He turned back to the TV. "You kids always get what I want confused with what your mother wants. You mean your mother called." He hit the channel select, and Mr. Rogers face popped onto the screen. "Look there, Mel. Mr. Rogers. Did you hear he died? Why, I was floored. That guy's younger than me!"

Confused, Mel looked down into her lap. What was going on with her father? He *seemed* fine, just like old times, but lately he'd taken to saying or doing odd things, then refusing to admit it later. Before she could ponder it further, she heard a noise, and then a yip-yip-yipping. Pete, newly clipped, came tearing into the room and launched up toward the foot of the bed, hitting the end of the mattress and scrabbling wildly with his rear paws. Once safely up, he stopped, startled, and looked at Mel as though she were a ghost. Then with a bark of glee, he came to the edge of the bed nearest to her and turned around in a circle, panting and wagging with excitement.

"Hiya, Petey," she said. She stood and reached over to pet the poodle's head, scratching him behind the ears.

From the doorway she heard her mother's voice. "Well, well, what are you doing here, Imelda?"

"Hi, Mom. I just stopped by for a visit on my lunch hour." Her mother had only ever called her by her given name, and Mel hated it. When she was 14, the shoe queen, Imelda Marcos of the Philippines, went on trial. Ninth graders are a rude lot, and Mel was teased. She decided that once she grew up, at her first opportunity she'd change her name. Of course, that was back when she thought she might get married one day and easily obtain a new name. By age 20 she knew that wasn't a reality, and she'd never gotten around to filing the paperwork to dump her old-fashioned name.

She stepped away from Pete, and the little dog turned and scurried the few feet to nestle under Nathan's arm next to the remote.

Agnes stayed in the doorway. "I suppose you'll be wanting something to eat then." It wasn't a question. Her mother's dark eyes looked Mel up and down, inspecting, scrutinizing in the same way that had always driven Mel crazy. "I see you've taken off some weight. Looks good on you. Now if you'd just let your hair grow out." Her mother disappeared from the doorway leaving Mel to bite her tongue. Dropping thirty pounds as the result of chemotherapy for first stage breast cancer wasn't her preferred method of weight loss. She knew exactly how she looked: haggard, bones emerging from her like knobby sticks with precious little flesh attached. But the doctors thought she had beaten it, so that was all that mattered. That—and the fact that the illness had drawn Calli closer to her. After all the horrors of the last year's treatments, it was clear Calli was hers for life and vice versa.

She met her father's eyes and he grinned up at her. "Guess you'd better go help your mother, Mel."

With a nod, she left the bedroom, wondering how her father, who was usually so kind to his daughters, had managed to stay with his wife for nearly forty years.

In the kitchen, Agnes, now clad in an apron over her pantsuit, was all business. She kicked the fridge shut, her arms full of containers and jars. Arranging them on the counter, she said, "Did you prepare something for your father?"

"Who, me?"

"Yes, you." She opened a drawer and pulled out a mean-looking butcher knife.

"I only arrived a few minutes ago. I haven't even been in this room 'til now."

Agnes set down the knife and turned to point at the microwave. "Open that." Arms crossed over her chest, she set her face in the angry grimace Mel had come to know so well over the years.

She pulled on the door to the ten-year-old silver appliance, and it clunked open. She bent to look inside. "I think a hotdog or sausage died a very ugly death here."

Her mother snorted. "Do you think it would have been so hard for him to clean up afterwards?" She turned back to the counter and hacked away at a hunk of salami three-inches in diameter.

Mel slid the plastic garbage container across the floor and used two paper towels to scrape out the mangled hotdog remains. She dampened the towel and wiped out the interior, then closed the door and returned the can to its regular space.

She heard a swishing sound as her father came up behind her in stocking feet. A second later, the click-click-click of toenails on linoleum announced Pete's entrance.

The bottom of a glass jar smacked against the counter. "Nathan, why on God's green earth can't you tidy up after yourself?"

Her father frowned. "Now what are you blatting about?"

Agnes pointed at the microwave. "If you're going to make hotdogs, you have to pierce them so they don't blow up all over the place. And when they do explode, kindly consider cleaning up afterwards."

"Hotdogs? What are you talking about? I didn't monkey with any hotdogs." His rheumy blue eyes came to rest on Mel. "Ask your daughter about this, Aggie. She looks like the guilty party to me!" He pivoted and stomped out of the room in a huff.

Agnes turned back to the sandwiches on the counter. Mel waited for some comment, some response. When one didn't come, she said, "Mom, what's going on with him? And I told you I haven't been in the kitchen."

With a sigh, her mother wheeled around and crossed her arms in front of her. "I know, I know. *He's* the one with the mustard stain down the front of his shirt, not you. I'm sure I'll have a dandy time trying to get that out." She paused as if debating her words. "The doctor says he has some memory loss due to mini-strokes."

"What?"

"For goodness sake, don't blame me, Imelda. He's old. He's 79 now. This sort of thing happens."

"I wasn't blaming you. I just didn't know." Mel's hands went cold, and she felt shaky, as though she wasn't getting enough air. "When—when did this happen?"

"How should I know? It just did." Agnes opened the cupboard door, took down three plates, and stacked a sandwich on each.

"But, but—strokes? Plural? How many strokes?"

Agnes ignored the question, instead handing her daughter a sandwich on a plate and a bowl of potato salad with a silver spoon sticking out of it. "Here. Go sit down and eat."

Mel did as she was told, using the opportunity to take the deep, calming breaths a past counselor had taught her. Two bites of the peppery potato salad anchored her, made her feel solid again, but she watched her mother, waiting, knowing that Agnes had heard her question. She picked up the sandwich. The small bite of salami and cheese on rye went dry in her mouth, and unexpectedly, her eyes filled with tears.

Agnes moved through the room, skirting the breakfast table where Mel sat, and disappeared down the hall. A moment later her parents returned to the kitchen, her father first and her mother nagging at him from behind.

"I do *not* need slippers," Nathan said.

"But the A/C is cranked up high."

"It's goddamn summer out! I'm not an old man who can't make decisions, Aggie."

"I was just asking if you wanted any. I didn't mean a damn thing by it."

"Hmpph!" He jerked the chair away from the table and planted his behind in it. The expression on his face was so petulant that Mel suddenly choked out a laugh, which she quickly repressed. *Oh, no.* She closed her eyes for a few seconds, realizing that she was back on the merry-go-round again, one minute feeling teary, the next slightly hysterical. *How do they do this to me?*

Her father looked down at the plate and bowl before him, and in an instant broke out in a smile. "Well, look here, my favorite! Tuna and cheese." He picked up half of the sandwich, took a bite, and grinned again. "Excellent, Aggie. Just excellent."

Agnes stood, one hand on the hip of her dark blue pantsuit. "That's salami and cheese."

Mouth full, he looked up at her in amazement. Between chomps, he said, "Of course it is. What do you take me for—a moron?" He glanced at Mel, then back to his wife. "Oh, boy, you two are in rare form today. What did you have? Another fight?"

Mel met her mother's eyes, and for the first time in years, her mother's face showed helplessness. Anger, too, but also a silent plea for help. Before Mel could respond, the expression was gone, replaced by a narrowing of eyes and a sharp retort. As Agnes berated her husband, Mel blocked out the volley of harsh words and tried to calm her rapidly beating heart. Looking down at the cheery, plastic table cover, all pink fuchsia and deep purple violets on a white background, she realized she felt thirteen again. In the past three years—ever since Calli came into her life—she thought she'd progressed so much, and now here she was once again, sitting like a wooden horse in the kitchen as her father and mother exchanged insults. Horses up, horses down, 'round and 'round, never reaching any sort of destination. From experience, she knew the merry-go-round would slow for a while, but inevitably, it would resume. Sooner or later the bizarre tune always returned.

"What's that damn noise?" Nathan hollered.

Mel's head came up fast as she heard the same peel. She rose smoothly and hustled through the kitchen, to the short hallway, and out to the living room where she pulled her daypack open and grabbed her phone. "Yes?"

"Mel, honey, it's me."

"Calli." She let out a sigh of relief.

There was silence on the phone for a couple seconds. "Mel? What's the matter? Where are you?"

"I'm at my parents' place."

She heard a warm chuckle. "You must be a glutton for punishment. My parents last Sunday, now yours."

Mel looked around the living room, then lowered herself to the rose-colored couch. It made a whooshing sound as she sunk into it, and though she couldn't see any dust, she felt a tickle in her nose and thought she'd sneeze. She said, "I thought you were painting today," as she rubbed her nose.

"Quick job after all. We just wrapped it up, and I'm off for the rest of the day. I got home, took a shower, and thought I'd call and check on you."

"Good idea."

"I get the impression that you can't say much, hmm?" Mel could tell Calli was smiling.

"Bingo."

"The only thing you really need to know, hon, is that the doctor's office called, and they need to reschedule tomorrow's blood draws. They can get you in today at 3:30 or else you have to wait until a week from Friday."

"Imelda?" Agnes stood in the doorway.

Mel wondered if her mother's x-ray eyes were scanning her slacks and blouse to see if any harm would come to the davenport. "Calli, will you give them a quick buzz for me and tell them I can come by for the blood draws today?"

"Sure."

"I'll be home right after."

"Okay, love. See you in a bit. Try to get out of there with your humor intact, and I'll take you to the movies tonight."

"Deal." Mel met her mother's eyes, and frowned.

Calli said, "Love you."

"Mmm hmmm..." Mel disconnected with the sound of Calli's purring laugh in her ear, and it gave her heart. "I've got to go, Mom." She hoisted herself up from the depths of the davenport and glanced back at it, thinking it was, after all, an engulfing, uncomfortable monstrosity.

"Wait a minute. What blood draws?"

Mel looked down toward her left breast, then looked away quickly. "Just another check for the—"

"Oh, I see." Her mother's voice was high and fast as Mel bent and dropped her cell phone in her bag. "Sure is lucky these days how they can excise the little problems so easily. Not like in the early days when that disorder was so dangerous to women."

"I'm not sure how much safer it is now, Mom. All I know is that chemotherapy is no fun."

"Well, dear, that's another thing you're lucky you didn't have to have." Mel's quick intake of breath caused her mother to pause and frown. "What? I'm no dummy, Imelda. Chemotherapy makes a woman go bald, and your hair looks fine, though you have always kept it too short."

Mel couldn't keep the look of disbelief from her face. The chemo she'd been through and the drugs for side effects hadn't caused much of her hair to fall out, but she'd gone through days of fever, vomiting and chills. Obviously her mother had not been paying attention, nor had she been listening to Izzy's progress reports. Mel scooped up her bag, stepped away from the rocking chair, head down, and made for the door.

"You want me to wrap up the rest of the lunch?"

"No, thanks, Mom. Let Dad have it. He seemed pretty hungry."

"It's probably better that you don't eat all that salami anyway. Too fatty, and now that you've finally got your figure where you want it, you don't want to run to seed." Agnes came close enough to reach out and touch Mel on the chin with a blue-veined finger. Her hand dropped away as she said, "You and your sister look so different. If only I had known. Look at those cheek bones, that nose, the eyes...maybe I should have named *you* after Isadora Duncan."

"Might have been a good idea, Mom. I'm never going to be the saint Imelda was, and Izzy won't ever dance."

"Ha. As if you ever dance," her mother said coyly.

Mel made sure her face didn't betray a thing, but inside, she was shrieking, *Yes, I do dance, and I'm damn good at it!* She pulled the door open. "Will you tell Dad I said 'So long'?"

"Sure will."

Mel stumbled to her car, thinking about names, and dying, and Catholic saints. In the year 1333, a day before Saint Imelda Lambertini's eleventh birthday, the little girl saint had died. She received her first Holy Communion and immediately afterwards dropped over dead, reportedly filled with ecstasy and joy. Saint Imelda was Mel's mother's patron saint. It occurred to Mel now, as she drove away from her parents' merry-go-round house, that little Imelda had probably killed herself after a run-in with her mother.

LATER IN THE afternoon Mel walked out of the doctor's office picking at the sticky tape holding down a piece of gauze in the inside crook of her left elbow. She'd never expected to become such a pin cushion. If the cops ever arrested her, she was sure they'd think she was a junkie and not the law-abiding owner of an art gallery in Lowertown St. Paul.

She wandered out into the hot parking lot, her mind full of thoughts about her mother's comments regarding her father's strokes. He didn't appear unhappy, and except for when his wife nagged at him, he seemed content. Yes, he was 79, but he looked just fine physically, though today he had been a bit bleary-eyed. His cataract surgery five years earlier had been successful, but Mel thought he might need the procedure again.

She got in her Honda Accord, started it up, and adjusted the air conditioning vents. The warm, humid air quickly cooled. With it blowing on her, she actually felt too cold and turned it down to low.

All the way home she worried about her father, and when she walked into the townhouse she shared with Calli, she felt tired and wrung out. She found Calli in the kitchen assembling a salad.

"Hiya, sweetie," Calli called out. "Thought we could have something to eat, then go see what's playing at The Lagoon." Mel stepped into the kitchen, and Calli wrapped her in her arms. "Bad visit, huh?"

Mel sighed and pressed her lips against Calli's soft neck. "Yeah. No fun at all."

The phone rang, and Mel let go to look at the caller I.D. "Hey, it's the Venture Capitalist." She picked up the phone and said, "Nate! What's happening? How are you, bro?"

Her brother's voice sounded guarded. "We're fine here, just fine." He cleared his throat. "I called to let you know that I just talked to Mom."

She leaned against the fridge and watched Calli set the table. "Oh, so she told you about the strokes?"

"Ah, well, yeah. That came up. Actually, she asked me to tell you that Dad had a little accident in the car today."

"What! I was just there at noon! Is he okay? What happened?"

"Slow down, Mel. He's fine."

"Is he in the hospital?" Her heart raced in her chest, and she was glad to be leaning against something.

"Nope. Home resting already. He wrapped the Buick around a tree. Lucky that old boat is so huge. He was on the way over to the market and must have had a dizzy spell. He ran up on the sidewalk and into a maple in someone's yard. Bumped his head a little, but he's fine."

Relief spread through her at the same time that she was struck by the circumstances. "So she called you in California to report this?"

"Yeah, sorry about that. She said the docs gave Dad some meds for pain that will make him sleepy. She wanted me to call you and Izzy to tell you what happened and ask you both to let them be. He can't see anyone right now, but he should be fine by tomorrow."

*What a chickenshit thing to do.* For a moment she thought she'd said it out loud. "Nate, thanks for calling. Sorry you had to do the dirty work."

"That's what big brothers are for, right?" She let out a mirthless chuckle. "I promised I'd call Izzy, too, so I'm going to let you go. The kids and Sheila say hi."

"Give them our love, too." They said goodbye and hung up.

Calli stood by the kitchen table, watching Mel with a quizzical look on her face. "What now?"

"Dad cracked up the car, and instead of Mom calling us to report this little fact, she called Nate to have him do it."

Calli shook her head. "Families. Can't live with 'em — can't kill 'em."

She strode over and put her arms around Mel, who tightened her hands into fists, then hugged back. "I am just so damn mad, Cal."

"I know," she said. "I know." Leaning away, she said, "Skip the movie?"

"Yup."

"I'll put the salads in the fridge and we can have them when we come back."

EVEN THOUGH NATE had phoned Mel before he called her twin, Izzy lived closer and arrived at their parents' home first. As Calli steered into the driveway, Mel saw Izzy disappear into the house.

"You staying here?" Mel asked.

Calli nodded and patted Mel's thigh. "You don't need another body in there for the inevitable showdown. I'll keep the car cool for you." She squeezed Mel's knee and made her jump. "Don't break a leg, sweetheart."

"If I do, it won't be mine that gets broken." Mel got out and shut the car door, thinking how she talked a good game, but knowing her mother could snap her in two with little more than a few choice words. She marched to the front of the house and let herself in, pausing a few steps into the living room. She heard whispered hisses in the kitchen, and after a moment, she could make sense of the words.

"He's fine," her mother said in a hoarse stage whisper.

"I'd like to see for myself, Mother."

"Isadora, I asked you not to run over here. He needs quiet and rest until tomorrow."

"Right. And thanks for the personal touch. Having Nate call long distance was swell of you."

Agnes responded, but Mel tuned it out. No way was she entering the kitchen now, not when Izzy was fighting the good fight. All through their youth, she had marveled at her sister's ability to meet their mother head on. Mel couldn't remember a single time she herself hadn't folded.

Moving across the room like a man walking the plank, she stopped in front of the fireplace.

On the mantel were four elaborate German steins, two to the left and two to the right of the nautical clock in the middle. For all the years of Mel's life, her mother had hated those steins, which Mel's father had brought into the marriage. Nathan Bauer missed active duty during World War II, but was stationed in Germany the year after the war ended. He always said the steins were the only souvenirs he'd bought, and he intended to keep them. "I may even take 'em with me to the grave," he once said in the midst of an argument over them.

The steins featured delicate hand-painted reliefs of German scenes: castles of Bavaria on one, dancers flanking a colorful crest on the second, and a beer wagon, Bavarian hat, and pretzel on the third. Mel reached for the fourth, which was her favorite. Inset, a three-dimensional swan was delicately carved. The plumed tail feathers made up the handle on the left. A baby swan nestled under the breast of the bird, and on the right, the swan's head was bent gracefully, making it easy to grasp the overlarge stein and drink from it. Not that anyone ever drank from the foot-tall pieces of art—except for Henry Altamont, who, unbeknownst to Izzy and Mel, had filled the swan stein with cheap Annie Greensprings wine. This was 1991, while Agnes and Nathan were away from Minnesota visiting a dying elderly relative, and Mel and Izzy had used the opportunity to throw a summer party.

Mel turned the stein around. The crack in the baby swan's wing was still there, though she and Izzy, in desperation, had glued it back on. She tried to remember how long they spent hoping and praying no one would notice the crack—or the spot in the carpet near the couch where they'd had to cut away some of the shag rug because Tyler Schmidt gave Henry Altamont a bloody nose in response to Henry's carelessness with what he called "that damn antique mug." Tyler's protectiveness had earned him Izzy's heart. Thirteen years, one extravagant wedding, and two kids later, they were still together. Mel hadn't heard from Henry since he'd graduated from high school and was lost to the romance of the California cocaine trade.

She set the stein back in its place, turned it so the crack wasn't noticeable, and wondered why her parents had never asked about the swan's injury. Certainly neither of them ever mentioned it if they had noticed. She wondered if she could confess now. What would they say? What would her father think? And how long would it be before her father forgot he had ever possessed the mugs?

Just then Izzy rounded the corner into the living room and stopped abruptly. "I didn't hear you come in, Mel." Her face was bright red. Mel looked beyond to see their mother standing in the doorway, with an equally angry face and her arms crossed tightly over her chest.

"Uh, hi, Mom."

"I see you can't follow simple directions any better than your sister."

"Nope. Guess it's genetic."

"Your father is just fine. Come back tomorrow if you like."

Mel nodded. With a huff, Izzy grabbed her forearm and

pulled her across the room. Without even a goodbye, they slammed out, letting the screen door slap shut behind them.

Mel looked back. Agnes stood behind the dull gray screen. In a hoarse voice she called out, "Don't think I don't know about your guilty fascination with your father's steins, Imelda."

Izzy pushed her forward. "The hell with her! Get in your car. You and Calli meet me over at the Caribou Coffee on Grand." She flounced off to her car, leaving Mel to wondering how many years her mother had known about the swan cover-up.

THE NEXT TIME Mel approached her parents' house, she arrived with prearranged reinforcements. Izzy sat in the Honda's passenger seat, toying with her long, straight hair, and gabbing about Mikey and Ashlee. Calli had graciously agreed to watch Izzy's two kids while the twin sisters spent the morning visiting their parents to talk about plans for the future. It had been two days since their father's accident, and after considerable discussion, the two sisters formulated a plan to suggest that their folks sell the house and move into an assisted-living center.

"Okay," Izzy said as they turned on their parents' street, "we have to do this good cop/bad cop style."

"Right. I suppose you're the good cop, as usual."

Izzy laughed. "I'm older, so shouldn't I get to pick?"

"Ten minutes shouldn't make that much difference. Besides, I'm a crappy bad cop."

"All right. You be the good cop, and I'll try to be the hellion. If that doesn't work, one of us gives a signal, and we can switch roles."

As Mel pulled up to the curb in front of the weathered house, she saw a green blob on wheels down the street. Like an over-sized alien, it weaved toward them.

"Oh, geez!" Izzy said. She pointed, her finger almost touching the windshield. "It can't be!" She grabbed the door handle and hauled herself up and out.

The green figure drew closer. Mel exited the car, shaded her eyes, and squinted into the sun. She met her sister's gaze over the top of the car and shouted, "What in the hell is Mom thinking?"

They slammed their car doors and stood waiting as their father wheeled up. A black, curly-headed Pete nestled between Nathan's bright white t-shirt and a heavy, forest green work shirt which was buttoned only halfway up.

"Dad," Izzy said. "What do you think you're doing?"

He applied the pedal brakes on the one-speed Schwinn and

gingerly stepped off to straddle the bike. With his right hand, he reached up to his chest and patted Pete. The poodle gazed upward with a look of rapture on his face as his pink tongue darted out and licked Nathan's chin.

"Hi, girls. You must have gotten my transmission."

Mel glanced at Izzy. "Transmission?"

"Yes, sirree," he said. "I asked one of the men to make contact. Little did I know that he would send it out in JN-25 code, but I always knew my girls were smart. The Imperial Navy has nothing on our forces." He looked down at Pete. "Glad you figured it out. That's how we'll win the war—smart civilians and officers like me getting it done."

Mel pointed at a dark purple lump on his forehead above his left eye. Bisected by an inch-long slice, the wound was held together by two butterfly bandages. "How's your head?"

"No problem. You don't think the Japs and Krauts could get to me, do you?"

"What?" Mel wanted to step over and feel his forehead to make sure he wasn't delirious.

He smiled. "Don't worry a bit. We've stepped up our security on base."

Izzy frowned. "Oh. I see. Well, Dad...hmmm." She glanced toward Mel again. "So, have you had any lunch—I mean, been to the mess hall lately?"

He leaned forward and whispered, "No. Afraid the sergeant will stick me with KP."

"Don't worry about that," Izzy said. "You know I outrank the sergeant."

He let out a guffaw. "Nice try. Not *this* sergeant!" He leaned the bicycle to the side and dragged his right leg over to dismount. The Schwinn nearly toppled, but Mel leapt forward and grabbed it while Izzy steadied their father.

Mel said, "I've got it, Dad. I'll put it away for you—return it to the Motor Pool, that is. You go on into the house."

He shuffled over to the curb, stepped up, and took slow, even steps toward the front door. Mel waited until he was out of ear-shot, then turned to her sister. "Wasn't dad a soldier after World War Two?"

Izzy rolled her eyes. "Yeah. And where did he get all that stuff about codes and the Imperial Navy? He didn't have anything to do with that in the 40s. He was never even an officer. I'll bet he's been watching the History Channel."

Shaking her head, Mel rolled the bicycle up over the curb and to the driveway. The garage door was locked. Without a word, Izzy went to the front door and disappeared inside. A moment later the automatic door rumbled up. Mel put the bike away, went into the house, and paused at the front door to press the garage remote.

Izzy stood in the doorway to the kitchen listening to their mother's sharp voice.

"...supposed to do? Handcuff him to the bed? I didn't even hear him leave."

Mel squeezed next to Izzy in the doorway and said, "Mom, that's the point. You can't just let him roam the neighborhood. Two days ago he's in a car accident. Today he's on that old bike. He could have fallen or been hit by a car."

"And hello to you, too, Imelda," Agnes said in a tight voice. She stood holding a wooden mixing spoon in her fist. A spotless white apron covered her tan housedress. An array of spices, flour, and sugar sat on the counter next to her Kitchen Aide mixer.

With a sigh, Izzy said, "Mel's right, Ma. You've either got to watch him closer or he needs to be placed somewhere where they'll supervise him 24 hours per day. We had an idea. We think you should consider an assisted-living complex."

Mel thought her mother was going to attack. For one brief moment, her eyes resembled the piercing black gaze possessed by the swooping red falcon out in the living room curio cabinet. Agnes smacked the wood spoon on the counter, then confronted her daughters red-faced and angry. "You want to send him to a home then? Just farm him out? He's *fine* and I can take care of him."

Izzy stepped forward allowing Mel to relax against the frame of the door. "He's not fine, Ma. The strokes have done something to him. He thinks he's back in the war."

Agnes waved a hand and picked up the wooden spoon. "Pshaw! Foolish nonsense. So he gets a little confused. He's 79, for God's sake. That's no reason to send him to an old folks' home when I can take perfectly good care of him. We're doing fine."

Mel shook her head. "But Mom —"

Agnes released her full fury. "You don't come around here for months at a time, Imelda, and then when you do show up, you think you can just walk right in and tell me how to take care of your father? Don't you try to tell me what you think is best! You, who don't even *have* a husband." She took two steps forward, shaking the spoon. "You have no right. None!"

Mel stood up straight, her face flaming, but she forged on, forcing the words to come out. "You always have to make things like this into something about *me*, about my lifestyle. You just can't do that anymore, Mom. Calli has nothing to do with this problem, so leave her out of it."

Izzy raised a hand, but before she could speak, Agnes shouted, "I'm 68 years old and have every right to make judgments for my life and your father's, too." She shook the spoon in the air. "When you have a husband, only then can you tell me you know what's best. You're just damn lucky we didn't disown you over your—your—oooh!" She spun away, facing the kitchen window over the sink.

Mel closed her eyes and let out a long sigh. With a flash of insight, she realized that no matter what she did, or said, or how she acted—or even if she begged—her mother was never going to accept her relationship with a woman. Certainly Agnes would ordinarily be polite, though distant, but when her back was against the wall, Calli would never be accepted like Izzy's Tyler was. In her heart, Mel had always known this, but staying away from her mother had allowed her to avoid confronting the fact. In the past, she would have left in a rage long before this point in the argument, but now she merely felt deflated. Tears squeezed out as she heard Izzy's next statement.

"You're being unnecessarily cruel, Ma. Mel's right. This isn't about her. It's about Dad and what's best for him."

It was clear Agnes wouldn't back down. She let out a gasp of exasperation and jammed the spoon into the silver bowl on the counter.

Izzy said, "Ma! I've got a husband. Are you going to listen to me or is that just an excuse you're using to hurt Mel?"

"Get out."

Izzy turned and met Mel's eyes. She said, "Ma, you can't—"

"I said get out!" Agnes didn't turn around, but it was clear to Mel that the conversation was over. She backed up into the living room, facing Izzy as her sister came through the doorway shaking her head in anger and frustration. Izzy gestured to the left, and Mel wiped her eyes on her sleeve as she followed her down the hall to their parents' room.

Nathan lay on his side, his green work shirt untucked, with Pete curled up next to his slumbering body. Mel stood there long enough to see their dad's chest rise and fall, then whispered, "At least he's got Pete." When Izzy nodded, Mel saw the tears in her eyes. "Let's just go, sis."

Mutely, Izzy nodded, and they left the house, back into the humid morning. The heat took what little energy Mel had left, and she couldn't help the tears that welled up. They got in the car and sat quietly for a moment before Mel started the car and turned on the A/C. "What a big mess." She crossed her arms over the top of the steering wheel and let her head drop against her forearms. The touch to her right shoulder was firm.

"Don't let her get to you. She doesn't mean it." Izzy sniffed and let out a sigh.

"Yes, she does." Mel's voice was muffled, but she went on. "What's wrong with her? How can she be like that?"

Izzy shrugged. "Maybe it was her childhood, something with her parents — hell, I don't know!"

"Me neither. She knows just how to get to me, and she never wastes an opportunity."

"Mel, listen to me. You aren't going to get what you need from her. You never have and you never will. Daddy always loved you best, and she always loved Nate the most. Look at the bright side. At least you were *somebody's* favorite."

Mel sat back against the hot upholstery and stared at Izzy. She gasped out, "That's not true."

Izzy smiled. "Sure it is. And that's why it's extra hard on you — because sooner or later we're going to lose Dad, and he's the one that has always gotten you through. Maybe he won't die for a while, but we're losing him still. And then we'll be stuck with our cranky, mean-spirited mother, and there'll be no buffer at all."

The tears came, and Mel couldn't stop them. "How can you be so matter-of-fact about this?" she choked out.

"That's my job as the older sister — to look at the bright side."

"There's no bright side in this mess. It's a disaster all around. And what about you? Dad loved me, and Mom loved Nate best? You got screwed!"

Izzy shifted to the side in the awkward bucket seat and took Mel's face into her soft hands. "No I didn't, little sister. I always knew *you* loved me best. That's the bright side."

## SX Meagher

S X Meagher was born in East St. Louis, Illinois, and has since lived in Chicago, Los Angeles, and New York City, where she now happily resides.

Her love of reading was fostered by the absence of a public or school library and parents who were loath to purchase books. Scarcity bred fixation, and S X hoarded her allowance to purchase Nancy Drew mysteries.

When S X was fifteen, she began the first of many part-time jobs, spending much of her earnings honing her tastes in fiction. Salinger, Pynchon, Updike, Mailer, Sinclair, Dreiser, Dostoevsky, Koszinski, Fitzgerald, O'Connor, and Faulkner were high school favorites, and she continued to read across genres and cultures until she got hooked on lesbian fiction when she was in her thirties.

The accessibility of the Internet led S X to give writing a try, which she did in 1997 when she began working on a story about two college-aged women from vastly different family backgrounds. That story, *I Found My Heart In San Francisco*, was published in 2002. S X expects to have two more books published this year, and hopes to continue writing for the rest of her life.

# That Way

## Fiction by S X Meagher

GRACE JENSEN PUMPED her legs, gaining purchase on the small hill at the edge of town, determined to be the first to the top. The boys were all a little taller and a little stronger, but she weighed less and had as big a will to win as any of them. Panting, straining, feeling the sweat trickle and twist down the middle of her back, she leapt onto the small plateau, beaming with pride when she hit it with her left foot just before Jerry Swenson swept past her. "I'm the king!" she crowed, jumping up and down, ebullient in victory. The gangly boy with the dust-brown hair — styled with the aid of a cereal bowl — and beady, close-set eyes gave her a push, dispatching her onto the seat of her shorts. But Grace didn't care. She'd won! She'd won, fair and square, and she lay on her back, taking in the cloudless, unspeakably blue hue of a summer sky in North Dakota.

She put her hands behind her head, then crossed an ankle over her raised knee. Jerry, Tommy White, Eric Torgerson, AJ Schmidt, and Bobby Nymoen all sank to the ground, mimicking her. The others had all slowed down when it was clear the race was between Grace and Jerry, but now that it was over, there wasn't a word spoken about it. All six kids lay on the ground, letting the still-cool earth diffuse the heat of their small bodies.

The sun was so warm and so blissfully welcome — they were all grateful for its comfort and the freedom that came with its return. It had been a brutal winter, the worst one Grace could recall, even though she really couldn't recall much at all, being five-years-old. It seemed the bitter cold had come early and stayed late, with more days than she cared to remember spent sitting in the small house on Prairie Street, watching the snow drift across their small yard. None of her friends could go out during a blizzard either, but she knew it would just take one generous adult to allow one child to go outside, and all of the others would follow.

Not, of course, that she was the leader of the group. That title belonged to Eric, the oldest, tallest, and coolest of the clique. Eric had been just one week short of the cut-off for first grade this past year, and he had much older brothers — giving him a depth and breadth of knowledge the other kids couldn't dream of matching. He even had a brother who smoked — the coolness of that alone was awesome — not to mention giving him ready access to the matches his brother always hid between his mattress and box spring. As soon as the tall grass was dry, they had plans to start a fire — something Grace spent nearly every night dreaming about. She could just imagine the orange and red flames whirling and surging across the prairie and feel the nearly constant wind from the northwest whip it into an inferno that would burn for miles and miles and miles.

Bobby, his black, tightly curled hair cushioning his head from the damp earth, was obviously thinking the same thing. He asked no one in particular, "How much longer till we can set the fire?"

"A while," Eric decided. "Still too wet." As if to illustrate his point, he scrambled to his feet, then grasped the hem of his T-shirt while turning his head to look over his shoulder. A large wet spot, muddy on the edges, marred the orange material, and he yanked it off and stuck it into the waistband at the back of his shorts. Each child joined him, Grace nearly rapturous to finally be able to take her shirt off and feel the hot sun on her back and shoulders for the first time since the previous summer.

They'd just started to play king of the mountain, with AJ giving Jerry a shove when Bobby said, "Gracie! Your gramma's coming!"

Without waiting for more information, she slapped Tommy on the shoulder and ran headlong down the hill, away from her grandmother's path, yelling tag at the top of her lungs. The boys took off after her, the group serpentining down the hillock and trading tags, until Jerry roared past her, tagging her as he did. They were on level ground now, and Bobby turned to face her while staying out of tagging range. "I think she saw you," he said, not needing to add of whom he spoke.

"But I didn't see her," Grace replied, smiling with the smugness of the technically innocent.

THE DAY CONTINUED to heat up, and during one of the group's pass-bys of the alley behind Prairie Street, Grace noticed that her grandmother's car was in the garage. "I'm gonna get somethin' to drink," she declared. Her comrades waved and continued on, knowing she'd catch up with them later in the day.

The little girl opened the screen door and ran up the three steps to the kitchen, delighted to find her mother there. "Hi!" she mouthed since her mother was on the phone. When her mother scooted the kitchen chair back and patted her legs in invitation, she dashed and climbed onto her lap.

There were a lot of times Grace was supremely happy: when she was running the streets and alleys with her friends, when her mother came home unexpectedly early, when her grandmother made a white cake with chocolate icing, when the Christmas toy catalogs arrived, when her mother read her a story, and when she sat on her mother's lap. It was so remarkably soft and cushy and comforting, sitting there on her mom's denim-clad legs, her own feet swinging freely. She didn't have words to talk about the feeling, but it was the sweetest thing she knew.

She wasn't sure who her mom was talking to, and in fact, it was very rare to find her on the telephone. Her mother had friends, none of whom Grace knew, but Luanne saw them at school and didn't often speak to them once she got home.

Luanne put her lips on Grace's neck and gave her a quiet kiss, then a playful, gentle bite. Grace giggled and squirmed, then her thirst propelled her from her mother's lap. She slid off and went to the refrigerator, pointing at it with a questioning look. Her mother nodded, and the girl opened the big door and carefully took out a pitcher of water, using both hands so she didn't break it—again. She carried the pitcher to her mother, then handed her a glass. She wasn't taking any chances.

"No, there really isn't anything new going on here," Luanne said as she poured the cold water and handed her daughter the glass. "I don't think anything new or interesting has ever happened in Voltaire." She laughed, but Grace knew her mother wasn't kidding. She wasn't supposed to know, but she'd heard her mother talking with someone earlier in the year and confiding that she planned on leaving North Dakota as soon as she was finished with her degree. Grace didn't really understand why her mother wanted to leave. Voltaire was a really nice place if you were a kid. She reasoned that there must be something about it that adults didn't like, since her grandmother also seemed to hate it. Of course her grandmother seemed to hate just about everything except "the Lord."

Grace gulped the water down, then her mother put her still-cold hand on her bare back, making Grace giggle and dance away "Go play, honey. You can stay out until dinner time. Put your shirt back on if your shoulders get pink."

Nodding, Grace started for the door, but she couldn't bear to have something as exciting as a phone call from a stranger going on without snooping. She'd developed very impressive skills in the art of eavesdropping, and she used a favorite ruse. "I have to pee," she said, shifting her weight from foot to foot to underscore the urgency of her need.

"Go on," Luanne said, putting her hand on her back and shooing her in the direction of the bathroom. Grace ran around the corner and noisily closed the bathroom door, staying outside of the room. Stealthily, she tiptoed back toward the kitchen and crouched down, for no reason other than it seemed like something a spy should do.

Her mother's voice was low and soft, but she could make it out. "I wish I could come now. My mother's about to drive me crazy! But I don't have any other choice." There was a pause, and Luanne continued. "No, it doesn't make any sense to leave before I get my degree. As bad as my mother is, she lets us live here and watches Gracie all day. Nobody's gonna do that for me in San Francisco. Besides," she added, "I'd have to take extra classes if I transferred now. I'm just gonna have to stick it out."

There was another substantial lull, then Luanne said, "Yeah, she's gonna have to start school here. I wish she could start in San Francisco, but the only way I could do that is if I held her back a year."

Grace was so shocked by this statement that she nearly fell over. *Stay back a year? Have everybody start school but me? No! NO!*

She breathed an audible sigh of relief when her mother continued, "But she's as a smart as a little whip, and she'd be bored to tears just running around for another year. She knows her ABCs, and she can spell a lot of words. I read to her every night, and I really think it's made a difference."

Grace put her hands together in prayer, just the way her grandmother had taught her. "Thank you, Jesus," she said quietly.

"So," Luanne said, her voice a whisper, "have you seen Dan around?"

The child's heart began to hammer in her chest. She wasn't sure how she knew it, but she knew that Dan was her father. Even though her grandmother had told her she didn't have a father, she knew she did and that his name was Dan. She was still a little sore at her grandmother for telling her she didn't have one. It wasn't just that it made her different; she was plenty different. But she had mentioned to her friends that maybe she was like the baby Jesus and didn't have an earthly father. Eric had laughed at her and, of course, all of the other boys had joined him. He told her that she had to have a father—even if no one knew who he was. He then proceeded to describe where babies come from, based on the research he'd done with the magazines his brother kept next to the matches. Grace was still reeling from that conversation, and she knew that somehow, her grandmother was to blame for the whole mess. She'd snuck a look at the tiny bit of sunlight she could see between her mother's legs when Luanne stood with the sun at her back, and Grace had decided that Eric must be crazy. And if he wasn't, well ... the whole idea made her sick to her stomach.

"Is he ... uhm ... what's he up to?" Another interminable pause and Luanne said, "Does he have a job?" A beat passed. "Really? How long has he been doing that? Working at a print shop is a good, steady job." Another few seconds and Luanne said, "And he's really not dating anyone? You can tell me, Jen, really." Grace inched her head around the corner, being careful to keep it close to the floor. Her mother's face bore a smile that wasn't completely happy, but it was pretty darned happy. Satisfied and pleased with herself, Grace tiptoed back into the bathroom and flushed the toilet, then ran the water in the sink and marched back into the kitchen, being extra noisy to avoid suspicion.

She waved at her mother as she passed, then jumped down each of the stairs, trying to get as high as she could with each jump. She wasn't allowed to practice this trick when her grandmother was home, so she had to make use of every opportunity.

When she was back outside, she went to the alley and stood quietly for a minute, listening for any signs of life. For a few seconds, all she heard was the buzz of gnats floating around her head. Then she heard a boy's voice in the distance, and she took off in its direction. It might not have been one of her friends, but in Voltaire, everyone knew where everyone was, and whoever it was would direct her to the gang.

GRACE AMBLED DOWN the alley, kicking a can, when she spied her grandmother walking down Independent Avenue, heading home. She was pretty sure her grandmother hadn't called to her when she was on the hill, and she could honestly report she hadn't seen the older woman. But sometimes she got into trouble for things that were completely illogical. She decided to wile away a few minutes waiting until her grandmother went into the house and griped to her mother if there was griping to be done. She hated to have her mom get yelled at, but she figured it wouldn't do much harm, since her grandmother was always yelling at her mom for some reason or another. The only thing she could recall having her grandmother be happy about was the fact that she was named Grace. She wasn't sure what grace was, but she knew it had something to do with "the Lord." Grace was still smug about the fact that she knew a big secret her grandmother didn't know. Just this year, her mother had told her she was actually named after a singer she liked—not the other kind of grace. Her mother had even shown her an album cover with the singer's picture. The woman looked a little strange, and her last name was Slick, a word that didn't seem like a real name. But she kept her opinions to herself, knowing that her mother must have had a good reason for picking this lady's name. She'd forgotten her misgivings immediately because her mother had sworn her to secrecy—something Grace loved. There were few things that made a kid feel more powerful than having a really good secret, especially when she knew that there'd be hell to pay if she revealed it. She wouldn't, of course. Wild horses couldn't have dragged that secret out of her.

She tired of standing in the alley, so she opened the creaky gate in the back of the yard by the garage. She'd found that if she opened it really, really slowly, it didn't make much noise at all. Once inside the yard, she crept across the grass and squatted down by the door to the storm cellar. The kitchen window was right above her head, and she felt a stab of pain right in her heart when she heard her grandmother yelling at her mother. But much to her surprise, her grandmother wasn't yelling about being ignored earlier in the afternoon. Once again, Gramma was angry about something that made no sense at all.

"I'll not have it," Ida Jensen said. "It's bad enough that she runs around like a wild Indian with that bunch of boys. I've a good mind to put a stop to that, too!"

"Mama, those are her friends! You can't make her stop playing with them! There aren't any girls in town Gracie's age!"

"Then she can play with older girls or younger girls. But no matter who she plays with, she's gonna wear a shirt! If I ever see her running around town showing her bubbies again, I'll take her over my lap!"

That kind of startled Grace, and she put her hands on the grass to steady herself. Times like this made her feel really bad about her gramma—and about herself. She felt mad and helpless and embarrassed all at once. The worst thing was she didn't know exactly why.

"You promised you wouldn't hit her!" Luanne shouted, sounding madder than Grace had ever heard her. "That was part of the deal!"

"Somebody has to take her in hand! She doesn't even know she's a girl!"

"Oh, don't be ridiculous!" Luanne said, sounding a little calmer, and making Grace shiver a little less violently. "She's just a tomboy."

"Tomboy, my eye! She's not right, and you know it, Luanne. You must have ruined her with all of them drugs you took. She's not a normal girl, but she's gonna be one before I'm through with her!"

Grace could hear a chair thump its way across the floor. She imagined her mother had been sitting at the kitchen table doing her homework. Her grandmother liked to stand to yell, so she guessed her mother was getting up so she could look her in the eye. "What do you think you're gonna do?" Now her mom's voice was low and sounded calm ... too calm.

"I'm gonna do what you should have done since she was born. I'm gonna make her into a normal girl. She's gonna play with dolls and have tea parties and play house like the other little girls do."

"She *is* a normal girl! That's just not what she likes," Luanne said. "She's never been interested in things like that. When she was just a little thing, she would only look at a doll to tear it apart. You can't make her be something she's not, Mother."

Momma only called Gramma "Mother" when she was fightin' mad, and Grace knew this scrap wasn't over by a long shot.

"Oh, yes, I can," Ida said, her voice topping her daughter's in volume and shrillness. "There's a woman from church, lives in Velva, who has a perfectly normal little five-year-old daughter. She's invited Grace to play with her. She's gonna go play dolls and imagine what it's gonna be like to grow up and get married. Unlike some people around here," she added with her voice full of disgust. There was nothing Grace hated more than the way her grandmother talked to her mother about not being married. It broke Grace's heart, but her momma had told her not to let it bother her. It still did.

"You can take her anywhere you want; you know I can't stop you. But neither Gracie nor this other girl are gonna have fun playing dolls. For one thing, Gracie'll probably experiment on the other girl's dolls by taking their heads off or giving 'em a haircut. And if she can't do that, she'll just sit there and stare with her arms crossed over her chest and her chin nearly touching her arms. She's not the kind of girl you can push around, Mama."

"Any adult who says you can't make a five-year-old do what you want is just plain stupid! You and your big city ways. Think you always know best. Well, I'm not gonna have my only grandchild grow up to be that way!"

There was something about the way she said "that way" that made Grace's skin crawl. She didn't know what it was, but for the first time, she knew her grandmother was naming some-thing — putting a tag to the way she'd always felt. She *was* differ-ent from the other girls, but she wasn't a boy. She didn't want to be a boy. She'd never talked to anyone about this, because she didn't know how. But she knew, sure as shootin', that her grand-mother knew what it was. And she was certain that it was bad. Very bad.

"You don't know what you're talking about," Luanne said dismissively. "Besides, it doesn't matter to me who Gracie is when she grows up. If she's different, I'll still love her."

"I should've known you wouldn't care," Ida snapped. "Well, I'll tell you right now, girl, if Grace turns out *that way*, she can just keep her butt outta Voltaire. We don't need those types around here."

"Gracie is too smart for this town," Luanne said, sounding awfully confident to Grace's ears. "She's gonna make something of herself."

"She can make something of herself after I finish making her into a regular girl," Ida yelled. Grace heard quick steps, moving from linoleum to carpet. She knew her grandmother had put on her ugly face — the one where the ends of her lips looked like they wanted to touch her chin — and stomped out of the room. She also knew that by the time she got to the living room, Momma would be crying. So Grace stood up and waited for the pins and needles to leave her legs, then dashed back across the yard and into the alley. She didn't want to find the boys or to play. She just wanted to go to the railroad tracks and hope that a train came by. Maybe the man in the little house on the back of the train would wave at her. That always made her happy — for a while.

IT WAS BARELY dark when Grace lay in bed that night, her room dimly lit with the dying embers of the summer sunset. She'd put her shirt on before she'd come home, and no mention had been made of the new rules her grandmother had talked about. Actually, not much talking of any kind went on at dinner. Grace had asked about her mother's day at school, but Luanne simply said nothing much had happened, and that was the end of that.

Grace had only given half of her attention to the television that night, even though her two favorite shows were on. Besides being distracted by the tension in the small room, she had to admit that she didn't like "The Brady Bunch" as much now that cousin Oliver was on every week. She knew she'd never ask Oliver to play if he moved to Voltaire.

By the time "The Partridge Family" was over, it was time for bed. Luanne tucked Grace in and gave her a kiss, but she didn't even offer to read her a story. She seemed to be thinking of something or someone else, and Grace imagined she was thinking about Dan.

So instead of thinking about the fire they were gonna start, or about putting pennies on the Soo Line track, she spent a little time thinking about the future. She'd miss her Gramma—a little. She knew she should love her more, but she just wasn't able to love her or Jesus as much as she should. But she loved her momma more than anybody loved anybody, and she knew she'd love her daddy when she met him.

She thought of what life would be like in San Francisco, but the only thing she could picture was that big orange bridge. She'd never been on a big bridge—only the little one that went over the Souris River on the road to Velva. She knew they wouldn't live on the bridge, but that was the only picture she'd ever seen of the place. So she thought of riding in a car, going across that big, big bridge. Her daddy was driving the car, even though she couldn't make out exactly what he looked like, and her momma was sitting next to him in the front seat, looking at him like she looked at Grace when she was really happy about something. They wouldn't be like "The Brady Bunch"—even before Oliver got there. She didn't want a bunch of brothers and sisters, anyway. She just wanted her momma and daddy to come tuck her in at night, and tell her that everything would be all right. Even if she was "that way."

## Radclyffe

Using her pen name in honor of feminist lesbian author Radclyffe Hall, the present-day Radclyffe burst onto the writing scene in 1999 and has not let up her pace. Since 2001, she has written and published seventeen books with many more on the way.

Radclyffe, who was born in New York in the Fifties, now resides in Pennsylvania with her partner, Lee. She is a surgeon by day, fiction and erotica writer by night, and the person who most influenced her writing was Ann Bannon, particularly with her Beebo Brinker stories. Radclyffe says, "I first began writing love stories about women more than two decades ago because the very act of giving form to the characters that populate my imagination is a personal pleasure. I would write even if there were no one else to read what I have written. Several of my published works are expanded versions of those early private stories. In addition, there weren't many romances involving two women available at that time, and I longed to see our stories told. Today, we are fortunate to have many writers and presses bringing us a vast array of fine lesbian fiction."

In 2002 and 2003/2004 Radclyffe won much-deserved Alice B. Reader's Appreciation Awards.

# Don't Ask, Don't Tell or...The Day My Mother Broke the Silence

## Memoir/Essay by Radclyffe

THE HISTORY BOOKS are likely to give President William Jefferson Clinton the dubious credit of coining the phrase "Don't ask, don't tell." The kinder chroniclers will say he was forced into accepting this compromise regarding gays and lesbians in the military by forces within Congress and the Pentagon too powerful to fight during the early days of his presidency. The unkind ones will simply say he was a coward and reneged on his campaign promises, as so many politicians do after the election is over.

While I tend to agree with those who take a harsher line on Clinton's performance, I have to say I'm not certain he deserves the credit for the philosophy behind the policy. I'm pretty sure that mothers and daughters have been practicing the same approach to secrets and silences for millennia. Perhaps the same unspoken and uneasy truce exists between fathers and sons as well, but I can only speak from experience. It's entirely possible that this is a genetically programmed parent-child behavioral interaction designed to preserve the place of outliers in the social structure. "Outlier" is a more palatable way of naming ourselves when the alternative designation is "outcast."

I would tend to cast my vote in this instance with the nature rather than the nurture supporters, because I'm quite certain I was practicing the policy almost before the age of reason. I clearly remember my first crush on a woman. I was five years old, and she was a space commander on an after-school children's show. She wore a uniform with some sort of generic Star Trek-type symbol over her rather ample breasts. I can't to this day decide what it was that captured my heart: the uniform or the fact that she was a woman in command. Whatever it was, I can remember the urgency with which I awaited the magic hour each afternoon, seated on the floor in front of the television well before it was time for the program to begin. I was enchanted for those sixty minutes every day, saddened each time the program ended, and consumed with thoughts of her until our next meeting.

I also understood it wasn't something I should talk about. I knew that as instinctively as I understood that I shouldn't put my hand in the fire or that there were things one did not tell one's mother. I didn't at that time have a concept of my feelings being wrong, but I definitely understood different. And along with that knowledge came the instinctive concept of "Don't tell."

Somewhere between five and twelve, without any specific instruction, I embraced the self-protective covenant of silence wholeheartedly. I can't give my mother any credit or blame for this, because she was still laboring under the understandable assumption that I would eventually turn out the way most girls do. Or at least, nine out of ten. I don't believe the truth became apparent to her for a few more years, and then the collusion began.

Beginning in seventh grade and on into high school, I had girlfriends. Well, two specific girlfriends to be precise. All girls that age have girlfriends, I'm told, but I'm fairly certain most don't have girlfriends the way I did. At the age of twelve, I somehow became best friends with the prettiest girl in the school, the one most likely to be named a future prom queen. She was somewhat delicate and definitely a femme. I was definitely not delicate, and to call me a tomboy would've been an understatement. Nevertheless, we spent hours on the phone every evening, ostensibly doing our homework, but actually finding anything and everything to talk about just so we wouldn't have to say good night. I would have done anything for her. I longed to be the knight to her fairy princess. I didn't quite have the words for that, but I was very aware of the feelings, and I didn't need to be told I was definitely over the line of "different" at that point.

By the time I truly fell in love at the age of fifteen with the second girl to claim my heart, I knew without a doubt that if asked, I should not tell. I still don't know precisely how I came to understand that silence was the better part of valor, or maybe just survival, but I did not voice the consuming passion I harbored for her. I grew up in a very small town in the pre-Stonewall era, before the word "gay" was used to refer to homosexuals, and was raised by unsophisticated but instinctively intelligent parents. I have absolutely no doubt my mother "knew" at just about the same time I did that I wasn't headed for the straight and narrow path.

I can't even imagine how my life would have evolved had she asked me then and if I had had the courage to answer. But she didn't, and I hadn't. And it was years before either of us did.

It's terrible to live with a secret, especially when what you're hiding is the heart of your existence and should be the foundation upon which you build your life. When I was eighteen, I was foolish enough to think that just because I didn't speak of something, no one would know. Apparently, people still believe that or would have you believe that they do. Hence, the ridiculous nationally endorsed policy of "Don't ask, don't tell."

I stopped believing in that pretense the first time I brought a lover home.

I went away to college, not very far, but far enough to save my life. I planned to start anew and create for myself a true and honest life. I had no idea what that would be, of course, because I had yet to see beyond my own self-constructed wall of silence. I had never heard the word "lesbian." I *did* know there were women who loved women, and I knew what they were called. I had never heard one of those words used in a positive way. I also knew, although I had yet to say the words to myself or acknowledge the truth, that I was one of them.

But I was lucky. I fell in love, and this time, I did tell.

I have to smile now when I realize that the telling of it here will sound like — well, a romance novel. I literally saw her for the first time across a crowded room, and, yes, it was love at first sight. I was a freshman and she was a sophomore, and it was the first dorm meeting of the year. I had no idea what her name was and couldn't remember ever having seen her before, but the moment I did, I couldn't see anyone else. She was like no woman I'd ever seen. She had long, long dark hair and incredible blue eyes, and she was wearing blue jeans and her father's maroon shirt. I think it was her father's shirt that made me realize she was different from any of the girls I'd ever known — that, and the fact that she didn't seem to care what anyone else thought of her. It was that mixture of independence and self-confidence, and a healthy dose of femme butchness, that captivated me. She was beautiful, and she was strong, and she was everything I had ever dreamed of.

Then and there, I determined I would know her. Must know her. I set about making myself indispensable, which initially translated into making myself a pest. I walked her to class; I hung out in the student center waiting for her between classes; I ate every meal I possibly could in the dorm cafeteria with her. I thought about her, dreamed about her, every second of every day. It took a few months, but eventually, she realized I wasn't going away. And not only that, she began to return my unspoken affection. Halfway through the second semester, we were alone in her room, and she was upset about something. I remember moving to the arm of her chair and her leaning into me. The next thing I remember was kissing her. And close upon that came terror.

I loved her, you see — adored her with the passionate innocence of first love. I would have thrown down my cape for her to walk across a muddy street, if I'd had a cape and the streets weren't paved. I would have given my life for her happiness. I would certainly have died before making her *unhappy*, and I feared I might have with that kiss. So, I did the only reasonable thing. I ran like hell.

Fortunately for me, she was braver and also more practical than I. It took her until morning to discover my hiding place, whereupon she unceremoniously instructed me to get my coat because we were going for a walk. Once outside in the chill March morning, nearly alone on the deserted campus, she said the words that would set me free and forever define my life. Instinctively, she knew exactly what I needed to hear, and I will be eternally grateful to her for that and so many things.

She looked at me as I stumbled along by her side, wondering when she was going to say something to bring my world crashing down. What she said instead was really very simple. "I don't know what happened last night. But I know that nothing that happens between us can be wrong."

Those simple words from that particular woman were all I needed to hear to understand that I was fundamentally okay. That the things I felt and desired and longed for were right and good. It didn't take us very long to return to the dorm and take the next step. Thankfully, some things come naturally and don't require much discussion.

Of course, being young and in love, I wanted everyone to know about it. Since that wasn't possible, I at least wanted to bring her home to meet my parents. Foolishly, I thought that when I did, we would be able to keep the true nature of our relationship a secret. I hadn't counted on the fact that anyone looking at us would be able to tell. Certainly, my mother could.

It was close to the end of the semester, and we knew we would be separated for the summer. The mere thought of being apart from her consumed me with despair. I remember very clearly sitting at the picnic table in my parents' backyard on a sunny May morning. Her hair was shining in the sunlight, a deep rich brown that fanned across her back, nearly halfway to her hips. She'd just washed it, and I was helping her untangle the long tresses, running them through my fingers as we talked.

My mother stood in the kitchen door, watching us. I know now that everything we felt for one another must have been clearly apparent, but it took me by surprise when I walked into the house and the first words my mother said were, "What's going on between you and..."

Turning point. I cannot to this day fathom what prompted her to confront me. We'd never had the kind of relationship where we discussed difficult issues. But the question was out, and I had seconds to make a decision. I will forever wonder what would have happened had I answered differently. My answer to that question would define the nature and boundaries of our relationship for decades.

The "right" answer to this question and the right time to ask or answer it is almost certainly different for every mother and daughter. It's a decision we each must make, mother or daughter, based upon what we are willing to risk and what we might ultimately gain. It is easy to say that honesty is always best, but we all know honesty can be accompanied by loss. I wish that were not the case. I wish we never had to consider in our own lives and in our relationships with those we love, the policy of "Don't ask, don't tell."

It's a policy that's been around for a long time, but as each mother, motivated by love and compassion, dares to ask, and each daughter, raised to trust, answers without fear, we can make it obsolete in all aspects of our lives. I know that when I said to my mother, "You know that I'm a lesbian, don't you, Mom?" and she answered, "Yes, honey, I do," we embarked on the best years of our lives together. Looking back, I regret that it took me twenty years between the first asking and the telling, but ultimately, I'm grateful she asked, and that I told.

## J.M. Redmann

Biloxi, Mississippi was the birthplace of writer J.M. Redmann. She now resides in New Orleans and likes to say that she "lives, works, and frolics in that city in a swamp." A voracious reader, J.M. expresses sincere gratitude to "all the writers who came before me, especially the women."

The wildly popular Micky Knight mystery series, featuring a plucky and complicated lesbian detective based in New Orleans, has received many awards and accolades including Editor's Choice of the San Francisco Chronicle, three shortlists for Lambda Literary Awards, and a Lambda win for her third book, *The Intersection of Law and Desire*. The fourth novel in the series, *Lost Daughters*, was published by W.W. Norton and will soon be reprinted along with the third book by J.M.'s latest project: a new press called Bywater Books, co-founded along with author Marianne K. Martin and publisher Kelly Smith.

Bywater Books will be publishing the fifth installment in the Micky Knight series, *The Death of a Dying Man*. Meanwhile, J.M. Redmann continues to work on Micky's further adventures and other novels as well.

# Lost Daughter

## Memoir by J.M. Redmann

*February 1, 1921 – February 29, 1984.*

I FINALLY WENT back to the grave, to see the red clay become green grass, the scar in the earth turn verdant and smooth. It was ten years then, it is twenty years now. I was nineteen when they first diagnosed the cancer, away in college. My mother didn't call me home, the daughter of German immigrants, she would not so burden her daughter. Not until there was no choice. I saw the scar, the smooth place on her chest where her breast had been when the cancer came back, in the year that I cared for her. I was twenty-six then. The cancer took her life in slow inches. I was twenty-eight when she died.

She was the youngest of eight children, ten really, but only eight made it beyond the cradle. The first to die, of those that survived. The rest of her sisters and brothers, my aunts and uncles, are still alive or made it to a much older age. Aunt Edna, 99, Aunt Lena, 94, Uncle Carl, 97, Uncle Herb, 91, Uncle Frank, 87, and Aunt Marie and Uncle Art are still here. The youngest, Naomi Ruth, but she went by Ruth, was 63.

I never came out to my mother. I didn't have to. She knew. I couldn't see it then, I was just stepping into the muddy waters of sexuality and had only the perspective of a bare twenty-some years. I wasn't old enough to think that the past could so predict the future. Looking back now, I think how could she not know? I was a tomboy's tomboy, the few dolls given to me were fodder to be run over by the tanks and trucks that I asked for. There are more pictures of me in torn jeans and t-shirt than dresses — and those were the days when we took pictures when we dressed up. I did, in my early twenties — when I was ready — tell her that I was a lesbian. She shrugged and asked me what else I was going to do with my life. She told me about her roommates during the war, two of them were a couple. It was a brief conversation, nothing had really changed, except that I knew she knew. I lived in New York City then. She remained in the small town on the Mississippi Gulf Coast where I had grown up. Our visits were holidays mostly. Phone calls now and then, more after my father died. I was busy being young and living in Manhattan. There would be time, she was the youngest of eight and her older sisters and brothers were still alive.

They all came to her funeral.

I want to ask her how she knew with such ease, how did she come to terms with her dyke daughter before I did?

WHEN I WAS in eighth grade, my teacher assigned us to ask our parents about their history, specifically what person they most admired. My mother named Eleanor Roosevelt. As most eighth grade assignments tended to be, it wasn't long, so I merely completed the requirements, let my mother name Eleanor Roosevelt, and mentioned the war. The Second World War, the one safely in my past, the one that shaped my parents and their future—even to the end of their lifes. My father and mother are both buried in a veteran's cemetery, earned by my father's service in the South Pacific.

But I know the history now, know how Eleanor Roosevelt stood up to the DAR when they refused to let Marion Anderson sing in their hall, I recently saw a picture of her, with a broad and confident smile on her face, sitting in the cockpit of an open plane behind one of the Tuskegee Airman who was piloting it, proving that black men could fly as well as white men. In ninth grade, the year after my mother named Eleanor Roosevelt as the person she most admired, my school finally, fully integrated. It was 1969, the year that all the Mississippi schools realized that they had lost every court battle.

I want to ask her what it was like living in a small Southern town, moving there in 1953, staying there until the day she died. How did she handle my New Orleans grandmother, who insisted on using one cab company because they hired only white drivers? How did I know, at eleven, when I heard my grandmother say those words that she was wrong? (And at eleven, I went along with the wrong, didn't confront my grandmother. Now I wonder if that isn't original sin, a wrong so heavy in the air, that no one escapes it. How could I confront the mother of my father at eleven? Yet . . . how could I not? I didn't. The sin remains.)

AFTER MY MOTHER had graduated college, she moved to Chicago, lived there working on a newspaper. With no plan or thought, I have followed the arc of her life, moving to New York

City after college. I want to ask her what her life had been like there, what other ways had I followed her footsteps beyond that broad outline? She met my father there. They both wanted to be writers. I went to Chicago a few years ago, walked the streets, they were unfamiliar to me, only a few names that I had heard in passing conversations between my parents. The Art Institute, Michigan Ave., the lake during a thunderstorm. But they were only memories that I had heard with the impatience of a growing child who couldn't imagine how fiercely I'd want to know, were you here? Did you walk this block? What places did we have in common, forty years apart?

I want to ask her about her life there, the turmoil and tumult of the war, a brief passing reference to being thought a German spy. She didn't say by whom or whether it was a passing comment or a serious accusation.

I WAS A daughter when I left home, off for college at eighteen, on the cusp of adulthood, not yet fully there. When I came back to care for her, when the cancer came back, I was a daughter who had become an adult, but my mother was ill, racked with the pain of a cancer that had spread to her bones. She took morphine every four hours for the pain. The questions I wanted to ask, thought that I would have decades to seek the answers, were lost in the tangle of her illness. Instead, our intimacy became one of physical necessity, washing her, the scarred place where her breast had been, placing suppositories in her vagina, my hand gloved, not to be clinical but to show respect even as I invaded this private place, also aware that it was the lesbian daughter with my hand there. Changing the bag of urine, emptying the bedside toilet, ointment on the sore where her chin rested on her collarbone, her head too weak to turn away.

Then the day came when I couldn't wake her. I walked outside to watch the sunrise, knowing soon that I would call the doctor. She lived a week beyond that. I never asked what finally killed her, her failing kidneys, the calcium from her bones overwhelming them, or the fragile bones breaking, her neck, her ribs into her lungs.

And I wondered, if my father and mother are both dead, am I a daughter anymore?

WHEN MY SISTER and I cleaned out the closets, in the back, on the top shelf, I found the poetry that she had written as a young woman, as a woman of my age then. I also found the journal she kept after the diagnosis, when she knew that the days she had planned to have, after retirement and my sister going off to college, would not come. The dream deferred and deferred, so faint, until it could only be a bare flicker passed down to the next generation.

I want to ask her what she dreamed of writing, I want to ask her how she got that dream from the Indiana farm she grew up on. I remember the books she read to us as children, but I want to ask her about the books she read as an adult, which ones inspired her, spoke to her, changed her life.

I want to tell her that she passed her dream on to me.

I had written some things, a few short stories, some plays, but never sustained it. Not in her life did I ever show the will to sit down and write and write and write and re-write until a book appeared. And then another book and then another. Even the few scraps that I did produce remained scattered sheets of paper, haphazard piles in a battered old file cabinet. I published nothing in her lifetime.

I STOOD AT her grave, with my third book in hand, the one I thought she would be most proud of. The one with the inscription that says, *To N. Ruth Redmann, February 1, 1921 – February 29, 1984. Too late, of course.* The lesbian daughter, the lesbian book, would she have been proud?

The grass was green, the sky gray, the only sound the wind.

## Jean Stewart

Jean Stewart is the author of one stand-alone novel and five installments of the Isis sci-fi/fantasy series. She has twice been a finalist for Lambda Literary Awards and has had several short pieces published in anthologies including a story called "Scoring," which is featured in the just-published anthology, *Back to Basics: A Butch/Femme Anthology* from Bella Books.

Jean was born and raised in the suburbs of Philadelphia. She says, "My sixth grade teacher, Bill Redfern, told me, 'You could be a writer.' That simple expression of his confidence in me changed my life."

Jean loves books, music, movies, dogs, and people who laugh. She was a teacher and a coach for a while, but now she writes. She lives near Seattle with her partner, Susie, two badly behaved dogs, and a reclusive Maine Coon cat named Emily Dickinson.

# World Without End

## Memoir by Jean Stewart

MY MOTHER WAS named Henrietta, after a character in a book. Neither of us ever knew what book or character that was. My grandmother had come across a story she liked, and so the name was there in her head in mid-March of 1920, when my mother was born.

My mother never liked her name. She thought it old-fashioned and even more than the polysyllabic length, she disliked the inevitable nicknames, Henny or Etta. I always thought it was an interesting name. Henrietta; it sounded musical and a little amusing. People smiled when they said my mother's name, and that seemed somehow quite fitting. My mother was that kind of person; a person who, without much effort on her part, made people smile. The uniqueness of her name suited her.

My mother spent her childhood and youth in southern Delaware, about twenty odd miles or so from the Atlantic Ocean. She had three brothers and two sisters. George, the brother born before my mother, died of diphtheria before he reached his third birthday. Coming into the world a year after his death, my mother was the last child. My grandfather was a telegrapher for the B&O Railroad, a secure job of skill and expertise in those days when radio was in its infancy. Yet in the months after Black Friday, he and every other man in town ended up out of work. Their family began to move from place to place, as my grandfather went anywhere he could to earn a wage, and the Great Depression settled over the nation like the sub-zero temperatures of an Arctic wind.

Mom told me once that they moved eight times in the course of three years, usually just staying ahead of the creditors. At one point, my grandfather tried to start his own business, and made gin in the bathtub, but my grandmother was a staunch Methodist. She pulled the stopper one night, sending the profits down the drain, and that was the end of that enterprise. At this time my mother had two dresses and one pair of shoes. My Aunt Stella and Uncle Bill went around to the finer addresses in town with their red wagon, picking up and delivering the baskets of clothes that my grandmother washed and ironed for an income. My grandfather had a rifle and spent most of his unemployed days "traipsing around" the pastoral southern Delaware countryside, hunting rabbits, squirrels, and quail. The family made meals of whatever he managed to bring home. My mother said my grandfather was not a good shot. There were many meals that consisted of canned beans and bread. Surprisingly, Uncle Bill, a teenager himself, learned to shoot incredibly well. It was a good thing, for during the worst years of the Depression, while Hoover was still President, they had no other meat than what sat on the table laced with birdshot.

My mother said she had eaten terrible things in those days. Luckily, she'd been made to eat so much spinach and okra that she never in my entire life served it to us. She said she had even eaten muskrat once; the meat was black and tasted awful. My grandmother taught her how to season with a little salt, a little pepper, or dill—or, if you could barter for it, butter—cooking long and slow, so that the toughest old rabbit melted in your mouth. She always said the simplest food could taste like a royal feast if you seasoned it well and let it cook long and slow. And she said if you were hungry enough, you'd try to eat just about anything.

When I was in college, she told me once, "At least my kids never knew what it was to go to bed hungry." It did not strike until years later how much of her early experience was revealed in that remark.

Even more clearly, I remember the wonder in my mother's voice when she described how her family had moved to a town with a free library. From then on, no matter where they moved, she was always on the lookout for the closest library. In the library she could sit and read, and let the worries and uncertainties slip away from her. As a child, she was afraid she would come home from school one day and find her family's meager furniture and belongings stacked up on the street. She saw families all around her being evicted for rents owed or defaulting mortgages, and she knew anything worth a few dollars was being repossessed by banks when loan payments weren't made on time. But in the library, poor as she was, my mother was truly free. She filled her head with stories and history and dreams. She read her books and convinced herself that if she worked hard she could survive hard times.

My grandfather moved the family to Philadelphia in the late Thirties, and my mother left high school with a year unfinished. She took a series of clerk and salesgirl jobs, then qualified to be an operator for Bell Telephone. She was a working woman in the Forties, independent and goal-oriented, and steadily becoming increasingly well read. Though later in life she pronounced that she didn't believe in "Women's Lib," she was a feminist front-trunner. According to my Aunt Stella, my mother did what she wanted and went where she pleased. She was an attractive woman, but uninterested in men, because according to her they only wanted someone to cook and do laundry and clean up after them.

Then she met my father.

He was a Scot who emigrated to America after serving Britain in World War II. He was looking for a new life and a job, and had fallen into a habit of watching my mother coming home each night, walking along the alley that ran along the back of his sister's row house. Intrigued, he asked my Aunt May to introduce them. According to Mom, my father and Aunt May had stood by the picket fence, my father dressed in a suit and wearing a wide tie. Mom was with her mother, passing by on their way to the 69th Street trolley. My mother thought nothing of the meeting at the time, though she was caught by the soft Glasgow brogue and his dapper attire. A few days later, on her way home from work in a driving rainstorm, my father unexpectedly appeared at her side and walked her home. My mother said he was wearing that suit and tie again, and this time he was soaked through. She learned years later that he had been circling the block for a half an hour, trying to make their meeting appear to be a fortunate accident, when it began to rain.

My mother loved my father. There was no other person in her life who meant what he did to her. I did not understand the connection until I found my own love, but that's the way of monumental things, isn't it? You have to find out for yourself.

They married and began working to build a life together. My mother left her job when she became pregnant with my older brother. Then fourteen months after my brother was born, I arrived. My parents had saved up enough money to make a down payment on a little Cape Cod style house in the Philadelphia suburbs, near Swarthmore. It was a peaceful, green section of the world filled with grassy lawns, tall old oaks and maples, and children. My younger brother came a few years later and completed our family. My mother told me she was surprised to realize how happy she was. With a home and her own family she had stumbled upon something she had always been searching for, without ever knowing it. She spent the next three decades settled in that one place, putting down roots she had not known she wanted.

She told me many times that those were the best years of her life.

During the Fifties and Sixties, for one week each summer, my family went to the southern Delaware seashore for a vacation. As we drove along in the '49 Ford, and then later the '57 Pontiac, with the windows rolled down and the hot, moist summer air swirling in, Mom stared at the passing scenery and grumbled aloud. She found it hard to accept that the Delaware she saw before her was not the same place she had known as a girl. The landscape had changed. The flat, dusty roads were paved. Long, narrow tomato fields and small truck farms were giving way to vast fields of corn and soybeans. She didn't like the honky-tonk of the boardwalk, the junky tourist shops selling seashells and Coppertone, the kiddie carnival rides, the sno-cones and cotton candy. She would tell my Father, my brothers, and me of how, when she was young, Rehoboth, Lewes, Fenwick Island or Bethany were each just a cluster of fisherman's houses and a gas station or two. She missed the quiet serenity of the old towns, where small houses of white-washed clapboard had been perched at the brink of the Atlantic for the past two centuries, enduring hurricanes and hot summer sun without much change. We thought she was crazy. We liked the jazzy-feel of the resort town that Rehoboth was even then becoming, and we loved the adventure of traveling to somewhere that seemed to exist simply as a place for people to go have fun.

Mom would say that all she needed to enjoy herself was a place to sit and watch the water rolling up on the shore.

The ocean was the one constant: always the same, unchanging and ever present, for her and for us. After we arrived at the beach and moved the luggage and the brown paper bags of groceries from the car trunk into the little rented cottage, Mom let us run down for our first look at the ocean. One year—I think I was eight or so—I remember clambering up a dune at the edge of the roadway. When I reached the top I stood, breathless, struck absolutely through with what I found. My brothers rushed by me, intent on charging down to the water's edge, and my father went after them, leaving me on my promontory of sand. The bright morning sun glinted on swells of jade-green water, and a fresh July wind gusted into my face, filled with that strange mix of brine and sun and intangible things. I remember feeling suspended in time, feeling pierced with some unknown poignancy. I think I knew, even then, that this was something precious, and I knew just as irrevocably that the moment would not last. My heart felt as if it had inflated like a balloon, filling up my chest and pressing against my ribs. Some part of my spirit was dying to get out and soar. At last, my mother came alongside of me and took my hand. We looked at each other, grinning, then both gazed at the sea. I felt so much it was painful, and I understood none of it. There were no words that would not diminish the power of the vast landscape before us, and so we didn't speak. Instead, we just stood together and looked our fill.

I have all sorts of memories like that flickering through my head just now, images emerging from the shadows into light, and then disappearing again. Snapshots of moments when my mother stood with me and together we looked at something, long and deep, acknowledging the gems of glory that were tossed in our paths each day by whatever unseen Benefactor might be with us out there in the everlasting night surrounding our small planet. I understand, now, long after the gift was given, that my mother gave me the way I pause every once in a while and savor the world. She gave me the way I live my life, the way I open my heart.

We stood many an evening in my backyard on Villanova Avenue, among the clipped lawns and tall trees of what was then Rutledge. On hundreds, if not thousands, of occasions, we lingered to watch the setting sun hover in red and golden skies beyond tall trees. Sometimes, if my father hadn't gone too crazy with the trimming sheers the autumn before, there were lilacs blooming nearby, and sometimes there were bumble bees buzzing among the clusters of sweet-smelling tea roses lining the picket fence. Sometimes my father was about ten feet away, checking the tomato plants. Sometimes my brothers were yelling at me to rejoin the game of wiffleball underway, and our wonderful, brown dog Candy was there, that happy grin on her face as she stood by my knee, waiting to see what I was up to and where I would go. This was the same back yard where the clothes blew on the line each afternoon for thirty years, where the robins hunted for worms, and where we children were sent on dandelion-digging details by my father when we misbehaved once too often.

In the summer, we swam in the three-foot blue pool, and my mother brought us Ritz crackers and glasses of Kool-Aid on a little tray when we had to get out at 4:30 or so, before my Dad got home from work. We played at being cowboys, or soldiers, or rustlers, or gladiators. The kickball world series was enacted every day. My mother often checked on what we were doing through the back window, her voice issuing through the dark, opaque screen like God's when we were caught in some mischief. I can still hear the tone that would stop me in my tracks. One word. One command to obeisance. "Jean!"

In the autumn, my mother and father raked orange and red leaves into huge piles, enlisting us children to load our wagon with them and move leaves out to the curb. We usually lost control at some point and dove into the leafy stacks, rolling around laughing until we could barely catch out breath. When I look back on it my mother was always there, always the center of the fun, always laughing with us then organizing us back to work so that the job was eventually done. At the end of the day, we burned the monstrous piles of color by the curb. We would stand together, usually tired, cold and hungry, watching the little flames flicker over the leaves, consuming them. A mild autumnal breeze took the smoke up and away, into the deepening blue of a late afternoon sky.

In the winter, we built snow forts in the yard and pelted each other and the neighbor children for hours, or until someone who wasn't a Stewart was crying. I developed a wicked sidearm. We weren't allowed to take our coats or scarves off if we worked up a sweat, yet we always did, flinging our garments away with the mad amnesia and abandon only a very over-heated child has. I lost a lot of mittens in those days.

In the midst of it all, I knew I was happy, and I knew I was blessed. And I thought my beautiful childhood would never end.

But as I entered puberty, my father changed. In an effort to improve his weekly salary, he left a job he enjoyed and took a new job down in the city. The new job turned out to be a grinding and grim experience for my father. He didn't like the hard men he worked with, and he didn't like his bosses. He tried to find another job and could not. I am sure he felt trapped. Gradually, he became deeply frustrated. I only know he rarely smiled after he made this change. And he was angry all the time.

I am not sure when I became the catalyst for the anger his life circumstances brought him, but at some point I did. By then, I was beginning to suspect there was something different deep inside me, something the rest of the world didn't want me to be. Always talented in sports and fiercely competitive, I was given the message in a thousand subtle, painful lessons: instead of besting the boys in the neighborhood in a thousand of subtle, painful lessons: instead of besting the boys in my neighborhood, I would do much better sitting on the sidelines and cheering for them. An intelligent, fun-loving, insatiably curious, and adventurous girl, I was given the message that these were not ladylike qualities. At one point, it seemed like everything I was, I was not supposed to be. I read too many books, I was too good at games, I was too talkative with strangers. What started as a disheartening entry into adolescence became a nightmare as I realized that the rest of my life would be lived under these increasingly strait-jacketing constraints.

By virtue of genetics, I was not a girly girl. I was tall, lean and favored boyish clothes like Levis and large hand-me-down cotton oxford shirts from my older cousins. During that time, I wasn't even sure I liked girls. The girls I knew in the neighborhood and in school seemed to spend much of their time obsessively worrying about their appearance, or being cruel to one another. I avoided them. Without understanding why, I felt more and more uncomfortable. I only knew I didn't seem to fit in anywhere. There seemed to be no one else even remotely like me on the planet.

Awkward and aloof, I had few friends.

At the dinner table, and in the living room watching the one television set in the house, my father waged a campaign of criticism, venting his own unhappiness by finding fault with me. His blunt comments and my sullen silences became our only dialogues. Within six months I had retreated completely from any social interaction with my family, going upstairs to read, or out on long, rambling walks with the dog in order to separate myself from the painful encounters with my father.

About this time, my mother insisted I help her each night after dinner, drying the dishes while she washed. I wanted to play the radio, to listen to the latest soul or rock tunes while we worked, but she wanted to talk, and so talk we did. During those nightly half hours together, alone in the kitchen, I told her all my youthful dreams and heartaches and uncertainties. We usually started out talking about incidental things and by the time I finished, I had revealed the secrets of my heart. In the midst of my adolescent angst, against my will, and sometimes without my knowledge, I revealed who I was and what was important to me. She maintained her purpose in making me help her each night was to teach me how to do kitchen chores and to create in me a work ethic. She all-knowingly informed me I would need both when I married, one day. However, she taught me far more than that during those sessions together over the soap suds and dish rack. She taught me that I was important to her, that my feelings and plans mattered.

She also made it a point to tell me that my father loved me. As with any truth sent through a messenger, I was never actually reassured on that fact. To be frank, looking back on it now that I am the age my father was then, I think my father knew I was a lesbian. I also think the knowledge disgusted him. I believe he abhorred me, and I believe from the moment of his realization of my true, if latent, nature, he was rejecting me in an almost primal reaction. No one in those days wanted kinship with something as horrific as a queer. Certainly not my father, who became more openly prejudiced and narrow-minded as he grew older. He didn't like anything that did not reflect his own social dynamic. He defined the world by his own points of reference, and anything outside his understanding, he despised.

In my mother's kitchen, I came to understand that my mother would always love me, no matter what. However, she would not put her marriage or her relationship with my father in jeopardy. I became the sacrifice my mother made to my father's anger.

When I was fourteen, my father began beating me. Sometimes once or twice a month. Sometimes every day. It happened most often when my mother wasn't around; for years, I feared coming into the house and realizing I was there alone with him. There were times when he found what he considered to be a good reason to hit me, and he roared about it, working himself into a frenzy before he cornered me. Just as often there was no good reason. Those times the beating began with a long, icy stare; I have never seen anything as awful as the hate I saw in my father's eyes. The silent beatings were the worst—as if the event was stripped of any excuse or trappings of cause and effect, and he hated me for knowing he could not be anything but the man I saw at that moment.

By the time I was fifteen, I had given up trying to placate his wrath with good behavior or compliance. Instead, I tried to keep a low profile, trying to stay as far away from him as I could. I hid in my room, reading an unending parade of library books or writing in the journals I filled with line after line of left-handed scrawl. I stayed out after school each afternoon, playing sports, volunteering for projects, or just walking for hours. By then, I was also becoming adept at recognizing the signs. My father gave unconscious cues that told me he was in a rage about something that had happened at work, or about the Phillies or the Eagles losing a game he had bet on, or some event I knew nothing about that had left him feeling powerless. There would be something in the set of his mouth, in the glaring brilliance of his eyes. When I saw it, I learned to go absolutely stock still, to blend into the paint on the wall, to try to do everything possible in order to prevent him from noticing me. I was living a shadow life, trying to disappear from our family, in a quietly desperate effort to avoid the increasingly frequent explosions of violence.

Only once did I stop him. I was standing by the kitchen counter one night, pouring a glass of milk and in the process emptying the half gallon carton, when he came into the kitchen. As I had developed a habit of never turning my back on a door, I saw him as his pace quickened, and he moved in on me. He shouted, "Selfish pig! That's the last of it!" as he swung at me. I was a month shy of eighteen, and I had had enough. I blocked the blow with an elbow, flung open the refrigerator door and grabbed the half gallon I had brought home earlier that night at my mother's request. When I showed the full, unopened carton to him, he actually got visibly angrier, confirming my belief that my supposed selfishness was just another pretext. He advanced on me, and I set the carton aside and for the first time did my own yelling. "What is wrong with you?" I demanded. Astounded, he stopped. And then in a voice that seemed to pour out of my lungs, full of power and fury, I stated, "It ends now. The next time you hit me, I'm hitting back." My fists were balled up at my sides, trembling. The blood was pounding in my head like a drum and oh so badly I wanted him to start the first fair fight between us. Both enraged, we stood there, a few feet apart for so long it seemed like a breach had occurred in the cosmic continuum of time. Minutes slid by. I think neither of us knew what to do; the usual order of things had changed abruptly. In a quieter and far less intimidating aside, he finally muttered that I was "getting a smart mouth," and then left the room.

He never tried to hit me again.

I didn't realize until I was in college that most families did not live like this. When I did finally comprehend, during my training to become a teacher, that what I had endured was child abuse, I was too ashamed to speak of it to anyone. Instead, too poor to afford therapy, too proud to admit I was emotionally scarred by what had happened, I read dozens of self-help and psychology books. In the next ten years, I worked hard not to become a duplicate of my father. I struggled to set aside my fears, and then gradually my anger. I slowly discovered I could become who I wanted to be, I could love whom I wished, and I could create my own life.

Somewhere along the way, in a deliberate act of self-preservation, I put my venomous father, whom I had once loved with all my heart, out of my realm of human acquaintance. I had succeeded in forgiving him, but for me he was still such a harmful personality that there was little use in trying to interact with him as I once had—as father and daughter. He was forever embittered, forever the man he evolved into when I was fourteen.

When he died suddenly one autumn twenty years ago, I did not cry. I felt relieved.

My mother was a far more difficult relationship to understand. During all those episodes, when my father sometimes hit me so hard that he knocked me to the ground, Mom did not once intervene. I might be huddled in a ball at his feet, sobbing in stark terror as he kicked me, and she stood in the background, wringing her hands, looking upset, and not saying a word. My mother never made an attempt to intercept him when he grabbed me and hauled me away. My mother never stopped his hand as he casually delivered a slap across my face at the dinner table. Worse, she never let on that the way my father treated me was wrong or cruel, or even that it angered her. And when I was finally old enough and enlightened enough to comprehend the enormity of her betrayal, I'll admit, it left me feeling utterly devastated.

There was a period of time in my early twenties, when I walked away from my family and I did not look back. For years, I stayed away, at Thanksgiving, at Christmas, and all the special birthdays in between. My mother called every once in a while to talk about family things, but I never spoke with her long. I always found a reason to end the call. I never called my parents. This wasn't because I was still angry with my father. True, I had given up on ever having anything resembling a father-daughter relationship with him. One can do that, you know. Hurt someone who loves you long enough and hard enough and they will simply not be able to love you anymore. No, the reason I stayed away from my parents for years and years was because I could not forgive my mother for her part in what happened to me in our home. I couldn't forgive her for her passive choice to let my father run our family, even when it meant I dwelt in hell.

Once I figured out what she had done, it took me nearly fifteen years to get over it.

But I eventually did forgive her. Though it sounds like a weak defense, I finally accepted that she was doing what she thought best according to the family dynamics of the time. She was as much a product of her generation's preconceived notions as I am. However, by the time I fully forgave, I was on the other side of the continent, completely involved in a caring, vital relationship with the woman I love. Finding love does that; it gives you the strength and good will to reach out and reconnect, even with people who have hurt you.

Still the difficulties of travel logistics and work demands prevented me from getting home much. My mother had ended up returning to the countryside of southern Delaware, living alone in a ranch-style home about twenty miles west of Rehoboth Beach. I managed to spend one week a year with her, sometimes more, but not often. We spoke every Sunday on the phone, though, and wrote letters and cards. In the odd way that distance promotes honesty and effort, we became very close. When we spoke, it was as if I was once more in the kitchen with her, methodically drying the dishes that she had washed, and showing her my heart.

Another fifteen years slid by in the slipstream of time.

And then one October afternoon this past autumn, she passed away in her sleep after a short illness. She told me a month before the end that she was more than ready to go. Surprisingly, ever the optimist, she confessed she did not believe in an afterlife, but that it didn't matter. Except for the sudden loss of my father twenty years before, she thought she had had a good life.

I told her I believed God gave us more than one chance to get things right. I thought we'd both be back, and if I was lucky, we'd meet again. She laughed a little at that. I told her I thought my father would be there to greet her when she crossed. She only shook her head then, her gaze turned inward with such a look of defeat that it silenced me. As I sat there with her in the warm sunshine, I realized I truly wished she would find after death the one person she cherished above all others. And that's when it struck me that I loved her entirely, beyond any bruise my own soul might still bear from those times. I loved her enough to forget that the man who owned her heart had purposefully hurt me. I guess it's true. Love forgives all things.

Not so long ago, I stood with my brothers and their grown children on the Indian River Inlet Bridge, releasing my mother's ashes into the wind. Caught in a swirling updraft, white-gray dust danced gracefully up and away, then drifted down and surrendered to the churning water rushing below us as the tide went out to sea. As she wished, my mother has merged with the land and sea off Rehoboth. And now I sit here trying to write of our relationship with truth and mercy. It is perhaps the most difficult thing I have ever done.

When I was a girl growing up in the Fifties and early Sixties, the world was a much more strictly defined place than it is now. People were categorized in groups and lived their lives within the boxes those groups defined. Men, women, boys, girls, black, white, Hispanic, Asian, Native American, heterosexual, gay, lesbian, bisexual, transgendered, and an infinite collection of other clearly defined sub-categories. So many of us spent our days trying to hide who we were, for good reason. Many Americans spent large quantities of time being afraid of or despising the groups in the other boxes. There are some people who wouldn't mind if our country again embraced the way things were then. I guess some people need a group to exclude, a societally condoned exercise in discrimination to make them feel better. It's strangely like the way my father needed someone who he could hit. Cultivating hate seems to be as much a part of human nature as expressing love is.

But America today is not the same place where I grew up. The boxes are breaking down, and the groups are merging. The prejudice that was commonplace forty years ago is still around, but it is not quite so acceptable anymore. In a thousand acts of defiance and persistence, I — and a million others like me who will not be treated as less than their brothers or sisters — have helped to cause change.

My father wouldn't like the place America is becoming. But I know my mother was all right with it. She told me once that she loved my partner Susie and thought of her as her daughter-in-law. But then my mother was a loving woman, and my father was a prideful man. If America is ever going to grow into the land I think it eventually could be, it will be due to people who love. The hard part is this: love is a verb.

America has changed a great deal since the 1920s, when the coastal towns of Delaware were small fishing villages. The roads weren't yet paved, and boats were the main means of transport from one town to another. In those days, people had so few changes of clothes that most bedrooms had no need of closets, and when an airplane engine was heard chugging overhead, it was such an event that everyone ran out of the house to try to see it. While living in a tiny rented house in a little one street town, my mother discovered a free library; she wandered inside and opened a book. As the fear and desperation of the Great Depression swirled around her, she returned again and again to the nourishing peace where thousands of glorious tales and millions of beautiful ideas were contained in the pages of books. Row upon row of books. Enough for a lifetime of contemplation. The library became her church.

Henrietta was a dreamer. And she raised me to be a dreamer, too.

World without end, Amen.

## Cate Swannell

Born in Birmingham, England, Cate Swannell now lives on the Gold Coast, Australia, after becoming an Australian citizen in 1985. She received a Bachelor of Arts from the University of Queensland and majored in English Literature and Semiotics, with a dash of journalism and psychology for good measure. Since then Cate has enjoyed a career in journalism including stints as a copy editor and page designer.

Partnered for seven years to a Midwest American, Cate has long been familiar with the issues and difficulties distance and travel present and says that she and her partner "qualify as members of that unique phenomenon of the Internet age—the long-distance relationship." This has afforded her the chance to visit the United States on numerous occasions for book and writing opportunities. She is currently at work on the beginning stages of her third novel.

# Damaged Goods

## Fiction by Cate Swannell

"OKAY, IT'S OFFICIAL. I now want my mother."

I looked over at the older woman sitting next to me and I knew, just knew, that I was being pathetic. Delaney's blue eyes didn't say it, but the bleating little voice inside kept telling me so. *Quit being such a baby. It's just a cut finger.*

"Do you want me to call her?" she asked.

I looked back at my left hand, which I was holding gingerly with my right. I could feel the blood pooling inside the light wrapping the doctor had left me. It was pulsing out of my body at a rapid rate, and the sensation left me scared and nauseous.

*You don't want your mother*, the calm part of my brain said. *What you want is for the woman next to you to quit looking at you like you're a freak, and put her arms around you and tell you it's going to be all right. What you want is to rest your head on her shoulder and know that someone else is in control.*

I swallowed hard and tried not to puke on the floor of the emergency room.

"No," I answered, my tongue feeling about 17 sizes too big for my mouth. "By the time she gets down here it'll all be over anyway. Better to wait till we find out what the damage is, I guess."

"Okay." She stayed where she was, sitting next to me, but apparently not inclined to touch me. Not that I could blame her. I was a mess.

Living alone for a long time had left me inclined to strange solitary habits ... like sleeping late, wandering about my house naked and letting the housework slide from time to time. So when I sliced my finger wide open one Saturday, severing an artery, a bunch of nerves and, for all I knew, the tendon as well, I was bare-assed and in that fascinating place—a locked, messy house with nothing but a cell phone and a list of acquaintances to call.

I'd managed to do what I'd needed to do, in between fainting twice. I'd crawled into clothes, contacted Delaney, and gotten myself out of the house. But by the time she pulled up in her car, I was covered in blood, sweating like a racehorse and still barefoot. She was lucky I was wearing underwear—shoes were not an option.

In the emergency room another wave of nausea hit me and I had the bad feeling I was going to pass out again. I slid down in the seat, stared at the ceiling, and tried not to think about the buckets of blood pumping out of my finger. Then I felt a hand on my shoulder, and it patted me tentatively.

"You'll be right," Delaney said quietly. It wasn't quite what I was looking for, but who the hell was I to ask or expect anything from someone who was more a colleague than a close friend? I was lucky she was there at all.

"My mother would be bloody useless in this situation anyway," I muttered, trying anything to take my mind off things.

"Yeah?"

"Yeah. She's worse than I am when it comes to the sight of blood," I explained. "At least I'm okay around other people's blood. It's just mine that freaks me out. But she goes pale and wan at the slightest suggestion of claret."

"Mmmm, that's probably just because it's her daughter's blood." Her hand had long since withdrawn from my shoulder.

"Did you go all weak at the knees when your boys were bleeding?" I asked. Her three sons were grown and out of the house.

"Nope, but then I love all this medical stuff."

"I got that impression," I said wryly. She would have been sitting out in the waiting room at that moment, but had expressed an interest in seeing the inside of my finger at close quarters. I was secretly delighted to have her nearby.

I made the mistake of moving and felt the fuzzy vision that had been a precursor to fainting begin again. "Uh, Del?"

"You're about to pass out again, aren't you?" I nodded. "Hang in there. I'm going to go and roust the doctors."

Less than a minute later I was flat on my back on a gurney, with a nurse and two doctors gathered around me. I could just see Delaney leaning against the wall, behind the doctors.

"If you really want to see, Del, you should come around this side," I told her.

The senior doctor said, "We need to put some local anesthetic in this."

"That's going to hurt," the nurse said helpfully. "But don't anticipate it."

*Yeah, right.* I bit down on the outside of my right thumb, anticipating like a son of a bitch.

"Okay, here we go," the medic said.

I wrapped my right leg around the raised metal rail on that side of the gurney, trying hard to get as far away from my injured hand as possible. My eyes were squeezed tight, and I bit down harder.

"Yeowww shiiitt," I yelped as the first needle dug in. I knew I'd jumped.

The doctor said, "Okay, we've got a few more of these to go before we can cover the whole area. But hopefully the anesthetic will start to kick in soon."

"Yeah, hopefully so," I muttered around a chunk of my thumb. Another yelp and I began to wonder if I wasn't in fact the biggest wuss on the planet. Did other people gnaw off their good hand just because they had three needles sticking in an open wound? Just then I felt gentle fingers wrap around the hand I was biting down on.

"Here," Delaney said. "Squeeze on my hand instead. You'll do less damage." She looked as self-conscious as I felt as she rearranged our hands into a more comfortable position. Maybe it was the rainbow ring the doctor had taken off my injured finger that was making her nervous. It was obvious to the room where my preferences lay. Perhaps she thought they believed we were partners.

I couldn't help it; I enjoyed that thought.

But it was only fleeting, as another needle bit deep. I didn't squeeze, though. Instead I found my thumb gently rubbing across the back of her hand.

"You're supposed to be squeezing," she reminded me, a half-smile playing across her lips. *Why on earth am I looking at her lips?*

The doctor announced, "Okay, we're going to give those a couple of minutes to take affect, and then we're going to put some stitches in to see if we can stop the bleeding."

"Oh, goodie."

They left us alone for a few minutes and Delaney kept holding my hand. It felt nice, soft and warm, a delicate contrast to the sharp stinging sensations the other side of my body was experiencing. I tried to remember the last time anyone had touched me and found I couldn't pinpoint it. My brain was working triple time, adding more significance to her touch than it could possibly deserve. *Why do I crave it so much?*

The doctors returned.

The senior resident said, "Right then. I'm going to drop a

couple of internal stitches in there to see if we can't pull the two ends of the artery together."

"How will you know?" Delaney asked. I was beyond caring. I just wanted the tendon to be okay. And it wasn't about the pain, or the surgery it would require. It was all about my mother. Having to call my mother down from the mountain to look after my cat, and tut-tut about the state of my house — that was what was making me will the universe to see things my way, for once.

"Well, if we manage to catch it with the stitches, we'll take the tourniquet off and it won't bleed," the doctor explained. "If it bleeds, then my guess is both sides of the artery are cut, and that," he put a hand on my shoulder, "will take some microsurgery to fix, I'm afraid."

*Great.* Delaney gripped my hand a little tighter, and I returned the squeeze, turning my head away from the sight of the doctor approaching the gaping cut in my finger with what looked like a large crochet hook.

"Here we go," the doctor warned.

I swear it hurt. I swear that despite five needle-loads of lidocaine, it still hurt. I'm fairly certain I cursed. But all I did was chafe the back of her hand with my thumb. I couldn't bear to grip too hard.

Finally it was done and the doctor removed the tourniquet as we all held our breath.

"Is it bleeding?" I whispered, still not keen on looking at the mangled lump at the end of my finger.

"No," Delaney said, her fingers wrapped around mine. I could hear the smile in her voice. I breathed out, happy that the first hurdle had been leaped.

"Okay, good," the doctor said. "Now let's see what you've done to the tendon." He rooted around with gay abandon, and for once I dug my fingers into the palm of Delaney's hand. She didn't wince, bless her.

"I want you to bend your finger," he said, pressing against the top pad of the offended digit. "Push back against my pressure." I did my best, though it didn't feel like any finger that belonged to me. "That's good, that's good," he urged. "I think you've just nicked the edge of the tendon. You wouldn't be able to bend it like that if you'd done more than that. So I'm just going to sew up the outside, and then you'll be done."

All I could think of was, thank God my mother doesn't have to see the pile of dirty dishes in my sink, or the remains of last night's Chinese meal, or the toilet that needs a good scrubbing. Oh yeah, and avoiding surgery was an added bonus.

In quick time the doctor inserted a line of stitches across the wound. As soon as he stopped, Delaney very deliberately put my hand on my stomach and let go. *Like a psychotherapist whose internal alarm clock's gone off near the end of a session.* My disappointment was palpable and, I'm sure, written all over my face. She raised a quizzical eyebrow at me before she retreated to lean against the wall, waiting as the nurse fussed around me.

The nurse gathered together the bandages and betadine and God knew what else she needed to dress the wound, talking all the while about doctors and politics and how the local newspaper had recently misrepresented the hospital.

"What do you do for a living?" she asked as she wrapped my finger in tight white cloth.

"I'm a writer," I replied, flicking a glance at Delaney, whose eyes were laughing at me from the corner. While we had been waiting for attention, we'd agreed not to mention we worked for the local newspaper, for just this reason.

"Oh really? How interesting. What do you write?"

"Lesbian romance fiction." The words were out of my mouth before I'd even considered that my honesty might make Del even more uncomfortable than she already was. But the nurse was very pleased with my answer.

"Oooo, really? Anything I might have read?" She looked at me candidly.

*You just never know when you're going to run into family.* I smiled wryly and threw on my most attentively flirtatious expression—not easy when you're covered in your own dried blood. "I doubt it," I demurred. "My stuff is published in America—hard to get here."

"That's a pity," she said. "I'd love to read your books some time. Now, here are some extra dressings." She stuffed the bandages and tape into my jeans pocket for me, which was quite disconcerting. I could feel myself blushing. "You need to go see your own doctor on Monday, just to make sure you haven't picked up an infection, and those stitches will need to come out in about two weeks." She patted my arm. "You're done." She glanced over her shoulder at Delaney. "And your partner can take you home."

I snorted. "I should be so lucky."

"I'm not her mother either," Delaney piped up from the other side of the room. "Before that occurs to anyone." It suddenly hit me that maybe that prospect was more bothersome to her than being considered a lesbian.

Five minutes later she was driving me home. It was dark and quiet in the car, and I rested my head back, eyes closed. My hand was pleasingly numb, though I knew that wouldn't last.

"Thank you," I said quietly. "Not the most fun way to spend your day off, I know."

"Oh, I don't know, it's been exciting so far," she said dryly. "Aren't you having fun?"

"Oh yeah. An absolute ball."

"Well, I'm going to take you home and cook you dinner."

*Oh shit.* "Uh, you don't have to do that, honestly," I said hastily. "The place is a mess, what with the blood, and everything. And ..."

"Casey," she said quietly, forcing me to look at her. "I'm not your mother. I don't care if the house is a mess or not. You're one-handed, I know you're hungry—I can hear your stomach rumbling from here—and so am I. I'm cooking us dinner, and I'll help you clean up the blood, as well."

I didn't know what to say. She wasn't taking no for an answer and that really wasn't the response I wanted to give her anyway.

"Thank you," I said again, wondering just what had made me pick Delaney's name out of my cell phone's memory.

Two hours later, the worst of the bloodstains were out of the carpet, and we had full bellies. I sat on the floor, leaning back against the couch, my head resting on the cushion. She relaxed on the couch, to my right. She'd raided my wine cellar and poured herself a glass of red, while I'd preferred to stay off the alcohol as long as there were weird drugs still floating around in my system.

"How's it feeling?" she asked quietly.

"S'beginning to throb a bit."

"I bet," she murmured. There was a pause as she took another sip from her wineglass. "Can I ask you something?"

"Sure." I glanced over my right shoulder at her. She was swirling the wine around, looking into its ruby depths.

"Did you really want your mother today?"

*Holy shit, where did that come from?*

"God, no."

"Why not?"

*I could give her the flip answer or I could lend the weight to it that the issue actually has for me,* I thought. *Opening a can of worms, though. Then again, I trust her. And she's here.* "Having her drive down would have been great in some ways, but it would have come with some strings attached."

"What kind of strings?"

"Well, for example, I couldn't have said 'thanks for coming and holding my hand, Mum, but please don't come in the house' like I did with you."

"Why wouldn't you want her here?"

I chuckled. "Because her disappointment and disapproval at my lack of house-pride would have been written all over her face. And I just don't handle that well."

There was a silence as she thought about that. "You let me in."

I nodded. "Eventually, yes. But you don't come with the same strings attached. Or if you do, you hide it better than my mother." I smiled up at her.

"I'm not your mother," she confirmed. "Besides, this place wasn't so bad."

"Well, thank you for not recoiling in disgust." That brought a laugh from her. I decided I very much liked to hear her laugh, and watching it was even nicer. The faint lines around her eyes crinkled and deepened, somehow intensifying their sparkle. I liked that a lot.

I rested my head back and closed my eyes. My finger was throbbing nicely, now.

"What would have been good about having your mother there this afternoon?" Delaney asked, surprising me again.

*What a good question.* "To be honest, I'm not sure how she would have reacted. I guess the idealized mother, the one in my head, would have held me and taken charge, and let me be a hurt child, instead of someone pretending to be a strong adult." I swallowed around the lump that had suddenly materialized in my throat. "Whether my mother would have actually done those things, I'm not really sure."

Even though I kept my eyes closed, I could feel Delaney looking at me.

"Didn't she do those things for you when you were a kid?" she asked.

I sighed. "I don't remember, honestly. She probably did, but I don't have clear memories of it. I have fuzzy things that might be memories, but, then again, they might be what I want to remember, and not the truth." I turned my head and looked at her. "She'd be devastated if she was listening to this conversation, by the way. I think if she didn't do those comforting things, then it wasn't out of malice."

"What was it, then?"

"Her own fears, I guess. I know some of the emotional games her mother played on her." I smiled wanly. "The beauty of hindsight."

"But you didn't know those things when you were little. So it must have had an impact on you."

"I didn't know them explicitly," I agreed. "But her mother lived with us from the time I was about two, until she died when I was 12. So, I suspect I probably absorbed some of that knowledge, one way or another."

"Ah."

We lapsed into another comfortable silence, and I let myself drift, happy to let her take the conversation wherever she wanted to go.

"Casey?"

"Mmmm?"

"If you didn't really want your mother there, why did you say 'okay, it's official, I want my mother'?"

*She's got you there, kid. Nailed to the wall.* "Um, well, I guess I was trying to lighten the mood a little."

"And?"

I swallowed. "And, I was probably hoping you would take the hint and act as a substitute." *Hoo, boy, the conversations I get myself into.*

"And I didn't do that, did I? I'm sorry."

I shook my head emphatically. "No, don't be sorry. You did what you could and what you were comfortable with, and frankly, I felt very lucky to have had you there at all." I looked at her, disconcerted to feel myself blushing. "You'll have gathered that this mother/daughter thing is a difficult issue for me, and it was unrealistic to pin those kinds of expectations on you. You were great and I'm very glad you were there."

She leaned forward and put her empty glass on the coffee table. With a sigh she rested back again.

"I wasn't very comfortable," she admitted quietly. "And I'm not very sure why that was."

"I have a few hypotheses." She raised an eyebrow, silently telling me to go on. "The lesbian thing?"

She smiled. "You know me better than that. We've had this conversation many times."

I shrugged. "It's one thing to have done the schoolgirl experimentation thing and enjoyed it, and a whole other beast to be in a room full of strangers who are probably thinking you're one half of a lesbian couple. That would make plenty of people squirm."

"Maybe," she murmured, half-conceding the point. "I think it's more likely that I recognized that you wanted mothering. And I didn't want to do that."

"In case I misinterpreted it." I nodded, swallowing the disappointment in myself that I felt. *One of these days, Case, you're going to learn how to do this.*

I heard Delaney sigh again, and then she was sliding down to sit next to me on the floor, her left shoulder pressed against my right. I blinked at her, feeling slightly off-balance.

"You're right," she said, blue eyes calm and cool. "I didn't want you to misinterpret my actions." My stomach slid even further. "But not the way you think." I raised my eyes to hers again, wondering just where this conversation was going. I must have looked as confused as I felt because she smiled at me gently. "I don't want you thinking of me as a mother-figure," she said softly. She leaned closer and her right hand reached up. I felt her fingertips caressing my cheek and couldn't believe what was happening.

"N-no?"

She shook her head slowly.

"No. So let me put any misunderstanding to rest, right now."

The kiss was soft and light and so full of promise it tugged at every cell in my body, it seemed. I didn't respond for several moments, the shock enough to paralyze my senses. But then I fell into the warmth of her, the nearness of her, and it was all I had ever imagined it could be. I kissed her back, letting her know that this was wanted, needed even, but allowing her to set the pace. Finally she pulled back and we sat inches from each other, just breathing the same air.

"Not a lot of room for, uh, misinterpretation there," I murmured.

"I would hope not."

I grinned. "I may need further clarification, however."

She chuckled. "I think that can be arranged."

I had so many questions for her but for this moment we were just content to rest our foreheads together.

"I'm sorry," she whispered finally.

"For what?"

"I should have done more than just hold your hand this afternoon. But I was self-conscious, and that was silly of me."

I smiled. "Don't worry about it."

"Tell me more about your mother," she asked.

I winced. "I actually try very hard not to think about my mother when I'm kissing a beautiful woman," I said, trying to lighten the total weirdness of that statement.

Delaney brushed my fringe off my forehead with a slow finger.

"But there's a fine line for you, isn't there? You really need that nurturing, don't you?"

I nodded, my tears close to the surface. The aching loneliness and skin-hunger had been a constant for me in recent years, seeming to gather intensity as I had grown older. She had found that void inside me in the course of one conversation. And had dived in.

"Where does the need to be mothered stop and the attraction start?" I whispered. "And for me the line is not so much fine, as ... hard to locate."

She kissed a stray tear from my cheek. "You worry too much about these things," she said, not unkindly. "In the end, does it matter? You're not in any doubt how you feel about me, are you?" She kissed the corner of my mouth, a feather-light contact that sent chills through me.

"Not in the slightest," I husked.

A smile. "Good. And presumably, you don't feel the same way about your mother."

"God, no."

"I'm guessing the feelings couldn't be more opposite." I nodded. "In fact, my guess would be that what attracts you in women like me is the possibility of finding the kind of nurturing that you never got from your mother. Would that be a fair assessment?"

"Yes, Doctor. How much do I owe you?"

"Another kiss."

"I can do that."

Our second kiss was longer than the first, infinitely more mutual, and every bit as wondrous. But the day was catching up with me.

"You look exhausted," Delaney said softly when we broke apart.

I nodded. "Finger's hurting like crazy too."

"Want me to go home and leave you in peace?"

"No," I answered, honestly. "But if you want to, I understand."

She shook her head and smiled at me. "I don't want to. Why don't you rest your head here." She patted her leg. "And we can watch a movie together. If you fall asleep, great. If not, at least you'll have somebody to help take your mind off the ache."

"Sounds wonderful," I replied. "It's been quite a day."

"It has, hasn't it? Thank you for calling me."

"Thank you for answering."

### Therese Szymanski

D.C. writer Therese Szymanski was born in Michigan in 1968. She's a writer, editor, playwright, reviewer, designer, type-setter, proofreader, chief cook and bottle washer—whatever will pay the bills.

As the author of six gritty Brett Higgins Motor City Mystery/Thrillers, Therese has been a Lambda Literary finalist twice. She is also an award-winning playwright. Therese is very excited about an anthology she recently edited, *Back to Basics: A Butch/Femme Erotic Anthology*, just out in February 2004.

Therese is hard at work on a variety of projects now—in between the panoply of odd jobs to keep her flush with pens, paper, and ink.

# Disconnected

## Memoir by Therese Szymanski

WHEN MY OLD friend Maria visited Michigan recently from her home in Alaska, she took a little road trip to visit me in D.C. and I did what I always do with out-of-town friends: I took her toy shopping. Fortunately for me, she came just before I had a deadline on a short story I was supposed to write. This one.

C'mon, growing up with Sally Sue and Roman, I'm lucky I ever got laid!" Maria said, referring to her parents, as we went down the escalator at the Dupont Metro. "I never saw them touch or kiss or anything. They were the most repressed people I ever knew."

"Are you totally forgetting my folks?"

"Oh, yeah. Right. At least you knew your father had sex."

"Well, I didn't discover that 'til years later." Turns out that when mom stopped putting out, my father turned elsewhere— namely toward his secretaries. Or maybe that had started before mom stopped.

Maybe Maria sensed my upcoming brood. She looked down at the bag in her hand. "I don't think I would have believed anyone who told me we'd *ever* go toy shopping together.

Just like anyone who said you'd wind up dating an Eskimo woman eleven years younger than you would've been nuts, eh?" Maria had just come out two years before with Nu, the daughter of one of her best friends. (Nu's real name was some long Eskimo/Indian thing I could never remember.) Whenever I taunted Maria about robbing the cradle, she turned the phrase about, insisting that she was the seducee, not the seducer—so it was more that Nu had mugged Maria in the old-age home.

Nu's mother wasn't happy about the relationship. Whenever she got drunk, which was quite a frequent occurrence, she would call and threaten Maria. Or else show up at her place and threaten her. Nu and Maria had decided that moving from Nome to the great Metropolis of Anchorage might add a touch of sanity to their lives.

"Will you quit bringing that up, Reese?"

I considered it for a moment before replying. "Nope, don't think so. But of course, you keep saying it, too, so ya really can't blame me."

Maria's 33 and I'm 34 and we've known each other for 21 years. A few years earlier, just before she came out, she had called me several times for advice because she was straight, and a younger woman was making the moves on her. After all, I was her really queer (as in "professional queer" at the time, since I worked at a national gay rights organization) friend. I lived far enough away to be her real true advisor in potentially gay times.

There were four of us back when we all got together in junior high—Maria and Jackie were in the seventh grade, while Ethel and I were in the eighth grade. If we had been in a teen movie, we would've been the geeks, and that's why we were together. Well, that and the fact we were all in the band. Which I guess automatically qualified us for the nerd squad.

IF MY PARENTS had kids, I wouldn't be here today." Jackie was the adopted one in our group. She's also the proof of nature over nurture, because her also-adopted sister, Stephanie, grew up to become a drug abuser. Stephanie's birth mother, whom Stephanie met once, was also a drug abuser.

Jackie never looked for her own birth mother. She never felt the need for such a thing. She found the parents who raised her to be all the parents she ever needed.

Jackie is now a high-school teacher in Kalamazoo, Michigan. A few years ago, one of her students asked during class, "Ms. Lemanski, can I ask you a question?"

"Yes."

"Well...you own cats, you ride a Harley, you live by yourself, and you say boys are icky. Are you a lesbian?"

"Would it really make a difference to you if I was?" she asked.

He thought about it a moment before he finally replied, "No."

She can pull stunts like that because, although she would love to be a lesbian, she can't stop drooling over boys' bodies (per her own words. Not that she has anything for underage types, I think she just uses the word to display the condescension she has for the sex.)

She also knows lesbian teachers, and wants to help them.

A few years ago she was quite happy to take me and my lover to our first Michigan Wimmin's Music Festival (giggling all the while that we were the virgins, and she was the experienced one). Every time I visit her, she takes me to the local gay bar.

It's almost like she's a member of the family.

ETHEL'S PARENTS WERE both high school teachers. She and Jackie had the nice parents, whereas Maria and I had the freak shows that put the dys in dysfunctional. Since Ethel and I went to the same school, we took a lot of the same classes and made fun of the same teachers. We were geeks-in-arms, together in the honor society, Mu Alpha Theta (the math club), and eating lunch in the library.

Ethel got her Master's in Art history and now teaches at some small Michigan college. What I noticed at our 10-year reunion, just before she got married to a boy, was that she was toning herself down to fit with him, to make him happy. Where we would be the outspoken ones always cracking jokes and acting out during high school, she was now allowing him to take the spotlight.

I wonder if she was following in her mother's footsteps, or just doing what's expected of her.

When I told Jackie about Ethel's personality and attire at that event, Jackie said that was a major reason she dated bikers — so she wouldn't have to tone herself down for them.

The idea of Ethel in a cocktail dress cracked up everyone I told.

MARIA WAS THE one most likely to be grounded when we were growing up together. The one most likely to have false accusations thrust upon her. While my parents ignored what I did, hers watched her like a hawk.

She had one brother, a half-brother, who was older. I never knew just how much older he was, though it was at least a decade from what I could surmise. He was the fruit from her mother's first marriage. Literally. He died from AIDS when we were in high school. Her parents did all they could to cut off communications between Maria and her brother when he came out, and when he died, Maria was not allowed to attend the memorial.

I only learned about her brother when one weekend she was acting all whacked, and Jackie gave me the 411 on the situation. Maria couldn't tell me herself.

There are some key moments that define relationships, just as there are some things that you clearly remember years later. I remember that, when we were in high school, Maria was once apparently not listening to her mother, so her mother did the

only reasonable thing she could and threw a grapefruit at her —
with amazing accuracy.

At least mine never did that.

But my father did slam me out of my chair one night during
dinner when I was fourteen. He had been repeatedly sticking his
finger in my face, lecturing me throughout the meal. I finally
asked how he liked it. And I stuck my finger in his face. He
didn't care much for that.

I stopped eating with them after that.

"I ALWAYS SEEMED to get along well with everyone's parents," I said to Maria Friday night, while we were drinking the
night away in my apartment. "But then I think they saw my evil
side —"

"No, actually, my mother needed to blame someone for the
fact she and I weren't getting along. You were an easy target."

"Well, there was the time Ethel's dad asked her why half the
family car's hood was clean, while the other half was dirty.
Before she could come up with some excuse, he said he knew it
had to do with that 'Polack.'"

"Oh, hell, he was always a trip! Wasn't that after the night
we went through the McDonald's drive-thru with you on the
hood? In the middle of the winter?"

It was a really cold, Michigan night. "Yeah, it was. The night
before I was gonna start managing there." I took another sip of
my beer. "It did start that job with a bang for me. At least I
wasn't labeled a goody-goody for a change."

In other words, Maria and I were taking a drunken trip
down memory lane. Remembering the times when we were each
other's best friends, confidantes...family.

JACKIE AND MARIA went to a private Catholic girl's high
school and grew apart after a while. Maria was in track and other
running sports, while Jackie was more involved with theater.

Ethel and I went to the local public high. She was my closest
at-school friend — and even after we four split to different
schools, we still got together a bit.

My senior year of high school, my best friend was a co-
worker at McDonald's. So much of my time (40 hours/week) was
spent at work that my old friends weren't with me so much.
Plus, I had it bad for a girl, Donna, who was a green-eyed blonde
with a wicked sexy grin.

ETHEL AND I made the mistake of rooming together our
frosh year at University, and since then, we haven't been in

touch. (I can't remember what tossed us off—if it was the fact that she was a total slob who left all her used tissues behind the couch; maybe her falling in with a crowd who had her searching through all my private stuff, including my desk; or maybe it was that everything of mine was up for share-time, while her stuff was hers, and hers alone. I guess no matter how much she bitched and moaned, she really was mama's little girl.)

We four were all writers to some extent. When Ethel and I were in the ninth grade, the four of us started doing an annual writing project (The Books of Weird and Demented Things) for fun. We bonded through our geekiness—that we never really fit with others. Occasionally, some folks hung with us a bit, but they'd fall away because, well, they weren't quite nerdy enough for us. After all, there's many different types of otherliness.

For instance, my pseudo-boyfriend Tom hung with us for a bit. He came into our group because his parents bought the cottage next to the one my folks had.

Now, whenever my mother asks me about Tom, wondering whatever happened with him, and why I don't go back to dating him, I don't remind her about the many times she stopped our dates. Instead I look her right in the eye and say, "The last time I saw him he was snorting a line of Coke in the women's room of a gay bar." One must be direct when dealing with my mother. Nope, no namby-pamby stuff for the wicked old Polack without emotion.

MY PARENTS WERE 45 when I popped out. When I was eight, my mother started telling me I was a mistake—that she only wanted four kids.

I have three brothers and one sister, all older. My sister and one of my brothers are my godparents. We're a good Catholic family. Five kids, and the nearest in age from me is six years my elder, while the oldest is 18 years older. In some ways I might've been an only child, but nothing can ever be easy.

My parents mostly noticed me when I was an inconvenience. In so many ways I was simply an object to them.

When I was 13, I developed the linguistics to properly reply to my mother's blaming my existence on me. I stood at the bottom of the stairs and yelled up to her, "Actually, mom, you fucked dad one day, and I'm here because of it."

My friends of the time would have been amazed to hear me use the F word. One day Ethel complained to our Trig teacher that my parents didn't even look at my report card, and hers would corner her and ask for reasons. A few days later, I got a test back with a B at the top and replied simply that I'd have to work harder the next time. Mr. McAleer looked at Ethel and said that's why my parents didn't care about my report cards.

But that wasn't the reason.

My mother may be 79 now, but she's actually 9. When I was 11, my sister wanted to fly me out to New Mexico to spend time with her. My mother claimed I wasn't old enough to fly by myself, so she had to come with me. But I was the one who had to lead mom, find the gates, and make sure she kept track of all her belongings (she still managed to leave her jacket in Dallas).

When I was 18, my folks decided I could travel by myself. And I learned to never, ever let them pack my carry-on bag again. For that particular adventure, where I had a layover and all, they put five pounds of kielbasa, a six-pack of Stroh's, and a brick into the carry-on I was carting across the country (it was a very nice brick—my brother's belated birthday present—complete with a hand-made cover—but my bag weighed more than me!)

When we moved into the house in Warren, my sister Sheila still needed a room. She had a little bit of college to finish. There were three bedrooms in the house—one for me, one for Bruce, and the master bedroom for the folks. Sheila didn't want to keep me awake all night with her studying, so she camped in the basement, and dad built her a room down there.

When Bruce's room was being painted, he took my room, and I stayed in the basement because there were spiders down there. Apparently I had more of a tolerance for them than Bruce.

My mother's sole reason for my existence was to take care of her when she got older. After I graduated from college, I couldn't find a job in my field immediately. (All of my folks' kids paid our own way through college. Mark lived in the family house for a while after college, until he got kicked out. The rest ran far away as soon as they were done.)

Mom bribed me into moving back in with her. That lasted all of like six months, then I moved out. I couldn't stand it. She didn't fight my moving out because just before I moved out, I came out on the CBS evening news, and she managed to see it— as well as the previews, where they showed me saying, "I'm looking for the woman I can take home to meet my mother and say, 'But Ma, she *is* my Mr. Right!'" while doing a three-snap.

GRADUATING HIGH SCHOOL, and leaving the Schoenherr McDonald's broke ties for me. Rather like leaving home does. I lived with Ethel my frosh year, and still kept in contact with Maria, Jackie, and Donna, my hottie co-worker at Mickey-D's. But Donna and I fell off slowly that year, especially with the death of former co-workers and the relatives thereof. But the killing blow was felled when I came out and realized I loved her.

It was kinda like being disowned by one's family when one comes out.

By my junior year, I no longer roomed with Ethel. And I wasn't talking much with Maria or Jackie. And not a word with Donna, for the most part.

IN 1991 I called my mother to tell her I was going into the hospital for a few days. (I had a bad incident with what turned out to be Cujo Cat—a cat that got in at least a dozen bites before we got him off me.) Turned out dad was going into their local hospital for a day or two as well. When I got released two weeks later and called them, dad was still in.

Although I had sworn never to visit my father in the hospital again, my girlfriend of the time talked me into it a few days later. Turned out, dad had been released from the hospital that day, and mom forgot to let me know. That day I saw him at the house and knew he was going to die soon. It was the only time in my life I saw him cry.

When I left that day, my mother came to me in the driveway. She noticed I was wearing suspenders. "Don't buy too many of those. After all, if anything happens to your father, you can have all of his."

BY THEN, I had come out. And I found my family within my family. When I first played nice with my mother's brother's family, mom was worried. After all, they were the underachievers, the ones who got in trouble, and...

"If you hang around with Raymond, people might think you're like that." Ray was the token queer in more than 35 first cousins. But not for long.

He and his lover, Jeff, held my hand through my coming out, and for years thereafter. They became my new basis for understanding of family. And thus I was allied with the black sheep.

MY MOTHER'S PARENTS had nine children, my father's, three. All of my grandparents came over on boats. My mother still speaks with an accent, although I don't notice it. She always said I had a different bearing, a different accent. And she remarks on people being "Americanized," down to Jill, my brother's ex-fiancee, who was Japanese; and all of the blacks on TV. It doesn't matter that they've all been here longer than us.

Now that I live in the Nation's capital, people remark on my accent. But when I lived in Michigan, where I had lived all my life, people kept asking me where I was from. Because of my accent.

At this moment, my mother has four grandchildren. At the most, she might end up with one more. We're a Catholic family...the greatest truth of how we were raised is that we're not reproducing at the rate good Catholic children ought to.

Unconsciously, we're stopping the trend. Five kids, maybe five grandkids. Max.

Don't get me wrong. It's not like we have feelings. When my brother's girlfriend told him they either had to get engaged or break up, I was the third person he called. He called our two sisters-in-law first, figuring they would be more likely to have actual feelings — emotions — than we did.

Then he called me. Figuring I was the most likely of our parents' kids to have emotions. And thus to understand what he was feeling, going through.

It was that brother who first, unbeknownst to me, taught me about unconditional love.

My mother always talks about family always being there for you, and that you have to pay attention to family and be with them so that it's the one constant in your life. Apparently she forgets how great biological family was to me when I first came out.

"OH GOD, I almost forgot about the VCR!" Maria says, sitting in my apartment in the here and now, laughing as she leans back into my futon with her whiskey and water. "I still can't believe that!" Our random drunken reveries brought me back, and made me remember yet other things, in the way beer-thoughts go.

"I was just so thankful you were there." My father had just kicked the bucket, about a month after the suspender incident, and although my brother Mark lived five minutes from mom, she kept calling me with her problems. I lived an hour and a half away, worked full time, and went to college full time.

That particular night she first called me because the clock on her VCR was blinking and SHE COULD NOT LIVE WITH THAT. I talked her through that crisis, telling her which buttons to push, what to do to fix it. (No wonder I was so good at telephone tech support later in my life.)

Then she called back because she wanted to watch a video on the machine and it wasn't working. It wasn't taking the tape.

"Yes, is Maria there?" I asked Sally Sue when she answered the phone.

"One moment please."

"Hey, how's it going?" Maria asked a few moments later.

"Big, big favour to ask. My mom's got this problem..."

"I mean, Reese, all I had to do was push the tape into the machine!" Maria now says.

"I know. And I knew it then. She was just lonely, and wanted me there."

"Isn't that when you moved back in with her?"

"Yeah. I gave in and moved in with her. I was there for like a month when..." I turned to look at Bruce's wedding picture on one of my many bookshelves. "We know I can't lie. I came out to her. I had moved in with her, even though it gave me a huge commute, in summer with a car without air, to school, but I did that for her. And she freaked."

"Didn't she disown you?"

"Yeah. Not that night, but shortly thereafter." I went into the kitchen and grabbed another beer. I couldn't stay put discussing this. I needed to pace and move and walk. Maria kept silent 'til I continued, "I came out, and then she told me dad had been fine and suddenly gave up—and now she knew why. She told me I killed my father. She disowned me." I grinned and extended my beer-holding hand toward her. "And ya know, that's something you'll hear a lot of in this life. It's gotten easier, and nicer, and folks keep coming out younger and younger, but..."

"But you still talk with her..."

WHEN I WAS sixteen, Mom and I had a huge argument. It lasted about an hour, and had me digging through our encyclopedias and other reference tomes to prove my point.

It ended when mom said, "Oh, Alaska's a state now!"

She had been insisting there were 49 states.

SINCE I GOT my driver's license, there have been three times I have been in a car with mom and allowed her to drive. Once, when I was sixteen, I was too drunk. She believed me when I said I was too tired to drive.

The other two times were when I had my wisdom teeth taken out, so I was on serious drugs. The second of those times was awful because I had to pull my brain out of my drug-induced state to tell her not to go the wrong way on one-way streets. Although she had lived most of her life in that area, she was still confused about it.

When I suddenly needed outpatient surgery years later, on the 22nd of December, she would not drive me. It was out of her way. And even though I could be called from further away to fix her VCR at 11 pm, she could not, with several days' notice, drive me for surgery.

The girlfriend of an ex-boss ended up doing it.

That same Christmas, my mother told me we'd be celebrating Christmas on the 26th, when my brother Kirk came to town.

Kirk got in on the 25th, and mom only called me after that day's festivities to ask where I was. She had forgotten to tell me about Christmas.

And yet my mother still tells me to pay attention to family, because they are the only ones who will always be there.

THIS PAST CHRISTMAS, I flew to L.A. From there, my sister and I drove to Denver, skiing along the way at Vail, Aspen, and such, and then spending Christmas with my brother in Denver. This is the second time we've done such a thing.

And it was the second time my sister asked me to change my flight plans at Christmas for her. This time I did. Under guarantee that my sister would not have some guy going with us. (The first time she wanted me to fly into L.A. and out of Denver. She ended up having her male friend, whom she liked, fly into Denver and accompany us on our drive from Denver to L.A., with all the skiing that involved. He was an obnoxious pig who wanted to control everything.)

This time I had planned on simply spending all my time in Denver, in order to get to know my new niece.

My sister and I were as close as we could be—considering that she's thirteen years older and lived in a different state—until I came out.

"We raised ourselves," Sheila said this past Christmas, flicking the windshield wipers. "Isn't it amazing to watch Nancy with Peyton? The way she cuddles her and tells her she loves her?" Nancy is my brother's mother-in-law, and Peyton is my brand-new niece. First one in eighteen years.

MARIA HASN'T COME out to her folks, but it's no big because she doesn't even see them annually. They're not an active part of her life.

It took me a while to realize that my mother needs me more than I need her. More than I ever needed her.

Yes, she wants the perfect little cheerleading daughter—but one who can also fix her car, mow the lawn, shovel the snow, and perform household repairs. Without tools, for she gave all dad's tools to my brothers when dad kicked, so I have to use my car toolbox to fix anything at her place. Even though my brother lives less than a mile away.

But the trouble is, she still won't admit to her own need.

BECAUSE OF WHO I am (a writer), I have helped many young women come out. It is always tough for me to answer questions about whether or not they should tell their family. After all, I cannot unequivocally tell them they should.

AFTER ALL, WHAT I want is for her to say she's sorry for telling me I killed my father.
And I know that will never happen.

"ONE OF MY worst fears," Maria says, referring to Nu, "is that her mom will get roaring drunk some night and call my mom and tell her all about us."
I can't lie worth shit, so I always support honesty, and telling folks what is. Nonetheless I replied, "Be grateful you live in Alaska."

SOME THINGS HAVE changed, and we may now be legal, but other things may never change. Some parents will love their queer children, others won't. Sometimes you'll meet your sib's potential in-laws and discover they couldn't be happier than to realize they'll have a lesbian novelist in the family soon.
Sometimes people see one of my mother's sides and think she's cool, but then they'll hear her tell people at a play, "I wanted two boys and two girls. I got three boys, one girl and one I don't know what." (One of my exes almost clobbered this seemingly sweet, Smurf-like 4'10" woman when she walked by her and heard that.)

WE'RE BORN WHO we are, and we can either fight against it, or try to be reprogrammed for a short period of time, but in the end, we are who we are, and to find love, we have to be who we are. Whether we are gay/straight/bi or something else, and whether we need to tell folks or not, or if we're a roaring nutcase, or have emotions, or whatever, the road to happiness is in who we are.

WHEN MY FIRST play premiered, for a two-night run, at the Wharton Center for the Performing Arts, with the bill footed by Michigan State University, my mother, Maria, and Jackie came for closing night. I cooked them all dinner before we went to the show—a real Polish meal of pierogis, kielbasa (cooked in beer, then browned in the oven's broiler—my father's recipe, which leaves the cook quite happy), sauerkraut, and blood sausage.

This last item has some cool Polish name, which I can never remember. It's really fun to serve to guests — you fry it up with mushrooms and onions and put it on the table, without telling anyone what it is. They are never happy later on to discover what they just ate.

Jackie almost had a heart-attack when she saw me: I, wanting to muck with folks' stereotypical images, was in drag, with make-up, skirt-suit, and curled hair.

After the play, before the cast party at my apartment, I cleansed my face, donned cut-offs and tank top, and combed out my hair. Jackie was thankful for that, because then I was the Therese she knew and loved.

At that time, I wasn't out to my mother about being a smoker, so folks kept joining me outside for cigarettes. The party continued until about four a.m., after several cases of beer and a few games of Trivial Pursuit. At some point, Maria crashed on the floor of the spare room, with my mom on the bed; my girl and I slept in our room; and Jackie ended up on the living room floor with a boy whom it took a bit to hook her up with. (Because she was an old friend of mine, he assumed she was gay. And the first time she saw him, he was kissing another man (during the play). It took some work to make them realize they were both het, and...I gave them condoms.)

Later the cast informed me they had been expecting my mother to be evil incarnate, and they didn't see that.

But skin is only so deep. As are appearances.

I STARTED PAYING for my own food and clothing when I was sixteen. I went to college when I was eighteen, and, since then, except for six months, I have been self-supporting, living on my own.

But it wasn't till I was 30 that I really and truly ran away from home — that's when I got out of Michigan. A two-hour drive is nothing for a lesbian daughter when her mother needs help. But nine hours is another thing — it is enough to give me freedom for moments.

She no longer cries on my answering machine telling me that her children have abandoned her, since she knows I will not come running.

MOM TELLS ME family is everything. But as a writer I know words can be five cents each, or less.

During my last trip to Detroit, my mother proudly displayed the homophobic flyers she had been passing out in church — she showed me the hatred that she had been helping to proliferate, even while she tells me to "be careful" because of what people think.

Family is those closest. There are some blood relatives I call on a regular basis, and some I want nothing to do with. But there are also friends who are closer than any which I am related to— these are the folks who understand and accept me no matter how dysfunctional I am, no matter how lost in my muddles I may be...and they also turn to me in their times of need.

We make our own families. And mine has changed, as one's life does, from school days to adulthood. But there are some who stick with you, and others who don't. Those who understand, and those who don't.

I will never forget the mother of one of my girlfriends, who, soon after finding out we were together, patted me on the shoulder and thanked me for taking care of her daughter.

MARIA LOOKED OVER her drink at me. "Do you remember when you were in the shopping cart and I ran it into a curb?"

I got up to grab another beer while I growled. I had forgotten about that.

"Hey, c'mon, we were about to be run over!" she called from the living room, referring to a night when the four of us had a sleepover at my place. Mine was the place we could leave for midnight adventures without my parents knowing.

Actually, Jackie hadn't been at the full sleepover. We just went a-knocking at her bedroom window in the middle of the night and kidnapped her. Took her with us for our midnight adventures, which my parents never knew happened.

I leaned against my entertainment center, which was actually the bookshelf my parents bought me when I was eight. Since then I have butchered it to make it into an entertainment center. "I think I told you, back when you first called me for advice, that you'd do whatever you wanted. And later on, I laughed at the idea of two women ever being able to casually date. I knew you couldn't just screw her and move on!"

"But why didn't you tell me before?"

I shrugged, and sat down on my La-Z-Boy. I had told Maria earlier that I wasn't going to jump her bones, and in my drunken state, I was way too...horny and seductive to be allowed into the general population. "Have I mentioned that young women can be wicked hot, but older women...who know what they're doing, and what they're about, can be so hot?"

"Are you sure you're not just saying that because we've been talking about mothers and families all night?"

I got what she meant. "You've seen my mother. Would I ever

even think of a woman in that way?"

"Point taken," she said as she drunkenly saluted me. "Not everything can be interpreted by a misogynistic old German, who probably suffered seriously from Oedipus Complex and Penis Envy himself."

You're stuck with your mother. And no one can ever replace her, no matter how much you wish it so. And we build our own families. And I could only reach such a conclusion while stumbling drunk, with someone with whom I had no blood connection, who was still family without any reason for me to consider her so. I stared at her for a few moments.

Finally, she said, "What?"

"Can you really get me a copy of *Once More with Feeling*?"

## Talaran

Talaran was born in New York in 1961 and continues to live there, happily married for the past 15 years to Barbara, the woman she calls her rock. In real life, Talaran is computer programmer and analyst for a Fortune 500 company. She also designs book covers, graphics, wallpaper, and logos for Just-Cuz.com. The cover to this anthology was designed by her.

With a background and education in Electronics and webpage creation, Talaran is imaginative and analytical, able to approach both business and creative projects with a unique point of view. She is currently contemplating writing a second book and perhaps a sequel to her crime novel, *Vendetta*.

# Ramblings of a Lesbian Daughter

## Memoir by Talaran

IF YOU ARE lucky enough to be loved by your mother, then you are among the most fortunate of people. A mother's unconditional love is one of the treasures one can only hope to experience in this life. So many people in this world are not so lucky. I am happy to say that I can be counted among the fortunate. I have never truly doubted my mother's love, even when she said the worst thing in the world to me – that she wished I was dead. At the time those words tore through me like a knife, but I do not believe deep down they ever really shook my faith in my mother's love. When my anger and hurt subsided and when I had an opportunity to digest the exchange between us, I knew she did not truly mean what she had said to me.

Without a doubt that was a very turbulent time in our history. It took place twenty-three years ago. At that time my mother's parents had passed away only a year a part from each other, one quickly and one agonizingly slowly. This was unbelievably stressful for my mother, as she was very close to both her parents. That was also the first time in my life when I was exposed to the unbearable pain of loss. The grief we both felt over the losses did not bring us together. It polarized us more than ever.

During those dark, turbulent years I was a lost soul in many ways. Not only was I mourning the loss of two very important people in my life, but I was at an age when my sexuality was blooming, and I was very confused and wracked with guilt over my sexual preference. All those years ago, gay culture was not widely known about, unlike today, where gay characters, albeit sometimes one-dimensional ones, abound on the small screen. During those tumultuous years I would have sacrificed a limb to have had someone, anyone to identify with. The emotional turmoil of that period of my life has left the time very hazy to me, as are many of the years that followed. The mind often chooses to forget painful experiences, and those years were fraught with confusion and pain. But I knew I would not be able to continue to survive with the secret I had kept for what seemed like an eternity. I had known from a very young age that I had no interest in boys other than as friends. Having to endure the constant questions as to why I wasn't dating made my life that much more stressful. Though I wanted to, fear kept me from telling my parents who I wanted to be dating.

After surviving many school girl crushes that I kept completely to myself I found the courage to tell my mother about my secret and the fact that I was in love with an older woman. I was not surprised when she did not embrace me. I wasn't foolish enough to expect a joyous celebration at my revelation because I suspected that she would be devastated. She did not disappoint me. She let me know that with my declaration, I, her only daughter, was dashing all of her hopes and dreams for me. (Apparently getting married to a man and bearing his children is the only worthwhile thing a woman can do in this world, or at least that was how it seemed twenty years ago.) When I told her my secret all I wanted was her acceptance and her love. I know she loves me, but I don't think she has ever truly accepted my choices nor has she been happy about them. What I have from my mother is a tolerance and a false understanding of what it means to be a lesbian. Perhaps that is the best I can hope for.

I think it may be unrealistic to expect that any heterosexual, even my own mother, can have a true understanding of what lesbian love is, what it means to be a lesbian, what struggles we contend with, not only within ourselves, but also with society. At that single moment in time, when I bared my soul with the most painful secret I could have had, I created a chasm between my mother and me that has never completely gone away. At that moment and during many moments since, she felt she didn't even know me, yet I was the same person I had always been. But she couldn't know that since she never knew who I really was to begin with. So for my mother not to understand me is in itself understandable, though not acceptable. I know that the belief that my life would be much more difficult as a lesbian was a large part of my mother's fears for me. She knew that life would not be easy for me and she was not entirely wrong. I think that I have fared better than many, but there were certainly difficult roads to traverse along the way. Of course, not being a parent myself makes it hard for me to see things from my mother's point of view. Yet, it always makes me wonder why my mother cannot simply be overjoyed that I turned into a healthy, happy adult. Shouldn't that have been her most fervent hope for me? Sure, she wished me to be a thousand other things, too, but shouldn't those two have been at the top of her list? I know if I had a child they would be. But these are answers I will never have.

As much as I love my mother I cannot bring myself to have any type of insightful conversations with her. We have tried before and we have failed, usually in a heated argument or a long stretch of not speaking to one another. The chasm is still there. It's not to say that we can't enjoy one another's company. In order to spend such time together, we cannot discuss topics such as finances, proper house cleaning techniques, or her viewpoint on what my responsibilities are. We can go from enjoyment to an argument in the blink of an eye if the wrong comment is made. Usually it's my mother saying something to me that sounds like she is chastising me because she is unhappy with something I've said or done. And it is because I have always felt like I have never quite made her happy that my hair bristles at any such encounters.

Even with our occasional confrontations, I will always have many fond memories of times we have shared. I've learned many things from my mother. She is a very loyal, compassionate, and proud woman. She taught me the lessons all mothers should teach their children: treat people fairly, tell the truth even if it hurts, be a hard worker, eat all your vegetables because they will make you strong, get plenty of sleep, wear proper winter clothing, don't do drugs or abuse alcohol, and respect your elders. My mother also instilled in me a love of music, movies, golfing, and shopping. I grew up listening to her favorite singers and watching the grand musicals of the fifties and sixties. West Side Story, Three Coins in a Fountain, Rock Hudson, and Doris Day movies will forever rekindle sweet memories for me.

It saddens me to think that I have spent a lifetime trying to earn my mother's acceptance and understanding. At various times in my life, I even thought I had them, but there were also many times when I was realized that I did not. What I have learned is that I do not need her acceptance and understanding in order to be a happy and fulfilled individual. I'm not sure why I ever thought that I did. I do not know why her approval was and still in some ways is important to me. I was always trying to do my best so she would be proud of me, proud of how I turned out. The reality is that in some ways my lesbianism shadows that pride. For all her attempts at understanding me, she has fallen short because she still feels she failed me; that something she did or did not do caused me to be "this way." Knowing that is how she feels makes me realize she will never understand who I really am. Unless she can accept the fact that she is not to blame, that no one is, and that it is okay for me to be who I am, she will never truly accept who I am.

Thankfully, that no longer matters to me. Twenty years ago it did, but time does many things. It heals wounds, it makes us forget things, and it ages us, but with age comes wisdom. The journey has been long, but I know now that my whole life I was striving to achieve my mother's approval to validate my life and the choices I have made. More than anyone else in my life, her opinion, her approval mattered the most. But now the only opinion of me that really matters is my own.

And I know that I turned out just fine. Maybe I *have* grown up after all.

## Julia Watts

Raised in rural Southeastern Kentucky, Julia Watts has always had a hankering to write. She received an M.A. in English from the University of Louisville and went on to become a professor. At the age of 27, her first novel, *Wildwood Flowers,* was published, and since then her short fiction has appeared in *The Journal of Kentucky Studies, The American Voice,* and the anthologies *Countering the Myths, Dancing in the Dark,* and *Common Lives/ Lesbian Lives.* She won the 2002 Lambda Literary Award for Children/Young Adult fiction for her novel *Finding H.F.*

With Karin Kallmaker, Julia has most recently co-edited a collection of four novellas, including one of her own, for *Once upon a Dyke: New Exploits of Fairy Tale Lesbians.* About her fiction in this mother collection, she says, "This story is dedicated to the memory of Thelma Windham, who provided the real-life inspiration for the fictional character of Theda."

Julia spends her non-writing and non-teaching time in her current residence in Knoxville, Tennessee where she juggles parenthood and writing.

# Girl Talk

## Julia Watts

"I KNOW, I know. I'm your friend from work, and we can't sleep in the same bed," I recited for the tenth time. "God, Judy, for such a big, bad butch, you sure are a closet case."

"Stop calling me that. Am I a closet case even though I'm out to everybody in the universe except my mom?"

"No comment." We were driving through the depths of south Alabama, with nothing in sight but endless scrub pines and the occasional barbecue stand. The Melissa Etheridge song on the CD player was our only reminder that we were still on a planet where people like us existed.

"Di, you just don't know what it's like being the child of old parents. It changes things — it's like dealing with two generation gaps instead of one."

Judy had been what old Southern women call a "change-of-life baby" — and an only child to boot. Her mother had named her after her favorite film star, Judy Garland, in hopes that her daughter would grow up to be as glamorous as her namesake. I think it was Judy's name that first drew me to her. A big butch dyke named after an icon for gay males deliciously unexpected.

Judy and I had been dating for six months, and as far as I was concerned, she was the woman I had been waiting for ever since the moment I caught my first glimpse of Diana Rigg on "The Avengers" and realized I wasn't like all the other little girls.

Judy, however, wasn't as quick to commit. I had been pestering her to move in with me for the past three months, and she kept hemming and hawing about how she wasn't sure her dog and my cat would get along and what a pain it is to divide up household chores.

Recently, I had backed off on the issue, figuring that dating Judy happily ever after was better than no future with her at all. And then, like a bolt out of the lavender, she invited me go with her to visit her mother, on the condition that my true identity would not be revealed. Still the invitation could be interpreted as a sign of commitment...kinda, sorta.

I had heard dozens of entertaining stories about Judy's mother — about her days as a debutante in Birmingham, about the time during the war when she slashed a soldier's face with a broken beer bottle because he had made a lewd comment to her, about the four husbands she had married and buried: the first two for love, the last two for money. I was excited about meeting her, but also a little terrified.

Reading my mind, Judy said, "Don't be nervous about dealing with her, hon. When in doubt, just compliment her on her appearance. She won't give a damn whether you like her cooking or think the house looks nice, but if you tell her how thin she is or what a nice manicure she has, she'll be your friend for life."

I surveyed Judy's stout, muscular body, and gnawed-to-the-nubs fingernails. "How did a woman like her end up with you for a daughter?"

Judy shrugged. "Never say that God lacks a sense of humor."

The house was a large red brick rancher with a porch lined with rocking chairs. It was the kind of house that wouldn't draw much notice in a city, but was palatial by the standards of a small, south Alabama town. Judy led me to the back door, explaining, "Mama always insists that family and friends use the back door. That way, if the front doorbell rings, she knows it's somebody who's trying to sell her something or give her a *Watchtower*."

The back door swung open before we had a chance to knock. Standing before us was a striking, elderly woman with white washed-and-set-at-the beauty-shop hair, Lauren Bacall cheekbones, and Joan Crawford shoulders. Her long nails were painted shell pink, and the ring finger of each hand glittered with an obscenely huge diamond. She gave Judy a once-over, then said, with an accent that masked malice with magnolias, "Well, look at you. You're sure not getting' any thinner, are you?"

Judy didn't miss a beat, which gave me the impression that what I had just heard was a traditional greeting. "Mama, this is Diane, a friend of mine from work."

"It's a pleasure to meet you, Mrs...Mrs...." I stalled. Judy's last name was Wyler, but her mom had had two husbands since Judy's dad. How could I have forgotten to ask Judy her mom's current last name?

"Just call me Theda, honey." She smiled, a little Mona Lisa smile. "I've had so many last names I barely remember 'em myself." She patted Judy on the shoulder. "You girls come on in."

Before I could even orient myself to my new environment, Theda announced, "Well, I guess we'd better go ahead and eat. The Braves game starts at eight."

I was confused. The kitchen, which was decorated in the dark browns and avocado greens of the '70's, showed no signs that any cooking had been done there in recent history. Despite the cave-like quality the color scheme bestowed on it, the kitchen was spotless in the way only a non-cook's kitchen can be.

My questions were answered when Theda began rifling through the freezer. She produced three packages of Lean Cuisine frozen dinners and declared, "All right, I've got spaghetti with meat sauce, vegetable lasagna, and macaroni and cheese. Who wants what?"

I got stuck with the macaroni and cheese. We sat at the kitchen table, each with a little box of micro-waved food, a can of Diet Coke, and a plastic fork. I was amazed. Before I took Judy home the first time, my mom called me on three different occasions for the sole purpose of discussing possible menus. I glanced nervously at the bottle of ketchup and jar of pickles which sat in the center of the table, fearful that I would be considered rude if I didn't find some use for them.

"So, Diane, you must eat a lot of these low-calorie dinners," Theda said. "You've got a cute little figure on you." She pronounced figure "figga."

"Uh...thanks," I said, uncomfortable with the idea that my lover's mom was scoping out my bod.

"If there's anything a man likes, it's a cute figure," Theda went on. "Put on some stockings and heels, smile and cross your legs real pretty, and a man'll do anything you want."

"Mama!" Judy protested.

"Judy always thinks I shock people. I'm not shockin' you, am I, Diane?"

"No, ma'am."

"Well, I figure it's just us girls together. What can we talk about if not men?"

What indeed? I stared down at my food, confident that if I caught Judy's eye, I'd have a giggling fit the likes of which I hadn't had since I was twelve years old and forced to sit quietly in church.

"I always tell Judy she could do better in the looks department," Theda was saying. "She may have got her daddy's stoutness, but she's still got my eyes and mouth, don't you think, Diane?"

"Um...yeah." I shifted uncomfortably. Given my rather intimate knowledge of Judy's mouth, I certainly didn't want to think of it as belonging to her mother.

"Yes, she could turn some heads, all right," Theda said, staring at her daughter's face. "Put on a dress every once in a while, let those awful fingernails grow out—"

"Mama, I fix computers for a living. I can't have long nails that are gonna get stuck in the machinery."

"She's such a tomboy, Diane. Always been more interested in fixin' things than in fixin' herself up. When she was little, I wanted her to take dance lessons, to be like Judy Garland—that's who I named her after, you know." She pushed her half-eaten spaghetti away. "But all she wanted to do was follow her daddy around and help him build things. Birdhouses, bookshelves, kitchen cabinets—you name it, they built it."

"I think it's great that Judy's so..." I searched for a word. "Handy."

"Oh, it's wonderful for a woman to know how to do things for herself," Theda said. "Of course, that's no reason for her to let her looks go. And sometimes, when you're around a man, it's good to let on you don't know quite as much as you do."

"It's not 1950 anymore, Mama. Women don't have to play dumb to get what they want."

"Oh, don't they?" Theda paused to admire the diamonds on her fingers. "Well, we've been havin' this argument since you were sixteen years old. You get your power your way, I'll get mine my way." She turned to me. "Now, Diane, what you need is some color on your lips and eyes, and you've got to do somethin' about those eyebrows."

In terms of bushiness, my eyebrows do lie somewhere between Brooke Shields' and Brezhnev's. But I've always had a very minimalist beauty philosophy: Don't mess with what's already there; just make sure your teeth are clean and you don't smell bad, and you're good to go.

Even though I hate baseball, I was relieved when the Braves game started. Theda and Judy were riveted to the screen, Judy gnawing her nails and Theda smoking cigarette after cigarette with Bette Davis aplomb.

Judy and I live in Atlanta. She took me to a Braves game once in the early days of our relationship. She was so transfixed by the action on the field she appeared incapable of conversation, so to relieve my boredom, I kept downing little plastic cups of beer. By the end of the ninth inning, I was so drunk I fell down the steps as we were leaving our seats. When my coworkers inquired about the Ace bandage on my ankle the next day, I proudly told them it was a baseball injury.

After the game was over, Theda stood up, stretched demurely and announced that it was her bedtime, with the implication that it should be ours, too.

After she was safely out of the room, Judy whispered, "She's a piece of work, isn't she?"

"I'll say." I looked around to make sure we had some privacy. "Hon, why were there pickles and ketchup on the dinner table?" Those non-sequitur condiments had been bothering me all night.

"You don't think we're trash, do you?"

Apparently, this was supposed to answer my question. Since inappropriate condiments seemed to be a sensitive issue, I decided not pursue it.

Judy stood and stretched. "Well, time for bed.'

"Really?" It was an hour and a half before our usual bedtime.

"Yep." She walked right past me.

"Judy!" I barked, then lowered my voice, "Don't I get a kiss?"

She blew me a kiss from several feet away and then padded on down the hall. Thank God this was just a weekend visit. If I had to spend a week at Judy's mother's, I'd die from lack of affection.

## Marie Sheppard Williams

Born in Minneapolis, Minnesota in 1931, Marie Sheppard Williams has lived through over seven decades of tumultuous times. She received an English degree from the University of Minnesota, then went on to get her Master's in Social Work. She married, divorced, and parented one daughter, Megan, who is now an architect in London. After a sometimes grueling career as a social worker, she retired and went back to school for an art degree.

Over the last twenty-five years, Marie has been publishing stories and poems in literary journals like *The American Voice* and *The Alaska Quarterly* where she has championed her own particular take on pacing, tone, and punctuation. She takes inspiration from everyday occurrences. For instance, in this piece, she says, "I was very much influenced by my little cousin's death (mentioned in the story) and by my father who told stories just as I tell them now—from 'The Everything but the Kitchen Sink School.'"

Marie's short fiction has been nominated for the Pushcart Prize a dozen times and won twice; she has received a Bush Grant; and she was a finalist for the Minnesota Book Award for *The Worldwide Church of the Handicapped,* from which the title story was recently made into a play by Kevin Kling. Marie continues to work on stories, poems, and novellas from her home in South Minneapolis.

# The Corn Broom

## Fictionalized Memoir by Marie Sheppard Williams

ONE DAY MAYBE a year ago my mother and I went to visit my Aunt Anna and my cousin George, who is Anna's oldest son. George and Anna live in a very small house, three rooms, on Colfax Avenue North in Minneapolis, and George takes care of Anna. My mother and I do not visit Anna and George very often, although we live in the same city.

Anna and my mother are sisters. Anna is the oldest of the five girls: oldest surviving, that is. Mary, who went to be a nun at seventeen, was really the oldest; then came Catherine, who is said to have been the beauty of the family and whom I remember only as a faint, sweet voice; then Anna. After Anna, my mother, and then the baby, Irma. All are dead now except Anna and my mother.

The two of them don't get on awfully well. Not all the time. Once after Irma died they didn't speak to each other for a whole year. My cousin Tildy got them to talking again, and at the time that I am writing about they were pretty good. Good buddies. On the phone to each other three or four times a week, for example. At least.

Anyway, Anna and George had just come back from grocery shopping when my mother and I got there on that day I'm talking about, were in fact just driving into the garage in back of the house as we were knocking on the front door.

When we walked around to the back yard—we heard them drive in and that is why we walked around—Aunt Anna was crossing the yard carrying a broom in her hand; she was using it as a cane, and George was carrying her real cane, a sturdy wooden one with a crook.

*Um, um, um,* she was groaning with each step. My Aunt Anna is diabetic and has a lot of neuropathy in her feet and legs, and the legs and ankles are badly ulcerated. Walking causes her a great deal of discomfort and is besides just simply difficult and slow because Anna's body is swollen and very bent and her balance is poor. And so on.

She negotiated the back yard and the one step up to the back door and went into the house, groaning and grumping, and we followed her, holding our hands at the ready in case she should fall over and it certainly looked like she might fall over, any second, and she went into the living room and positioned herself by her favorite chair, still holding on to the broom, which was an old-fashioned corn broom. She backed up to the chair, slowly, and we held our breaths, at least I know that I did and George looked like he was holding his — I don't know about my mother, actually she may not have seen well enough to be aware of any of this, her eyesight is very bad — and then Anna let herself fall down and backwards, heavily, sickeningly, and she somehow hit the chair just right and suddenly was seated there, triumphant, with the corn broom held aloft in one hand like a strange sceptre.

She thumped the floor with it.

Look at this broom, she roared.

Just look at it!

Anna speaks very loud because she is deaf; at least, I think that is why she speaks very loud.

What a terrible broom! she screamed. They don't make good corn brooms any more!

Look at that!

What's the matter with it, I said.

It's *thin*! she shouted.

It's not fat like it should be!

They don't make them fat any more!

And the straws are too thick!

Like sticks!

Puff-puff.

Not thin like they should be!

Huff-puff.

Why, you might as well try to sweep the floor with *a bunch of sticks!*

I can get you a real old-fashioned fat corn broom with thin straws in it, Aunt Anna, I said. I think I know just the broom you want.

You can? she said, her dim old half-blind eyes sparking up for a second: I guess there is nothing like the possibility of having a dream fulfilled to perk up even a very old life.

Yes, I said. At the hardware store.

AT THAT TIME I worked at Gelle's hardware store, which is one of the last of the great old-time hardware stores where quality is still champion and service is a small god, and they sell everything and repair everything, etc., etc., well, you know the kind of store I mean.

I worked at Gelle's for five months after I quit my job as a social worker at the Minneapolis Society for the Blind, and before I started into a commercial art sequence at Minneapolis Vo-Tech. I am the oldest would-be artist in my class, which is I guess neither here nor there but which is nevertheless true and which I thought might interest you.

When I went to sign the papers for my school loan at the bank the clerk said: Is it for you? Certainly it's for me, I said.

That's the kind of crap you get when you are old. Oldish.

When I told my mother I was going to quit my job and go to art school she said: That's good, you had so much talent when you were a girl, I always thought you should do something with it.

Honestly. I nearly fell over. I expected instant resistance: how can you do that, what will the neighbors think, what will the family say, your brothers, the cousins, blah, blah, blah, well, you know. But: *That's good*: she said. She surprised me so much: well, I nearly changed my mind, that's what a shock it was. I nearly didn't quit my job to go to art school.

Sometimes it seems to me that my mother might be another person than the person I think I know.

SO ANYWAY I promised to get Anna a real old-fashioned corn broom and to bring it to her within the next month.

You won't, she said. You'll forget.

I won't forget, I said.

People forget, she said. They always do.

Not me, I said. I won't forget. I absolutely promise to bring it some time within the next four weeks. The next month. I absolutely promise.

Well, she said. Maybe you will.

You were always a good girl, Joan, she said. You were always good to me. I remember the time you gave me the bottle of Chanel No. 5...

*Oh, one thing in life I always wanted* – a memory of her haunted cracked crazy voice came to me down the years – *oh, the one thing I always wanted* – her voice remembered was a comic, self-aware, cackling wail, her voice that was once low and soft they say, as soft as my mother's, as Catherine's – *is a little bottle of Chanel No. 5! Just a little bottle! Oh, I always wanted that...*

Well, of course I got it for her.

Oh, Anna won't like that, said my mother. Anna only likes

practical things.

No she doesn't, I said; yes she will.

No, said my mother. Anna is hard. Anna doesn't like anything very much.

No, I said. Anna is easy. Anna likes beauty. And luxury. And things that are really good.

I suppose you think you understand Anna better than I do, my mother said.

Yes, I said. I do think that.

I think my mother has always been a little jealous of Aunt Anna where I was concerned—you know how it happens sometimes. Anna and I are a lot alike, and my mother and I are not alike. Anna and I are *simpatico*.

You know how this happens. Sometimes. In families.

How much will it cost? said Anna.

The broom, she meant. We are back to the broom.

Oh, I don't know, I said.

More than ten dollars?

I don't think so, I said. Not more than ten dollars, probably not.

All right, she said. It's worth it. To have a real corn broom. You buy it for me, Joan, and I'll pay you for it.

Okay, I said. I will.

I don't really think you will, though, she said. I don't really think so.

You'll see, I said. I will. Inside of a month.

Maybe I'll see, she said.

Did you hear that, George? she said. Joan is going to bring me a real corn broom...

That's good, my cousin George said. Soberly. But I thought I saw a certain hilarious light in his good eye. George, I forgot to tell you, has had sight in only one eye from birth.

Honestly. We begin to sound like some kind of disabled crew, don't we?—old, deaf, blind, diabetic, one-eyed. Well, that's life—a far cry from the TV.

George is honest to god some kind of saint. I really think so. He is so good to Anna.

WELL, I BOUGHT the broom. I almost forgot to buy it, a month is too long to remember anything these days; I think that I too am getting old although it is hard to credit that because I have all these mothers and aunts; I almost forgot but I did not quite forget. About three weeks later the idea of the broom popped into my head, just in time, and I went in to the hardware store and hefted one broom against another and weighed the prices against the heft and balanced it all in my mind — as I knew Anna would want me to do — and I finally settled on a broom for seven-ninety-nine. Sort of midway between thin and overweight. Fairly high in the price range — there was one for nine ninety-nine that I considered but it seemed to me that it was just too heavy for her, too fat. And the straws in that very fat one were I thought perhaps not quite thin enough.

What do you think? I said to Charlotte in the store. Because of my working there with her. Charlotte knew quite a bit about Aunt Anna and the rest.

Well, I think you've made the best choice, said Charlotte. The other one is too heavy. Also it is too expensive. It would go over ten dollars with the tax.

That's true, I said. With the tax.

A good broom, said Charlotte. Not too heavy. And with nice thin straws. Just right.

Oh, you know about thin straws? I said. I thought only my family cared any more about thin straws.

I know about thin straws, said Charlotte. Sure. And laughed.

I'm from New Ulm, she said. Remember?

I do remember now. Char, I said. And laughed too. New Ulm, Minnesota — I know this because I lived in New Ulm once myself, back when I was married, before I was divorced — is as strange a collective as my family is. Or almost.

But that's another story.

ALONG ABOUT THE fifteenth of September, within the allotted month, but barely, I told my mother that I had the broom. I said that we would take it to Anna the following Sunday, in two days time.

How much did you have to pay for it? said my mother.

Seven ninety-nine, I said. Plus tax.

Plus tax, said my mother.

Yep. Plus tax, I said.

That's a lot for a broom, my mother said.

Oh, I don't know, I said. For a good corn broom? I think that's a good price.

Well, my mother said.

I suppose I'm behind the times, she said.

Then she said: Anna's birthday is next week. Thursday.

Oh, right, I said. Thanks. I would have forgotten.

I know you would have, said my mother.

I said I would have didn't I? I said, nettled and furious suddenly. My mother can get to me like nobody else can—even now with eight thousand dollars worth of therapy under the bridge. I try very hard to ignore what I consider—of course, you understand this—to be her deliberate baiting, but I ignore it at my peril: inside I burn. I almost never argue with my mother or tell her that I am mad at her. She is old, I say to myself. She is deaf. Almost blind. What kind of a person argues with an old deaf and blind woman? And a mother. Apple pie. God and country. In my heart I still buy it all, I am sort of embarrassed to say.

Once when my daughter carried the flag at the Bluebird Flyup, I actually cried when the little girls all sang the Star Spangled Banner, *Oh say does tha-hat star-spangled ba-han-er-her ye-het way-have*, and Margaret marched up to the front holding perilously and shakily aloft the heavy flagpole and the vaunted banner.

Cried.

Is there any hope for such a person as me?

Are you going to give Anna a birthday present? my mother asked me.

Oh, I don't know. Mama, I said. Maybe I will. Maybe I won't.

She's your godmother, my mother said.

Mm. I said. Not paying a lot of attention, as you can probably see.

You should give her a present, my mother said.

Mother, I said. Sometimes I give Anna a present and sometimes I don't. And Anna understands that. Anna is okay with that.

I suppose you think you know Anna better than I do, she said.

Absolutely, I said. Not arguing, though. Just saying it.

Huh, said my mother.

I think you should give her a present, she said. Tildy always gives Anna a present.

Well. Maybe I will, I said.

Listen, maybe I'll give her the broom for her birthday, I said. Maybe.

You'll give her the broom? my mother said.

Commitments are hard for me: Well, I don't know, I said. I'll think about it. Maybe I will.

Oh that will be nice, my mother said.

Maybe I won't, I said. I'll think about it.

That will be nice if you do, she said.

Well maybe I will I said.

Tildy will give her a present, said my mother. Tildy always does.

Well hooray, I said. Good for Twinkie.

What does that mean? said my mother.

It means: Good for Tildy, I said. Good for her.

I really like my cousin Tildy a lot. I can't imagine why I do sometimes, the way my mother goes on about her. Tildy this and Tildy that. Well, you know.

Tildy never forgets my Aunt Anna's birthday. Or mine. Or my mother's. Or anybody's. Tildy probably sends a birthday card to goddamn President Bush, for God's sake.

THE NEXT SUNDAY I drove my mother and the broom over to Aunt Anna's little house.

Are you going to give Anna the broom for her birthday? my mother said.

I guess so, I said. Yes I am.

I told Tildy you were, my mother said. Tildy was very impressed.

Tildy was impressed? I said. I laughed. By a broom? For goodness sakes. Why?

Well, said my mother. A broom is an expensive present. Tildy always gives Anna a little present. Like a tea-towel. Maybe.

I see, I said. A tea-towel.

Honestly.

Do other families have this kind of conversation?

SO, FOLKS, WE get to Anna's house with the corn broom one bright cool Sunday in September. Anna as usual is sitting in her big hard chair with the straight back that her other son Billy and his wife Laura gave her and that is easier to get in and out of than a softer chair would be. It is important to Anna to be able to get out of her chair by herself, without help. Every time she does it, it looks like an excruciating effort. I don't offer to help her. My mother offers. *Do you need any help Anna,* my mother says, and Anna always ignores her.

This Sunday Anna is sitting in the chair when we come in. In the living room: which is the major room in this little tiny house. This is the fourth in a series of houses that my aunt has lived in since her oldest son, Paulie, drowned in the Mississippi when he was six years old.

Besides the living room, the house has only a bedroom and a

kitchen. Well: and a bathroom. There is a basement, but no attic. I mean, it's not much bigger than a lot of garages. Anna has the bedroom—the double bed from her life as a married woman almost fills it up, you can hardly turn around in that bedroom—and George makes do with a couch in the living room that opens out into a bed: that same couch that my mother and I sit on when we come to visit.

You know, I have lived in Minneapolis all my life except for the twelve years in New Ulm, and a summer in New York City when I was going to break away and go big-time, become an editor on a magazine or something, but it didn't work out, I came back here and got married instead and went to New Ulm. But what I was going to say, in all that time I have never once seen the river without thinking of Paulie and seeing in my mind his little drowned body dressed in its blue snowsuit under the ice. I see his white face with the blue wool helmet like little kids wore in those days, and the blue baby chin strap under his chin, so that the helmet never came off in the water, but the mittens did, and they say fish nibbled at his fingers. I was younger than he was, just a baby when it happened really, but I don't forget. I won't ever forget, I don't believe that I will.

There are a lot of family stories about Paulie's death. My mother says that is when Anna's voice took on that queer cracked crying sound; and they say that she wouldn't live in the house by the river any more after that, she made my Uncle Luke, her husband, buy another house, and then another, and another, each house smaller than the one before; until Luke died and she bought by herself this last house, the smallest of all.

The family says that Anna has had a very sad life. Paulie dying; and then also they say that she loved a man and did not marry him, the family did not approve of him; I remember her from when I was a child, years ago, sitting by an old hand-cranked phonograph, playing sad love-songs, tears slipping silently from her eyes and dripping down her face.

Anna is thinking sad thoughts, my mother would say gently; in those days: Leave her alone, my mother would say.

But you know, I married my true love—against my mother's wish—and that didn't work out any too well either.

WELL. ANYWAY. *Comme ci, comme ça.* Or whatever.
Back to the broom.
Hello, Anna, I say. Look what I brought you. I promised you a broom and here it is. And right on time too. I wanted you to know that sometimes people do keep their promises.
Well. Says Anna. Some people do. You do. I guess you are

different.

Let's see it.

I wave the broom under her nose. Look! Corn! I say. A real corn broom. Charlotte in the hardware store said it was the best one for the price.

Nice thin straws, I say.

See?

And fat *enough*, I say. Not *too* fat.

See?

Hm, yes, says Anna. It's a good broom. Look, George, she says. A real good corn broom. Joan brought it like she said she would. You're a good girl, Joan, she says. Elizabeth, Joan is a good girl.

Girl. I am fifty-two years old.

Oh, well, my mother says. Pleased though; you could tell that she was pleased. A little.

You're lucky, Elizabeth, to have a daughter like Joan, says my Aunt Anna. Who is so good to you.

Now that was going too far—I knew my mother couldn't buy that.

Oh, well, my mother says. I don't know about that. I was never lucky in anything else.

That's enough, Anna says. It's enough to be lucky in your daughter.

I guess so my mother says.

Damned if it is, I hear.

I think you're lucky to have a son like George, Anna, my mother says. Who stays with you. And takes care of you.

Oh, ow. A hit.

Lucky, lucky, who is luckiest? Who has won the biggest prize from the one-armed bandit, life, who takes away with his one hand, and takes away and takes away? Look at them: one wouldn't think either of them could be called lucky...

Deaf and blind and sick and old and crippled.

A son is not the same, says Anna.

George sits and smiles through all of this. Honest to God. Like I said. A saint. I really like my cousin George a lot, though everybody else including my mother I think underestimates him badly. He is in a way quite shy; when he was a kid in school they said he was mentally retarded and put him in a class for retarded people. He is not retarded, he never was; but being in that class I think made him feel shy and different; and I think it made him not expect anything much from the world. He used to trap with my brothers when he and they were young. My brothers have given it up, but George still traps. And he has learned (by mail) taxidermy; sometimes when he catches a particularly beautiful animal, he does not sell its skin but instead stuffs it. His trophies are in the basement under the little house: pheasants and ermine, for example. A mink.

I don't approve of trapping, I think it is cruel and barbaric, but somehow it's okay with me that George does it. Because he's family? I guess so, maybe.

What do I owe you for the broom, Joan, Aunt Anna says.

Nothing, I say: I mean it to be a birthday present.

Oh, no, says Aunt Anna. I asked you to buy it and I want to pay you for it.

No, I say, really, it's for your birthday, I want it to be a birthday present.

Oh, well, says Aunt Anna. If that's what you want.

That's what I want, I say.

The conversation veers to other subjects. The two sisters, Anna and Elizabeth, talk to each other. Neither one of them can hear much. They both wear hearing aids, and the hearing aids give them a lot of trouble a good deal of the time.

Looking at the two of them, listening to them, it is tempting to conclude that hearing aids are more trouble than they are worth.

George and I listen and smirk at each other: middle-aged (no, young; as long as they are alive we are young, we are children) superiority and health and strength — well, relative health, relative strength — radiating between us, sending unspoken messages back and forth:

God, isn't this funny?

Isn't this awful?

What can we do?

George smiles, shrugs his shoulders.

Aunt Anna says: I've had a terrible week, Elizabeth!

My mother says: No, I'm not. What makes you think that. I'm not.

Anna: Turn the thermostat down, George.

George: (Loud; he is used to this) *Why?*

Anna: Elizabeth says she's hot.

George: *No she doesn't.*

Anna: (Yelling at my mother) *Elizabeth didn't you say that you were hot?*

Elizabeth: *Hot?* No, I 'm not.

Anna: See? She's hot. It's too hot in here.

Me, loud: No, Anna, she says *no*, she says that she is NOT

HOT. NOT. HOT.

Anna: Not hot. Oh I thought she said she was hot.

Me: NO.

Anna: Why would anyone say that they were *not hot*?

George gets up and adjusts his mother's hearing aid. She has the kind that is attached to a battery pack that is held in the hand, and George takes it out of her hand and twists dials.

Oh, that's better, she says. Oh that's much better. *Say something Elizabeth*, she roars at my mother.

What did you say? my mother says in her soft murmur. My mother cannot shout, never could that I can remember, her voice is like a sweet soft flute, cracked and breathy now. Her breath weaves softly through the holes in her voice.

*I Said Say Something Now, My Hearing Aid Is Fixed,* Anna yells.

My mother looks blank.

Let me see your hearing aid, Mother, I say. I twist and bend myself around behind her as she sits on the couch in the tiny crowded room: I peer at the little levers and dials on the aid, which is a Sony Monaural Model #4733, one of the best models in that line. It fits behind her ear. It has numbers 1 through 8 on a little wheel to control the volume. She is supposed to turn the little wheel with her finger. But she doesn't remember to do it, or she can't, or something. And sometimes it turns by itself, or so it seems.

When the aid is set on 1, there is hardly any amplification. Set on 8 there is a lot. I turn it to 6. I push the ear mold firmly into her ear, none too gently by this time.

How's that? I shout at her.

I don't think that helps, she says.

Well it's on 6 for god's sakes, I say.

Let me see, I say. I twist behind her again.

Oh for god's sake, I say.

It's turned off. I say.

How can this have happened?

Helpless wrath is beginning to boil up in me.

I don't think I can stand this, I say to no one in particular. I begin to giggle. I think I'm going crazy, I say.

I turn her hearing aid on: flip the tiny switch at the bottom that somehow has flipped to "0" — when it should be on "M".

God only knows what "M" means.

"0" means Off.

Maybe the couch turned it off? like maybe it caught on the couch or something? She was hearing ok before, at least I thought she was.

My cousin George laughs.

Oh, that's good, my mother says.

A nerve-grating whistle begins.

It's whistling, she says.

It whistles on 7, I say. It must have slipped to 7. I twist around behind her again, I turn the little wheel to 6.

There, I say.

Eventually both aids are adjusted, and the two sisters can talk to each other.

Oh, it's terrible to be old. Aunt Anna says to my mother.

Oh, well, says my mother, we have to accept it.

I don't want to accept it, Anna wails.

You have to anyway, says my mother.

The grim realist.

I'm ready to die, says Aunt Anna. I'm ready any time.

Oh I'm ready too my mother says.

This conversation goes on and on. It is never any different. It is always the same conversation.

Aunt Anna always says: I am ready to die.

My mother says she is ready too.

My cousin George smiles: always.

And I am always — always — going crazy.

FINALLY IT IS time to go.

George, give Joan some money for the broom. Aunt Anna says. How much did it cost, Joan?

No, Anna, I say. I told you. It's a birthday present.

I want to pay you for it, she says.

No, no, I say.

Yes, she says.

No.

Yes.

No.

How much did it cost?

Something in me snaps. I have been through this so often before, this is not an argument, this is a ritual dance. I am not going to dance, damn it. Seven-ninety-nine, I say. It cost seven-ninety nine. I begin to laugh, catching my cousin George's eye. He is laughing too.

Ha-ha-ha-ha.

Oh, ho, ho, ho.

Some voice in me is screaming in agony: Plus tax! it screams. Plus tax!

Give Joan eight dollars, Anna says. To George.

I give up. I mean, you can see how I might give up about

now?

Okay, I say. Give me eight dollars, George. All right. I am licked, I give up. Uncle.

George still smiles.

His smile expresses perfect sympathy with me: he knows exactly what is happening. But he nevertheless does what Anna tells him to do. He gets out his wallet, opens it, counts out eight dollars and gives it to me.

George works in a car wash half-days. Has since I can remember; certainly since he came back from his service in the Korean War.

Conflict. The Korean Conflict. They didn't call it a war. But people killed each other in it just the same.

George had an injured back when he came out of the Conflict and he was never able to work much after that, or do any heavy stuff.

So he works half-time in the car wash and takes care of Anna.

I put the eight dollars into my purse. What can I do? I say to George. What else can I do?

Nothing, he says. You're trapped. He laughs.

I get ready to go: I put my coat on, move toward the door, take my mother's arm, urge her out the door.

I embrace my Aunt Anna: I kiss her fine old wrinkled cheek and I love her more than I can say and I forgive her for everything that has happened or that ever can happen.

I forgive my mother nothing.

Goodbye, Anna, I say.

Goodbye, George. *Arrivederci*. I say.

Goodbye, George says.

Come again, he says. Please. My mother likes it when you come. He says.

I will, I say. I will. Soon this time. I promise. I swear to God.

If I come three or four times a year it's a miracle.

His eyes are full of pain and acceptance of pain. Perhaps he accepts so deeply that he does not call it pain any more?

WHEN WE WERE children, George and his brother Billy had a sort of shack that they built out in their back yard. Little — about the size of a big doghouse. The three of us could get into it; one other person could be shoe-horned in, but not two. One day, probably a Sunday, I was usually over there on Sundays, we were in the shack and two of George and Billy's friends came by: two little girls, Annie and Zetta. One of them can come in, Billy said. Billy was the leader even then, though he was younger by a couple of years.

The other one has to go home. He said.

And then, to me: You choose.

*Me?* I said. *I* have to choose?

Yes, you're the guest.

But I don't know them, I said. So Bill presented their cases.

Annie's the most fun, he said. Annie's the best. Annie's true blue. She'll never let you down. She tells the truth no matter what. She won't rat on you.

Zetta's a pain, he said. She's a sneak.

I stuck my head out the shack door and stared at the two girls.


ANNIE WAS RED-HAIRED, with pigtails down her back. She had a funny cheerful face with freckles all over it. She had braces on her teeth.

Zetta looked like a picture in a magazine. Long straight blond hair fell to her waist in a shining cascade. She wore a spotless and unwrinkled blue dress. She smiled a secret little smile.

I'll have Zetta, I said.

Zetta! said Billy. You *can't* have Zetta. She's awful.

You said I could have anyone I wanted, I said.

Zetta! said George. You want *Zetta?* I *hate* Zetta.

Why do you hate her? I asked.

I just do, he said.

And one other time when we were all out for a drive in my father's 1936 Chevy on a Sunday and someone said: Let's go to Wayzata.

No, said George. Not Wayzata.

Why not.

It reminds me of that goddamn Zetta, he said, pushing his nose flat against the car window.

But we went to Wayzata anyway, and I guess we had a good time. We usually did when we were together.


I AM HOLDING my mother's arm and giving her an assist down the front steps when the thunderbolt comes.

That's the worst thing I have ever seen, my mother says.

That is just terrible, she says.

*You are a terrible person*: she says.

I stop dead. She keeps saying it: You are a terrible person. Terrible. I have never seen anything so terrible.

I shake her arm to make her stop.

*What!* I say. *Be quiet.*

I *won't*, she says.

But why are you doing this, I say. Why is this happening?

Can't you hear it, folks, Adam and God, Job and God: why are you doing this, why? An old joke's punch-line ricochets in my mind: Something about your face just pisses me off...

To make somebody pay for their own birthday present, she says: how could you do that?

Mama, I didn't...I begin. But hopelessness rises in me. Stay here, I command her. Don't move an inch. I leave her standing on the sidewalk. I run back up the steps to where my cousin and my aunt are watching, hearing all this in the open doorway.

All this hasn't taken a minute, you know. Anna and George still have their hands raised — frozen, I guess — in farewell.

I open my purse and get the eight dollars out of my wallet, and my hands are shaking and I can hear myself beginning to stammer and I push the money into George's hands, H-here, t-take it, don't argue, don't say anything for G-G-God's s-s-sake...

But. But. He says.

It's your money, Joan, my aunt says. We owe it to you.

*Ohhhh*: I hear my voice beginning to wail. Take it, Anna. Please. My mother will hate me forever if you don't take it...

Please...

George takes the money.

I run back down the steps to where my mother is standing. I grab her arm and rush her toward the car. My turn now, folks.

I'm so mad at you, I say. I'M SO MAD AT YOU...

Well. I was right, she says. Prissy, prim, righteous. Fifty-two years of rage erupts in me. Mount St. Helen's of Minneapolis.

I push her into the car and close the door. I tear around to the other side and I open the door and slam myself into the seat. Slam the door shut.

No you weren't right, I say. I start the car violently and jerk it away from the curb.

Oh, be careful, she says.

You were wrong, I scream.

You didn't have all the facts, I scream.

You were absolutely wrong! I scream. Yes. At the top of my voice. I really got going. I really got into it. I began to enjoy it. It was the first time in my whole life I ever really yelled at her. I yelled all the way to her apartment. The time came when I wasn't mad any more and I was screaming just for the sheer pleasure of it.

So finally I stopped.

Excuse me, I said. And began to laugh as I pulled into a parking place in the lot by the hi-rise building where she lives.

Don't yell at me when we are going in, she said. Don't raise your voice. The neighbors will think we are fighting.

So then of course I got mad all over again. But this time I shut my mouth and nearly bit my tongue off instead of expressing, as they told me I should in my therapy, my feelings.

THE JOY REMAINED, though. All the way home, driving to my house in South Minneapolis, I felt clean and clear and refreshed and absolutely justified.

I was ashamed of myself later, of course, but it didn't matter: it was worth it. It was absolutely and totally worth it. And Aunt Anna loves the broom, still uses it; every time my mother and I go over there to see her in her little, little house she shows it to me, shows me how fat it is, how well it sweeps, how splendidly thin the straws are.

My cousin George smiles.

My mother sits, quiet and remote behind her blind eyes, her hearing aid; her soft, soft voice is for this moment stilled.

## Kelly A. Zarembski

Born and raised in Ohio, Kelly Zarembski attended Cleveland State University where she was a Philosophy major. She currently lives in Cleveland with her partner of fourteen years and their cat, dog, and turtles. When not reading, writing, or indulging in her love of travel, Kelly works as a purchasing agent.

Asked what has sparked her writing, Kelly says, "My seventh grade honors English teacher influenced my creativity." In terms of authors she emulates, it is "most importantly Anne Rice. Her style and imagination are my inspiration."

In 2003, Kelly's second novel, *Embers in the Sky*, won the Stonewall Society Pride in the Literary Arts Award. She is at work now on her fourth novel.

# June Hunter

## Fiction by Kelly A. Zarembski

SITTING QUIETLY ON the edge of the bed I looked down on my sister lying motionless, surrounded by bottles and tubes suspended above her. She is a shell of what she once was. My sister and I were never close, not until six months ago when she called me from out of the blue to tell me she was dying.

My mother died the same way, breast cancer. It swept through her body so fast; one day she was my mother, the next she was a frail shell like I see before me now.

I reach for Jeanie's hand, and it is cool to the touch. She looks at peace, but from what I remember of my mother, this is not typical.

Holding her hand I wonder where all the years went. All the senseless arguing and fighting...it all seems so pointless now.

I think about and ache for my mother every day, and seeing Jeanie lying here brings back vivid childhood memories.

"WHY DO YOU keep hanging around me? Mom! Glory will not leave me alone!" Jeanie yelled, as she stood in the hallway outside our bedroom door.

"It's my room, too, Jeanie!" I screamed.

"Girls, don't make me come up there," my mother yelled from downstairs in the kitchen.

"Fine!" I whipped around, grabbing my basketball. "Have it your way, Jeanie. I'm gone." I dribbled down the hall, then down the stairs, a trick I'd been practicing, then through the kitchen.

"Glory, not in the house."

I watched my mother mixing brownies in a glass bowl with a big wooden spoon. "I'm going to the playground. Jeanie kicked me out of our room again." I leaned against the counter, while I continued to dribble.

"I'll have another talk with her, but you have to give her

some space, baby. She's seventeen and boy crazy," she said, giggling.

"Whatever." Jeanie was only two years older than me, and mom was right, she *was* boy crazy. I watched the ball all the way to the palm of my hand.

"Glory," she stopped my ball, "help me finish these brownies and I'll spot you five out back."

"Five? Mom! Make it seven."

"Seven it is. Get me the brownie pan from under the sink, baby."

My mom was the best, not only did she make the best brownies, but she had the tightest three pointer of anyone I knew.

"TWENTY-ONE. I better start dinner."

I sat down on my ball.

She ran her fingers through my long dirty blonde hair. "I'll tell you what, let me give your father a call so he can pick up dinner, and I'll whip your butt again. How's that?"

I jumped up off my ball. "Okay! Tell dad to get Chinese, steamed dumplings."

"We'll see, I think in the meantime you should practice until I get back."

"Mom!"

"Start with foul shots. The free ones make all the difference in the game."

"Okay."

"By the time you finish fifty, I'll be back."

I immediately lined myself up on our hand-painted foul line and concentrated. With each shot I made, and with every time mom would stuff the ball back in my face when we played, I knew I was getting better.

In the back of my mind I also knew every time I felt myself getting better I was raising myself up to Marcia's level. She was the best player on our team in high school. She was a year ahead of me, and she was amazing. Long curly black hair, and I felt closer to her than to anyone else my whole entire life.

We liked the same music, Bee Gee's of course; the same sports, too, and I followed her around all day, every day. Marcia Jones, she was my first crush.

She was the reason I woke up in the morning; she was when I knew I was gay. I had no interest in boys; I was in love with my best friend and scared to death.

I so wanted to talk to my mother about it, but I had no idea what to say.

"GLORY, HERE!" MARCIA yelled, as she jumped up and down.

With one hand I lined the ball right at her, one bounce right into her hand. She shot and we won.

I ran, jumping in her arms. "Great shot!"

She hugged me. "Great pass!"

The whole team ended up at the pizza parlor down the street from the gym, and I stood next to Marcia at the jukebox.

Nervously I patted my fingers on the glass. "The usual?" I asked.

"Yeah."

She smiled at me and my body tingled, as I punched A5 for *Staying Alive*.

Jeez, I wanted to talk to my mother.

SUMMER CAME, AND I thought I was going to die without Marcia around me. I begged my mom to put me in a basketball camp. If nothing else, I wanted to improve my game so when I did see her, I'd be able to impress her with my new skills.

"Glory, it's too expensive."

"But mom, please!"

"We'll see. Five hundred dollars is a lot of money, baby."

"My birthday's coming up." I was the poster girl for Independence Day. I was born on the Fourth of July, thus the name, Glory Independence Hunter. "If I get the money myself, can I go?"

"Yes, Glory. If you raise the money, of course you can go."

"Great! Thanks, Mom." I jumped in her arms.

"Don't thank me yet. That's a lot of money, Glory."

"I'm going to go to camp, Mom."

"I know you are, baby," she said, hugging me. I was almost as tall as she was.

Mom was a great basketball player in high school and I went to the same school she did. The name June Hunter was engraved on just about every plaque and trophy in all the glass cases in the gym. She was offered scholarships from colleges everywhere, but dad pressured her not to accept any of them. Instead, she became his wife and gave up all of her dreams.

I loved my mother.

"HAPPY BIRTHDAY, BABY!" My mother came and sat on the edge of my bed. "You're not going to sleep your birthday away are you?" She wiped some stray hairs away from my face.

I smiled, "No."

"Good, this is for you." She pulled a present from behind

her back. "This is just between the two of us, okay?"

"Our secret."

"Yes."

I slowly opened the box and inside was a bracelet, small hearts with X's. I looked up.

"I love you, Glory. You're my little firecracker. I always want to be with you. This way my heart will always be around your wrist."

I fell into her, throwing my arms around her neck, crying.

"Don't cry, baby. Now get dressed. I have blueberry pancakes waiting for you downstairs."

Before she left I yelled, "Mom!"

She turned.

"I love you."

She smiled while she stood in the doorway. "I love you with all my heart, baby. I always will."

I LEANED BACK in my mother's arms while we all sat on a blanket watching the fireworks after the annual Fourth of July carnival. She whispered, "Your future's as bright as these fireworks, baby. Remember that. You can be whatever you want to be."

I held her arms tight around me. "I'll never forget this birthday, mom. Thank you."

"It's your sixteenth, you shouldn't. Hey, look. Marcia's here."

"She is?" I sat up.

"By the Ferris wheel," she whispered.

"Mom, I . . ."

She squeezed me. "Go ahead, baby. Go to her."

I turned and looked in my mother's hazel eyes, and they looked just like mine. We stared at each other and at that moment I knew she knew. "Mom . . ."

Her hand lay gently on my cheek. "I know, I've always known. I love you, Glory."

I fell into her, hugging her. "Mom, I wanted to talk to you, but I didn't know how. I'm so confused. I've always known I never liked boys like Jeanie does. Then Marcia made me realize why."

"Does she know?"

"No! God no. I would just die if she didn't feel the same way."

"Well she's here now. Maybe she does feel the same way and just doesn't know how to tell you."

"Do you think?" I asked, hopefully.

"Only time will tell. Take things slow, baby. Now go to her."
She smacked my butt, pushing me forward.

"I love you so much, Mom. I was so afraid of having this talk
with you. I never want to do anything to make you hate me."

"You could never. This is nothing, Glory. This is only one
part of your life. There's so much more to you than who you
choose to love."

I smiled at her, then ran to her again, hugging her. I stepped
back feeling great because I knew how much my mother loved
me.

I turned and started forward, then looked back at my
mother. She was beautiful and tall, with blonde hair.

Just like me.

"Glory!" Marcia yelled.

"Marcia, hi. I didn't know you were here."

"I knew it was your birthday." She gestured forward with
her head.. "There's a great spot just ahead to watch the fireworks."

"Okay." I followed her, my heart racing. I was so nervous.
Her hair bounced as she hurried through the crowd.

"Marcia, where are we going?"

"Just up ahead."

She stopped at the edge of a grassy clearing.

"Here?" I stopped.

"Yeah," she looked up at the sky. "Here, it's perfect."

I looked at her. "It is."

"Glory, I wanted to wish you a happy birthday. Here."

I didn't know what to say.

She moved closer to me and hugged me.

My arms went around her and it was the best feeling. I
didn't want to move.

Her head lay perfect on my shoulder, then she stepped back,
staring. After a moment, she leaned in to kiss me.

Her lips were soft, and it was everything I ever dreamt of.
The kiss was quick, and she pulled back slightly to stare in my
eyes. I didn't move. I couldn't. Then I pulled her back to me,
kissing her again.

She didn't pull away, so I opened my mouth and she slipped
her tongue in.

She pulled back when we both heard a noise. I watched Marcia while she watched me. "Happy Birthday, Glory."

Then she was gone. That quick.

I ran back to my mother.

"Hey baby, you're back already?"

"Yeah, where's Jeanie and Dad?"

"One last ride on the Dutch Shoes. We're going to be leaving soon, okay?"

"Sure, let me help." I reached for the cooler as my mother started clearing the picnic table.

"Where's Marcia?" She looked up at me as she folded the tablecloth.

"She left."

"That was fast."

I took the tablecloth from her. "Mom . . ." I held the tablecloth with both arms; I wanted to tell her about Marcia, about my first kiss, about my first amazing kiss. My first kiss and I wanted to share it with my mother.

She grabbed my hands and pulled me to the picnic table. "Tell me all about it, baby."

"Marcia and I, we . . ."

"Did you two kiss?"

I looked up, shocked.

"Glory, it's fine. You're sixteen years old now, and you like who you like and you'll fall in love with whomever you fall in love with. Marcia's a great girl. I'm so happy for you. So, how was it?"

"Oh, Mom, it was perfect. I'm so glad we talked. What about dad?"

"You leave your father to me," she said, while she put her arm around my shoulders.

I felt like my whole world was coming together. My life was perfect.

"WHY DOES SHE get to go to camp?"

"Jeanie, your sister paid for camp on her own, that's why she gets to go to camp. Besides, it's basketball camp. If you really want to go, Jeanie dear, I'll be glad to send you."

"Oh please!" She turned in a huff and stomped her way upstairs.

"Mom, I'm going to miss you so much." I hugged my mother, almost on the brink of tears.

"Glory, this is going to be good for you. All this practice could lock you into a college scholarship. Enjoy yourself."

"Okay."

"But you better write me," she tugged my ponytail. "You hear me?"

"I will, I promise. Where's dad?" I asked.

"At work."

"He wouldn't be if it was Jeanie who was leaving for camp."

"Well, if he was here, then I wouldn't be able to give you

this." She pulled a box out from one of the kitchen cabinets.

I hurried to open it to find a brand new pair of Nike basketball shoes. "Mom?"

"Hurry and tuck them away before your sister sees them. Now get all your bags. Your ride will be here in a minute."

"Okay. I love you, Mom."

She smiled. "You be careful, baby. I love you."

THE CAMP WAS at an area college, and everyone stayed in the dorms. I unpacked and was headed downstairs to look around when I saw Marcia coming out of one of the rooms down the hall. "Marcia!" I yelled.

"Glory."

"I had no idea you were going to be here," I said, as I hurried closer to her.

"Well, I knew you were going to be here. Your mother told my mother."

"She did? I didn't know that. I didn't even know they knew each other."

"I didn't either, but everything turned out okay, right?"

"Yes, Marcia, about the night at the carnival..."

"What about it? Didn't you like it? The kiss, if..."

"No, God Marcia, no. I thought..."

"I mean, I wanted it to happen. I planned it to happen just like it did. Glory, I like you, a lot, more than just friends. I really like you."

"I, me, too." I felt relief, and I wanted to throw my arms around her.

"We have an hour before we have to be in the gym. Why don't you come inside and we can talk." She held her door open.

I walked inside, and she reached for my hand, pulling me to the bed. "Let's sit."

I sat next to her and my body was pulsing. "I'm so glad you're here. I was so afraid of missing you this summer."

"Now you won't have to." She ran her hand through my hair. "You have beautiful hair."

"Can I kiss you, Marcia?"

"That's all I've been thinking about since your birthday."

I hugged her then kissed her, softly at first, then passionately as we fell back on her bed. We lay side-by-side kissing and hugging until we had to leave. Neither of us wanted to but we knew we were together, just us and our passion, and basketball for four weeks.

TWO WEEKS FLEW by, and Marcia and I played basketball non-stop all day and made out on her bed all night. It was one of the many nights we spent together kissing in Marcia's bed when she pulled back. "Can I touch you?"

I'd wanted her to touch me for days now, but I was scared. Nervous. "Yes." I stared in her brown eyes and she kissed me. Her tongue searched for mine and her hand slid under my t-shirt. I wore no bra. I never did. I never really had to. She touched me so soft and slow I felt my breath stop. My breaths were heavy against her cheek, and I let out a soft moan. I was embarrassed at first until she didn't stop, so I followed my instincts. I touched her. She was bigger than I was, and I couldn't help it. I moaned again.

She leaned back to look at me.

I paused, "I'm sorry, am I doing something wrong, I've never..."

"No, you're not, you're doing everything right. I never did this either. Is everything okay? Does it feel okay?"

"Oh, yes it does. I was afraid that...well, I was making sounds."

"I like when you make sounds."

Her hand kept touching me and my eyes started to close. "Kiss me some more, Marcia."

I ARRIVED BACK home just in time for school to start, and I was the happiest I'd ever been and thought I could ever be in my whole life. I was in love. I knew I was in love. I was in love with Marcia and she was in love with me; she told me so.

I threw my luggage from camp on my bed, and was glad Jeanie was out with friends when I got home. I didn't want anything spoiling this day for me.

My mother yelled from the kitchen, "Glory, family meeting at dinner, so I don't want you to be late, okay?"

"Sure, Mom. No problem." I bounced my basketball through the house, then outside. I couldn't wait for school to start. I would be able to see Marcia every day and play basketball with her all afternoon.

Mom came outside just as I finished a lay-up, and she started tossing me the ball for some outside shots. "So how was camp?" she asked.

I released the ball, and it fell short, hitting the rim and bouncing into the bushes. I felt myself blushing.

"That good, huh?" She grinned, as it was my turn to toss her the ball for some three pointers that she was so good at.

"It was." My face was still red. "Mom, thanks for talking to

Marcia's mom. How do you know her?"

"We talked a few times after some of your games." She released the ball and swish, she was white hot. "Don't you know your mother is a social butterfly? I just don't stay home and bake brownies all day." Swish, again. Man, she was good.

"Well, thank you for talking with her so Marcia could come to camp. We had a great time."

"I guessed that from all the blushing you're doing. So, is she your girlfriend?" She dribbled twice, and then swish.

"Mom, if you keep this up, I'm never going to get a chance to shoot!"

"Are you trying to change the subject, Glory Hunter?" She walked up to me. "Let's go a short game to eleven. Show me what you learned at camp, and I am talking basketball here."

"Mom!"

"I'm just happy for you, baby, that's all." She put her arm around my shoulder and we walked to the foul line. "Go ahead, you take it out."

"How much are you spotting me?"

"Are you kidding? You just got out of basketball camp. Now show me your moves. Basketball, that is," she said again, laughing.

"Mom!" I shouted, embarrassed.

I MADE IT to the table just in time for dinner. "So, what's this all about?" I asked while I sat at the dining room table.

Everyone passed the mashed potatoes when my father stopped. "Jeanie, Glory, I'm just going to come right out and say this because I know you're both adults. Your mother's sick."

I turned. "Mom?"

"Glory, shhh...let your father talk." She gave me a small smile.

"Yeah, Glory, shut up!" Jeanie said, "Go ahead, daddy."

I folded my arms across my chest and slammed back in my chair with a pout on my face.

"Girls, this is very important. Your mother is very sick and will be in the hospital for a while."

I stared at my mother who was staring down at the dining room table.

"Now I expect you girls to help out around here. We all need to make things easier for your mother."

I nodded.

"Okay, daddy," Jeanie said.

"What's wrong?" I asked. "Mom, Dad, what's wrong? Why do you need to go into the hospital, Mom?"

"Glory, you don't need to worry about that right now," my father said. "Let's just finish our dinner."

I watched my mother put her hand on my father's forearm. "I found a lump a few days ago. I have to go into the hospital to have it removed."

"Mom!" I was scared.

"It's okay, baby. Everything will be all right. They just need to remove it and make sure it's not cancerous."

"June!" My father's head shot up.

"They need to know everything, dear."

"So, you don't know for sure?" I asked. "If it's..."

"No, baby. It quite possibly could be nothing. The odds are in my favor."

"Mom . . .I'm scared."

She stood and came to me, putting her arms around my neck. "There's no need, baby. Everything will be fine." She pulled my sister into the circle, and with one uncovered eye, I watched my father sitting at the head of the table, playing with his fork.

My eye closed, and I wanted to stay forever in my mother's safe arms.

I STARTED SCHOOL at the same time my mother started chemotherapy, and nothing was the same. Her cancer was aggressive, and she quickly deteriorated from the energetic woman she once was.

Where dad and Jeanie followed her path, I became the strong one. I took care of her. I wouldn't have had it any other way. I wanted help from no one, especially my father, not that he ever offered.

"Glory, Marcia's at the door," Jeanie yelled, from downstairs.

"I'll be right back, Mom. Okay?" I wiped her mouth gently after helping her with some water.

"Glory, go. Have a good time with Marcia. You never leave my side anymore."

"Mom, this is where I want to be. Let me get rid of Marcia and I'll be right back."

She reached for my hand. "Baby, take the afternoon and have a good time. Please, I promise I'll sleep while you're gone."

"You sure?"

"Yes, Jeanie's home. Now go and tell Marcia I said hello."

I kissed her forehead. "Okay, but I won't be long." I hated leaving her; I felt like I had little time left with her, and I didn't want to miss a moment.

She smiled at me and I ran down to Marcia. "Hi," I said, as I reached her side.

"I haven't seen you in ages," she said, with concern.

"I know, my mom..."

"That's okay, I just wanted to stop by for a minute to see you. I've missed you."

"I miss you, too. I have about an hour while my mom takes a nap. Want to go somewhere?"

"Sure!"

We drove around for a while in Marcia's old Escort, barely talking. I felt guilty leaving my mom. Suddenly she stopped by the lake. "Want to walk?" she asked.

"Yeah."

We walked around on the beach for a while, then I reached for Marcia's hand. "This is the best I've felt since this all started."

"How is your mother?"

"Dying."

"Glory?" She sounded shocked.

"It's the truth, she knows it and I know it. Jeanie and my dad pretend there's nothing wrong. Like she has the flu or something."

"Maybe they can't handle it."

"No, they don't want to handle it. It's easier that way."

We stopped. "Come on," she tugged my hand. "Let's go somewhere private, I want to hold you."

"I need that."

I SAT AT my mother's side in the hospital. The end was near and she knew it. She asked for me. I gently took her hand in mine and kissed her softly. "I love you, Mom," I said, holding back the tears.

"I know, baby. Where's your father and Jeanie?"

Her breaths were short and quick. My heart was breaking, but I wouldn't break down, not in front of her. "They're outside in the lobby. Do you want them?"

"No. It's you I want by my side. I'm going to miss you, baby," she said, giving a soft smile. "You're everything I wanted to be when I grew up. You're tough, and you know what you want out of life. Tell me your dreams, baby."

"I dream of you being healthy again and being in my life forever."

"Oh baby, I will be in your life forever. I may not be with you but I'll always be in your heart."

"I miss you, Mom."

"Tell me more. Don't stop talking to me, Glory."

"I also dream of spending the rest of my life with Marcia. We plan on going to the same college together."

"I'm so happy that you found someone to love, baby. Things aren't going to be easy for you. Being gay is a tough road, but I know you can handle it. Never give in, baby, and never hide who you are. Be proud. I'm proud of you. I will always be proud of you." She stopped, struggling for air. "Your father isn't me, though. He's not that understanding, be tolerant with him, he does love you and he does mean well."

I looked down. "I know he does. Does he know?"

"I tried to tell him but he walked out on our conversation. He's old school. He'll come around, though."

"Mom, I don't want this to happen. I know what's going to happen but I don't want it to." I couldn't hold tough any longer, and tears rolled down my cheeks and off my chin. "Mom..."

"Oh my, Glory," she said, softly and patted the bed next to her. "Come here, let me hold you."

I crawled in bed with my mother, and my chin rested on her shoulder with my ear to her chest. I listened to her shallow breathing while she stroked my hair. "Tell me more of your dreams."

I choked back the tears. "I want to be a doctor. I want to help people, Mom. People shouldn't have to go through this."

"I love you, Glory," she whispered.

I was so content I could have fallen asleep right there, with my mother's arms around me.

My head rose when I stopped hearing her breaths, and when I couldn't feel her chest rising up against mine any longer. I sat there, just looking at her. She was beautiful. Still after everything she'd been through, she was beautiful.

After several minutes, a nurse came in. "Honey, you should go get your father." She went to my mother's side, then looked up at me. "Your father should be here."

I left and found my dad and Jeanie in the lobby. Dad, you should go in mom's room."

"What's wrong?" He stood, then walked away.

Jeanie came toward me. "Glory?"

"Mom died."

My sister and I held each other for the first time in years. Mom had brought us together, again.

JEANIE'S EYES OPENED as I sat on the bed next to her the same way I had sat next to my mother so many years ago. "Jeanie, you're finally awake."

"Glory," she whispered. "I'm glad you're here."

"So am I. I'm glad you came here, Jeanie. I built this hospice in memory of Mom."

"Mom always said you would make something of yourself."

I smiled. "Where's dad? Is he coming here today?"

"I asked him to but..."

"But he won't come if I'm here, right?"

"Glory, he was never the same after mom died. He's still upset over the fact that she wanted to be with you when she died. That's why he treated you like he did."

"By calling me a dyke and telling me to leave as soon as I turn eighteen?"

"I never said anything, Glory. I never told dad about you and Marcia."

"You knew?" I was shocked.

"A long time ago, I saw you kissing her at the carnival. I never said anything, Glory. You were a brat, but I loved you, you're my sister."

I traced her cheek with my palm. "I've missed you, Jeanie. Why did you stay away?"

"I don't know, I took care of dad and I guess I just didn't want to upset him. After that, I don't know."

"Yeah, it seems like the years went by so fast."

"What you've done here, this hospice, Glory, it's amazing. Mom would be so proud."

"It was all for her, and it means a lot to me that you're here. Now get some rest I'll be right back with something for you to drink."

I looked back at her from the doorway and felt relief. The door closed, and I walked the hallway of the June Hunter Hospice Center and felt pride. It meant a lot when Jeanie said Mom would be proud of me. I hoped she was. I felt her in my heart every day.

After medical school, I raised enough money to build this hospice. I wanted everything to be perfect, and I wanted it to be named after my mother. I had visions of this building all through college. I had a dream, and it came true, and Marcia was by my side the whole time. She still is. It's been nineteen years, and we're still in love. I still tingle when I see her.

"Dad!" I stopped short, almost bumping right into him.

"Glory. You look good."

"Jeanie's down the hall. I was just getting her something to drink. I can have a nurse take you to her."

"Why don't you take me?"

"Um, all right." I was shocked, not only that he was here,

but that he was talking to me civilly. I watched him as we walked, and he looked so old, so worn out.

We walked side by side to Jeanie's room, saying nothing.

His hand rested on the door. "Your mother would be proud of what a wonderful woman you've become," he said, and then he stepped through the door.

I stopped, stunned.

MY FATHER AND I stood at Jeanie's gravesite holding hands, listening to the wind in the trees. "In spite of everything that's happened, I do love you, Glory," he said.

"I know, Dad."

Jeanie was buried next to my mother, and I bent down at my mother's grave to lay a single white lily on her headstone. I felt my father's hand on my back.

"You were her life, Glory. I was so jealous of what the two of you had."

I turned to him; twisting around my wrist the bracelet my mother gave me.

"She loved you so much. When she was in the hospital and wanted to see you, the bitterness ate at me, and I took it out on you. I'm sorry for that. It wasn't your lifestyle, not really. Your mother told me about that long ago. She was proud of you coming out to her. I never understood that, but it was your relationship with her that angered me."

"How could a daughter's relationship with her mother anger you?"

"Because I was never close to you that way, or your mother for that matter. The two of you had something so special; you wouldn't let anyone else in. Even the day she died, she wanted only you by her side."

"I'm sorry, I had no idea."

"It was just as much my fault. I could have tried harder."

We stood quietly for a moment. "I miss her every day," I said.

"So do I."

# Contributor Bibliographies

**Cameron Abbot**
*To The Edge*, romantic suspense, The Haworth Press, Alice Street Editions, 2001
*An Inexpressible State of Grace,* romantic suspense, The Haworth Press, Alice Street Editions, 2004
<u>Website</u>: hometown.aol.com/cameronsabbott

**Georgia Beers**
*Turning the Page*, romance, Regal Crest, Yellow Rose Books, 2001
*Thy Neighbor's Wife*, romance, Regal Crest, Yellow Rose Books, 2003
<u>Website</u>: www.georgiabeers.com

**Meghan Brunner**
*From the Ashes*, urban fantasy/romance, AuthorHouse, 1st Books Library , 2002
*Into the Storm*, urban fantasy/romance, AuthorHouse, 2004
<u>Website</u>: www.faire-folk.com

**Carrie Carr**
*Destiny's Crossing*, romance, Renaissance Alliance Publishing, Yellow Rose Books, 1999/2001
*Hope's Path*, romance, Regal Crest, Yellow Rose Books, 2001/2004
*Love's Journey*, romance, Regal Crest, Yellow Rose Books, 2001
*Strength of the Heart*, romance, Regal Crest, Yellow Rose Books, 2002
*Something to be Thankful For*, romance, Regal Crest, Yellow Rose Books, 2003
*Destiny's Bridge*, romance, Regal Crest, Yellow Rose Books, 2003
*Faith's Crossing*, romance, Regal Crest, Yellow Rose Books, 2003
<u>Website</u>: www.carrielcarr.com.

**Caro Clarke**
*The Wolf Ticket*, historical romance, Firebrand Books, 1998
<u>Website</u>: www.caroclarke.com

**Katherine V. Forrest**
*Curious Wine*, romance, Naiad Press, 1983
*Daughters Of A Coral Dawn*, sci-fi/fantasy, Naiad Press, 1984
*An Emergence of Green*, fiction/romance, Naiad Press, 1988
*Dreams & Swords*, short stories, Naiad Press, 1988

*Flashpoint*, fiction, Naiad Press, 1994
*Daughters Of An Amber Moon*, sci-fi/fantasy, Naiad Press, 2002
Kate Delafield Mystery Series
*Amateur City*, mystery, (originally Naiad Press), Alyson Publications, 1984
*Murder At the Nightwood Bar*, mystery, (originally Naiad Press), Alyson Publications, 1987
*The Beverly Malibu*, mystery, (originally Naiad Press), Alyson Publications, 1989
*Murder By Tradition*, mystery, (originally Naiad Press), Alyson Publications, 1991
*Liberty Square*, mystery, Berkeley Publishing Group, 1996
*Apparition Alley*, mystery, Berkeley Publishing Group, 1997
*Sleeping Bones*, mystery, Prime Crime, 1999
*Hancock Park*, mystery, Berkeley Publishing Group, 2004
<u>Anthologies Edited</u>
*The Erotic Naiad: Love Stories by Naiad Press Authors*, anthology, Naiad Press, 1992
*The Romantic Naiad,* anthology, Naiad Press, 1993
*Diving Deep: Erotic Lesbian Love Stories*, anthology, Naiad Press, 1993
*Diving Deeper: More Erotic Lesbian Love Stories*, anthology, Naiad Press, 1994
*The Mysterious Naiad: Love Stories by Naiad Press Authors*, anthology, Naiad Press, 1994
*Deeply Mysterious: Erotic Lesbian Stories*, anthology, Naiad Press, 1995
*All in the Seasoning: And Other Holiday Stories*, anthology, Odd Girls Press, 2002
<u>Website</u>: www.art-with-attitude.com/forrest/forrest.html

**Jennifer Fulton (Rose Beecham )**
*Passion Bay*, romance, Naiad Press, 1992
*Saving Grace,* romance, Naiad Press, 1993
*True Love*, romance, Naiad Press, 1994
*Greener Than Grass*, romance, Naiad Press, 1995
*Passion Bay, Expanded 2nd Edition*, romance, Regal Crest, Yellow Rose Books, 2004
*Saving Grace, Expanded 2nd Edition*, romance, Regal Crest, Yellow Rose Books, 2004
*The Sacred Shore,* romance, Regal Crest, Yellow Rose Books, forthcoming, 2005
*A Guarded Heart,* romance, Regal Crest,  Yellow Rose Books, forthcoming, 2005

**Writing As Rose Beecham**
*Introducing Amanda Valentine,* mystery/romance, Naiad Press, 1992
*Second Guess,* mystery/romance, Naiad Press, 1994
*Fair Play,* mystery/romance, Naiad Press, 1995
Website: www.jenniferfulton.com

**Gabrielle Goldsby**
*Wall of Silence,* mystery/romance, Regal Crest, Yellow Rose Books, 2002
*The Caretaker's Daughter,* historical romance, Regal Crest, Yellow Rose Books, 2004
Website: www.gabriellegoldsby.com

**Ellen Hart**
Jane Lawless Series
*Hallowed Murder,* mystery, (originally Seal Press), St. Martin's Press, 1989
*Vital Lies,* mystery, (orig. Seal Press), St. Martin's Press, 1991
*Stage Fright,* mystery, (orig. Seal Press), St. Martin's Press, 1992
*A Killing Cure,* mystery, (orig. Seal Press), St. Martin's Press, 1993
*A Small Sacrifice,* mystery, (orig. Seal Press), St. Martin's Press, 1994
*Faint Praise,* mystery, (orig. Seal Press), St. Martin's Press, 1995
*Robber's Wine,* mystery, (orig. Seal Press), St. Martin's Press, 1996
*Wicked Games,* mystery, St. Martin's Press, 1998
*Hunting the Witch,* mystery, St. Martin's Press, 1999
*The Merchant of Venus,* mystery, St. Martin's Press, 2001
*Immaculate Midnight,* mystery, St. Martin's Press, 2002
*An Intimate Ghost,* mystery, St. Martin's Press, 2004
Sophie Greenway Culinary Series
*This Little Piggy Went to Murder,* mystery, Fawcett Books, 1994
*For Every Evil,* mystery, Fawcett Books, 1995
*The Oldest Sin,* mystery, Fawcett Books, 1996
*Murder in the Air,* mystery, Fawcett Books, 1997
*Slice and Dice,* mystery, Fawcett Books, 2000
*Dial M for Meat Loaf,* mystery, Fawcett Books, 2001
*Death on a Silver Platter,* mystery, Fawcett Books, 2003
Website: www.EllenHart.com.

**Lois Cloarec Hart**
*Coming Home,* romance/drama, Renaissance Alliance Publishing, 2001
*Broken Faith,* romance/drama, Regal Crest, 2002

*Assorted Flavors*, short stories, PD Publishing, Inc., 2005
<u>Website</u>: http://members.shaw.ca/ljchart

**Karin Kallmaker**
*In Every Port*, romance, Naiad Press, 1990
*Touchwood*, romance, Naiad Press, 1991
*Paperback Romance*, romance, Naiad Press, 1992
*Car Pool*, romance/light mystery, Naiad Press, 1993
*Painted Moon*, romance, Naiad Press, 1994
*Wild Things*, romance, Naiad Press, 1996
*Night Vision: Daughters of Pallas 1*, science fiction/paranormal,
Naiad Press, 1997
*Embrace in Motion*, romance, Naiad Press, 1997
*Christabel*, gothic historical, Naiad Press, 1998
*Making Up For Lost Time*, romance, Bella Books, 1998
*Watermark*, romance, Naiad, 1999
*The Dawning: Daughters of Pallas 2*, science fiction/paranormal,
NaiadPress, 1999
*Unforgettable*, romance, Naiad Press, 2000
*Frosting on the Cake*, short stories based on previous novels characters, Bella Books, 2001
*Sleight of Hand: Tunnel of Light 1*, historical fantasy, Bella Books,
2001
*Sugar*, romance, Bella Books, 2004
*Substitute for Love*, romance, Bella Books, 2001
*Seeds of Fire: Tunnel of Light 2*, historical fantasy, Bella Books,
2002
*Maybe Next Time*, romance, Bella Books, 2003
*Once Upon a Dyke: New Exploits of Fairytale Lesbians*, Fish Out of
Water, fantasy novella, Bella Books, 2004
*One Degree of Separation*, romance, Bella Books, 2004
*All The Wrong Places*, erotica, Bella Books, 2004
*Just Like That*, romance, Bella Books, 2005
*The Forge of Virgins: Tunnel of Light 3*, historical fantasy, Bella
Books, 2005
<u>Website</u>: www.hometown.aol.com/kallmaker/kallmaker.html

**Marcia Tyson Kolb**
*Living Wabi-Sabi: An Imperfect-Perfect Life*, (forthcoming)
<u>Website</u>: www.dragonflycottage.com

**Lori L. Lake**
*Ricochet In Time*, romance/drama, Regal Crest, Yellow Rose
Books, 2001

*Gun Shy*, police procedural/romance, Regal Crest, Quest Books, 2001
*Under The Gun*, police procedural/romance, Regal Crest, Quest Books, 2002
*Different Dress*, romance, Regal Crest, Yellow Rose Books, 2003
*Stepping Out*, short stories, Regal Crest Enterprises, LLC, 2004
*The Milk of Human Kindness (editor)*, anthology, Regal Crest, 2004
*Have Gun, We'll Travel*, adventure/thriller, Regal Crest, Quest Books, 2005
Website: www.lorillake.com

**SX, Meagher**
*I Found My Heart In San Francisco*, romance, Fortitude Press, 2002.
*Arbor Vitae*, romance, Fortitude Press, 2005
Website: www.sxmeagher.com

**Radclyffe**
*Safe Harbor, 2nd edition*, police procedural/romance, BookEnds Press, 2001
*Above All, Honor, revised edition*, action/romance, BookEnds Press, 2001
*Love's Melody Lost, 3rd edition*, romance, BookEnds Press, 2001
*Honor Bound*, action/romance, Regal Crest, Yellow Rose Books, 2002
*Innocent Hearts*, romance, Regal Crest, Yellow Rose Books, 2002
*Shield of Justice*, police procedural/romance, Regal Crest, Quest Books, 2002
*A Matter of Trust*, romance, Regal Crest, Yellow Rose Books, 2003
*Love and Honor*, action/romance, BookEnds Press, 2003
*In Pursuit of Justice*, police procedural/romance, Regal Crest, Quest Books, 2003
*Beyond the Breakwater*, police procedural/romance, BookEnds Press, 2003
*Love's Tender Warriors*, romance, BookEnds Press, 2003
*Tomorrow's Promise*, romance, BookEnds Press, 2003
*Passion's Bright Fury*, romance, Regal Crest, Yellow Rose Books, 2003
*Love's Masquerade*, romance, BookEnds Press, 2003
*shadowland*, romance/erotic drama, BookEnds Press, 2004
*Fated Love*, romance, BookEnds Press, 2004
*Justice in the Shadows*, police procedural/romance, BookEnds Press, 2004
*Honor Guards*, action/romance, BookEnds Press, 2004
Website: www.radfic.com

**J.M. Redmann**
*Death by the Riverside*, mystery, (orig. New Victoria), Bella Books, 1990
*Deaths of Jocasta*, mystery, (orig. New Victoria), Bella Books, 1992
*The Intersection of Law and Desire*, mystery, (orig. W.W. Norton), Bywater Books, 1995
*Lost Daughters*, mystery, (orig. W.W. Norton), Bywater Books, 1999
Website: www.jmredmann.com

**Jean Stewart**
*Return To Isis*, sci-fi/fantasy, Rising Tide Press, 1992
*Isis Rising*, sci-fi/fantasy, Rising Tide Press, 1993
*Warriors of Isis*, sci-fi/fantasy, Rising Tide Press, 1995
*Emerald City Blues*, fiction/drama, Bella Books, 1996
*Winged Isis*, sci-fi/fantasy,, Bella Books, 2001
*Wizard of Isis*, sci-fi/fantasy, Bella Books, 2004
Website: www.jean-stewart.com

**Cate Swannell**
*Heart's Passage*, romance, Regal Crest, Yellow Rose Books, 2003.
*No Ocean Deep*, romance, Regal Crest, Yellow Rose Books, 2005.
Website: www.kotb.net

**Therese Szymanski**
*When the Dancing Stops*, mystery, (orig. Naiad Press), Bella Books, 1997
*When the Dead Speak*, mystery, (orig. Naiad Press), Bella Books, 1998
*When Some Body Disappears*, mystery, (orig. Naiad Press), Bella Books, 1999
*When Evil Changes Face*, mystery, (orig. Naiad Press), Bella Books, 2000
*When Good Girls Go Bad*, mystery, Bella Books, 2003
*When the Corpse Lies*, mystery, Bella Books, 2004
*Back to Basics: A Butch/Femme Erotic Anthology* (editor), Bella Books, 2004
*Once Upon a Dyke: New Exploits of Fairytale Lesbians*, A Butch in Fairy-Tale Land, novella, Bella Books, 2004
Contact email: tsszymanski@worldnet.att.net

**Talaran**
*Vendetta,* police procedural/romance, Regal Crest, Quest Books, 2001
Website: www.talaransrealm.just-cuz.com

**Julia Watts**

*Wildwood Flowers,* romance, (orig. Naiad Press), Bella Books, 1996

*Phases of the Moon,* romance, (orig. Naiad Press), Bella Books, 1997

*Piece of My Heart,* romance, (orig. Naiad Press), Bella Books, 1998

*Wedding Bell Blues,* romance, (orig. Naiad Press), Bella Books, 1999

*Mixed Blessings,* fiction/drama, Jacobyte Books, 2001

*Finding H.F.,* drama/romance, Alyson Press, 2001

*Once Upon a Dyke: New Exploits of Fairytale Lesbians,* La Belle Rose, fantasy novella, Bella Books, 2004

Contact Email: JuliaW7590@aol.com

**Marie Sheppard Williams**

*The Worldwide Church of the Handicapped,* short stories, Coffee House Press, 1996

*The Weekend Girl,* novellas, Folio Bookworks, 2003

Contact Email: number1giraffe@hotmail.com

**Kelly Zarembski**

*Visions of Sarah,* romance, Writer's Showcase Press, 2002

*Embers in the Sky,* romance, Writer's Showcase Press, 2003

*Love and Pork Chops,* romance, iUniverse, 2004

Website: www.kzarembski.com

## Permissions